BY THE SAME AUTHOR

The Pearl of France
The Fair Maid of Kent

THE QUEEN'S SPY

CAROLINE NEWARK

Matador
9 Priory Business Park,
Wistow Road, Kibworth Beauchamp,
Leicestershire. LE8 0RX
Tel: 0116 279 2299
Email: books@troubador.co.uk
Web: www.troubador.co.uk/matador
Twitter: @matadorbooks

ISBN 978 1789014 440

British Library Cataloguing in Publication Data.
A catalogue record for this book is available from the British Library.

Printed and bound in the UK by TJ International, Padstow, Cornwall
Typeset in 11pt Minion Pro by Troubador Publishing Ltd, Leicester, UK

Matador is an imprint of Troubador Publishing Ltd

In memory of
Howard Liam Harbord
1963–1986

LIST OF MAIN CHARACTERS

Edward II — *King of England*
Isabella — *his estranged wife*
Edward, Earl of Chester — *his son and heir*
Edmund, Earl of Kent — *his half-brother*
Sir Hugh Despenser — *his chamberlain*
Eleanor Despenser — *Hugh's wife and the king's niece*

Margaret, Lady Comyn — *a widow serving Isabella*

Thomas, Lord Wake — *Margaret's brother*
Henry, later Earl of Lancaster — *the king's cousin*
Jeanne de Bar, Countess of Surrey — *the king's niece*

Roger Mortimer, Lord of Wigmore — *the king's enemy*
John of Brittany — *Earl of Richmond*
Charles IV — *King of France and Isabella's brother*

Madame of Evreux — *Charles's third wife*
Robert of Artois — *Isabella's cousin*
Jeanne de Valois — *Countess of Hainault*
Philippa — *her daughter*
Sir John — *the Count of Hainault's brother*

Adam Orleton — *Bishop of Hereford*
Thomas, Earl of Norfolk — *Edmund's brother*

Alice, Countess of Norfolk	*a coroner's daughter*
Margery, Lady Abernethy	*Margaret's friend*
Sir Thomas Gurney	*Lord Berkeley's man*
Sir John Pecche	*Constable of Corfe Castle*
Sir Ingelram Berenger	*a Despenser adherent*
William, Lord Zouche	*his friend*
William Montagu	*a friend of Edward Earl of Chester*
Nicholas Langeford	*Margaret's gaoler*

Prologue

Sir Hugh Despenser watched as his wife let down her hair. After nineteen years of marriage she no longer aroused him the way she once had but he remained acutely aware of her latent sensuality and its value to his current plans.

He spoke quietly. 'There is something I need you to do.'

Eleanor paused, a hairpin held lightly in her fingers. Somewhere in her slanting green eyes it was possible to detect a flicker of alarm but the gentle rise and fall of her breasts remained constant and nothing altered the slight upward curve of her lips. Living with a man who reminded her of one of her uncle's caged beasts had taught her early the wisdom of stillness.

'My lord?'

'The task is a little more delicate than usual.'

Eleanor Despenser raised her elegant eyebrows. Her husband was not known for his subtlety. In her opinion it was his only weakness. He was ruthless and violence came easily but he lacked *finesse*.

'Is my uncle proving difficult?' she enquired.

'Not at all. He may be king but he is my servant in all things and does what I require of him. My concern is the interference of the queen. I need her out of the way.'

Eleanor's position as the queen's senior lady allowed her unprecedented insight into her mistress's private feelings and, although nothing had been said, she knew Isabella both disliked and mistrusted Eleanor's husband. To Isabella the king could do no wrong thus any infringement of her position as her husband's consort and chief counsellor was the fault of her husband's chamberlain, Sir Hugh Despenser.

'I have arranged for her to go to France. She will negotiate a peace accord with her brother.'

'You wish me to accompany her? Report on whom she meets, what letters she receives?'

'No, that will not be necessary. I need you here.'

'And my task?

'I wish you to be kind to the king.'

She blinked in surprise.

'You wish me to be kind to my uncle?'

'Perhaps I didn't make myself plain. Did you not understand?' A slight edge of menace had crept into her husband's voice.

'Oh no, my lord. I understand completely. How kind would you like me to be?'

'How kind would you think?'

Eleanor thought rapidly. Kindness towards another man would mean bestowing favours normally reserved exclusively for a husband. But her uncle?

'My lord, I realise the king has needs which the queen does not meet.'

'Yes? His voice was dangerously quiet.

Eleanor wondered if what she'd learned from the servant she paid for information, was true. She thought it probably was. 'Do you not satisfy his requirements in that department?' She paused. 'It is said …'

Hugh Despenser's face betrayed nothing. He knew exactly what was said about his closeness to the king and it pleased him to keep his wife guessing.

'As I told you, I have him precisely where I want him.'

Eleanor was aware that her husband's desires and ambitions had no boundaries and he would always do what needed to be done. To her it was what made him a worthy husband.

'And my role?'

'With the queen absent, the king will lack female companionship. You will be his *chère dame*. There will be no-one else. I need him to be soothed, to be compliant and you will of course be very, very kind. You will provide him with whatever he wants. Can you do this?'

'Yes, my lord. It will be my pleasure.'

She showed no hesitation. She'd always done what Hugh asked of her, however distasteful. But this? Was not a connection with an uncle forbidden by the church? Naturally a bishop's disapproval would not worry Hugh. He was not overly concerned with the salvation of his soul but the fear of eternal damnation lay ever uppermost in Eleanor's mind. And there were others to consider.

'My uncle has a certain tenderness for me, my lord, but what of his brothers? What if they should object to our closeness?'

'Thomas is a wild young fool and can be bought.'

'And Edmund?'

'Edmund bungled the peace negotiations in Paris last year and has made a mess of the war in Gascony. He's in disgrace. You'll get no interference from that quarter. But my lady, do not forget whose interests you serve. I should not like to be forced into administering a reprimand.'

FROM A LETTER DATED 1ST DECEMBER 1325
WRITTEN BY EDWARD II TO HIS ESTRANGED
WIFE, ISABELLA

"Lady, oftentimes we have sent to you,
both before and after the homage, of our great
desire to have you with us, and of our great
grief of heart at your long absence; and, as we
understand that you do us great mischief by
this, we will that you come to us with all speed
and without further excuses. Before the homage
was performed, you made the advancement
of that business an excuse, and now that
we have sent, by the honourable Father the
Bishop of Winchester, our safe conduct to you,
you will not come for the fear and doubt of
Hugh le Despenser ... Wherefore we charge you
as urgently as we can that, ceasing from all
pretences, you come to us with all the haste
you can."

"Most dear and potent lady, the whole country is disturbed by your news, and the answers which you have lately sent to our lord King; and because you delay your return out of hatred for Hugh le Despenser, everyone predicts that much evil will follow. Indeed, Hugh le Despenser has solemnly demonstrated his innocence before all, and that he has never harmed the queen, but has done everything in his power to help her; and that he will always in future do this, he has confirmed by corporeal oath."

1

PARIS 1325

I crept through the darkened room as far as the half-closed door. Despite the silence, I glanced over my shoulder to make sure I hadn't been followed. It was early and most in the palace were asleep or at their morning prayers, but it was always wise to be careful especially in our current circumstances. I took a step closer.

A man's voice. 'D'you think she calls him uncle while he's fucking her?'

The reply, a smothered high-pitched giggle.

'Course she'd hardly call him, your grace, would she? Not with her skirts up round her ears.'

'You're lying. A king would never, not with his niece.'

'It's true, as God's my witness. Mind you, mightn't be the lady. Might be the lady's husband.'

'But he's a ...'

'A what? A man? You're a big lad, you've heard of men like that. Anyway, he's an Englishman. Bumfuckers the lot of them.'

They were talking in the local patois and their words were utterly disgusting but after six months I was accustomed to their way of speaking and could understand them easily enough.

The deeper voice again. 'There's many likes both. Not inclined that way myself. Never fancied a man. A pretty young boy? Well, that's a different matter, 'specially if he's got a tight little arse like yours.'

More giggles, a scuffle and then silence.

I despaired. If the servants were talking then by tomorrow the state of the English queen's marriage would be common currency on every street corner in Paris.

Treading softly I moved away from the door and retraced my steps, thankful to be done for the moment with the disagreeable business of spying. However glorious my present surroundings, and I had to admit the rooms were truly magnificent, I was weary of Paris, weary of the fabled palaces of the French king and weary of the constant discord and malicious gossip which pervaded our daily life. I would have liked to go home to England but my place was with the queen and we both knew it was much too dangerous to return.

I walked quickly through the outer rooms, hoping to reach the queen's chamber unobserved, but at the head of the stairs had the misfortune to encounter the heavy bulk of the countess of Surrey, Lady Jeanne de Bar.

'Lady Margaret,' she purred in her low confiding voice as she deliberately stepped into my path. 'We must talk.'

'Countess.' I inclined my head. I liked Lady Jeanne, you could even say we were friends, but I was reluctant to have private words with her in case I repeated something I'd regret. Spying for the queen meant keeping secrets and the countess was well known for her loose tongue and equally easy manner.

'You must tell me,' she urged, leaning a little closer and placing a surprisingly firm grip on my arm. 'What is going on?'

The countess had been out of England for most of the past ten years - escaping from her English husband so everyone said - and must know little of how things stood at home.

'In what way, my lady?'

'The king and the queen. Their marriage. This intruder Isabella speaks of. Who is it?'

'I'm sorry, my lady, but I don't know.'

She gave me a shrewd look from her deep-set brown eyes. They were placed rather close together and gave the unwarranted appearance of slyness.

'Come, Lady Margaret, that cannot be true. When you were in England you practically lived in the queen's privy chamber. You will have heard things. I cannot ask Isabella. There are conversations which even the most intimate of friends do not have and this matter of her marriage is one of them. But you must know and I insist you tell me. Is it the king's niece, the Lady Eleanor?'

I didn't like Eleanor Despenser. She was a green-eyed serpent with a poisonous temper who had made my life a misery with her spiteful insults. She had served Isabella from the earliest days of the royal marriage and regarded herself as the queen's most senior lady.

'I believe the king has a great affection for the Lady Eleanor,' I said cautiously. 'But he is her uncle and what doting uncle does not love his niece. He showers her with gifts and there is talk that he dines in private with her away from the court, but ...' I paused, wondering how blunt I should be, '... whether there is anything improper, my lady, it is impossible to say.'

The countess pursed her lips, savouring for a moment the thought of Lady Eleanor's likely impropriety. Then

3

said sharply, 'I have also heard mention of Eleanor's husband.'

'Sir Hugh Despenser? Yes, he is the king's chamberlain and his very special friend.'

My words had the immediate effect of arousing her suspicions. 'How special a friend can a chamberlain be?'

I doubted Lady Jeanne was privy to servants' tittle-tattle but there had been a steady stream of visitors from England to the French king's court these past months, ready to drip poison into the ears of anyone who would listen. And Lady Jeanne was a very good listener.

'Sir Hugh is constantly at the king's shoulder, my lady,' I said. 'The king favours him above all others and, as you know, the king is famed for his generosity. When the spoils are given out he rewards Sir Hugh with the lion's share and people grumble Sir Hugh now owns half of England. It is said he is favoured beyond what anyone would expect of a chamberlain.'

'But nothing more? No familiarity? He does not overstep the boundaries of what is proper? He does not … touch the king?'

It was difficult to explain to the countess how any familiarity came not from Sir Hugh but from the king himself who was constantly placing his hand on his chamberlain's arm or on his shoulder or around his manly waist. Perhaps in private, when the candles were doused and the bed curtains drawn, he placed his hand on other parts of Sir Hugh's body but that was something nobody could know for certain. There were rumours and the bishops were said to be unhappy but …

'The king appears very taken with Sir Hugh, my lady.

It is said his chamberlain has only to ask for something and it is given willingly. There are times when Sir Hugh is impatient for his reward and doesn't ask, he just takes. Then woe betide anyone who gets in his way. Yet the king does nothing.'

'The king does nothing?'

'No, my lady.'

All this was perfectly true. My late husband's sister had been menaced and I knew of a lady whose legs had been broken by Sir Hugh Despenser's henchmen because she refused to part with her lands.

'Did the queen not tell you about the dowager countess of Lancaster, my lady?' I asked in all innocence. 'Sir Hugh threatened her with burning?'

'Alice de Lacy? Jesu!' Lady Jeanne was understandably horrified. 'What kind of man would do such a thing?'

'A greedy man, my lady. A man who is impatient for wealth.'

Even Lady Jeanne could understand that.

'But there has been no intrusion? I mean, how could there have been? Isabella would never, not with a man like that, not with any man. And as for the king?'

Her cheeks were flushed and her breathing quickened as unwanted images skittered through her mind. I realised she had shocked herself with where her thoughts had taken her so I moved quickly to relieve her anxieties. 'Oh my lady, that would be quite impossible, surely?'

'The king is a good man,' she said hurriedly. 'He was kind to me when I was young, when my husband and I experienced a little difficulty in our own marriage. I know he would do nothing to harm dearest Isabella. Besides which, as you say, I mean, his chamberlain? It would be impossible.' Her eyes sought mine for reassurance. 'Quite impossible.'

The Despensers were much too close to the king for anyone's comfort and it had been the king's refusal to listen to any of his advisors other than Sir Hugh and his father that had pushed the queen to the brink. Deprived of her long-time servants, half her income and her husband's loving presence, what woman would not make a stand? But Isabella was no fool and had wisely waited until a stretch of sea separated her from her husband and his dangerous friend to issue her ultimatum.

The previous day she had proclaimed in front of her brother and the whole of his court that someone had come between her and her husband, someone who was trying to break the bond of their marriage. She declared she would not return to England and resume her marriage until this intruder was removed.

I'd heard the audible in-drawing of breath from the Englishmen present, the shocked looks and exclamations of horror. Who could the queen possibly mean? But apparently everyone knew who the queen meant. Even the servants knew.

'She must go back to England,' said Lady Jeanne firmly.

'She is afraid.'

'Of what? She is the queen. She has no reason to be afraid.'

But I knew she had every reason to be afraid.

'I cannot return,' she had said to me. 'The king is incapable of saving our marriage. He would let Sir Hugh Despenser destroy me.'

Later, after the household had broken their fast, Isabella took my arm as she often did in our occasional private moments. We were walking round the little courtyard garden followed at a discreet distance by her other ladies.

'What have you discovered?' she said once she was sure of not being overheard.

'The servants are talking.'

'Of course they are. What are they saying?'

I gave her an account of the conversation I'd heard that morning, sparing her none of the lewd details and yet she barely flinched.

'What else?'

'The countess of Surrey thinks you should return to England. She says the king is a good man, which of course he is. How could he be otherwise, being your grace's husband?'

Isabella gave a twitch of her pale pink lips. 'Is she not concerned for my safety?'

'She has a little difficulty in accepting the rumours but she believes the king will protect you.'

'Whereas you and I know he will not. You and I know he will do whatever that creature wants. He may value me, but he values Hugh Despenser more.'

These were the moments when Isabella and I were closest, when she admitted her inner fears and looked to me for comfort.

'Sir Hugh Despenser will try to harm you if he can, your grace. He is careful but he is a dangerous man.'

'He is a malign influence.'

Of course he was. He was the most evil of men and married to a witch.

'What of Lady Eleanor?' I asked, wondering if Isabella believed the rumours.

'My spies in England tell me she has put herself at my husband's disposal.'

'She has served your grace for a long time.'

'And her husband for longer.'

'You think she is no longer loyal to you?'

'I *know* she is no longer loyal to me.'

I wondered what else Isabella knew that she wasn't telling me.

She gave a little sigh. 'There are times, Margaret, when I think you are the only friend I have.'

But I wasn't her friend however much I wished I was. I might be loyal but friendship required something more. I'd served her for five years and in all that time she'd kept her true self well hidden from me. Even those who'd been with her the longest only saw what she wanted them to see. Her husband must know what she was truly like yet it was from him that she was estranged.

As the days grew short we entered the darkest part of the year, cold and grey with the prospect of snow filling the air. Riding out into the streets of Paris on an errand for the queen I was barely able to feel my fingers. I longed for a pair of gloves with soft warm fur on the inside but my funds would not run to it. As a widow in possession of just two small manors I often found myself regrettably short of money.

Returning some hours later, I found Isabella in her chamber. She was dressed in what she had described to me that morning as her robes of widowhood and mourning:

8

a gown of exquisite black velvet and an enveloping black veil. She was positioned against a backdrop of silvery-white curtains where the candlelight made her look as fragile as a Christmas rose.

She was undeniably the most beautiful woman in Paris. Her face was a perfect oval, the skin luminous, the cheeks and lips coloured with a delicate blush. Her eyes were grey-blue flecked with amethyst, fringed with thick dark lashes; eyebrows arched and plucked into a narrow line setting off the broad sweep of her brow to perfection.

Beside her on a small embroidered stool sat her elder son, Edward, duke of Aquitaine, earl of Chester, count of Ponthieu and Montreuil, heir to the throne of England. In the early autumn he had come to Paris to pay homage to his uncle for his lands in France and had not yet returned to his father. He was thirteen years old and a handsome boy, quiet and well-mannered, with a pleasant disposition. As I entered I saw mother and son were reading, their heads close together, a picture of perfect maternal and filial devotion.

Isabella was very careful of how she appeared to others and just at this moment it pleased her to be seen as a beautiful, wronged woman in need of a champion. Not that I thought she would find one at the French court. Nobody, least of all her brother, would want to rattle the door of the English king's cage. To do so would set a most unwelcome precedent.

I'd settled down with my sewing when a messenger appeared with what I assumed was yet another letter for Isabella. Our days were punctuated with letters from her numerous French kin or from whichever bishop had last been sent out from England to remind her of her duty. There were also frequent vituperative letters from her husband demanding the return of his son. He had, it seemed, resigned himself to the fact that his wife was staying exactly where she was on this side of the Narrow Sea, a favoured guest at the court of her brother, the king of France, but he was not going to countenance the loss of his heir.

I was mistaken. The letter was for me. I raised my eyes to the queen for permission.

'May I?'

'Certainly, Margaret.' She didn't smile and despite our supposed closeness she was clearly displeased. 'We cannot wait to know who wishes to communicate with you.'

I broke the seal and quickly read the contents. It was from Thomas, Lord Wake, my brother, my sole companion of our long-ago nursery days.

I passed the note to the queen to reassure her that it was not part of some evil plot against her person. Even here in her brother's realm she was nervous of her husband's intentions and terrified of what the Despensers might do to her. Last night she'd clung to my hands and with tears in her eyes, begged me, as a friend, not to desert her. Many were leaving now that she could no longer pay their wages. Her usher had left that morning and half a dozen squires were already packing their boxes.

She waved her hand. 'If Lord Wake wishes to see you - go! I shall manage very well without you. But Margaret, when you return, bring him with you. We should like to have sight of this elusive brother of yours.'

She was right to describe Tom as elusive as I'd set eyes on him just twice in the years since he was a boy: once at our mother's funeral and again on the occasion of my marriage. He hadn't attended to my welfare when I was widowed and yet now he was expecting me to run to his whistle.

Tom was lodged in a distant part of the palace and by the time I'd crossed a dozen courtyards, walked the length of a magnificently tiled cloister and passed under a score of narrow archways, my fingers and toes were frozen and I was almost weeping with cold. At last the man showing me the way stopped outside a steep flight of steps.

'*Ici, madame.*' He bowed and indicated that I should proceed.

I climbed slowly up the steps and stopped. At the top, waiting for me, was Tom. It was said he resembled our father and I would have recognised him anywhere, even after all this time. He held out his hands.

'Sister, greetings.'

I curtsied, made a formal greeting, then stood on tiptoe and kissed his cheek. 'What brings you to Paris?'

He took my cold hands in his.

'You.'

'Me?' I found that hard to believe. I was certain he seldom thought about me. He had only ever thought of his own advantage, never mine.

'Yes. I have something with me I know will bring you pleasure. A little persuasion was involved but it is a gift of great value.'

What was he talking about? He knew nothing about me. We were practically strangers.

'I wasn't aware I was in need of anything,' I said carefully.

He guided me in the direction of a half-open door 'Would you like to see what it is?'

He indicated to his boy to open the door wider and ushered me into his room. I looked around with curiosity, wondering how he lived. It was plainly furnished, only a single threadbare hanging which I recognised from our childhood. There was a hearth and a table and … a man. He hadn't come alone.

Leaning against the far wall with his arms folded as if he didn't have a care in the world was someone I knew only too well. A tall young man with dark golden hair and eyes the colour of a cloudless summer sky. It was nearly two years since I'd last seen him. Two years with no letters, no messages, no words - nothing. Not even a hastily scribbled note. It was two years since I'd promised to wait while he travelled to Paris on royal business. Two years since he'd said he was mine.

We neither of us moved. Within the room, a half-charred log in the hearth shifted and settled while from outside came the relentless grinding rumble of a heavy cart and a single shouted curse. Behind me, the door closed with a soft muffled thud, leaving us alone.

One look at his face told me he'd changed his mind. I'd always known it. In the company of his French cousins he'd probably panicked at what he'd almost promised me. It was only to be expected and yet that last time as we'd stood in the shadow of the little church of St Peter ad Vincula, when we'd neither of us known what the future would hold or if we might see each other again, he had asked me to wait for him and I had truly believed he would be constant.

2

It had been a most singular courtship.

Of course I'd seen him many times at a distance and once or twice close to when he'd visited the queen's chamber, but we'd never spoken. I doubted he knew my name.

We met on the day the earl of Lancaster died, when the uprising against the king was finally over. The ringleaders were either dead or in prison and the king's cousin had paid with his life for his many treasons over the years. A great deal of blood had been spilled and for miles around the roads were full of fleeing Lancastrian knights, discarding their armour and their fine garments as they ran. Better to wander bare-arsed begging your bread, it was said, than be named as one of Earl Thomas's men.

Apart from the hall where the king's men were noisily celebrating their victory with food and wine from the earl's storerooms, the rest of the great Lancastrian fortress of Pontefract lay brooding and silent in the moonlight. The castle was unfamiliar and, taking a wrong turning, I lost my way. Lit by torches all buildings looked alike and I couldn't find the entrance to the queen's rooms. At the joining of two walls I saw an archway with a flight of steps leading upwards but there was no velvet padding on the hand rail. The stones were clean-hewn and paler than the rest, and the treads were unworn. This must be the new tower which the earl of Lancaster had built and where he'd been confined the night before his execution. The king had ordered his cousin locked in the self-same room which the earl had intended as a prison for his king.

I placed one foot cautiously on the bottom step, curious as to how it would feel to be a man facing his end. But it didn't do to dwell too long on such matters, not at a time like this. Ahead of me, the stairway was cold and dark and uninviting. I peered upwards. The frost had returned and the earl must have spent a bitter and uncomfortable last night in his tower room repenting of his sins.

I heard a noise, a small scrape, and turned round. A black shape moved fast, blocking the light from the torch on the wall. Whatever sort of creature it was, it filled the recess and where a head should have been was a flaring crown of flame.

I wasn't a woman much given to imagining demons, I left that to my maid who saw hobgoblins round every corner, but that night at Pontefract I felt the hairs on the back of my neck start to prickle. I told myself I was not afraid of the dead. This could not be Thomas of Lancaster returned. I held fast to the rail, squashing down a terror which threatened to engulf me.

'What are you doing here?'

The dead do not speak, or if they do, they do not ask questions like that. I couldn't tell who it was because the man's face was in shadow and I didn't recognise the voice. As he moved towards me, I froze.

'Who are you?' he demanded.

'I …' The words died on my tongue.

14

'Let's have a look.'

He reached out and grasped my chin. I jumped as if I'd been struck.

'Well, if it isn't Lady Margaret, Isabella's little lapdog.'

It was Lord Edmund, the younger of the king's two half-brothers.

'My lord.'

With one foot still on the step I tried to lower myself into a curtsey, all the while seething with fury. The king's brother should know better than to insult one of the queen's ladies.

He moved away from me and positioned himself against the entrance to the recess with one of his boots resting on the opposite wall, blocking my escape. If I wanted to leave I would have to climb over his leg because it was obvious he had no intention of moving.

'Do you often go wandering about strange castles in the dead of night, Lady Margaret?' he enquired. 'Or are you on a commission for the lovely Isabella? Does she crave a memento of her late departed uncle: some rag he wiped across his face or a half-chewed crust of bread bearing the imprint of his teeth?'

'The queen is at prayer.'

He was watching me carefully. He could not have been more than twenty, several years younger than me. Close to he bore little resemblance to his brother, the king. His face was finer-boned, the skin drawn taut, the mouth wider, the lips firmer. His hair was more the colour of dying beech leaves than ripe golden wheat, and his eyes were blue like the sky on a bright summer's day when the sun shines hot and your heart lifts with joy. He was not much like his other brother either, the one whose hair was night-black and was said to be a seducer of young women in Norfolk.

He removed his foot from the wall and took a step towards me. 'Are you frightened, Lady Margaret?'

My heart was racing. 'No, Lord Edmund. I am not frightened.'

But I was. He stopped just a hand's breadth away, his toes almost touching mine. I could hear his breathing and inhaled the scent of some rich aromatic perfume. The folds of my green velvet gown brushed the creases in his brown leather boots and I felt the heat from his nearness. If I'd been so minded I could have put my fingers on the beating pulse just above the collar of his fine linen shirt.

He wore a single jewel on his right hand, a magnificent ruby ring, which gleamed as it caught the light. His fingers touched my cheek, smoothing away a tendril of hair which had come loose.

'You must not be dishevelled when you return.' His voice was low, the words slurred. 'Or they'll think I have dishonoured you.'

My tongue was thick in my mouth. I could smell wine on his breath and knew he was drunk. The tell-tale signs were there: the over-bright eyes, the flush high on his cheekbones and the slight tremor in his hands.

'You have beautiful hair,' he murmured, his fingers easing under the cloth of my headdress and gently caressing the soft strands above my ear. 'Yes, quite beautiful.'

I felt a pit open beneath my feet and I shivered.

'Are you cold, Lady Margaret? Shall I warm you?'

I was terrified of what he might do. I'd seen too much drunkenness in my life to dismiss the danger to a woman like me from a man like him, even here just a stone's throw from the royal apartments.

'I must return to the queen.'

'Why? Does my brother's wife require you to perform some humble intimate task?'

I tried to move away but he took another step, trapping me against the stairway. 'Killing one's own kin gives one an appetite, Lady Margaret. Did you know that? Perhaps you might care to undertake an intimate task for me? It so happens I am in great need of comfort tonight, the kind of comfort that only an obliging young woman like yourself can provide.'

It was too much. I slapped him hard across the face before I realised what I was doing. 'You're drunk, my lord. And you're disgusting.'

He winced and rubbed his cheek with the back of his hand. 'I suppose that depends on what disgusts you.'

'*You* disgust me. You insult the queen, you insult me, and if I were a man I'd …'

'You'd what? What would you do to me, Lady Margaret?'

He lifted one of my hands to his mouth and, without taking his eyes from mine, gently bit the soft cushion of flesh at the base of my thumb.

There was a brief moment when neither of us moved. Then I wrenched my hand from his grasp and shoved him hard. He stumbled and fell back against the wall. I ducked my head, pushed past and ran out into the courtyard as fast as I could.

You fool, I thought. You fool! You fool! You fool!

Of course that wasn't the end of our acquaintance. The following morning he sought me out and in front of a giggling audience of two of the queen's damsels made his stilted apologies.

'I have very little recollection of what occurred between us last night,' he began, 'but I'm told I was drunk.'

He looked like a man who hadn't slept. There were dark smudges under his eyes and the sides of his mouth were white with fatigue.

'Yes, you were.'

He stared at me in surprise. He had probably expected a dutiful surrender, not an attack.

'I have been advised,' he said slowly, fumbling for the thread of his speech. 'I have been advised that I should offer an apology for any harm I did you or for any harsh words I spoke.'

I wondered who had advised him and just how much he, in fact, remembered of last night. His eyes were a clear steady blue but he wasn't smiling.

'I have already confessed my sins of yesterday and done penance, and this is all that remains on my conscience. Is there is anything I can do to make amends, Lady Margaret?'

'Amends?'

'Some service I can do for you, a matter which needs attention?'

I spoke before I could change my mind. 'Yes, Lord Edmund, there is something you can do for me.'

He frowned. It was obvious he'd thought a quick apology and a meaningless offer of service would be all he'd have to suffer. But I had remembered my neighbour's children at Loxton near Sherwood and realised the king's brother could discover things I could not.

'Well?' He was clearly anxious to be gone from this humiliating encounter. 'What is it you want done?'

'I had a friend whose husband rode with the earl of Lancaster. She died last summer leaving seven children behind. I would like to know if their father is alive or dead.'

He looked horrified. 'You expect me to trawl through stinking dungeons looking for your friend's husband?'

'No, Lord Edmund,' I said, thinking how transparent his thoughts were. 'I'm sure you have a man to do that for you, some menial who can dirty his feet on your behalf; someone who will happily travel from one castle to the next inspecting their rat-holes for signs of vermin. You need not even get straw on your boots.'

He looked relieved. 'What is this husband's name?'

'Everingham. Lord Everingham. He has a manor at Loxton, near Sherwood.'

'And what is he to you, this Everingham man?'

I lowered my head, not wishing him to see the slight flush which I was certain had stained my cheeks. 'Nothing. He is nothing to me. I was a friend of his wife. They were neighbours. That is all.'

'Everingham,' he muttered under his breath. 'Very well I shall see what I can discover.'

As he walked away, I sighed. I knew he would disappoint, like all men. He would forget Lord Everingham's name before he had reached the foot of the stairs and once back with his friends would not give a second thought to what he had just promised.

We left Pontefract with its hideous memories and seven weeks passed before I saw him again. If I thought of him during that time it was to acknowledge that he had forgotten me and my awkward request. I'd hoped he would remember but why should he? I was no-one of importance, merely an impoverished widow who had the good fortune to serve the queen.

One afternoon, as I hurried across the inner courtyard of our lodgings in the friary at York, a man approached me with a note. There was only the slightest of breezes to cool the heat in my cheeks and the note was very short.

'You may thank your master,' I said politely.

'Is there no reply?' He seemed genuinely surprised.

I shook my head. 'No.'

Once he was gone I swiftly unfolded the note again. It was nothing, just a few lines in the neat crabbed writing of a clerk. A space left at the top for a formal flowery greeting, which had been omitted, and no indication as to where the letter had been written or from whom it had been sent, nothing but a scrawled signature at the bottom.

"He is alive and well, but four hundred marks the poorer in exchange for his liberty. And my boots are still clean."

I smiled with pleasure. He had not forgotten his promise. And he had remembered our conversation. I tucked the note in my purse telling myself to forget him because nothing could come of it. He was the king's brother.

But at the back of my mind hovered the image of the pretty little coroner's daughter from Norfolk. She had lived in a house with a curtained-off area at the end of the hall for the bed she shared with her sisters. Pewter cups sat on her family's board and there were only a handful of servants. But with the help of her wily father she had danced and flirted her way to a countess's coronet.

Now she sat at the queen's table and graced the castles of her husband, the king's dark-haired half-brother, the earl of Norfolk, eating off his silver plates and sleeping in his great high bed. She had exchanged rough wool and plain linen for the finest brocades and richest of velvets, and her sensible workaday caps had given way to swathes of embroidered silk and golden cauls.

If such a thing could happen to her, it could happen to anyone. And if it could happen to anyone, it could even happen to me.

Two days later he found me in the gardens watching a group of boys play a game which involved balls and sticks and a great deal of noise. He came and stood beside me. For a long time he said nothing, he just stood there.

'You didn't reply.' His tone was peremptory. He wasn't looking at me, he was gazing at one of the boys swinging a bat.

'I presumed our dealings were at an end, Lord Edmund,' I replied. 'You had done as I asked and the debt was repaid.'

'You could have written to say thank-you.'

'I saw no need.'

'Had you no desire to prolong our correspondence?'

'Lord Edmund, I am a virtuous woman.'

I glanced sideways but he was still watching the boys.

'I don't know many virtuous women.' I thought of the tales I'd heard and was surprised he acknowledged the truth. 'As Everingham is alive,' he continued, 'and doubtless trying the merchants this day for a loan, you'd better tell me what he is to you.'

I knew I was blushing. 'He is nothing, my lord. As I told you, he was my friend's husband.'

There followed an uneasy silence and I wondered why he didn't go.

'Is he a good man?'

'Yes, I believe so.'

He hesitated. This was like no ordinary conversation. There were pauses and I sensed too much was being left unsaid. He wanted to say something but couldn't find the words.

'In my experience of women, Lady Margaret,' he began slowly, 'good husbands are dead husbands. Wives complain about their lords and it isn't until a man is safely in his tomb that he becomes a saint. So the remedy is this - a good man should never marry. If he does, he will become feckless, faithless and a cross to be borne, or else be doomed to an early death.'

I bent my head so that he shouldn't see me smile.

'Was your husband a good man?' he enquired.

John's face was fading in the summer haze, the blue of the sky so bright I could no longer see the warmth of his dark brown eyes.

'Yes. he was; he was a very good man.' I was aware how unsteady the ground beneath my feet had become.

'And has Everingham asked you to marry him?'

'Yes, my lord, he has.'

22

'It is all arranged?'

'No, my lord. The earl of Lancaster called him to arms before I could agree to the match.'

'But he will pursue you, now that he is free?'

'I think under his present circumstances, my lord, he will seek a woman with more wealth than I possess.'

'But you are the widow of Sir John Comyn who was heir to the lordship of Badenoch.'

'True, but I have only two small manors, and thirty pounds a year which I haven't yet seen.'

He looked shocked. 'Surely your husband left you better provided for?'

'My husband had not come into his inheritance, my lord, and most of his lands lay beyond the border. The king has been generous but I am merely one of many widows.'

'And have you no brothers or cousins to plead for you?'

'I have one brother, my lord, but he is married and has troubles of his own.'

'And cousins?'

I hesitated, wondering how much he knew about me and how much I should tell him. In these dangerous times it could be unwise to acknowledge one's kin.

'I have a cousin,' I said slowly. 'Lord Mortimer of Wigmore. I am sure you know him, my lord?'

He gave a short laugh. 'I do. You'll get no help there.'

Of course I wouldn't. Roger Mortimer, the son of my mother's sister, had been taken at Shrewsbury, accused of leading the lords of the Welsh Marches in rebellion against the king. He was currently languishing in the Tower awaiting judgement and with the king in his present vindictive mood I didn't hold out much hope for my cousin.

23

He grunted and looked away. 'I too am dependent upon the king's generosity, Lady Margaret.'

'You? But you're an earl.' I took in at one glance the costly cloth of his tunic, the fineness of his linen and the jewels he wore.

'An empty title.'

I murmured that I was sorry.

'Shall I tell you what the reward is for loyalty, Lady Margaret? The reward for a faithful brother who has done everything that was asked of him, a brother who has endangered his very soul - do you know what he gets?'

I shook my head, not daring to say anything.

'Three miserable castles. Three! And in Wales! And do you know what the king's chamberlain receives? Half the bloody country!'

He was furiously angry. I hadn't realised. What I'd taken for impatience was anger simmering beneath the surface.

'I have a charter, Lady Margaret, drawn up by my father and locked in my treasury box. It says I am to receive lands to the value of seven thousand marks. But what do I get? Three miserable Welsh castles!'

Three Welsh castles would have pleased me greatly but then I was not an earl. And seven thousand marks was a vast sum, enough to equip a king's army and keep a wife in fine style. No wonder he was bitter.

'My brother, the king, does not see fit to give me my inheritance but considers it perfectly acceptable to heap rewards on that … that turd!'

He kicked at a loose stone, sending it skittering across the path. 'I did everything he asked of me. I even condemned my own cousin to death. Yet still he won't give me what I am owed. His chamberlain gets whatever he wants while I must wait for my inheritance.'

With that he left me standing in the garden and strode off to vent his anger elsewhere.

There was nothing in it but I should have been more careful. He'd said he was unused to virtuous women and his interest in me was obviously not honourable. Doubtless he'd make his intentions clear before long and then I could refuse him and that would be an end to our acquaintance.

Even if he liked me the king would not allow him to make the same mistake as his brother and reject an important marriage alliance to pursue a woman of no worth. I would do well to forget him because soon he'd be safely married to a foreign prince's daughter and I'd never see him again.

I told myself not to be foolish.

Next morning he stopped me on my way back from mass. He was loitering in the shadows of the porch, unseen by the others, and pulled me in beside him before I had time to protest.

'Hush!' He put his finger to my lips. 'My brother's army is leaving for Scotland tomorrow and I wanted to see you before I went.'

I pushed his hands away, trying to stop myself from trembling. 'I cannot see why, my lord. I am responsible neither for your armour nor for your provisioning. And I don't ask for your attentions. I am not the kind of woman you seem to think I am so please leave me alone.'

It wasn't true. Even as I said the words I knew I didn't wish him to leave me alone.

'What have you heard about me?'

'Nothing you'd want to hear.'

'Oh but I can imagine: the drunkenness, the fighting, the women. What did you expect, Lady Margaret?'

How could I tell him what I wanted him to be when I couldn't even admit to myself that it mattered.

'Do you know what the good folk of the towns do when they know I am coming?'

'Lock up their daughters, I should think,' I muttered.

'Far from it. A man decks his daughter in her finery and sends her off to church, eyes demurely down, a flash of ankle, a bare wrist, hair alluringly unpinned as if by accident. She flaunts her charms before me until the father is sure the hound has caught the scent. Then he shuts her away in a back room with a couple of grizzled old women for company.'

'What happens after that?' I was amused by his air of injured innocence.

'The father sets out his stall in front of his door and waits. If he receives no offer he repeats the performance the following day.'

I smothered a laugh.

'You may well laugh,' he protested, 'But my brother has a lot to answer for. I like his pretty wife but my life would be easier if he'd taken Dona Maria as the king wanted.'

'The queen says it was the lady herself who refused the match.'

He laughed. 'Oh Lady Margaret, what young lady would be so foolish as to refuse the attentions of a brother of the king of England?'

I smiled at him. 'Perhaps if the lady is virtuous?'

'As are you?'

'Yes, Lord Edmund. As you have observed, I value my virtue.'

I managed to detach myself from the shadows of the archway and walk calmly away, half-wishing I didn't have to, half-wishing my position was different, half-wishing I had something to offer a man which would not simply involve an inevitable fumbling in the dark and a short spell of sweetness with someone who made my pulses race.

It was time for the Nativity celebrations. There was a king and a queen, as there always was in these matters, and a handsome young knight riding through the greenwood - a real greenwood with branches of laurel and holly which got tangled in the silks of the knight's garments much to everyone's delight. This was our first Christmas entertainment, although there'd been a rumour that two naked men had danced on a table in the king's private rooms the previous night.

After the failure of the Scottish campaign and the queen's ignominious flight from Tynmouth in the face of threats from the advancing Scots, not even the bishops could object to an evening of secular entertainment. And it was well known that the king loved mummers and playacting.

The side tables in the hall were stacked against the walls, and the benches pushed back to make space for the players. I had Lady Abernethy beside me, raised up on her toes to get a better view, and my shoulder was hard up against one of the king's hangings. Every time I rested my head against Queen Guinivere's elegantly shod feet, the coloured wools scratched my cheek and I breathed in the scent of long-forgotten fleeces.

The play concerned a knight's quest and involved much fighting with the forces of evil who were dressed in black.

'Did you think I had deserted you?'

The sudden whisper in my ear made me jump with fright, but the hand on my waist caused me even more alarm. The voice was low but unmistakeable.

'No, Lord Edmund,' I whispered, half-turning my head. 'You are usually to be found somewhere.'

I couldn't see him, just feel the warmth of his presence and hear the familiar sound of his voice. He kept his hand where it was, pressing against my waist. He didn't say anything else but I found breathing difficult knowing he was standing behind me.

The minstrels struck up a tune and from the players there was a lot of leaping about amidst gales of laughter from the audience. Nobody could see us, as the torches at the rear of the hall had been doused on the instructions of the steward. Lady Abernethy had her back to me and was too involved in the entertainment to notice what I was doing.

'Do you think virtue will win the day, Lady Margaret?'

I smiled to myself. 'Virtue has its own rewards, Lord Edmund. Good will always triumph over evil.'

'You are very sure of yourself.'

'Naturally.'

'You have tested your own defences, I trust? I should not like to think of your virtue being too easily overcome.'

I said nothing. I felt his hand tighten on my waist. For a few moments there was silence between us while the scene in front of my eyes blurred as the knight was attacked by a horde of small boys dressed in green.

'Are you betrothed to that Everingham man yet?'

'No, my lord. I told you, he needs an heiress. I'm not wealthy enough for him.'

'But you wish you were?'

Did I? However kind Lord Everingham had been and however much I cared for his children, I was quite certain that if I were an heiress I would set my sights higher. I would set them as high as they could possibly go.

'Lord Edmund, if I were wealthy I would not choose a man who had taken up his sword against the king.'

'Who would you choose?'

I smiled at this thought. 'Women do not get to choose, Lord Edmund. They do as they are bid. Fathers and brothers make choices for women.'

'Widows cannot be forced into marriage, Lady Margaret. You know that. You may marry where you will. You are more fortunate than me.'

I edged further round, being careful not to tread on the back of Lady Abernethy's gown. Now I was fully in front of him and could see his face clearly.

'How can I be more fortunate than you, Lord Edmund?' I whispered. 'You have an earldom and you have riches, however meagre you may think they are. You will marry a wealthy and beautiful lady. You are favoured and your life is blessed.'

He looked into my eyes. The flame of a single candle beyond where we stood flickered in the depths of his gaze and lightened the planes of his face. He looked incredibly young, much younger than his twenty-one years.

'My brother wishes to make an alliance with Castile. He intends to find another Dona Maria.'

Ice slithered through my veins and I caught my breath. Of course the king would marry him to a foreign princess; I'd always known this would happen. Anything else was mere daydreaming and folly.

'A good marriage,' I murmured.

'The lady he has chosen is reputed to be very beautiful: dark hair, black eyes, skin like a ripened peach.' He peered at me closely. 'Do you think she will suit, Lady Margaret? Is she a bride you can imagine me taking to my marriage bed?'

I turned my head back to the doings of the knight in the greenwood. He was climbing up a precariously built tower to rescue a long-haired maiden leaning out of a window.

'Do you think I shall enjoy my Dona Maria?'

By now I was trembling. I lowered my gaze to the dark folds of my gown.

'I have no idea what you enjoy, Lord Edmund,' I whispered. 'It is none of my business.'

'My brother, the king, would make me the richest noble in the land with a wave of his royal hand. But if I were free to choose …'

His hand left my waist and he thrust his fist hard against poor Guinivere.

Just at that moment there came a loud blast on a horn and everyone broke into a storm of clapping and stamping.

With no warning he left me, pushing his way through the press of people and disappearing into the crowd.

What had he been going to say?

'Wasn't that wonderful?' said Lady Abernethy.

I thought of the handsome young knight in the greenwood and the tests of his endurance. I considered the temptations of sin and the triumph of virtue, and I thought of his whispered words, the warmth of a hand, the hunger, the need and the cliff over which I was gradually falling.

'Yes,' I replied softly, 'It was.'

Frost came in the night and by next morning pale flakes of snow were falling fast from a sky the colour of pewter. He was waiting for me at the end of the cloistered passageway, sheltering from the cold. I'd been half-expecting him, wanting him to come yet all the while hoping he wouldn't.

He gave me no conventional greeting because we both knew time was too precious to waste on unnecessary words.

'The king is sending me away.'

My heart turned painfully in my breast and a lump rose into my throat.

'Are you not staying for the rest of the celebrations, my lord?'

'No, I cannot. Duty calls.'

He took my hand and I found myself unable to ask him to release me.

'Lady Margaret.' I stood completely still, not trusting myself to reply or to step away. 'Don't marry him.'

This wasn't right. He shouldn't dictate what I might do.

'My lord, I would remind you it is none of your business if I accept an offer of marriage or if I do not.'

He smiled at me.

'Two manors? I'd say not much to attract anyone you'd think worth marrying.'

'I didn't ask for your opinions on my prospects.'

'But you might find them interesting.'

'I doubt it.'

He still had hold of my hand and showed no sign of letting it go.

'There'll be danger where I'm going. Are you not concerned for my safety?'

'I'm sure you know how to keep yourself safe, my lord.'

'I do but it would be pleasant to think of you worrying about me.'

I was tempted to smile but bit my inner lip hard to stop myself. 'I have plenty to occupy my thoughts, I thank you.'

'But you would not refuse to say a prayer for my safety the next time you are in church. I wouldn't ask for a special visit. That would be presuming too much. But perhaps a candle? A small one?'

This time I couldn't prevent the smile. 'Very well. A small one. A very small one.'

'In that case, Lady Margaret, I shall bid you farewell. I don't suppose you would permit a kiss?'

'No, my lord; I would not.'

'I thought not.' He grinned at me. 'Till we meet again.'

He turned on his heel and sprinted off up the steps, leaving me standing speechless.

How had he done that? How had he made me do something I never intended to do? I knew now how much he liked me. I could see it mirrored in his eyes, an appreciation of something I possessed. But it could lead nowhere and yet each time we met I felt more and more tempted. It had been such a long time since John and sometimes in the dark, while the others slept, I longed to have somebody hold me. I knew this man would hold me but I feared he might also let me fall.

It was more than a twelvemonth before he returned, yet in the world I spun around myself I saw him everywhere: in the sudden turn of a man's head or the glimpse of a pair of bright blue eyes. And although we had never kissed, I tasted him on my lips each morning when I woke. But while I was day-dreaming the time away with idle thoughts of a man who could never be mine, everything was changing and the balance of power around the king was shifting.

The queen's fall from favour that year was so gradual that at first none of us noticed. The king no longer sought her advice, any suggestions she made were ignored and on several occasions she was denied access to his chamber. A crisis caused by an encroachment of the French into our lands in Gascony soured the king's relations with her brother and resulted in the queen herself coming under suspicion as a Frenchwoman. But all this was lies whispered into the king's ear by Sir Hugh Despenser. The queen was loyal. I knew she was.

She followed the king dutifully to Kenilworth for the Christmas celebrations and then to Sir Hugh's castle at Hanley, but by now it was obvious that the king's preferred companion was his chamberlain, not his queen. It was with Sir Hugh he sat listening to minstrels play interludes for his delight and it was Sir Hugh's company he sought when he wished to stroll round the gardens. And in the late evening, where once he used to visit the queen's rooms, he now retired with Sir Hugh to his privy chamber for refreshments and entertainments of a private nature.

Long dreary months passed and in all that time there was no news. Nobody mentioned the king's younger half-brother and, naturally, I couldn't ask. I had almost given up hope when, at the beginning of April when we were once again lodged at the Tower, he arrived without warning. The trouble in Gascony had deepened and Lord Edmund had come, we were told, to pay his respects to his brother's wife and meet with the men who were travelling with him to Paris. The king was sending him to talk peace with the queen's brother.

I could think of nothing but his presence in the royal apartments. At any moment I expected to meet him strolling through a chamber or surprising me in a dark corner. I wandered across the inner courtyards and found myself unexpectedly in the hall amongst the servants. I visited the queen's rooms on every possible occasion and offered to run errands in place of her maids. I loitered in the gardens and ran my fingers slowly up the rails as I climbed the stairs, pretending to be deep in thought. His men were everywhere, but he was nowhere to be seen.

Just when I had given up all hope, he appeared in the shadow of the little church of St Peter ad Vincula, somewhere I had no business to be. It was as private a place as one could hope to find in the inner precincts of the Tower where there were very few opportunities for privacy.

I kept my head bowed not daring to look at him. I knew my feelings were written right across my face and I didn't want him to know. We stood in silence as the last rays of sunshine stole away from the courtyard and the laughter of men lighting torches rose and fell and then faded into the distance.

At last he put out his hand and touched mine. A flash of fire ran up my arm. I flinched and he withdrew his hand.

'I'm sorry.' His voice was very quiet.

I began to tremble. To have him this close when I'd thought about him for so long was to be in the path of an incoming tide.

'I prayed for you,' I whispered. 'I didn't forget.'

His fingers reached out and touched the side of my face. Slowly, slowly, he traced the curve of my cheek caressing my skin until he reached my mouth. There he paused.

'Lady Margaret?' He seemed very young, very unsure, very uncertain of what to say next. 'Is there anyone? It's been more than a year and I wouldn't blame you if after all this time you …'

'There is no-one.'

He breathed a deep sigh and wrapped the fingers of his other hand around mine. They were warm and firm and I had no desire to pull away.

'Margaret,' he whispered.

Very gently he took my face in both his hands and kissed me. His lips were cool and firm and sweet. It was what I'd woken to every morning these past months, a taste of honey.

Slowly my mouth opened under his and I felt myself falling. From the moment I'd met him two years before

I'd known I was in danger but I'd allowed myself to be lured into his net. Now it was too late and I was caught fast.

I clutched at his sleeves, drawing him closer. He covered my face with urgent kisses while I tipped back my head, wanting the touch of his mouth on mine.

'Can you feel it?' he whispered into my ear. 'How I burn for you?'

Pressed against his chest I could have put out my fingers and seared them with the fire between us. If he was burning then so was I.

I had forgotten the joy of surrender: the thrill which ran down my body, the warmth which flooded my veins. During ten long years of widowhood there had been no-one else, not even a passing fancy. I was not like some of the younger women who gave away their hearts a dozen times a week. I had loved only once before and that had been for such a short time. Now there was this.

I reached up and touched his face: weather-worn, a small scar above the left eyebrow. I ran my finger across the puckered mark. It was fresh.

'Where have you been?' I whispered.

'In the North, keeping order for the king.' He lowered his mouth to mine.

'And now?' I kissed the corner of his mouth.

'Right now?'

'Yes.'

'Right now there is disorder of a most serious kind.'

I breathed in the rich deep scent of his clothes, felt the unaccustomed softness of his extravagant velvet against my fingers, and sighed. Wherever he had been, wherever

I had been, at this very moment we were both in a heaven of our own devising.

He pushed aside my veil and I felt the night air blowing cool across my skin.

'Margaret,' he murmured. 'I love you. I've loved you since I first met you.' He kissed my throat, 'Such a very long time. Oh Margaret. Christ knows but I love you more than life itself.'

Slowly he ran his hands down the full length of my clothing, from neck to thigh. He gripped me, leaning the full weight of his body against mine. It was the sharp jab of an iron peg on the base of my spine which alerted me to the perilous position I was in. With a great effort I thrust him away.

'No, my lord, please! No! I can't.'

'No?' He looked surprised. 'I thought you were saying, yes. Was I mistaken?'

'No, you were not mistaken but I cannot do this.'

His eyes softened. He understood.

'Virtue?'

I placed my hands against his chest. 'Yes. It is not that I don't love you because I do, you know I do. But an encounter like this is not right.'

He smiled with such tenderness I almost changed my mind.

'Sweetheart, I'm sorry. Of course, not here and not now. But my dear virtuous one, you must know there is no dishonour in any of this. I love you and I want you with me always. I cannot imagine being without you.'

He wrapped me in his arms and spoke of the life he could give me: the silks, the satins, the jewels, the furs.

There'd be fine horses in my stable and silver cups upon my board. I'd have servants to do my bidding and a house with a magnificent solar. And when the day was over and the candles were low, he would lay me in his great high bed and make love to me.

For a brief moment I allowed myself the luxury of hope but I feared the answer to the question which I knew must be asked.

'In what capacity would you have me in your bed, my lord?'

I held my breath praying he would not prove false, but as he hesitated, I knew my dreams were fast dissolving into dust.

'Oh Margaret, my dearest love, you know I would marry you if I could. But if I marry without my brother's permission I will lose everything and he would never agree to my marrying you.'

'Lord Norfolk married without the king's permission.'

'And got knocked across the floor for his pains. He'll not be forgiven and it cannot be undone. The king insists I make a good marriage. He says he depends on me.'

'I see.'

The clipped little words must have betrayed the injury he had dealt me and the vast wound to my pride. It was humiliating to be told that I was not worthy to marry Lord Edmund.

He hurried to soften the hurt.

'Margaret, this is not what I want but it is all I can offer.'

'I understand.' Even to myself I sounded defeated.

'Margaret, Margaret.' He pulled me close and held me tightly in his arms, my head resting against his shoulder.

'Margaret, you are the only woman I love. Do you imagine I want one of those hairy Infantas with their sloe-black eyes? It's you I love. I've loved you from the moment we first met. But we both know that love and marriage are separate. I do not need to love my wife, but I shall always love my mistress.' He gave me a little smile. 'Provided it is you.'

With that he proceeded to kiss me again. I put up no resistance for I was too tired to explain myself, too beaten, believed myself too much in love. I merely blinked away my tears and turned my mouth to his.

We stayed like that for what seemed like hours, holding each other, whispering words of love. He stroked my hair and made an inexpert attempt to pin back my veil which made us both laugh. Tomorrow was another day, another time; tomorrow was an enemy we both feared so we didn't mention the future again. It was sufficient for now to live like this.

It was the sound of a night owl which made me aware of the hour.

'When do you leave?'

'Tomorrow. At first light.'

'Will there be danger? Should I light another candle?'

He smiled. 'No, there's no danger. We're just talking and banging the table. I'm only there to add a bit of royal weight to the proceedings, to impress Cousin Charles.'

I didn't want him to go.

'Margaret.' He was talking into my hair, his voice slightly muffled.

'Yes.' I kissed the side of his neck.

'When I return ...'

'Shush, don't talk about it. Not now. Let us be happy.'

He pulled back, still holding my hands. 'Wait for me. When I return I shall talk to my brother.'

For a few moments I stayed where I was looking into his eyes, eyes which I knew to be blue but which, in the shadowed darkness, were pools of black. I stepped forward and kissed him gently on his mouth.

He took my hand and together we made our way across the courtyard to the safety of the archway leading to the royal apartments. The guards moved aside to let us enter. At the foot of the steps he pulled me into his arms one last time and kissed me until I could barely stand. Then he gave me a little push and I ran quickly up the stairs.

Next morning he was gone.

3

PARIS 1325

A wasteland between: two years with no letters, no messages, no words, nothing. I waited and I wept and I despaired. At times I feared he was dead and would never return; at others that he had proved faithless and was pursuing another woman. My birth was not exalted, my situation one of dependence on the queen, and already the years were beginning to show on my face. I was no virginal beauty trailing a fortune and men seeking wives ignored me, fearing an entanglement which would bring no benefit to themselves. Yet he had said he loved me.

By the time the second summer came to an end I acknowledged that our affair, if I allowed myself to call a tentative friendship by such a name, was over. Whatever had been between us was no more and my hopes of a future together had vanished in the warmth and the dust of an early French autumn.

Yet here he was in my brother's room in Paris on a cold December day, exactly the same man as before.

He inclined his head. 'Lady Margaret, you are well?' He spoke hesitantly as if afraid of what I might say.

I had some difficulty forming the words but was determined he shouldn't know how much he had hurt me.

'Yes, I thank you, I am.'

'Still serving Isabella?'

'Where else would I be?' I replied sharply.

His lips curved in the smallest of smiles. 'I wouldn't know; perhaps following some handsome French lord around the countryside, tucked up snug in his baggage train?'

I raised my gaze to his and looked at him levelly. I wasn't smiling. 'My lord, you insult me.'

'It was a joke.'

I paused a moment. 'I don't appreciate jokes about my virtue.'

He frowned, a puzzled look on his face as If unsure what to say next. I didn't like the silence.

'Have you made your glorious marriage with Castile yet, my lord?' I tried to keep my voice steady. I would be perfectly composed and treat him like any other man of my acquaintance.

He smiled at the question as if something only he knew about had been resolved. 'Would it distress you if I had?'

'What you do is of no concern of mine, my lord. You have made that abundantly clear.'

The smile broadened as if he was enjoying my discomfiture.

'Ah Lady Margaret, if only that were true. In the end I decided the Infanta was not to my liking.'

A wave of relief flooded through me. He hadn't made the marriage his brother had wished to foist upon him.

'The king must be disappointed,' I said. 'I believe he had invested a great deal in the proposed alliance.'

He put his head on one side and considered the matter. 'He is my brother, he will forgive me. And if he doesn't, so be it.'

This was a new Edmund. The old Edmund would have cared deeply about his brother's response, not wanting in any way to displease him. I wondered what had changed.

'You didn't write,' I said, unable to hold back the words any longer.

'No' he said slowly. I didn't write. I should have done. It was wrong of me but you must understand how difficult things were. My brother expected a peace accord with Cousin Charles and there was the war and Uncle Valois treating me like a turd. Gascony was a nightmare of a place; you can have no idea how dreadful it was.'

'I am sure you found plenty of diversions.'

'If you mean that story about the girl in Agen, it wasn't true.'

I had heard nothing of a girl in Agen, but for him to think I had, meant the story had currency.

'There was no girl?'

'Yes, there was a girl.'

'You were not in Agen?'

'No, I was there, but it wasn't as they made out. I didn't steal her from her father. She crept into my bed of her own free will. I didn't know she was there until I slid between the sheets but afterwards she made it plain she wanted to stay.'

'I don't suppose it occurred to you to throw her out.'

He put his head on one side and smiled. 'My dear Lady Margaret, you've been married, you know what we men are like.'

I knew exactly what he was like so why was I disappointed? Why did I feel as if my heart had been savaged?

'I was lonely without you,' he said.

'Indeed.' I was entirely unconvinced however much I would have liked to believe him.

He pushed himself upright and walked across the room. He came right up to me and stood there, his legs brushing against the skirts of my gown.

'Margaret.' He reached for my hand. His voice was low. 'You know how I feel about you.'

Yes, I knew. He had never lied. He'd said he wanted me but that marriage was out of the question; his brother needed him to make a foreign alliance and I was not worthy.

'You're not married yet? You didn't accept that Everingham fellow?'

'No,' I whispered, lowering my head so that he couldn't see my distress. 'He has married someone else.'

He was making certain there would be no outraged husband in the background because if I was a married woman there would need to be a pay-off to make a husband stand aside. Lord Edmund was not powerful enough to take another man's wife against the man's wishes.

Blessed Mary, Mother of Christ! I thought. How has it come to this? How have I arrived at this shameful point in my life where I am thinking of giving my body to this man in exchange for so very little? All because he stirs my blood and because I am tired of being alone. He promised he loved me and yet he left me and here he is speaking lover's words and smiling as if we'd parted only yesterday. This life he was promising me would be no glorious future free from poverty and fear, but a continuing shame, an unhappy reminder of my past foolishness.

'Margaret. I have something for you.'

He picked up a document from the table. He turned it slowly in his hands then held it out, offering it to me. It was covered in seals. I doubted I had seen such a weight of parchment before. This would be a gift, some pretty little manor he wished to bestow upon me to seal what he thought would be our bargain.

'I cannot accept anything from you, Lord Edmund,' I said trying to speak in my coldest voice but failing as my words faltered. Tears pricked the back of my eyes and I thought if I didn't escape soon I would weep.

I made the mistake of looking up into his eyes.

'Oh Edmund,' I said. 'I know what you want but it cannot be. I cannot be your mistress.'

'Read it,' he said.

I hesitated. Was I so sure I would let him walk away? I still loved him. How could I not love him?

'Margaret, you need to know what it says. Believe me, you need to know.'

I knew I should read it. It would be utter folly to do otherwise. This would be my security. Mistresses could be discarded at a man's whim but this would ensure I was well provided for no matter what should happen. It was important to have a document lawyers could chew over, something to protect me and any children we might have.

I wondered would I have to sign anything. I doubted it but I was totally ignorant in such matters. My brother would have attended to everything. Tom would have satisfied himself that I would never be left destitute because everybody knows one man's mistress can never be another man's wife. No-one would want her. I would be used goods patched together to look like new, presented as a virtuous woman. But no-one would be deceived. They would all know and of course I would not be welcome in the queen's presence again.

I held it in my hands. It was weighty and felt strange. The softest of parchment, the very best. I looked at the Latin words, beautifully written, beautifully phrased. I blinked. I read the words again and then a third time.

'It is a papal dispensation,' I whispered. 'For marriage, for those persons named who are related in the third or fourth degree.'

'Yes,' he said in the gentlest of tones.

'Given on the sixth day of October.'

'It has taken me a while to get here. Storms, poor roads, you know how things are.'

I was crying now and could not see him clearly.

'Margaret, dearest Margaret,' he said, removing the document and taking both my hands in his. 'The Holy Father has sanctioned our marriage, your brother has given his approval, I'm asking you to be my wife. So why are you crying? Was this not what you wanted?'

'Oh Edmund, it was. It is.'

He put his arms round me and, with the greatest of care, kissed me, not with urgency like he had the last time, but slowly and gently, his mouth warm and his lips inviting. A flood of sensation filled my very being and I could think of nothing but this moment of complete and utter happiness. I wouldn't ask who had changed his mind, what persuasion had made him take the honourable way. He was the shining knight of my dreams come to rescue me from the prison of my widowhood and that was all that mattered.

'Marriage?' Isabella favoured me with a beaming smile. 'How wonderful! And how good of Lord Wake to come from England with the news. Mind you, Margaret, he has been somewhat slow in arranging this. How long have you been a widow?'

This was Isabella at her sharpest. She knew exactly how long it had been since John's death and was telling me I should be grateful for any crumb, no matter how small.

'More than eleven years, your grace.'

'Indeed!' She raised her eyebrows. 'So long! Tell us, who is the fortunate man? He must be fortunate, must he not, ladies, for Margaret is a jewel amongst women?'

There was a murmur of assent from the others, all dying to know who I was to marry even though none of them regarded me as a jewel.

Isabella frowned impatiently. 'Come Margaret, tell us who it is. Can it be the emperor of Byzantium? I know he is in need of a wife but …' She smiled while the others tittered behind their hands at the outrageousness of her suggestion. 'Regretfully a widow in your circumstances cannot expect much when it comes to remarriage - an elderly knight perhaps? So tell us - who is it?'

'I am to marry Lord Edmund, the king's brother.'

There was complete silence. You could have heard a pin drop. No-one moved, not even an inch. Nobody laughed or gasped or giggled or even coughed. Isabella's eyes widened in disbelief, then narrowed with suspicion.

'That is a very poor joke, Margaret. It does not amuse me.'

I bit my lip. This was worse than I'd imagined.

'It is the truth, your grace. Lord Edmund and I are to be married.'

She drew herself up to her full height, stepped forward and slapped me hard across my face. The pain was immediate and shocking as I jerked my head away.

'You slut! How long has this been going on? How many times have you sneaked away from my presence to meet with him?'

Her face was white but two angry red spots blazed on her cheeks.

'I expected something better from you,' she spat. 'Though perhaps it is no surprise. Your father was a liar, pretending he was descended from some brave Saxon hero while all the time the man was a pot-scrubber from Normandy. Your mother lowered herself into the gutter when she married him.'

I said nothing. She was the queen and had the right to be angry if she chose. To her, I was merely one of her ladies, little more than a servant for all her pretty words the other night.

'If you think this marriage will go ahead,' she hissed, 'think again. It is an abomination, an impossibility. Lord Edmund's mother was my father's sister. The sacred blood of the Capet kings ran in her veins. Do you think I shall permit this insult to my family?'

She was trembling with fury, her fingers curled into claws ready to scratch out my eyes. I took a step back in alarm but she followed me until she had me against the table. She was in such a fury I thought she might strangle me with her bare hands. The other ladies huddled together, far too afraid to do anything other than mew.

'Get out of my sight and do not return,' she said in her coldest voice. 'I never want to see you again.'

Edmund laughed when I told him.

'Isabella will come to accept our marriage, sweetheart. She'll have to. You're going to be her sister-in-law.'

We were walking side by side in the inner court of one of the houses within the palace confines, the most my brother would allow in the circumstances. 'Your reputation must be spotless now that you are to marry the king's brother,' he had said, lecturing me on my behaviour as if I was an untouched girl of thirteen not a woman of almost twenty-eight who'd been married and bedded and borne a child.

In the centre of the tiny paved courtyard stood a little fountain where clear water still trickled into the shallow basin despite the danger of frost and ice. Here, where tall, pale-coloured buildings blocked out the raucous cries and foul smells of the alleyways, we had found a surprising peace. There was nothing but the gentle splashing, our muffled footsteps and the sound of our beating hearts.

'Tell me about your first husband,' said Edmund.

'Why do you ask? He's been dead eleven years.'

Edmund reached for my hand. 'A husband likes to know who his wife compares him with when he comes to her bed. It is man's nature to wish to be the best.'

I smiled. So Lord Edmund was nervous about his performance. Despite his dreadful reputation and his boasting about village girls and eager prioresses, he was still unsure.

What to tell him? John Comyn and I had married in our springtime, a boy and girl affair, just two young people exploring love. In the evenings as we'd sat by the fire, he'd told me of his father's murder at the hands of the king's

49

enemies, and of Badenoch, his boyhood home, high in the Scottish hills, a home he hadn't seen for more than six years.

'When I go back,' he'd whispered. 'I shall plant a garden for you with banks of thyme and pear trees like those in the queen's secret garden at Woodstock, where they shed white blossom across the grass.'

But he never went back. One sunny day he'd ridden away up the sandy track to Southwell, gorgeously arrayed in scarlet and blue as if off to a wedding. I never saw him again. He died beneath the Scottish pikes at Bannockburn and if I dream of Badenoch now, I cannot see the pear trees. There is no garden, no bank of thyme, no snow-white blossom on the grass; just the mute grey walls of a stone-built castle and the crimson blood of a thousand Englishmen spreading out across the ground, trickling away into the still dark waters of a Scottish loch.

'There is nothing to tell,' I said quietly. 'It is too long ago and I have forgotten.'

I could see my answer pleased him. He wanted no ghost hovering around our marriage bed and no opponent in the joust of love. He wished to be the undisputed champion who could claim the purse of gold.

He lifted my hand to his mouth and easing off my glove, kissed my fingers one by one.

'Only three more days,' he whispered. 'Then I shall have licence to remove your clothing.'

'I trust you will not be disappointed, my lord. I hope there will be no regrets.'

He risked a quick kiss. 'Margaret, how could I regret marriage with you?'

'Will the king be very angry?'

'Possibly.'

'But he won't confiscate your lands?' My voice quivered. How would we manage if the king withdrew his favour? Edmund wasn't wealthy and I had very little of my own.

'No, he won't do that but if he does, he'll give them back again. Why the concern? Would you not marry me if I was poor?' A sliver of doubt clouded his eyes. Did he really imagine me so faithless?

I stood on my tiptoes and forgetting my brother's orders, kissed his cold lips. 'I would marry you if you had nothing and were clothed in homespun, and I shall do my best to be a good wife.' And then, remembering what the duties of a good wife entailed, I promised that once we were married I would let him remove my gown.

A day later I was summoned back to the queen's presence. Isabella had decided to be magnanimous and forgive me for what she perceived as my presumption in daring to consider marrying the king's brother.

'She will be there to see you become my wife,' Edmund told me, fumbling with the ribbons on my winter cloak as we walked along the covered cloister, trailed by my maid and one of Edmund's grooms. 'There is little else she can do other than make the best of things as Cousin Charles has given us his blessing. If the king of France is to attend our wedding then you can be certain the queen of England will not wish to be left out in the cold.' He slipped the cloak off my left shoulder.

'Lord Edmund!' I said severely, pulling myself away

from him and rearranging my clothes. 'It is freezing outside. The river has iced over, the fires are barely warming the rooms and I am a virtuous woman who has no intention of removing any of her clothing before marriage, so will you please stop what you're doing or I shall have to go and walk elsewhere.'

I compared this fabulous wedding we were to have to the tiny gathering at Lincoln in that time long ago when John and I were wed. Apart from Aunt Mortimer and John's uncle, the earl of Pembroke, there was no-one there of any note: no finery, no glittering presents, no pomp or fuss, just a boy and a girl gazing at each other in wonder as an elderly bishop muttered the words of the marriage service and led us through into the chapel for the nuptial mass.

Later, as I entered the royal apartments and made my formal greeting, the queen passed her gaze across me in much the same way as she did to her lowest servant to show me I hadn't really been forgiven. Edmund was right. She had weighed up the situation and seen little advantage in continuing to oppose the match but I knew from the way she deliberately ignored me that she didn't approve.

I sat quietly with my embroidery on my knee near some of the younger ladies who had chosen my company in the hope of discovering more about my scandalous wedding. The colours of their close-woven gowns jostled one with the other as they squabbled for the seat next to mine and a faint scent of lavender rose from the folds of their skirts.

An elbow dug uncomfortably into my side as one of them placed her stool on the hem of my gown. Several shoulders were inclined in my direction while the ladies smiled and raised their eyebrows in mock sympathy. They told me they were unsure if my marriage would take place as the queen had threatened to have it stopped.

'I've heard your betrothed is wildly handsome,' whispered one, smiling hopefully at me, expecting a confidence in return for her interest.

'Has he kissed you yet?' asked the youngest, a small thin-faced red-head from Beauvais who reminded me disconcertingly of Eleanor Despenser.

'Why her?' I heard someone say to her friend. 'What has she got to recommend her that she should make such a good marriage?'

'She'll be sent home,' said the friend who had never liked me.

Isabella, who had been talking to her chamberlain, smoothed her velvet gown, and turned her attention to Lady Jeanne. I knew Isabella would pick on me before long so I kept my head bent and concentrated on my stitches. The air was heavy with the weight of unspoken words and my tongue felt too large for my mouth. My hands began to tremble and I nearly dropped my needle.

'It is a disaster.' the queen spoke in a voice loud enough for everyone to hear. 'I suppose he fancies himself in love. A wholly unworthy reason for marriage. Lord Edmund is not a plough boy, even though he may behave like one, poking with his stick in the furrows.'

A suppressed giggle from the girl next to me.

'No indeed, it is not acceptable,' agreed Lady Jeanne.

The queen smiled at her friend. 'Lord Edmund cannot please himself as to whom he will marry. He is my husband's brother and has responsibilities. I do not like to admit it but I fear he has taken leave of his senses. Some temporary madness perhaps?'

I jabbed my needle fiercely into the cloth wishing I could stab Isabella. I knew she was trying to provoke me so I set my lips together, determined to say nothing. But I couldn't escape her voice.

'Men who marry for love fall out of love just as easily and then what is a woman left with? You only have to look at the countess of Norfolk to see what lies in store for Lady Margaret. But in our charity we must pray for her as she is to be greatly pitied.'

The countess of Norfolk, for all her pretty looks, had been sent away to one of her husband's manors in the country. There, it was said, she sat stitching napkins for her lord and weeping into a bowl of pottage. The earl regretted his hasty marriage but could do nothing other than make the best of what his brother the king had said was a mess of his own making.

'A marriage cannot be founded on a moment of folly when the candles are dimmed, ladies. We all know that, don't we?' the queen laughed gaily, looking round for our agreement.

There was a murmur of assent, although I noticed one young lady was less eager to nod her head. She was doubtless dreaming of a lover in the greenwood while her father was tying up a betrothal contract with the dull middle-aged widower whose lands bordered his own. She knew better than to voice her opinion because no matter what she thought, the queen was always right.

'Love makes fools of men. And you do realise what he's like, don't you, Lady Margaret?' she said, dropping like a hawk onto its prey. 'He's a wild young man with very little to his name. I trust that was not your reason for pursuing him.'

She couldn't accept that Edmund was the pursuer. She thought me an avaricious harpy digging my claws into Edmund's unresisting royal flesh. I said nothing. With Isabella it was wiser to remain silent.

'If he marries you,' she continued, 'my husband will punish him. A thousand marks your brother, Lord Wake, paid for his presumption in marrying without permission. Just think how much more the king will wrest from Lord Edmund. If later my husband should feel inclined to forgiveness I'm certain his chamberlain will ensure he is steadfast. And don't look to me for help, I have enough difficulties of my own.'

It would have been impossible not to know about the queen's difficulties. She hosted daily gatherings where she complained of her situation to all those present. Her most devoted admirers - apart from her brother Charles and his new wife, little Madame of Evreux - were the elderly earl of Richmond and the queen's cousin, Robert of Artois.

The earl had come to Paris in the spring as one of the king's envoys but was refusing to return to England. Every time he received a command from the king to quit France the queen entwined her arm with his, looking up from under her lovely dark eyelashes, 'Go back to England? Surely you won't desert me, dear Britto? What would I do without you?

Who would advise me? Who would protect me?'

And so of course he stayed.

Isabella's kinsman, the gigantic Robert of Artois, count of Beaumont-le-Roger, lord of Conches, was the most ardent of her royal cousins. When he visited he caused the queen's ladies to withdraw to the side in case they got in his way. We'd had years of practice in sweeping our skirts out of the paths of large men like the count but I felt sorry for his wife who must endure being embraced by this great bear of a man.

'Isabella, dearest cousin,' he growled, a surprisingly low and tender voice in a man of such vast proportions. 'You know I worship daily at your shrine. Anything you want shall be yours. You only have to ask.'

The French ladies said the count had spent all his wealth in endless legal wrangling with his aunt so I doubted he had much to offer but perhaps Isabella didn't know. Perhaps she thought he had vast wealth to place at her disposal. I wasn't privy to the details of her finances but I knew she borrowed from her brother as well as from the bankers. Understanding a little of money matters myself, I wondered what they hoped to gain from an exiled and impoverished queen whose husband had taken everything that was once hers.

'Robert, dearest cousin.' She stroked him tenderly with her words if not with her fingers. 'I am in your eternal debt, as you know. I depend on you entirely and the days when you are not here are dismal indeed.'

This kind of exchange was commonplace as Isabella wove her web around those she wished to ensnare in her endless campaign against her husband and the Despensers.

The next day I could smell the excitement in the air. The queen's ladies fluttered about the chamber like a flock of panicked hens, smoothing their gowns, adjusting their girdles and checking each others faces for blemishes.

'What is happening?' I asked.

'Don't you know?' said one of the French ladies. 'Madame's cousin has arrived in Paris and is coming to pay her respects.'

There were dozens of these royal cousins littered across Christendom, from the shores of the Narrow Seas to the burning lands far away in the south where people's skin was darker than ours and olive trees grew like weeds. I wondered which one this was.

Despite the joyous occasion Isabella remained dressed in unrelieved black. Lately she had taken to wearing a conventual veil and the unflattering barbe which enclosed her face but oddly made her look more beautiful than ever. I swear she could have worn sackcloth tied with a rope and still stopped a man in his tracks, whereas we less fortunate women struggled to make the best of what God had given us, with silks and ribbons and pots of paste.

'The countess of Hainault is on her way to Perray, to her father's bedside,' the queen informed us. 'My uncle of Valois, is sick and, as befits a dutiful daughter, she wishes to see him.'

In the late summer while we'd been idly journeying around the French king's palaces and visiting holy shrines, the elderly count of Valois had been struck down with a malady which had left him confined to his bed, barely able to speak. The royal physicians were in despair. They had tried every remedy at their disposal but to no avail and now the king's astrologer was foretelling a death before the year turned. Nobody spoke of it, but the arrival of the countess must mean the end was near.

The countess was her father's eldest daughter and had travelled to Paris without her husband who, the queen's French ladies told me with much silly giggling, was riddled with gout and unable to sit on a horse. We were gathered at one side of the room in small groups, huddled together, with the younger ladies clutching each other in suppressed excitement. Who knew what good-looking young men the countess might bring in her train?

'I've heard the men from Hainault are particularly handsome,' whispered one.

'My cousin says they kiss with their mouths open,' replied her friend.

'*Sainte Vierge!*' squeaked the first, giggling into her hands.

I wondered if I was ever like these young women. Their fathers and brothers might shield them from unsuitable men to keep their reputations pure, but they were helpless when it came to a little flirtation taking place right under the queen of England's nose.

Madame Jeanne de Valois, countess of Hainault, breezed into the room with all the confidence of one who knew she would be welcome. She was small, plump and dark with a long nose. Accompanying her was her daughter, Philippa, a stout girl of about eleven years old.

Isabella rose in a rustle of the very blackest of brocades and, stretching out her arms, embraced her cousin with genuine emotion. Behind the countess, her many ladies and gentlemen crowded into the chamber hoping to be presented to the English queen, their black garments fluttering one against the other as they settled down to roost.

I watched the formal greetings and exchange of gifts and resigned myself to a lengthy ritual of presentations of the senior men, all dull flat-faced Hainaulters with burly bodies and short legs. There was not a single handsome young man for the French ladies to sigh over which was perhaps just as well. The younger ones could be extremely tiresome, wanting to send little notes and behaving in a very foolish way.

On the opposite side of the chamber, stretching all the way across one wall were the queen's favourite tapestries, a present from her brother: Guinivere and her women tending the dying Arthur. As my eyes travelled across the pale-coloured limbs of the legendary queen, marvelling at her woven elegance and womanly compassion, my thoughts drifted to Edmund and our wedding.

I was lost in a delicious reverie of sweet music and soft candlelight in which my husband was holding my silk-clad body close to his when suddenly I felt I was being spied upon. I lowered my gaze and looked around. Nothing but dozens of men, their arms neatly at their sides, all with their eyes fixed firmly on the queen and the countess. Then I saw a familiar pair of dark grey eyes looking at me.

'Lord Mortimer!' I put my hand over my mouth.

He saw me gasp and smiled, then turned his face back to the queen.

Roger Mortimer! Lord Mortimer of Wigmore! My cousin. Ten years older than me and the hero of my girlhood. Two years ago he'd escaped from the Tower and disappeared and I hadn't expected to see him here.

The countess was still presenting her people. When at last she came to my cousin, she smiled beguilingly at Isabella. 'See! I have saved the best till last. Someone I know you have been hoping to meet, someone who has been safe with me these past months - your loyal servant, Lord Mortimer.'

My cousin sank to one knee and pressed his lips to his queen's ring. Beneath the heavy black veiling, and probably unnoticed by the others, a faint flush rose in Isabella's cheeks. I couldn't hear what my cousin was saying, his voice was too low, but whatever it was took him an exceedingly long time. The baron and the queen were engaged in a very private conversation which precluded the rest of us, even the countess, who looked on in a most proprietary way.

'You see my friends,' she said, favouring us with a little smile. 'This is how I honour my dearest cousin, by bringing her exactly what she wants.'

The Hainaulters laughed. My cousin rose, giving the queen a final kiss on her slim white fingers, and moved backwards. The countess beamed as if she had just performed a miracle which, in the queen's eyes, I was certain she had.

Isabella had wanted a champion and who could be more suitable to slay her dragons than Sir Hugh Despenser's bitterest enemy, my cousin Roger, Lord Mortimer of Wigmore.

He bowed over my hand. 'Cousin, I barely recognised you. You were no more than a child last time we met.'

I looked carefully at his face: slightly older, thinner and more lined than before but still attractive; the same wide-set eyes, the full lips, the slightly curved nose and hair which was dark with hardly a trace of grey, just a slight touch at the temples. They said he was a brutal, violent man but to me he had never been unkind.

'You haven't changed one bit, my lord.'

'I think my time in the Tower may have given me a more sombre manner.'

'Your escape was the subject of much discussion amongst the queen's ladies. Lady Eleanor swore you had been changed by magic into a raven and flown from the window.'

He snorted. 'If anyone was flying around the walls of the Tower festooned in black it was my Lady Despenser mounted on her broomstick.'

I smiled at the thought of Eleanor Despenser dealing with the devil. I was certain she'd spied on the queen for her husband so I could believe her guilty of almost any foulness.

'The king had half the country out looking for you,' I said, wondering if he'd known. 'We were told you were coming to invade with an army of Frenchmen and no-one was safe in their beds.'

He laughed. 'I went to our de Fiennes cousins in Picardy. They took care of me, and King Charles has been more than generous. He sent me to his cousin in Hainault and my six months with the countess and her husband have proved most instructive.'

'Will you make your home there?'

'Of course not. How could you think such a thing? I intend to go back to England.'

I gasped in horror. 'You can't go back, my lord. You'll be killed. Sir Hugh Despenser will have your head on a stake before you're half-way to Wigmore.'

'You expect me to spend my life living in someone else's house?'

'N-no,' I stammered. 'I understand that would be impossible.'

He looked at me coldly. I remembered my cousin's displeasure from the days when I was young. I'd endured many a frightened hour at Wigmore hiding with the Mortimer children in the nursery while men's voices raged in the hall.

'I hear you are to be married,' he said, not seeming much interested. 'My mother said youth was your only advantage and she doubted you'd find another husband.'

I pressed my lips together, wondering yet again at the way people regarded my chances of a good marriage as so very low.

'Who has agreed to take you?' he asked.

I eyed him coolly. 'Lord Edmund, the king's brother. We are to be married on Saturday.'

He stared, his eyes widening in disbelief, then said with a broad smile. 'I congratulate you, little cousin. You've done well.'

Of course he realised that as the wife of the king's brother I would be one of the most important women in the land, only a step behind the queen. The Mortimers would bend their knees to me. After years of casual indifference when I was nothing more than another child under his feet or a needy young widow laying claim to his assistance, he now saw me as a woman of importance. There was a delicious warmth in savouring this moment of close kinship with the great Lord Mortimer.

To show his approval he kissed my lips and held me close. I breathed in the scent of his skin and his clothes, a smell I remembered from a day long ago in the hall at Wigmore when he was going away to Ireland. There was a time when this would have been the fulfilment of my dreams, to be held and kissed by my big cousin. But not now, not now that I had Edmund; not now that I so very, very nearly had Edmund.

I awoke to the sound of gentle tapping on the door and a muttered conversation. The bed was strange: oak posts hung with blue and green figured damask, golden cords and knotted tassels, and sweeping curtains of rose-coloured silk.

Strands of hair lay across my face and by some means I had lost my pillow.

There was a cough and a, 'My lord!' from beyond the curtains. Edmund lay sprawled on his back, half-entangled in the bed sheets.

Another cough.

Edmund opened an eye. 'Go away, damn you, this is my wedding night.'

'My lord!' It was the voice of Edmund's squire, William de la Mote. 'It is your uncle, the count of Valois.'

'Valois? What of the old bastard?'

'He is dying, my lord.'

'Again?'

'It may be he is dead already, my lord. The messenger says he has only a few hours left.'

There was a long silence before Edmund raised himself onto his elbow and said, 'God rest the old bugger's soul.'

'Her grace, the queen has requested you attend, my lord. She has already set out for Perray.'

Edmund muttered something under his breath, then sat up. 'Get the boy to lay out my clothes and ask the countess's maid to attend her shortly.'

At the sound of the closing door he turned his attention to me. Last night he had proved a surprisingly hesitant lover, treating me with a tenderness I'd not expected. Instead of the eager young prince impatient to prove his manhood, I'd found myself with a man, somewhat shy, almost a stranger, but one who came to our marriage bed full of kindness and generosity.

'I remember the day I first saw you,' he had murmured into my hair.

'You called me the queen's lapdog.'

'And you asked me to trawl through my brother's dungeons looking for Lord Everingham.'

I'd twined my arms round his neck, smiling. 'Were you jealous?'

'Yes, I thought you meant to marry him.'

'No, my lord, I meant to marry you.'

After eleven years alone I had forgotten the joy of a man's body and Edmund didn't disappoint me. By the time I had fallen asleep, wrapped in my new husband's arms, I felt truly married and glad of it.

But this morning was another day.

'Oh Jesu, Margaret,' he murmured kissing my bare shoulder. 'I'm glad I married you and not the Infanta.' He looked about him. 'And now for Perray and the family. I hope to God he's made a will.'

Our small world was covered in snow and ice the day the count of Valois died. It was as if God had shaped the frozen landscape to match the coldness which swept into our hearts. Requiem masses were sung in every church in Paris, the shops ran out of black cloth and only Edmund seemed unmoved by the death.

'My mother never liked him,' he remarked on our return from Perray. 'He was a bully. He once threatened to put me in a sack and throw me in the river.'

I was startled at such violence from a family member. 'When did he do that?'

'Two summers ago when our armies were fighting against each other in Gascony. He made me look a fool. We'd already surrendered and a worthy man would have been magnanimous. But not Uncle Valois. He wanted to rub my nose in our defeat. It would teach me a lesson, he said.'

'But it wasn't your fault.'

'Of course it wasn't. It was Despenser. My brother had a fleet ready to sail for Bordeaux to come to our aid, but Despenser stopped the ships saying the winds were not in their favour. Christ's blood! When were winds ever in anyone's favour? All he had to do was wait a week. I hope one day Hugh Despenser finds himself on the receiving end of adverse winds, then he'll know what it feels like.'

Throughout the days of the Nativity a heavy cloud of black mourning hovered over the palace on the Île de la Cité while everybody waited patiently for the funeral of the count of Valois. My brother left for England, telling us he dare not risk the king's fury by staying longer. His unlicensed marriage to Henry of Lancaster's daughter had already cost him a large fine and he had no wish to make matters worse. Being a supporter of the dead earl's brother was a risky affair but so far, to his relief, the king had made no move against him.

'Perhaps, we too should go,' suggested Edmund somewhat half-heartedly. 'Return to face my brother's wrath.'

I quailed inwardly at the thought of facing the king as his brother's new wife, an unworthy woman, married in haste and without permission.

'I cannot desert Isabella,' I said quickly. 'I promised her I would stay.'

'Very well, we'll wait until after the funeral. Then we'll go home.'

Apart from a small feast marking the homage done by the earl of Richmond to Lord Edward as duke of Aquitaine, our life was dull with no entertainments. I suspected the queen would have liked a little jollity but was afraid of displeasing her brother. He paid her bills and kept her safe so it wouldn't do to offend him.

After two weeks it was decided we should remove ourselves to the castle at Poissy which Monseigneur Charles had most generously made available to his sister. It was a day's journey away, far enough to be the answer to Isabella's present predicament. At that distance the men in her household who were paid to spy on her would be unlikely to report each appearance of a wisp of coloured ribbon or a small eruption of minstrelsy.

As a mark of renewed affection to one who was now married to her brother-in-law, she decided I might accompany her.

'You may *not* call me sister,' she said, with frost coating every word. 'In private and in the presence of others you will call me, your grace. I shall continue to call you Margaret.'

That was how she was to me. If for one moment I thought I was forgiven, the next I was left in no doubt as to where I belonged, and that was firmly crushed beneath the heel of her shoe. I might have been her sister-in-law but there was to be no sisterly feeling between us. I was allowed to take no liberties.

'I shall follow you in three days,' said Edmund, holding me close. 'Cousin Charles has matters he wishes to discuss.'

'Does he wish you to return to England?'

'No. He says he needs my advice on the subject of marriage.'

'Advice?' I teased. 'Truly?'

He kissed my mouth gently.

'Two weeks with you my dearest sweetheart has taught me all I need to know.'

Despite being a day's ride from Paris, the queen's admirers followed her to Poissy and each morning they crowded into one of the smaller chambers to continue their private discussions. Their adherence to the queen's cause must have been known to the king and to Sir Hugh Despenser and their hopes of a return to England were all but impossible.

With Edmund still in Paris and the countess of Surrey in attendance on Isabella I was alone when a man arrived with a summons to Lord Mortimer's rooms. It was, he said, a matter of great importance and would I please make haste.

Inside the room were the men I'd grown used to seeing gathered round the queen. As well as my cousin I saw the earl of Richmond, Lord John de Ros, Sir Thomas Roscelyn, Sir William Trussell, Sir John Maltravers and several others whose names I didn't know but whose faces were familiar.

'Countess.' It was the earl of Richmond who spoke first. 'On behalf of everyone here, I thank you for coming. You are, of course, acquainted with your kinsman, Lord Mortimer.'

I nodded. 'Yes, my lord. I have had the pleasure of knowing Lord Mortimer since I was a child.'

'And I believe most of us here are known to you if not by name then at least by sight.'

'Yes, my lord.'

'We have asked you to join us because we believe you have a greater knowledge of the queen's feelings in this matter, than we men. You have served her for a long time?'

'More than five years, my lord.'

'And you know her well?'

'As well as it is possible to know her grace.'

He coughed and chewed his lip. He was an old man, slightly stooped, and his present predicament seemed not to his liking.

'We find ourselves in something of a dilemma, my lady. Her grace tells us she despairs of the state of her marriage and desires to have Sir Hugh Despenser removed from the king's side but we do not know the means she wishes us to employ to achieve this end.'

I tried to recall Isabella's exact words when she'd last talked to me of her hatred of Sir Hugh Despenser.

'My lord, the queen wishes to return to her husband but cannot until Sir Hugh is gone. He has threatened her person and she fears the king will not be able to protect her.'

'Would she be content to have Sir Hugh exiled?'

'The queen does not believe exile is a sufficient safeguard. She says we should learn the lessons of the past.'

We all knew that four years earlier the king had been forced to banish both Sir Hugh and his father but had speedily contrived their return.

'It's true last time the king had Sir Hugh brought back,' agreed the earl. 'But if it is not to be exile, what does she envisage?'

I hesitated, knowing how much these men loathed the Despensers, yet not wanting to be the one to mention what we all knew must be done.

'How about a blade between the ribs?' said William Trussel.

'Assassins rarely succeed,' remarked the earl. 'And we have no proof the queen would sanction such a move.'

I chose my words carefully. 'My lords, despite her natural piety the queen would consider the death of Hugh Despenser an act of mercy towards the king. It is her belief that both Hugh Despenser and his father have usurped royal power and their malign influence has led to great misery for the king's realm.'

'How far would she go?' asked Lord John de Ros. 'Would she stand beside the man who struck the blow? Would she wield the dagger herself?'

Voices were raised condemning Lord John's question.

'You mistook my meaning,' he said bluntly. 'If a single assassin cannot carry out this deed then there must be more men, many more.'

'What if we were to return to England with a sufficient force to make the king agree to our demands?' William Trussel suggested.

There was a moment of silence.

'We are too few,' said the earl, shaking his head. 'Be realistic Sir William, we would never succeed.'

'Not on our own. But we would have support. Our friends would join us.'

'We'd not get halfway up the shingle,' observed Sir John Maltravers. 'Despenser has spies everywhere and the king's army would be waiting for us.'

'We'd need a goodly number of men if we were to succeed, and a fleet of ships,' mused Lord de Ros. 'And for that we need money which, regrettably, we don't have. Unless the queen has funds.'

My cousin, who had been quiet up till now, turned to me. 'How strong would you consider the bond between the queen and the countess of Hainault? You must have observed them together. Is it a deep and lasting friendship or simply one of convenience?'

'They seem close. They often talk privately with no-one else present.'

'Not even you?'

'Not me, nor any other of the queen's ladies.'

'Are you aware of the subject of their conversation?'

'My lord! Are you accusing me of spying on her grace?'

My cousin laughed. 'No, merely wondering how far your womanly curiosity might lead you.'

A blush spread across my neck and my cheeks. Of course I knew what the queen and the countess had been discussing. I wasn't that stupid.

'I believe they were discussing the marriage of the countess's daughter.'

'The Lady Philippa?'

'Yes.'

'And did the countess have any suggestions as to whom the Lady Philippa might marry?'

'I don't know, my lord.'

'Or the queen?'

'I don't know, my lord.'

'Countess.'

'Yes, my lord?'

'Next time, move a little closer.'

I itched to rebuke him for his rudeness but my years in Aunt Mortimer's household had left me with a great respect for my cousin's authority. Roger Mortimer was not a man to cross.

'I think it is time we went back to England?' I told Edmund that evening. 'After the funeral Isabella will release me.'

He hesitated. 'I now think it might be safer to remain here a while.'

'Safer?'

'I have received a letter. My brother is extremely angry. He has cut off my allowance.'

I gasped. 'Edmund! How shall we live?'

'My love, as my wife you do not need to worry about money. Rest assured, I shall not leave you to starve like your first husband did.'

'But the king?'

'It is not my brother, it is Despenser. These days everything is done to please him and Sir Hugh wants rid of anyone who has influence over my brother. He looks at me and considers me a threat. He is aware my brother is fond of me and - who knows? - in the future he might turn to me for advice. Despenser won't allow that to happen.'

'What of your other brother, the earl of Norfolk?'

'He has no love for Despenser either but won't wish to cross him. I believe he keeps to his manors.'

And so we stayed. I continued to serve Isabella and Edmund passed the days talking and riding with the other men exiled from England who would also have liked to go back were it not for the vicious rule of the Despensers.

In mid-January we returned to the Cité for the funeral of the count of Valois. Arrangements had been complicated by the fact that his many children must journey the length and breadth of Christendom to come and say farewell to their father. Seemingly dozens of daughters arrived daily together with their husbands and their retinues from Brittany, from Calabria, from Naples, from Blois and from Artois.

The count's two elder sons, Philip, now count of Valois in his father's stead, and Charles, count of Alencon, swooped down with their wives like a small flock of scavenging gulls. They were seen everywhere, dressed in black, as sombre and long-faced as one would expect of the recently bereaved. Edmund said they were squabbling over the rings on the count's fingers.

'They're wondering who'll wield power now their father's gone. It won't be Cousin Charles. He may have a crown on his head and he may think himself clever, but that doesn't mean much if nobody listens to you.'

Edmund was sprawled on a chair in the queen's outer chamber, dressed in his funerary garments and looking very smart.

'But he is the anointed king,' I protested.

'Ah yes, but his first wife, the beautiful Blanche, made him a cuckold and a man who cannot keep his wife is judged by others as a fool. They do not respect him.'

I sank into a curtsey as Isabella entered.

'Black doesn't suit you, Margaret,' she remarked in her usual icy tone. 'You look better in grey, it is more becoming to your pallor.'

This had the desired effect of making me feel unsuitably dressed for such an important occasion.

'Don't worry, Isabella. If the garment offends you, I'll remove it. If that's what you'd like?' said my husband carelessly, as if it were nothing to undress his wife in front of the queen.

'Edmund!' I said in horror. 'This is your uncle's funeral!'

'We've been burying him for months. I should imagine the gatekeepers of Purgatory are weary of waiting for his arrival.'

Isabella swept past, pretending she hadn't heard a word.

'Come wife,' murmured my husband. 'Everything is ready, you look beautiful and it's time to say farewell to my uncle.'

We entered the shadowy vastness of the church and sank to our knees in front of the embalmed corpse of the count of Valois. A hundred candles burned in silver holders placed round the bier and thirty black-veiled widows knelt in silent prayer. The count's bulky body was clothed in the finest of his fur-lined robes and his stern fleshy face stared upwards as if commanding God's angels to prepare a path for him. He would demand one strewn with the fairest of summer flowers and suitably lined with adoring and reverential crowds. He looked twice the man in death that he'd been in life and it seemed an imposition to leave his presence and return to the palace, but, after a suitable time on our knees, we made our final farewells and walked softly away.

Later, together with the king and queen, the widow and other members of the count's extended family: the sons, the daughters, the widowed queens, the innumerable royal cousins; and the dignitaries: the constable, the exchequer, the parliament, the bishops and numerous lesser clergy, we accompanied the count's body to the church of the Minorites on the Rue St Jacques. He was to be laid to rest between his first two wives, both long gone to dust. The third wife, blank-faced and trembling, stood clutching her husband's heart encased in an elaborate silver vessel. The entrails, Edmund whispered, had already been sent for burial to the abbey at Chaalis.

The day after the burial the queen made preparations to receive her kin. The daughters of the count of Valois came one at a time, together with their husbands, to greet their dearest cousin and to enquire how she did. Although nothing was said, it was perfectly obvious that their other purpose in coming was to look me over. I was an object of intense curiosity - a woman with no connection to any royal family who had somehow managed to capture a king's son. Sadly, they took one look and seeing no great beauty, decided I was not worth a second glance.

The countess of Hainault, the last of the day's visitors, stayed longer than the others and the afternoon lost its formality as the two women talked. The countess would soon be leaving Paris to return to her husband in Valenciennes and I knew Isabella would be sorry to lose her.

After a short while my cousin joined us. He nodded to me and then made his greetings to the queen and the countess.

'Handsome,' whispered one of the young French ladies in my ear. 'Such dark hair, and, *Sainte Vierge*! Look at those lips!'

'He is my cousin,' I replied frostily, not wishing to be drawn into conversation.

She laughed. 'My own cousin, he is very attentive. He tells me - best to keep it in the family.'

'His wife is my friend.'

'*Et alors*! Does the existence of a wife stop anyone? It does not stop your queen.'

'What do you mean?'

She regarded me coolly. 'Your queen, she is very taken with the handsome Lord Mortimer. Do you not see how she simpers at him? It is Lord Mortimer this, Lord Mortimer that. Oh Lord Mortimer how kind you are. Please to pick up my glove, Lord Mortimer.'

'She speaks in that way to all her admirers. Look how she treats the count of Beaumont-le-Roger.'

The young woman collapsed into giggles. 'Count Robert? He is a lecher. If she was not a queen he would have his hand up her skirts. But I do not think a crown will protect her where your Lord Mortimer is concerned. *Regardez*! You can see it in his eyes.'

I turned to look at my cousin as he talked to the queen. Their conversation seemed very correct but I noticed Isabella occasionally place her hand on his arm, too often for it to be by chance. He was listening to her but I couldn't see his eyes. If I could have seen his eyes I would have known his intentions.

The following day Edmund and I were required to visit Monseigneur Charles. Although this was a purely private visit, a royal command had been issued which was impossible to ignore. I was nervous. I had changed my gown three times until Edmund said if I didn't hurry he would take me in my shift.

'Don't be frightened. It's only Cousin Charles.'

'But what shall I say?'

'Men do not expect women to say anything sensible. You can discuss the weather or the state of the roads if you like.'

As we entered the royal apartments I felt my heart sink into my stomach. When I was merely one of Isabella's ladies, I had walked three paces behind her with my eyes fixed firmly on the hem of her gown. Now I was someone of importance, I was able to gaze at the gilding, the painted walls, the great circles of light and the slender white columns soaring upwards to the galleries above, but it didn't stop me from feeling nervous.

The king of France was a good-looking man with carefully curled fair hair swept back from a high forehead. His cheeks were plump and rosy, and his lips well-shaped. Today he was dressed in black velvet trimmed with miniver with a narrow circlet of gold on his head. He greeted Edmund, clasping his shoulders and kissing his cheeks.

'Cousin,' he said in a high silky voice. 'At last you have brought me your new wife. I was saddened to miss your nuptials but my uncle ...' He shrugged his shoulders and made a distressed expression with his mouth. 'I was summoned to his bedside, you understand?'

Edmund bowed his head in acknowledgement of the king's graciousness.

'And this is she?' the king regarded me with puzzled interest.

I curtsied as low as I could possibly go. '*Monseigneur.*'

He was wondering why Edmund had married such an insignificant and unworthy woman. It was written right across his face: no wealth, no position, no family of any note; an alliance of absolutely no value at all. Then the frown cleared and he smiled at me.

'I have the answer. It is simple. It is the *amour*, is it not?' He leaned down to raise me up. His hand was soft and slightly damp, not at all what I had expected. 'This is what you and my dear cousin have: the first love, the passion of youth. Ah, how well I remember those days: the sweetness,

77

the warmth, that first touch of the lips, the quivering of the senses. Honey and wine and soft words, is that not it?'

I blushed. 'Yes, *monseigneur*. It is as you say.'

'And you will give my cousin many sons?

'If God wills it, *monseigneur*.'

'If a wife does her duty and her conscience is clear, why should there not be sons?' His eyes slid sideways to where his wife sat with her hands folded neatly in her lap and her lashes lowered. 'My wife,' he said in the tone of voice one might use to say "my dog" or "my gloves". 'My wife has not yet performed this duty. She is suitably devout but there is clearly some defect. I watch her closely and cannot discover it, but my bishops assure me that failure in this respect is the fault of the woman.'

He looked sourly at his queen. 'My father had four sons.'

'*Monseigneur's* father was truly blessed.'

'He was. My brothers produced nothing but useless girls; not one living male child between them. And now this!'

Madame of Evreux flinched. Her failure was being touted round the court and flung in her face. I felt truly sorry for her. She and the king had not even been married a year and she had already given him a daughter but men are impatient for sons and this man was more impatient that most.

'*Monseigneur* has many years of fruitful marriage ahead,' I said delicately. 'I am certain God will soon bless your union with a son.'

'It is a great expense and inconvenience to rid oneself of a wife,' he grumbled. 'His Holiness's favours do not come cheap as I know only too well. But a king has responsibilities.'

I murmured something suitably reassuring.

'My brother England has sons.' This was not a question, more a statement of fact - an unwelcome fact.

'Two, *monseigneur*.'

'Why so blessed?' He turned to Edmund. 'I have heard strange things about my brother England.'

'If you are referring to the gossip about the Lady Eleanor,' began Edmund.

'Phh! If your king should wish to lie with his niece, what business is it of mine or of anyone else? If he lies with his chamberlain, which I have also heard is true, it is nothing. A king may choose how he wishes to pleasure himself. Provided he does his duty by his wife, the rest is ...' He waved his hand as if to indicate the unimportance of a king's activities outside the royal marriage bed.

'No, it is his - how would you say? - his liking for low people: these sailors, these carpenters, men with no lineage. It is *incroyable*. At first I did not believe it but I have been assured that it is true. I am told he entertained a barge-master in his rooms for four days. Four days? What conversation could they have? He is an educated man. He has minstrels to play for him, he rides like a whirlwind, he is skilled at *la chasse*. How can he find solace with ditch-diggers and fishermen? And now they tell me he likes to swim. To swim! In the rivers with common men! *Mon Dieu*! To think this is a king who has been blessed with two sons while I, Charles, great-grandson of the blessed Saint Louis, I am still waiting.'

Madame of Evreux lowered her face. Edmund looked amused which I thought unwise. The king was angry and it would be sensible to remember we were his guests.

'Your brother sends me letters,' he said crossly as if this was Edmund's fault.

'He writes to me too, cousin.'

'He complains that my sister will not return to his side. He asks me to send her back to him.'

This was not news. We all knew the English king wrote letters to his brother of France, as well as letters to His Holiness, the archbishops and anyone else he thought might bring influence to bear upon his wife. People were laughing at him behind his back. A deserted husband vainly trying to reclaim his runaway wife is a figure of fun and good for kitchen gossip. Even some of Isabella's ladies found the subject one of great amusement.

'Will you do that, cousin?' enquired Edmund. 'Send her back? Cease to protect her?'

The king spread out his hands in a gesture of helplessness. 'My sister says her life is in peril, that this man, *le Despenser*, has …' he glanced over to see if his wife was listening. In a lowered voice he said, 'has used her in some villainous way. She has not said more but swears he will harm her if she were to return.'

'Do you believe her?'

'She is my sister. Of course I believe her.' The words were robust but his eyes spoke of doubts. 'Nonetheless, it is a wife's duty to obey her husband. And there is the matter of the boy. He should be with his father. Sons should always be with their fathers.' He looked across at his wife whose face had sunk even lower into the front of her gown. 'If a man is fortunate enough to have a wife who gives him sons, she should ensure they are by his side.'

As we walked back through the endless corridors and courtyards of the palace I asked Edmund about his cousin's first wife, the one nobody mentioned.

'Ah yes, the delectable Blanche,' mused my husband. 'Very sweet, very enticing. Charles was besotted. I remember how I envied him. I wanted her.'

'How old were you?'

'Oh, twelve I think. Thirteen maybe.'

I raised my eyebrows. 'So young?'

'Old enough,' he laughed. 'And Blanche was particularly inviting. Charles was a fool. I'm not surprised she had him by the horns.'

'Who was the man?'

'I don't remember. Some equerry.'

'But in the palace? Right under her husband's nose? Didn't anyone notice?'

'Of course they did. The servants knew and somebody talked. Isabella found out and told her father.' He lowered his voice. 'Cousin Charles has never forgiven her.'

'What happened to the wife?'

'The old king threw her into a dungeon at Chateau-Gaillard.'

'*Sainte Vierge*! Is she still there?'

Edmund shook his head. 'I heard Charles had her taken to Maubuisson, to be enclosed in the priory.'

4

CONSPIRACY 1326

The queen of England's privy chamber in the French king's vast palace in the Cité was hidden beyond two outer chambers making it the most private place I knew. If one should wish to plot or make mischief or pass secrets from one person to another this would be an ideal spot because nobody outside could hear so much as a whisper of what was being said. When my cousin sent a note asking Edmund and me to meet him there, I knew we were going to discuss something of a serious nature.

Feeling rather awkward in the claustrophobic little room where there was hardly space to move, I sat down opposite Isabella. Edmund leaned against the wall eyeing my cousin suspiciously. They didn't like each other which was unfortunate.

Isabella patted the stool beside her.

'Edmund, please, sit here next to me. I cannot talk to you if you stand there looking fierce.'

Reluctantly, my husband did as he was asked.

She smiled at him the way she did to men when she wanted something from them: a little upturn of those beautiful lips together with a widening of her dark-fringed amethyst eyes.

'Edmund, I need your support in this matter, because I most assuredly cannot do it without you.'

'What matter would this be?'

Edmund knew perfectly well what Isabella was talking about. A return to England and the destruction of the Despensers had been the subject of numerous heated meetings at Poissy in the early weeks of January and gradually a plan had emerged. But the problems of such a venture were immense and I had grave doubts.

'How can I possibly return to England if you are not at my side?' she pleaded.

Edmund glanced at me and then back to Isabella. 'And how can I possibly take up arms against my brother?'

Isabella sighed. 'Edmund, he may be your brother but he is also my husband and I want nothing more than to be reunited with him. That cannot happen while Despenser lives. I have no more desire than you to take up arms but once we have Despenser caught, everything can return to how it was before.'

'I fail to see any advantage to me in your plan,' said Edmund. 'Give me one good reason why I should join with you.'

There was silence for a moment, then Isabella said, 'Suppose I promise you will have the rest of what my husband owes you? All the lands your father said should be yours. How much was it? Seven thousand marks? Ten thousand? Whatever your charter says. Suppose I were to pledge this to you if you agree to join me.'

Edmund said nothing, his face a mask of indifference. An onlooker would have thought his inheritance was of no importance to him.

'How much have you at the moment?' persisted Isabella. 'Two thousand? They can't be worth much, those few paltry castles of yours.'

'About a quarter of what I am owed.'

'You would be rich,' she smiled invitingly. 'Able to take your rightful place as the son of your father. Think of it Edmund. He never meant you to be impoverished and all because my husband has been remiss in his duty.'

'How will you persuade my brother to do this?'

'It will be a condition of mine for the resumption of our marriage. Once Despenser is gone we shall be reconciled. My husband knows, as I do, that it is our sacred duty to live together as man and wife.'

Edmund looked at me. 'Is this what you want, Margaret? Do you want us to ride with the queen and Lord Mortimer knowing that my brother and Sir Hugh Despenser will raise an army to greet us? Do you wish to set yourself against an anointed king?'

I turned to my cousin. 'What will you do with Despenser when you catch him?'

He inclined his head to Isabella. 'My lady, what would you have us do with Sir Hugh Despenser?'

She smiled, drawing back her lips to expose her small white teeth. 'Do with him? Why, if you hand me the knife, dear Mortimer, I'll slice him into small pieces. And before he breathes his last breath, I'll spit in his face. I hope he burns in Hell.'

'And my brother?' enquired Edmund. 'Your husband? What will you do with him?'

She had a ready answer. 'My husband will be better served by being rid of Hugh Despenser. It is folly to think otherwise. Everywhere you look England lies in ruins, brought down by Sir Hugh and his father. My sole desire is to rescue the kingdom for my husband and for my son who will one day wear the crown.'

'So my brother will not be harmed?'

Isabella's eyes widened in horror. 'Edmund! How can you think I would allow that? I have shared a bed with him. He is the father of my children and my dearest companion. As I told the Holy Father, it is my most cherished wish that we be reconciled. But as long as Despenser is in my husband's company, it is impossible. He has vowed to my face to destroy me. He has brought about the destruction of our marriage and I mean to be rid of him.'

'Very well,' said Edmund. 'Tell me what we are to do.'

Neither of them heard my cousin's sigh of relief but I was sitting next to him and almost felt the slight exhalation.

He smiled at Edmund as if they were already friends. 'The count of Hainault has promised ships.'

'How many?' enquired Edmund.

'Close on one hundred and fifty.'

I tried to imagine how large a fleet that would seem to a man on an English cliff top seeing our ships appear out of the mist. Would he light beacons and take up arms or would he run?

'The count's brother will organise the raising of troops and will take command.'

My cousin was visibly relaxed now he had Edmund safely netted. Watching him and knowing him well, I realised how much he and Isabella had needed my help in securing my husband. Edmund's presence would give added validity to Isabella's claims and perhaps he could persuade his brother Norfolk to join with them.

But Edmund was still wary. 'What happens when we reach England? If I'm to ride with you I have to know.'

My cousin nodded. 'The queen will ride at the head of our procession and we have many friends who will rally to her cause. They are waiting and are impatient for our arrival.'

'Will the king and Sir Hugh Despenser not also be waiting?' I asked, thinking of the man on the cliff top.

'They've been expecting me for two years,' laughed my cousin. 'I hear Despenser is scurrying up and down the coast ordering beacons and lookouts, garrisoning every port with his men and panicking each time he sees an unknown sail. Not that it will do him any good. Once we land there'll be nowhere for him to hide.'

I touched his arm. 'What will you do with Lady Eleanor?'

'I don't make war on women,' he said shortly. 'Unlike Despenser and the king I prefer to pick my fights with grown men, not women and young girls.'

Isabella was like a cat eyeing a bowl of cream. 'You may give her to me.'

My cousin smiled. 'Of course. A gift for your grace. How could it be otherwise? Whatever you desire, my lady, shall be yours.'

There was nothing in it. They were perfectly ordinary words for a lord to say to his queen but something in the way he spoke made me glance up. The look exchanged between the two of them was far from ordinary. On the part of Isabella it was intense, almost a yearning; and from my cousin, an unguarded expression I'd seen once before in the early days at Wigmore when he'd looked at his wife.

Edmund and I sat in our bed with the curtains drawn, huddled together like a pair of conspirators.

'Is your cousin involved?'

Edmund shook his head. 'Cousin Charles has declined to help. He'd dearly love to invade England but knows such a move would be dangerous for him. Yesterday he could talk of nothing but the injustice of my brother having a son like young Edward when all he has is one puny daughter.'

'I don't understand any of this,' I said. 'Her brother refuses to help so Isabella turns to the count of Hainault. But why? Why would the count agree to help when the French king will not? Where is the advantage?'

Edmund was as mystified as I was. 'I don't know. It's not as if Isabella has money to offer. My brother was once on good terms with the count; there was even talk of a marriage alliance. But the count favoured Cousin Charles in all things so my brother went looking elsewhere. And when the count welcomed your cousin to his court, my brother was furious. He thought the count was his friend and, as you know, considered Lord Mortimer his worst enemy.'

It was like a ray of sunshine breaking out from behind a cloud.

'Edmund! We've been blind! It's obvious why the count is anxious to help. Don't you see?'

He shook his head. 'I see nothing.'

'Isabella plans to marry her son, your nephew young Edward, to the count's daughter.'

'That's impossible. My brother would never agree.'

'Your brother isn't here. Isabella will do it without his agreement. That way she won't have to pay for ships or men or armaments. And think of the advantages to the count - a daughter who will one day be queen of England, a queen who will encourage her husband to favour Hainault in every way. It's a deal which suits them both.'

I could see how foolish Edmund's brother had been and how my cousin and Isabella had taken advantage of his foolishness. To send the boy to his mother, unwed and with no way of ensuring his return, had been the height of folly. And in that selfsame moment I realised that it wasn't Isabella who was enticing my cousin to do what *she* wanted, but *he* who was playing *her* as skilfully as a minstrel plays the strings of his lute. This had been my cousin's plan right from the beginning.

It remained cold and as we entered the long slow weeks of Lent I learned my cousin had begun secret talks with a party of Scottish envoys found hovering around the French king's court. Whatever they were discussing I doubted it would be to our advantage. The price for any of Bruce's promises would not be a scant handful of oatmeal.

But worse was to come. Edmund's brother, angered by his refusal to return to England, confiscated his property. Everything Edmund possessed was forfeit and we were virtually penniless. The earl of Richmond and John, Lord Cromwell received further orders to return home and were informed that if they did not do so, they too would lose everything.

But returning home was not without its perils. A letter, smuggled out with a silk merchant, said that Lord Beaumont - one of Isabella's supporters who had returned in the autumn rather than risk losing his lands - had been arrested and imprisoned. The lands he'd been so anxious to save had been confiscated.

A rumour that the English king's chamberlain had sworn to be rid of the king's wife, no matter what, reached Isabella who now went in constant fear of an assassin. Her personal cook prepared all her meals and pushed aside the serving boys to accompany the food to the queen's table. Still clad in his kitchen apron, he insisted on tasting each dish before allowing so much as a morsel to pass the royal lips. In that way he knew the queen was safe from a would-be poisoner and he was safe from accusations of treason.

But I could have told her that no man, however diligent, could guarantee her safety. My time with the herbalist at Wigmore had taught me the secrets of deadly plants which are tasteless and slow-acting. A victim would have no idea what caused the night-time cramps, the sweating, the purging and the sudden closing of the throat, until it was too late.

For Isabella the darkest day was the arrival in Paris of the Holy Father's envoys, the archbishop of Vienne and the bishop of Orange. His Holiness was displeased with the behaviour of all parties to the English queen's quarrel with her husband and wished to remove the obstacles which hindered their reconciliation. He was insisting a solution be found. This put a halt to the progress of my cousin's plans while Isabella negotiated several difficult interviews with her brother and the two envoys.

She dressed in a severe black gown, cut high at the neck, without ribbons or embroidery and, instead of her usual radiance, acquired a fragile pallor. Without Lord

Edward and the countess of Surrey giving support on either side of her, the slightest breeze might have blown her away. She solemnly promised the envoys to return to her husband, laying out perfectly reasonable requirements for her continued safety. She was careful to place all the blame for the breakdown of her marriage on Sir Hugh Despenser and none on her dearest and most beloved husband.

But everyone knew the English king would never agree to her demands.

Eventually, pleased with the apparent success of their mission, the envoys departed. Their next interview would be with the king of England and his favoured chamberlain after which they would report back to His Holiness.

One morning, not long after the departure of the papal envoys, I was leaving the chapel when I felt a note slipped into my hand. With a swift movement I drew it into my sleeve, wanting no-one to see. But I needn't have worried, the note was from Countess Jeanne asking me to break my fast with her.

She was very welcoming, offering me a plate of dried figs and some white bread.

'Countess, you wished to see me?'

She looked nervously over my shoulder to make sure I had brought no-one with me and then gripped my hand most painfully. 'I am worried, Lady Margaret. I do not know where to turn.'

'What concerns you?' I hoped the conversation was not to be about her faithless husband who was said to be hoping for a reconciliation.

'The queen, Lady Margaret. All these rumours, these treasons people are whispering. You must have heard them, surely? They are everywhere. Only yesterday I overheard two of the queen's own women discussing it.'

'Discussing what, my lady?'

'It isn't true. I know it cannot possibly be true. But how to stop people talking? Denials simply fan the flames and if there were to be a conflagration - where would we be? What if the Holy Father were to hear? Or her brother?'

'Countess,' I interrupted. 'What are you talking about?'

'Why, your cousin, Lady Margaret. Your cousin, Lord Mortimer.'

'Lord Mortimer?'

'They are saying,' she lowered her voice and leant forward so that her face was an inch from mine. 'They are saying that Lord Mortimer and the queen … that Lord Mortimer and the queen … that they …' She couldn't bring herself to say the words.

'What are they saying?'

'Oh Lady Margaret. You do not know what it is like. He is always there. Every morning when I greet the queen, he is there. Not doing anything in particular - just there. He is like a hound at her feet. He leans against her chair and gives his opinions on matters which are no concern of his - personal matters. And he is dreadfully familiar. I have never known her allow anyone the liberties she allows Lord Mortimer. It is …' She rummaged around for the right word. 'It is unqueenly.'

'And is there more?'

I had a horrible suspicion there might be as Lady Jeanne's face had turned an unbecoming shade of red with what I assumed was embarrassment.

'The women say she withdraws with him into her privy chamber.'

'But my lady, they have secret matters to discuss.'

'For so long a time? And when they emerge the queen's cheeks are said to be flushed and her gowns disordered.'

The countess had clearly drawn her own conclusions but I thought she was mistaken. If Isabella and my cousin were engaged in improper conduct in the queen's private room I wouldn't look at her gown but at her hair. It was my belief that the first thing a man did in any amorous encounter, was to loosen a woman's hair. He removed the pins, the ribbons, the veils and any pieces of restraining cloth so that he could run his fingers through those unconfined tresses which were so seldom displayed to men. For a woman to allow a man to fondle her hair was a mark of true abandonment. And I didn't think Isabella was about to abandon herself to my cousin.

'I am certain they are exaggerating,' I said firmly. 'The queen holds herself in too high a regard to consort with a mere baron. And even if she did not, I cannot imagine Lord Mortimer being reckless enough to try.'

But as I spoke, I knew this was untrue. My cousin *was* reckless. If he could lead an invasion against his king what was there to stop him from stealing the king's wife? Such a move would damage our campaign before it began but if my cousin wanted Isabella, I knew he would not think twice.

'Perhaps you could have a word with the queen?' I suggested. 'Tell her to be more circumspect?'

'I cannot. My husband is taking me back to England. He is loyal to the king and has declined to join this folly hatched by the earl of Richmond and Lord Mortimer. But poor Isabella! I fear she has been led astray. and I do not know what will become of her when I leave. She depends on me entirely.'

As soon as I could, I escaped from my duties and returned to our rooms where I waited impatiently for Edmund's return. At last I heard the sound of boots, the door opened and a draught of cold air blew across the floor. The fire flared into life and my wandering husband caught me round the waist, kissing me full on the mouth.

'Your lips are cold,' I protested half-heartedly.

'Whereas yours are delightfully warm, as always.'

'How are your cousins?' I said, trying to disentangle myself.

'Cousin Robert was in fine form but Charles is mournful. His wife has failed him once again.'

'Poor woman!' I murmured.

'And how about you, sweetheart?' said Edmund, kissing my wrist but with his eyes on my waist. 'Any news?'

'Not yet, my lord.'

'Perhaps we should practise some more?'

I gave him a look which promised much and then proceeded to tell him what Lady Jeanne had said.

'Do you think it's true?' I asked.

'Do you?'

'I cannot believe Isabella would consider my cousin as a man in that way. I think she looks on him as a stout champion who will give her what she wants.'

'And you think she doesn't want what other women want?'

'Edmund, she is a queen. She has a husband. No matter what she might want in that respect her position means more to her than anything else. She allows no-one other than her personal women to touch her.'

'And yet you say your cousin takes liberties and she doesn't object.'

I had a sudden image of my cousin with his hand laid possessively on Isabella's arm and of Isabella smiling.

'He behaves more like a brother.' I said hastily.

'But he is not her brother.'

'No, he is not.'

'You don't really think that she and he … that they …?'

'Do you?'

In truth neither of us knew what to think. The women who served Isabella since she first came to England might know something but they were saying nothing. Totally loyal, they'd have let their finger nails be pulled out rather than divulge any secrets.

Springtime came late to Paris that year and with the warmth and the scent of blossom came good news: Madame of Evreux was at last with child.

'Now Charles will have to give her a coronation,' said Edmund with a smile. 'I was beginning to think she'd remain uncrowned for ever.'

It may have been springtime in the hearts of the king and queen of France but in the rooms of the queen of England there was an undercurrent of unpleasantness. Mother and son were not in agreement. Lord Edward was thirteen and in the matter of the French queen's coronation his objections had become so loud we could all hear.

'I will not have that man carry my robes. I shall have Richard Bury. He is my tutor and serves me well.' He stuck out his bottom lip, planted his legs a little further apart and stared defiantly at his mother.

'Dearest,' said Isabella smoothly, tilting her head slightly to one side and smiling sweetly at her firstborn. 'We shall not quarrel over the matter. You know how much this means to our plans. If you and I are to return home we need Lord Mortimer.' She lowered her voice. 'If you were older you could lead our men yourself but for the moment Lord Mortimer's presence is necessary. And we must show that he is acting for us and has our trust. What better way than to place him high in the list of those who serve you? And he is your friend.'

'He is not my friend. He is …'

He couldn't say it. He must have heard the rumours. They were flying round Paris and by now had probably spread to the merchants who would carry them back to England. It would distress any boy to have his mother the source of such salacious gossip but for Lord Edward it was doubly hurtful. He loved his father. He also loved his mother, as indeed he should. All boys should love their mothers and Isabella could be very lovable when she chose.

She regarded him with a little frown. She was calculating how to please both my cousin and her recalcitrant son.

'Dearest,' she said at last. 'Lord Mortimer is loyal. Never underestimate the value of loyalty. Faithful friends are beyond price. And if occasionally we have to set aside our own self-importance in order to satisfy their very understandable need for recognition, then it is such a little thing to ask.'

The boy was wrong-footed. He looked warily at his mother. He didn't wish to be seen as churlish and he was being handled by an expert in the art of getting what she wanted.

He shuffled his feet. 'Very well,' he muttered. 'Lord Mortimer may carry my robes.'

'Thank you dearest,' said Isabella. 'I am very proud of you.'

If I thought that after the coronation of Madame of Evreux our path would become smoother I was gravely mistaken. No sooner were the celebrations over than we were plunged into a new and potentially even more dangerous crisis. Isabella's brother began avoiding her. He made excuses not to see her and failed to invite her to any of the court entertainments. She raged, and for those of us serving her, daily life became very unpleasant.

One afternoon, after yet another rebuff from the French king, I was forced into playing a game of chess with her. She knew I was a skilful player so I couldn't risk making too many foolish mistakes but Isabella must, of necessity, be the victor. I was manoeuvring to leave my bishop exposed on the board when we were interrupted by the heavy footfall of Monsieur Robert of Artois.

'Cousin,' said Isabella delightedly. 'How did you know I was missing you?'

'Where you are concerned, fair cousin, I know

everything,' fawned the count. 'You are constantly in my thoughts. And today I have brought news for you.'

Isabella clapped her hands. 'Good news, I trust.'

'That depends.' The count lowered his large bulk into the chair at Isabella's side and nodded to me. He rarely addressed me by name. Perhaps he had forgotten who I was.

'In my house I have an extremely fine piece of silverware,' he said, rubbing his large fleshy hands together at the thought. 'The finest workmanship. A tureen of vast proportions. I do not think I have received such an expensive gift before. It shines like the moon in the celestial heavens; it sparkles and glistens like the stars.'

'So did the thirty pieces of silver in the hands of Judas Iscariot,' remarked Isabella.

'The strange thing is,' continued the count, 'each member of our king's council has received a similar gift. Oh, not exactly the same, you understand; I do believe mine was the largest and the most expensive. But on every sideboard in the Cité you will find a pair of gleaming candlesticks or a wonderfully wrought sauce boat or some other extravagant trinket. And all from a man they do not know but who wishes to become their friend.'

'Tell me,' said the queen icily.

'Monsieur le Despenser.'

Isabella pursed her lips. 'What does he want?'

'Oh cousin, do you really need to ask? He wants you. You and Monsieur Mortimer, trussed up in a barrel on a ship bound for England.'

'They wouldn't dare. My brother wouldn't stand for it.'

'I would not be so certain, *ma chérie*. Your brother, you must understand, has a problem. He is besieged with letters from your king and from his special friend, Monsieur le Despenser - who incidentally expresses his devotion to your grace and says he has never harmed a hair on your head, nor ever would. Also letters from His Holiness who says a wife should live with her husband.'

'The ...' Isabella sought for an insult fitting for the occasion.

'I have a fine supply of words, dear cousin, if you cannot think of one suitable for today.'

The count leaned back in his chair, no mean feat for one of his proportions.

Isabella eyed him carefully. 'What can I do?'

'Do?'

'Yes, do? I have no intention of ending up in Monsieur le Despenser's hands.'

'Perhaps it is time to consider moving on.'

'Moving on? Where would we go? Mortimer says we are not ready. We need more time and more money.'

The count folded his arms across his capacious belly, and regarded Isabella with a little smile. 'Your lands in Ponthieu? Hainault, perhaps? Yes, Hainault. Not too far, and I do believe the air there is most agreeable for the young. The countess's daughters flourish, so my wife tells me. Rosy-cheeked, pretty girls. Just the sort of diversion for a boy who has become disgruntled.'

'Robert,' said Isabella, 'If my heart was not already in another's keeping, I would give it to you. You are magnificent.'

The count shrugged. 'It is nothing, *ma chérie*. And that

98

tureen will look very fine on my board at home in Artois. My wife likes such extravagances.'

As the days passed Isabella and I drifted into some semblance of our old relationship of royal mistress and favoured servant. But she couldn't forget my trickery in marrying her brother-in-law. Ours was by no means a comfortable relationship.

One morning, not long after Count Robert's visit she asked me to accompany her to the royal apartments.

'You have little to recommend you, Margaret, but a talent for keeping secrets can be useful in the hands of the right woman and today I require such a woman, one able to hold her tongue.'

Holding my tongue was a habit I had acquired in my years with Isabella. First I had been the butt of hurtful taunts from Lady Eleanor Despenser and her coterie of friends, and later, on occasions, from Isabella herself. My elevation to listening at doorways and reading other people's letters had taught me to watch what I said. Now I rarely spoke in the queen's presence without first carefully weighing my words.

'My brother is mourning his first wife,' she informed me as we walked down the long gallery towards the French king's chambers. 'The whore. The faithless Blanche.'

It was the first time Isabella had referred to her family's domestic scandal.

'She is dead?'

'Yes, praise be. Even her mother is glad to be rid of the reminder. You don't expect a child of yours to bring disgrace on your name in that way. If my father had not acted as he did, she would have had the girl strangled.'

'And Monsiegneur Charles?'

Isabella laughed. 'He keeps them chained now. Marie, the second wife, was watched day and night and Madame of Evreux dare not even cough for fear of what my brother might do. It's as well she's such a timid little mouse.'

When we reached the huge double doors of the royal apartments we were told the king was busy. Isabella scowled.

'My brother requested my presence and I do not choose to wait while he amuses himself with others.'

In his gilded chamber the king was indeed busy. With him were his cousin, Philip, the new count of Valois, and the bishop of Beauvais. The bishop was short, fat and expensively clothed, a huge amethyst gleaming on one of his plump white fingers. The count, in contrast, was a tall, thin man with broad but sloping shoulders. His long nose quivered like a greyhound's and his pale blue eyes had a soft pleading expression as if he'd been whipped once too often. Isabella's French ladies giggled that his wife ruled him the way she ruled their entire household: with a boot and a rod of iron.

The table was covered in rolls of parchment and Monseigneur Charles was drumming his fingers in annoyance. He looked up as we entered.

'Madam Isabella, my sister,' he said. 'How fortuitous. These men were just leaving.'

The bishop looked annoyed but there was nothing he could do in the face of a royal dismissal. He folded his hands across his ample middle, murmured gracious words and then backed out of the king's presence. The greyhound muttered a greeting and scuttled out, his long legs tangling themselves up in his haste to be gone.

'Brother,' said Isabella seating herself firmly in front of the table and not waiting for any formalities. 'I am far from pleased. I hear you have received another letter from my husband in which he demands my return.'

The king turned his gaze upon his sister. Just at that moment I moved into the light and he caught sight of me.

'Ah, my new cousin,' he said, rising and coming to my side. '*La petite amoureuse*. Greetings, *ma chérie*. Are you well?'

I swept to the floor which seemed the safest thing to do and whispered that I was indeed very well.

'You have not answered me, brother.' Isabella sounded irritated.

To my relief, Monseigneur Charles returned to his sister.

'Ah yes, the letter from brother England. Not the words of a happy man. He again commands your return to his side and complains bitterly of your conduct. He most particularly finds it offensive that you show favour to Lord Mortimer.'

'And why should I not?' retorted Isabella. 'Lord Mortimer is a loyal and faithful servant to me and my son.'

'Loyal and faithful servants are still servants and queens should be circumspect in how they distribute their favours. And, while we are on the subject of your son - your husband also finds it shameful that at the coronation of my beloved companion, Madame of Evreux, you permitted Lord Mortimer to carry Lord Edward's robes. A foolish move as you must by now be aware.'

'It was not foolish.' Isabella was growing increasingly angry.

'It gave rise to talk. Some of my council are not happy with the perceived closeness of Lord Mortimer to yourself and the way in which it reflects upon ourselves.'

'Exactly what are you implying?'

'Is there anything to imply? Is your behaviour all that it should be? You know what they say, sister. They say you lie with Lord Mortimer. They say you are his whore.'

I had never seen Isabella so angry. Her eyes glittered and her lips turned white with fury.

'How dare you! It is a foul untruth as well you know. I am as chaste now as the day I entered Paris a year ago. If you doubt my word, call back your bishop. Tell him to bring his Holy Book and I will swear to you that I have lain with no man other than my husband.'

'Ah sister, if only it were that simple. You see your husband involves my bishops already. The bishop of Beauvais has received a letter in which the king of England accuses you of sharing your lodgings with Lord Mortimer. A woman caught in adultery, sister. Can there be any greater sin?'

Beneath his smooth words lay the echoes of the distant scandal of the first wife. Monsiegneur Charles had not forgiven his sister.

'I have told you, brother - it is a lie. My conscience is clear.'

The king carried on as if Isabella had not spoken. 'And it transpires His Holiness also has been honoured with another letter from your husband.'

'As I told the Holy Father's envoys, I have been grossly slandered.'

'But it seems you are not believed.'

Isabella gasped. 'They doubt my word? The word of a queen?'

'It seems so. And it is not just a matter of your behaviour, sister. Your husband now regards me as one who is aiding and abetting you in your defiance. He looks upon me as his enemy. So I regret very much that I must ask you to desist in whatever plans you are making. I can no longer be seen as a party to such matters.'

'You are not.'

'But when rumours reach my ears of plots to murder my brother England and his friend, Monsieur le Despenser, and I learn that these plots emanate from the hand of Lord Mortimer who currently resides in your lodgings, then what am I to think? I fear you have gone too far, sister.'

'There is no plot.'

'My spies in England tell me otherwise. They say Lord Mortimer's men were caught in the act.'

'It isn't true.'

'Witchcraft, sister. Waxen images of your husband and Monsieur le Despenser. Evil deeds done in dark corners against the teachings of Holy Church.'

'It is a lie.'

'The men have confessed.'

'Men will confess to anything as you well know.'

'And there is also the question of our lands in the Aquitaine.'

Isabella's eyes narrowed. 'My son is the duke of Aquitaine. Gascony is his by right and you know it.'

'Some would disagree.'

They were face to face like the angry children they had once been.

'If you think you can steal my son's birthright you will regret it, Charles. You should pay heed to the fate of our two brothers: dead before their time and no sons to follow them. What do you think lies ahead for you?' She leaned across the table and caught his arm. 'If anything happens to you, God forbid that it should, who do you think will step into your boots? Long-nosed Philip? He's no Capet.'

'My wife is with child.'

'Mewling daughters!' spat Isabella, letting go of his arm. 'That's all you'll get from her. It's all you're good for. Believe me, our father will have only one true heir and that will be my son.'

Monseigneur Charles went white to the tips of his ears and hurriedly made the sign of the cross. 'You witch! Don't you dare ill-wish the child in my wife's belly.'

'I have no need,' said Isabella, rising to her feet. 'Your seed is already damned. Everybody knows you will never gain a living son. The Grand Master's curse pursued both our brothers into their graves and it will hunt you down too. There is nowhere to hide, Charles. Your bishops cannot help you. No-one can help you. The curse will follow you until the day you die.'

The king slumped back into his seat and closed his eyes. Isabella looked contemptuously at him. 'Weakling,' she muttered under her breath. Then, signalling for me to follow, she turned on her heel and swept out of the room.

It was more than ten years since the burning of the Grand Master of the Templar Knights, yet the echoes of his dying words still haunted Isabella's family. Cursed out of the flames unto the thirteenth generation; the Iron King dead within the year; Louis, the heir, cut down eighteen months later, his posthumous son living just five days; Philip, the next heir, dying in agony before six years passed and still no sons. Girl babies lived, boy babies died.

No wonder Monseigneur Charles was terrified of what lay ahead.

'She threatened him,' I said to Edmund once we were alone. 'She threatened all of them. She said the crown of France would one day belong to her son and that he was the only true heir of his grandfather.'

'Christ's blood!' said Edmund. 'She must be mad. I'd not kick up that hornets' nest for all the gold in Christendom.'

'Then let us pray Madame of Evreux presents him with a living son.'

5

HAINAULT 1326

We rode out of darkness into an uncertain dawn. A pale sky in the east together with the faint sound of distant bells heralded the start of a new day.

The warning had come in the middle of the night when our household was asleep. It was the earl of Richmond, dusty and dishevelled. Usually a scrupulously tidy man, tonight the hair beneath his black velvet cap was uncombed, his clothing all awry as if thrown on in haste. He had ridden through the streets of the Cité as fast as he could.

'You must be gone before daylight,' he said to Edmund. 'The Great Council has turned against you. Yesterday evening the queen's brother signed documents for the arrest of the queen and Lord Mortimer. They will undoubtedly come for you too. The three of you are to be sent under escort to Boulogne and thence to England.'

I put a hand over my mouth in horror.

'And Cousin Charles?' said my husband.

'At Chaalis with the members of his council. His Holiness has threatened him with excommunication if he continues to harbour the queen and Lord Mortimer. Count Robert rode to warn us. He couldn't go directly to the queen for fear of implicating himself so he came to me. He says the guards will come in the morning.'

'And Isabella?'

'The queen, her son and Lord Mortimer are leaving as we speak. They will meet you at Meru on the road to Beauvais.'

Edmund turned to me. 'One maid, one small bundle, and your travelling clothes. If we are riding fast we can't have our saddlebags cluttered up with your fripperies.'

He fired off orders for horses and men.

'Are you not taking your household?' asked the earl.

'I'll send them to Poissy. They can wait there until my cousin's men follow, thinking we are with them.'

'And you?'

'We'll go to Beauvais. Then north to Ponthieu.'

The old man looked relieved. 'I've sent men to rouse Lord de Ros and the others from their lodgings. They'll join you on the road.' He clasped Edmund tightly. '*Bon chance, mon ami*. May the saints keep you under their protection.'

'Will you not come with us?'

He smiled. 'No-one will harm me, I'm considered a friend. I even have a little influence in some quarters. I'll be of more use to her grace if I remain here but beyond that ...' He spread his hands in a gesture of helplessness.

We crossed the bridge in single file and rode beneath the walls of the Chatelet, a small group of men with two women dressed in sombre travelling clothes. My face was hidden by my hood while the men had swords and daggers concealed beneath their cloaks. We wound our way through the dark streets of Paris and, with a handful of coins, had the city gate opened.

'My master's wife has a fancy to visit her sister in Poissy,' grumbled one of Edmund's men to the gatekeeper. 'The Good Lord alone knows why we have to leave at this hour.'

Hopefully the man would remember the conversation.

We rode fast, not stopping for food or drink. Towards mid-day Sir John Maltravers joined us. We paused to attend to our needs but before long Edmund ordered us back into the saddle.

It was evening when we rode into Meru and I saw the welcome sight of a wayside inn. As we dismounted, my cousin was in the yard clapping Maltravers on the back and calling a greeting to Edmund.

'Where is Isabella?' I said. I didn't say "the queen" in case someone overheard.

'Inside, resting. It was a hard ride for her.'

It had been a hard ride for me too but my cousin was not concerned with my wellbeing. I wasn't necessary to him now that I had brought him Edmund.

The plan was to stay the night and press on next day for Beauvais. There, my cousin would strike out for Hainault with Maltravers, leaving the rest of us to make our way north to Amiens. Once across the border into Ponthieu we'd be safe and would wait there while my cousin arranged safe conducts for us to enter Hainault.

The inn, for all its size, was a poor place, ill-lit and ill-furnished. Edmund went up to inspect our rooms while my cousin talked to the landlord. We must have made an odd party because a prosperous-looking merchant was staring at us. He was one of a group of three eating at a table near the door. The younger man was likely his son as the resemblance was pronounced. The third, an older man, was perhaps his steward. The merchant seemed somewhat the worse for drink.

As we turned to leave he rose and came unsteadily across the floor. 'I beg your pardon for the intrusion, monsieur, but haven't we met?'

My cousin cast a quick glance at the man. 'No. Sorry. I don't know you.'

'Valenciennes? Last summer?'

'No.'

The man scratched his chin in puzzlement.

'I could have sworn. I said to my son … are you sure? Your face is familiar.'

'I was in Rouen last summer.'

'Oh well then, it can't have been you.' He looked at my cousin curiously. 'But he was very like you, monsieur. Perhaps your brother? Or your cousin?'

'I have no cousins and my brother was in Rouen with me. You are mistaken and now if you will excuse me, my goodwife and I …'

'Oh, to be sure.' He shook his head. 'I would have wagered a week's money. But if you're certain.'

'I am.'

The man still looked bewildered. 'And the voice. Your accent. But as you said, monsieur, you were in Rouen so it couldn't have been you.'

'No, it couldn't.'

'Then all I can do, monsieur, is apologise for my presumption.'

My cousin inclined his head. 'Where are you headed, you and your son?'

'Oh, Paris. Where else? And you?'

'My wife and I go back to Rouen. Now I must bid you goodnight.'

Together we climbed the stairs in silence. When we reached the top, my cousin grasped me by the arm. 'Say nothing to the others.'

'Did he know you?'

'Yes. I met him at a friend's house in Valenciennes. Once his head is less befuddled with drink he'll remember my name.'

'What will you do?'

He looked at me as if I were stupid.

'Don't ask foolish questions. You don't want to know the answers.'

That night Isabella and I shared a bed of sorts while the maids lay on straw near the door. Edmund and young Edward were in the next room with my cousin. I didn't ask where the other men slept but I heard my cousin detail a watch for the night in case we'd been followed. As I tossed and turned I tried not to think about the plump merchant and his fresh-faced son sleeping peacefully in their bed; or the French king's men-at-arms in their black cloaks with their hats pulled low, galloping through the night in pursuit of the English queen.

Next morning my cousin said casually to the landlord. 'I hear there are robbers on the roads near Gisors. Let's hope they don't trouble you. I should bolt your doors and shutters well tonight.'

The man grovelled and thanked the lord for his warning.

'When our friends upstairs rouse themselves from their slumbers, you might tell them we've decided to go to Rouen after all. The fat one was laying a bet I'd change my mind.'

'Friends upstairs?' said Edmund as we rode out of the inn yard.

My cousin drew his finger across his throat. 'Shutters open, table upset, bedding strewn about, empty purses lying on the floor, coins missing. The fat merchant was boasting last night of what good business he'd done. Clearly the work of robbers and thieves. I shouldn't wonder if the landlord takes better care of his customers in future. It doesn't do to get a bad reputation.'

I said nothing. But the thought of what my cousin had ordered done made me want to weep.

We waited a month in the safety of Ponthieu while Isabella raised money from her tenants and before we left I gave Edmund my news.

He dropped his gaze to my belly. 'Now?'

I smiled at his ignorance of women and babies. 'Not now but by the time winter comes I shall be as plump as a goose. You can display me at the Christmas feast.'

Edmund was quiet for a moment. 'Our son will be born in England?'

'Yes. But are you certain I have a son in here?'

'I shall be just as happy with a daughter. I'm not like Cousin Charles. All I want is for you to be safe, sweetheart, and for the child to be healthy.'

From Ponthieu we travelled slowly east through Vermandois to Cambrai in Hainault.

'It won't be long before we are back in England,' I said,

111

vainly trying to make conversation with the thirteen year-old boy riding at my side.

Lord Edward had grown this past year but he was still a quiet boy, self-contained, well-mannered, and a complete mystery to me.

'Yes, Lady Margaret.' He shot a glance at the folds of my skirts. 'I suppose I should call you "Aunt" but I have thought of you for many years as "Lady Margaret".'

'Lord Edward, you may call me whatever you want.'

He gave me a quick smile, still not meeting my eyes. 'Thank you.' He looked away seemingly intrigued at the sight of an expanse of deserted meadow. 'My lady mother tells me I am to meet my betrothed in Hainault. She says she has chosen a suitable bride and I shall be pleased with her choice.'

'I am certain your lady mother has chosen wisely. She will have considered the matter most carefully. She has your best interests at heart.'

'Was it the same for you, Lady Margaret?' he enquired politely. 'Were you chosen for my uncle in this way?'

I was surprised he didn't know, considering how loud Isabella had been in her objections to my marriage.

'No. It was different for me. Lord Edmund chose me himself.'

'I would have liked to choose for myself, but my mother says I am too young. She says it is better to allow those older and wiser to arrange such matters.'

'I am sure she is right.'

'What if I dislike the lady she has chosen? And what if the match does not meet with the approval of my father?'

He rolled the leather of his reins around in his hand. Hunching his shoulders slightly, he lowered his head. 'My father is not pleased with me. He has forbidden me to bind myself to a marriage without his consent. But what can I do?'

What indeed? A boy torn between warring parents. He loved them both but couldn't please them both. As far as he was able he would have to decide to whom he owed his loyalty and act accordingly.

'Her grace will not have chosen a lady who would be displeasing to you. She will have taken the greatest of care. She is the kindest of women and no mother wishes her child to be unhappy.'

He was silent for a long while and then turned his face to mine.

'Lady Margaret, may I ask you something?'

'Of course you may.'

'Is it true you are Lord Mortimer's cousin?'

'Yes, it's true. Our mothers were sisters. I spent the larger part of my girlhood in my aunt's house at Wigmore.'

He seemed satisfied with my reply.

'Do you know Lord Mortimer well?' He paused and bit his lip, hesitating over what he wanted to say. 'Would you consider him a good man? A kind man?'

Good? Kind? My thoughts flew back and suddenly it was yesterday. "Who is this little *bwbach**?" A pair of grey eyes level with my own, a grown man's hand in mine. Strong arms holding me close. And a knife. "Don't ask foolish questions, you don't want to know the answer."

---

* brownie, a mischievous good-natured spirit.

113

Indeed, I didn't. But what sort of man was my cousin, Roger Mortimer, Lord of Wigmore?

'Yes,' I said slowly. 'I think he is a good man. He is loyal and he cares for those who are in his keeping. What more can you ask of any man?'

'Thank you for telling me.' He paused. 'Aunt.' He flashed a sudden smile, pleased to acknowledge our closeness. 'I worry about my lady mother. I worry that she …' He was unable to say what he was thinking, but I could complete his words for myself. His mother was falling under a spell woven by my cousin, and her son feared, not just for her reputation and her dignity, but for her happiness. He wanted to know that whatever happened she would be cared for if he could not care for her himself.

Adultery is the greatest of sins for a woman but though Isabella might want my cousin as much as he wanted her she would not imperil her soul. When I was closeted with them in the days when we'd planned all this, the air between them had sometimes scorched with their desire. But I knew Isabella would be resolute She would deny herself because that was her nature. It suited her purpose that people should think they were lovers but as long as her husband lived, Isabella would not allow my cousin into her bed.

The weeks we spent in the flat green lands of Hainault were almost perfect, poised as we were between two worlds - our endless days in the halls of the French king and the unknown England to which we were returning. I liked to pretend our idle, luxurious life would continue for ever.

At Homs Isabella signed an agreement with Count William who, in return for a promise of recompense if any

114

were lost, agreed to lease her one hundred and forty ships. Once business was done he invited her to visit his family at Valenciennes.

How I enjoyed Valenciennes!

In the great galleried hall of the Hotel de Hollande we were greeted by the countess who proceeded to introduce her four daughters, the littlest barely out of short clothes. The girls were remarkably alike: all pretty, freckled and slightly plump. The elder two were already married and knew exactly how to behave with honoured visitors, smiling politely and lowering themselves to Isabella, but Philippa was like an unbroken filly, giggling and fiddling with the ribbons on her gowns.

Lord Edward was entranced. He stood beside his mother staring at these pretty creatures who smiled at him from behind their hands. As the minutes passed the poor boy began to blush.

The countess showed great thoughtfulness and suggested a walk in the gardens for the young people. Relief flooded Lord Edward's face as he and the four girls were shooed outside with their attendants to make friends away from the prying eyes of their parents. As soon as they'd gone the countess turned to Isabella and said, 'All will be well. Wait and see.'

And she was right. Friendship flourished in the gardens of the Hotel de Hollande and by the time we'd been eight days in Valenciennes, the signing of the betrothal contract promising marriage between the son of the English queen and Philippa, daughter of the count and countess of Hainault seemed a natural consequence and pleasing to everyone.

As we stood in the courtyard making our farewells, I could see a small red-headed girl with tears in her eyes, great fat glistening drops which rolled slowly down her freckled cheeks. She blinked several times and put up her fingers in a vain attempt to stem the flow. Her lips trembled and she swallowed hard, but the loss of her newfound friend was proving too much to bear and to her mother's obvious amusement, eleven-year-old Philippa began to weep in earnest.

Lord Edward paid no attention to those who were urging him to mount. He walked back to his future bride and took her hand.

'I shall write. I promised I would and I will. And in less than two years we shall be married.'

I thought he would kiss her but instead he squeezed her plump little fingers and gave her a tentative smile.

'Did you see how he looked at her? 'I whispered to Edmund. 'I swear it is a love match,'

'Like ours,' replied my husband gently, smiling into my eyes.

The night before, he had urged me to consider remaining in Hainault until our child was born but I had refused. I remembered a hot summer's day long ago when I had waved a husband off to fight and never saw him again. If Edmund was sailing to England in support of a cause he thought was just, then so was I.

At Brill, on the eve of the feast day of St Matthew, we dined with the Hainault court for the last time.

'Are you afraid?' said Edmund, holding me tight.

'Yes,' I replied, pressing myself closer. 'I am afraid we

do not have the support my cousin says we have; I am afraid there will be hundreds of armed men waiting for us the moment we set foot in England; and I am afraid your brother will not forgive us for what we are about to do. I remember the earl of Lancaster's fate at Pontefract and I am frightened for you. I do not want to lose you.'

Edmund kissed my mouth. 'You will not lose me, sweetheart.'

But Edmund was young. He didn't know how easy it was for those you loved to slip from life into death. But I knew.

Two days later, with a fair wind behind us, we set off up the wide channel towards the open sea. To begin with our ship moved slowly but as soon as the banks of the estuary fell away, the sailors pulled their ropes aboard and the barges, which had dragged us into deep water, disappeared. Up went the sail. The huge expanse of canvas bellied as it caught the wind and we surged forward like a hound unleashed. Ahead of us, somewhere beyond the horizon, lay England.

We had said our prayers and made our supplications to Saint Cuthbert before we left Brill and believed God would be with us, but we were wrong. We sailed straight into the clutches of a storm. One moment a multitude of gulls were following us, swooping and wheeling above our heads, their screams snatched away on the breeze. The next they were gone. The skies turned black and the rain began. Edmund ordered me inside and told me to stay there.

'Pray,' he said curtly. 'We may need it.'

Over the howling of the wind I could hear tremendous crashes of thunder. Torrents of rain lashed against our tiny cabin and in the dim light of the single swinging lantern, Isabella's eyes were wide with apprehension.

Outside huge waves crashed against our vessel and with each battering the oak panelling creaked and our ship's timbers shuddered. Sea-water had already breached the door, washing in malevolent dark swirls around our boxes and slapping up against the walls. Every so often the floor lurched and dipped as the ship rolled. At times it felt as if we were climbing up towards Heaven, at others, pitching down into the very depths of Hell.

Above the screaming wind and the noise of the rain I could hear men shouting and deep below us the awful sound of a shrieking horse. Tossed about like a tiny piece of wood with our sail useless, we were completely at the mercy of the storm.

Provided we remained still there was just enough room in the cabin, but the maids were already cowering on their knees on the floor, weeping and wailing, convinced we were about to die. Isabella sat rigid on the bed, her lips moving in prayer, her right hand holding her beads, her left clutching the cross she habitually wore at her throat. Our prayers at Brill had been in vain for no peace-loving saint could intercede with God to placate a tempest like this.

Against Isabella's wishes, my cousin had elected to travel in the lead ship with Sir John of Hainault, the count's brother. I didn't know where they were or if any of us would ever see land again. There was nothing we could do but pray we would not be swallowed by the heaving waves.

Isabella stretched out her hand to within an inch of my own but when she spoke it was with no hint of fear.

'The Day of Judgement may be closer than I thought and if I am to die here, in this ship, I do not wish to have sins staining my soul.'

She was so calm she might have been sitting in her privy chamber making her confession. 'I have examined my conscience and it seems to me that in all things I have behaved as I should. I have not sought beauty or riches or power but they have been freely given to me, and what I have received I have used wisely for the benefit of my family and my husband's people.'

She paused. Then her voice dropped to a whisper. Now I could barely hear her above the noise of the storm.

'I imagined that when I passed from the light of this world into the darkness of eternity I would be surrounded by those of my family who were dearest to me. But it seems God has seen fit to leave me with you. The rocks and fire of Purgatory creep ever closer but I am not afraid.'

There was a sudden crash of thunder. The lantern fell to the floor with a clatter and the candle went out. The maids screamed.

Isabella's voice spoke from the darkness. 'There is no-one to hear my confession, Margaret, so it will be to you alone I shall say these words. I have not behaved well towards you these past months. I was angry when I had no reason to be, and I would ask, now, before it is too late, for your forgiveness. I do not wish to die with the sin of pride upon my soul and these words unsaid.'

This was the Isabella of before, the Isabella of my early years, the queen who was also a friend.

'Your grace, there is nothing to forgive but if you wish forgiveness, it is yours.'

She said nothing but in return I felt a slight movement and the brush of her fingers on mine. We sat there with the storm raging outside and our hands barely touching.

'When I was a little child, not yet five years old,' she whispered, 'I fell and cut my knee. My mother would allow no-one to comfort me. I was sponged and bandaged but no-one put their arms around me as I wept. My mother said that when I was queen of England, no-one would touch me other than my husband. This, she explained, was the price you paid for being a queen.'

I wanted to touch her but didn't dare. Instead I said quietly, 'How loveless you make it sound.'

'Royal marriage has nothing to do with love. My purpose in marrying the king of England was to bear him sons and assist him in ruling his kingdom. My father had trained me well and I was skilled in the art of governance.'

'The king was fortunate to be given such a worthy wife.'

'I was twelve years old when I first saw him.'

'He was a fine man,' I said, remembering Aunt Mortimer's stories of the handsome young king.

'He was beautiful,' said Isabella wistfully. 'Tall and golden. Such broad shoulders. He could do everything to perfection. If only you had seen him in those days, Margaret. I had been told about him but nobody mentioned his beauty.'

I heard her breath catch as the ship heeled, the cabin tipped sideways and she slid closer to me.

'The first time he put his arms around me, I froze. No man had ever held me before that moment. He laughed and told me I was a funny little thing. Imagine! I, the Lady

Isabella, daughter of the king of France - a funny little thing!'

'Was he kind to you?'

'Yes, he was very kind. I tried to help him rule, as a wife should, but he cared little for governing his kingdom and when his friend, Monsieur Gaveston, was murdered he fell into a melancholy state.'

'It was a dark time.'

'Then our son was born. A fine baby. His father was proud of him. He gave him a great household and showered him with gifts and titles, and because I was the woman who had given him this magnificent child, he was kind to me. I think that for a while he loved me.'

The storm paused for an instant and except for the snivelling maids there was nothing but silence and Isabella's words 'I thought we had a good marriage but one day everything changed. My husband had acquired a new friend and the friend didn't like me. He mistrusted me and wanted my husband to himself, all the better to rule him. To my shame I was no longer necessary either as a wife or as a queen and my husband ceased to be kind. He never held me again.'

I thought how cruel the king had been to a wife who was blameless.

'It is wrong,' whispered Isabella, 'But I long to have someone hold me in their arms. I do not want to die alone.'

'You are not alone, your grace. I am here and if you like we can comfort each other. I would hold you, if it pleases you.'

A great crash rent the air, the ship shivered and rolled, the rain and wind rushed back in, and a small cold hand wrapped its slender fingers tightly around my own.

6

INVASION 1326

A day later our battered ship was sailing along a deserted coastline of dune-backed beaches, a part of England none of us recognized. After carefully studying the shore and consulting some odd-looking drawings, the captain said he believed this to be the demesne of the earl of Norfolk, my husband's dark-haired brother.

As we struggled ashore there were no signs of an army. At the top of the dunes, in an area of rough grass, the queen's servants had built a tent of carpets. It was big enough for several people so Isabella immediately sent for her clerk. She needed to write letters: letters to London, to York, to all the cities and towns of any importance, telling them of the queen's arrival and of her intention to rid the realm of the Despensers. She begged the citizens and the townspeople to lend her and her son their assistance.

According to Edmund, who had investigated further, we had landed near the manor of Walton on the banks of the River Orwell. With no sign of any of Sir Hugh Despenser's men I thought we had slipped ashore unnoticed but my cousin disabused me of any such notion.

'We may not have seen Despenser's spies but they will undoubtedly have seen us. Some local ruffian will have been paid to keep a lookout.'

All around were the familiar sights and smells of England but somewhere behind the windblown trees and the endless reed-filled marshes, were the men we had come to find. Beyond the deserted villages and the empty farmsteads they'd be massing their armies and preparing to attack. By now they would know we were here and it was only a matter of time before they came.

That night, safe in my brother-in-law's hall, my cousin gave orders for our ships to be sent back.

'We don't want Sir John and his Hainault friends creeping home before our job is done, do we?' he said smiling with his teeth at Isabella when she protested. 'Men who can't turn back, my lady, must go forward and fight.'

Bowing politely, he bade us good-night and returned to his men. It had been decided that once we were in England, my cousin's face should be seen as little as possible. This was to be the queen's campaign to rid the country of a hated favourite, not a rebel baron's attempt to topple his enemies.

With the noise and gaiety and banging of drums I thought our procession seemed more like a pilgrimage than an invading army. Isabella rode under the royal banner and with the blazing colours of England before her and her son riding at her side, she was an impressive sight. Everywhere we were cheered and nobody raised so much as a pitchfork to hinder our progress.

We advanced inland through a deserted Ipswich, to Bury and then Cambridge. At Dunstable we were joined by Lord Henry. Upon hearing the news of our landing, he had gathered his northern barons together, sacked the town of

Leicester, and hurried south. In his train he brought, not only my brother, but part of Sir Hugh Despenser's treasure he had seized from the abbey of St Mary de Pratis. Isabella was delighted.

But not all was as Isabella had hoped. My cousin was finding it difficult to keep Sir John's men in order. With no enemy in sight, the Hainaulters took the opportunity to plunder and terrorise the surrounding countryside. Isabella was kept busy pacifying the irate owners of cattle which had been seized, and handing out purses of coins to compensate them for their losses. She couldn't afford to alienate people before we managed to capture the Despensers.

'My friends, they want to fight,' explained Sir John. 'They did not come for this gentle progress through your so beautiful land, Lord Mortimer. They came to kill the Lady Isabella's enemies. And where are these enemies? First you tell me they are in London. Then you tell me they are fleeing to the West. So why are we plodding along, oh so slowly? Why do we not pursue them with greater haste?'

'All in good time, Sir John,' said my cousin. 'It is the same with warfare as it is with women. He who advances slowly and carefully will always gain his heart's desire.'

Sir John was not convinced and went away grumbling like an impatient suitor.

At Oxford the gates of the town were firmly shut but as we advanced down the road we saw movement ahead. Coming towards us, glittering in the afternoon sunshine, was a small procession.

'The good burghers of Oxford bearing gifts,' exclaimed Edmund. 'How fortuitous.'

Isabella extended her gloved hands and received the proffered silver cup. Then, escorted by the Oxford worthies and a cheering crowd of scholars and townspeople, she and Lord Edward rode under the gatehouse and into the town. We had arrived. The first of the king's loyal towns had fallen to us without so much as a single sword being drawn.

That evening my cousin brought the bishop of Hereford to pay his respects to the queen. Adam Orleton was a sharp-faced, grey-haired man with intelligent eyes. He was introduced as a long-time friend and supporter of my cousin.

'What a pleasure, your grace,' he said, settling himself comfortably in a chair. 'There are few sights more splendid than that of yourself. I am pleased God has delivered you to us in safety.'

Isabella inclined her head and smiled. She very much enjoyed praise.

'I have spoken with Lord Mortimer,' continued the bishop, 'and he suggests there is an opportunity for us. Tomorrow I preach in the church of St Mary the Virgin and would like to agree with you some of the finer points of my sermon.'

Isabella looked amused. 'And what text will you use, my lord bishop, to make these finer points?'

'I thought from the first book, the book of Genesis. '*I shall put enmity between thee and the woman, and between thy seed and hers.*'

'*And she will bruise thy head,*' quoted Isabella.

'You know your scriptures well, your grace,' said the bishop.

'*Bien sûr.* What is a queen for but to be learned in such matters?'

My cousin shifted himself impatiently.

'Well enough for your scholars, Orleton, but it won't do for the townsfolk.'

'Patience, Lord Mortimer.' The bishop dared to reprove my cousin which was not a thing many people did.

'We don't have time for patience.'

'You deal in the blood of battle, my friend. I deal with men's souls and the workings of their minds. My thrusts are fatal to the reputation of a man as yours are fatal to his human flesh. You need not worry. Between us we shall deal our enemy a mortal wound.'

'How will you do that?' enquired Isabella. She was enjoying the bishop.

'I shall tell the congregation that Sir Hugh Despenser is the snake in the Garden of Eden, the seed of the first tyrant, Satan. I shall tell them he will be crushed by the Lady Isabella and her son, the prince.'

'It is not enough.' Isabella's words were sharp.

'In what regard it is not enough, your grace?'

'To colour Despenser as a cruel tyrant is insufficient. For simple men you must paint him guilty of sins beyond their worst imaginings; those sins the church has forbidden to man. It is only in that way that you will stir their blood.'

'Of course,' said my cousin drily. 'Fornication, my lord bishop and in this particular instance, I think, sodomy.'

The bishop looked in surprise at his queen. 'You are certain, your grace? You do realise ...'

'Of course I realise,' she snapped. 'I am not a fool.'

'I hardly think fornication is something to disturb the majority of your congregation, Orleton,' said my cousin. 'Perhaps the goodwives of Oxford might cover their ears but not the men. A sin more noteworthy for its commission than in its absence. Sodomy, on the other hand, will give great cause for concern.'

He touched Isabella's hand. 'If the bishop speaks about Despenser in this way, my lady, you know what men will say of your husband?'

She smiled at him but there was no warmth in her eyes. 'The bishop may preach of bad advice given to my husband by both father and son. He may speak of their greed and their cruelty. But in this other matter, I will not have my husband named as the partner in sin of that vile creature who has destroyed my marriage.'

She turned to Edmund. 'You and I shall write to the people, a proclamation in which the blame for these matters is laid at the feet of Sir Hugh Despenser and his father. There are those who still feel loyalty to the king and I would not see him maligned. I wish people to know I am a dutiful wife. In this way, with the bishop's sermons and our proclamation, we shall bring all of England with us. Do you not agree?'

At Wallingford, which had once been Isabella's town, the castle opened its gates when they saw us approach. Here we found my cousin's son-in-law, Thomas Berkeley, the husband of my childhood friend, Meg Mortimer. He had been languishing in the castle prison for four years and was more than somewhat pleased to see us.

That same day Bishop Orleton preached an inflammatory sermon which threw Edmund into despair.

'He should not have said it. He had no right. My brother is an honourable man. Misguided, foolish, weak - yes. But he is not a tyrant and he is not a sodomite. God knows what that creature Despenser may be. He may deal in foul practices but my brother would not.'

'This is war, my love,' I said gently as one might to a child. 'The bishop only says what must be said.'

'He is my brother, Margaret. They are painting him as a degenerate monster. I shall withdraw. I shall refuse to put my name to any of this.'

'But Isabella's proclamation says nothing about your brother. It is perfectly respectful. It lays all blame on the Despensers and says only that they have disinherited the king and his son by taking to themselves powers to which they had no right.'

'You heard what Orleton said - "*The head of a kingdom should be taken off.*" What is that if not a command to kill the king? "*Sick and diseased*". That's what he called my brother.'

I did wonder if Edmund knew his brother as well as he imagined. We had never discussed the closeness of Sir Hugh Despenser to the king, but I knew secrets I would rather not tell my husband: words whispered in quiet corners by men who didn't know they could be overheard, and private letters carelessly left in unlocked coffers that I'd read whilst spying for Isabella.

Despite the news that London was in uproar and the queen's son, John, in the Tower with the Lady Eleanor Despenser, my cousin refused to allow us to be diverted from our main purpose. Sir Hugh and his father were said to be in the company of the king, heading for the Despenser strongholds of South Wales and that was the course we would take.

At Gloucester Isabella received a gift sent by the citizens of London: the blackened head of the bishop of Exeter nestling in a straw basket.

She stared impassively at the lifeless eyes and said carefully, 'I must thank the mayor for this act. It is an excellent piece of justice. He deserved to die. He was ever against me.'

I peered at the offering, noticing how the edges of the bishop's neck had been severed, not cleanly by a sword or an axe, but by a rough blade. I backed away in horror wondering if Lady Eleanor was still alive or if she, too, had fallen into the hands of the mob.

From Gloucester we travelled through marshy wooded country to Berkeley where the castle was restored to Thomas Berkeley, and thence to the town of Bristol, where our men had Sir Hugh Despenser's father, the elderly Lord Despenser, trapped inside the castle. It took eight days of siege and futile bargaining but eventually our men had the gates open and the old man in chains.

That same afternoon I stood watching as Isabella with her son led our men into the chamber for their first council meeting: Edmund and his brother Norfolk, Lord Henry with my brother Tom, Lord Beaumont, Bishop

Orleton and those of his fellow bishops who were loyal to the queen, my husband's friend, the archbishop of Dublin and three other men whose names I didn't know.

'Is this proper, my lord?' I asked my cousin who stood at my side. 'Is the queen permitted to hold a council meeting?'

My cousin turned his head to me. 'She is. We had news this morning: the king and Despenser have left our shores. They took ship from Chepstow and were last seen heading out to sea. Now we must pray for a strong south-westerly, then we'll have them.'

'So we've won?'

'Not quite yet but we have the advantage.'

'Lord Edward! Keeper of the realm!' I exclaimed, clapping my hands together.

My cousin laughed. 'It is such a waste you being a woman. You may have been a little *bwbach* but you've twice the mind of your husband.'

'Lord Edmund is a good husband to me.'

'Oh I'll admit he's a fine man but he's not like you, cousin. If I wanted someone at my side to advise me it would be you I'd choose. And yes, we shall have Lord Edward as keeper of the realm. Then we can get down to business.'

There was something very odd in all this. 'My lord, why are you not with the others? Surely you have the right?'

'I do, but I choose otherwise.'

My cousin was a clever man. From the beginning he had allowed Isabella to take the lead. This was her invasion, her revenge and this must be her council meeting. Lord Mortimer was merely obeying orders.

'Does the queen not do your bidding?'

He smiled. 'Let us say she takes my advice. She needs me. She has no idea how to manage these men. Without me they'd crush her to pieces.'

'But she won't always need you.'

He idly stroked his beard. 'I think she will, cousin; I think she'll need me for a very long time.'

On the day we left Bristol they took old man Despenser's body down from the forked gibbet and fed it to the dogs. He had suffered a death well-suited to his crimes and nobody had shed a single tear: drawn for treason, hanged for robbery and beheaded for misdeeds against the church. A fitting end for a traitor.

We were headed for Hereford but the count of Hainault's brother, Sir John, did not ride with us. He had been sent to London by Isabella, charged with holding the Tower in the name of the queen and with protecting her younger son. Soon he'd have the questionable pleasure of meeting Lady Eleanor Despenser.

In Hereford Isabella kept the feast of All Saints with great solemnity and then took her son to live with her in the Episcopal Palace as guests of Bishop Orleton. While the queen was praying, Lord Henry, who, since the council meeting now called himself "Lancaster", made preparations. He gathered his men and, with my brother at his side, disappeared across the Severn in pursuit of Sir Hugh Despenser. Their quarry was rumoured to have suffered adverse winds and been forced to make land at Cardiff. This news caused Edmund to laugh immoderately and call for more wine.

We waited but the next arrival was, not the king, but a very weary abbot of Neath on a donkey. He was accompanied by two Welshmen and came with an important message: the king wished to talk terms. My cousin was adamant. He would listen to no-one, not Edmund, not the queen and certainly not the abbot.

'No!' he shouted. 'No terms, no haggling, no concessions. Complete and total surrender. Nothing less. And I want both of them, not just Despenser.'

'Surely he can allow the king come in on his own?' I whispered to Edmund. 'That way there can be a settlement between him and Isabella and we would have Sir Hugh Despeneser in chains before the day was out.'

Edmund looked miserable. 'Despenser will have thought of that. He won't let my brother go. He wouldn't let him go to France to perform the homage and he won't let him slip out of his hands now. He'll not risk Isabella doing a deal behind his back. He'll keep Ned by his side, with a knife if necessary.'

A few days later we were informed by my cousin that Edmund Fitzalan, the earl of Arundel and one of the king's most stalwart supporters, had been taken. He was to be executed forthwith. There was to be no trial, just summary execution.

'Surely that is wrong?' I said to Edmund.

He shrugged. 'Your cousin does what he likes. Haven't you noticed?'

Edmund Fitzalan was the earl of Surrey's brother-in-law and with his death only one earl remained loyal to the king and that was Lady Jeanne's husband. I thought of her barely-concealed joy at her tentative reconciliation with the earl and her hopes for a new and prosperous life in England, and wondered if she regretted her decision.

Then came the news we'd all been waiting for: Sir Hugh Despenser had been captured and was, at this very moment, being brought in chains to the queen.

'And your brother?' I asked Edmund.

'He is being escorted to the castle at Monmouth where Cousin Henry is waiting for him.'

'What will happen to them?'

'For Despenser: trial, humiliation, execution. For my brother?' He laughed grimly. 'I don't know.'

'I suppose once Despenser has been dealt with, the king and queen will have to decide how they are to restore their marriage and be husband and wife again. It won't be easy.'

'I'm not sure I would want you as a wife if you had taken up arms against me.'

I frowned. 'No, I suppose not.'

We were both silent, trying in our own minds to reconcile the irreconcilable and imagine the unimaginable. Suddenly everything had become, not simpler, but more complicated

Dark clouds pressed lower when the day of retribution dawned for Sir Hugh Despenser. Isabella called her ladies together to ensure she was well-supported. When I arrived she was pacing the floor, clutching her hands to her breast and laughing gleefully.

'If you will excuse me, your grace,' I said politely, resting my hand on my belly. 'I do not wish to attend.'

Isabella stopped her pacing and raised her eyebrows. The laughter vanished in an instant.

'You do not *wish*?' She jabbed her finger in my face and hissed. 'Do you think I like seeing a man torn apart by the executioner? Do you think it gives me pleasure?'

Yes I did. Isabella might pretend to be above the enjoyment of watching a man suffer but I knew she'd been relishing the thought of what she'd do to Sir Hugh Despenser for more than twelve months. Now the hour was upon her, she could scarcely contain her excitement.

She was adamant. 'As the wife of one who passed judgement on the traitor you will sit with me. And I would remind you, Margaret - this is your duty. Although as the daughter of a mere baron from who-knows-where, I wonder if you know the meaning of the word.'

'I am fully aware of my duty, your grace, but I do not want my husband's unborn child affected by such a spectacle.'

'A spectacle?'

'The smell and the noise,' I said lamely.

'Today your husband's unborn child will learn what justice means. I came with God's blessing to rid England of a traitor and that is exactly what I shall do. Remember that and pinch your nose.'

Then, noticing how whey-faced and weary I looked, she relented. 'Very well you can sit with my women and hide your face if you wish.'

Sir Hugh Despenser's crimes were read out to him at his trial but, like Earl Thomas nearly five years earlier, he had not been allowed to speak. Not that he was in any condition to do so. People said he had refused food and drink on the journey from Llantrisant and was intent on cheating the queen of her plans by starving himself to death. Knowing Isabella's thirst for vengeance, in his position I would have done the same.

The crowd in the market square was vast and the noise overwhelming: clarions blaring, trumpets braying, shouts of "traitor", roars of approval every time Despenser's body was jolted on his final journey. If the crowd had had their way they would have torn him limb from limb with their bare hands before he even reached the gibbet, such was the hatred whipped up by his enemies.

They stripped him naked and wrote verses on his skin. If either the king or Lady Eleanor had ever looked upon Sir Hugh's body with enjoyment, neither of them would do so now: white wrinkled skin, caved-in ribs, shrivelled member, stick-thin arms and legs, and buttocks scarcely worth a whipping they were so scrawny. His eyes were sunk into their sockets but he was still alive and that was all that mattered to Isabella. Live men suffer and she certainly meant Sir Hugh Despenser to suffer.

The verdict given out at the trial had sentenced him to be hanged as a thief, drawn and quartered as a traitor, beheaded for violating his sentence of exile and, because he was always disloyal and had procured discord between the king and his queen, he was to be disembowelled. This was going to be a long and bloody affair.

From where I sat I could see Isabella's eyes burn with excitement. She ran her tongue across the tips of her teeth and twisted her fingers together as Sir Hugh was hustled up the steps onto the gallows' platform. He was shivering. So was she but I thought Isabella's shivers were caused, not by cold or fear, but by a sensuous anticipation of what was to come.

'We have waited a long time for this, Mortimer, have we not?' she murmured to my cousin.

I gripped the rail on the front of the ladies' platform and tried to squash the nausea rising in my throat. I told myself I was a countess and had no business behaving like a mewling girl.

First a rope was looped around Sir Hugh's neck and, to a mighty roar from the crowd, he was hoisted into the air. His legs kicked and his body jerked while his face turned from white to red to dark purple and his eyes began to bulge. But the hangman was skilled at his craft, watching the twisting and turning with a practised eye. He knew just how long to leave his customer up there: long enough to make him suffer but not so long as to kill him. Sir Hugh was still alive, just half-choked.

Next the crumpled body was tied to the top of a vast ladder, fifty-foot high if it was an inch, and one of the men called for a fire to be lit. The executioner in his leather apron, climbed up the ladder until he was level with his victim, his little piggy eyes glinting with pleasure at the thought of what he was going to do. The man seemed to be enjoying this almost as much as Isabella. But many men enjoy their work; it is not unusual.

The clerk, who held the written instructions passed down by the trial judges, began to read the sentence. He shouted loudly so that everyone could hear.

'You are a heretic and a sodomite, Hugh Despenser, and this is your punishment for involving our lord the king in your unnatural practices.'

The crowd groaned and swayed.

To a great cheer, the executioner removed a knife from his belt and brandished it in the air. At that moment I knew exactly what Isabella had ordered. I had heard of such mutilations upon a man's person but had never thought to see it done. I wanted to look away but there was a fascination in seeing this particular man deprived of his manhood. Looking at him now, a twisted wretch, I could see how evil and depraved he really was, and I trembled at the thought of how close I might have come to falling victim to his cruelties.

With his free hand the executioner grasped at his victim's groin and then with slow precision accompanied by a low growl from those watching, severed from between his thighs those very parts of Sir Hugh's body with which he had offended God's laws.

There was a moment of absolute silence and then a huge roar of approval from the crowd which almost drowned out the anguished screams from Sir Hugh.

'No cock-sucking now, you little cunt!' I heard the man below me yell.

'Let's see his guts!' shrieked the woman clutching his arm.

The executioner tossed the pitiful bloodied scraps down into the fire where they sizzled and spat. Then he set about splitting open Hugh Despenser's belly from chest to groin. When he had done this he reached in and pulled out his entrails, bits of bloody pulp and long slippery loops of pale stuff like chitterlings. As the heart was thrown down he yelled, 'False-hearted traitor!'

By now Sir Hugh was dead and all that remained of the entertainment was to see his head cut off and his body hacked into four. No dogs this time. Edmund said the head was to go to London and the limbs to York, Norwich, Lincoln and Salisbury. Everyone was to know that the rule of the hated Despensers was at an end.

I glanced over at Isabella. She had a rapt expression on her face. She was utterly captivated and enjoying every minute of this. I could imagine her and my cousin in the privacy of her rooms reminding each other of the particular refinement they had chosen for this their greatest enemy. They would laugh over his pathetic body and enjoy remembering the inhuman howl which had burst forth from his lips. If Hugh Despenser had laid a single finger on the queen in any way, she had had her revenge.

Afterwards my brother came to pay his respects. I had seen very little of him since he'd joined us at Dunstable but I could see how highly regarded he was by our cousin. Some of the more difficult tasks had been given to Tom, and Isabella had more than once commented favourably on his loyalty.

'I hear your father-in-law is to escort the king to his castle at Kenilworth,' I said, finding it oddly difficult to talk to a brother I hardly knew. 'I suppose the queen will wish to celebrate Christmas there with the king and with Lord Henry.'

He looked at me oddly. 'The queen is to spend Christmas at Wallingford with her friends.'

'Oh! I didn't know. I thought …' But I wasn't quite certain what it was that I thought. 'Will the king come to Wallingford?'

'The king will remain at Kenilworth.'

From those few scant words I sensed a whole host of others left unsaid. Plans which had been discussed and decisions taken when neither Edmund nor I had been present.

'Brother, is there something I should know?'

He sighed deeply. 'It is possible that because of who she is and because of what she once was to him, the king may, in time, forgive the queen for what she has done. She is the mother of his children and has occupied a position at his side for many years.'

'She had his welfare at heart. She only did what she believed was best for him and his realm. Sir Hugh Despenser was a fiend. His hold over the king was evil. Naturally, forgiveness, however deserving, may be slow in coming. But it will come.'

'For the queen? Possibly. But for Lord Mortimer and for me? Never. The king will in no way extend forgiveness to those of us who challenged his royalty and killed his friends. To believe otherwise is madness.'

'Could you not throw yourself on his mercy?'

Tom gave a bitter laugh. 'There would be no mercy. He would have us declared traitors and then he would have us killed.'

'The queen would not allow that. She would demand forgiveness for you and for our cousin. And what of Lord Henry?'

'My father-in-law remembers only too well the fate of his brother when he dared to rise up against the king. Earl Thomas was the king's cousin but that did not save him.'

It could not have been more clear if Tom had written the words large on the walls of Hereford: if we were to be safe, the king must remain a prisoner for the rest of his life.

What only this morning had seemed a clear path was now mired in a swirling fog with no obvious way forward. The king would stay in Kenilworth, the reluctant guest of Lord Henry, unable to rule as a king should, unable to summon parliaments or speak with his council.

But how could we have a kingdom with the king held prisoner? Who would wield power?

That evening in the bishop's palace, Isabella supped privately with my cousin and Bishop Orleton. No invitation was sent to Edmund which precluded him from hearing Isabella gloat over the final agonies of her enemy. Instead my husband took me to my room where he took off my outer robes and loosened my gown. Then he laid me on the covers of the bed and climbed up beside me. Very gently he wrapped me in his arms.

'Are you weary, my love?'

'Very.'

I felt very much a beloved wife as we lay there quietly. This was not passion, but comfort, a very domestic comfort.

'Edmund, what will happen to your brother? Tom says he is to remain at Kenilworth.'

'A prisoner in all but name.'

'Yes, but they can't keep him there. He is the king.'

'He may be the king, dearest, but Isabella holds the reins of power. After today, she and your cousin have everyone dancing to their tune and no-one dare lift a finger to help my brother. Despenser's henchmen have been destroyed and I believe even the earl of Surrey is hurrying to ingratiate himself with his queen.'

I laid my hand on Edmund's chest feeling the steady beat of his heart.

'Are we safe? You and I?'

'Yes, but be pleasant to Isabella. We mustn't anger her. She promised me my inheritance and I intend to hold her to her word.'

'And the king?'

'There is nothing I can do for him. Isabella has sworn not to harm him and soon they must meet and talk but I don't know when that will be. And in the meantime you must think of nothing but our child.'

I smiled at Edmund. 'Where shall I go for the birth?'

'How about a miserable Welsh castle. I believe I have three.'

I giggled, remembering the days of our courtship and thinking once more how fortunate I was to have a husband like Edmund, a man who not only loved me but cared for me.

Next morning I set my maid to packing my boxes. Isabella had given orders that we were to leave Hereford and make a slow progress towards Wallingford. This, she told me, would allow people the opportunity to cheer their queen who had rid them of the rapacious rule of the Despensers.

'There's a woman outside, m'lady,' said my maid keeping her eyes on the floor. 'Steward don't know her but she insists on seeing you.'

I sighed. This would be yet another woman seeking help. The town was awash with them, all anxious to prove their loyalty to the queen's cause.

I sat and waited. A moment later the steward ushered in a hooded figure in a voluminous black cloak. She was like one of those women you see skulking outside tavern doors, wrapped up so that nobody recognises them.

She put up her hands and pushed the hood back from her face.

It was the countess of Surrey.

'Oh Lady Margaret,' she wailed. 'I am in such distress. I don't know who I can count on as a friend.'

I nodded to the girl to fetch wine for the countess and waited while she seated herself.

'Forgive me for not rising,' I said laying my hand on my belly.

'You are *enceinte*?'

'I am.'

She looked wistful. 'How fortunate you are.'

'Countess, forgive me, but why are you here?'

Her hands fluttered in her lap like the wings of an injured bird. 'I cannot go to the queen or Lord Mortimer, not after my husband turned his back on them.'

'You have heard what has happened?'

'Yes, yes. The king taken and his chamberlain dead. Such folly!'

'You think it folly?'

'I do. The queen has upset the order of everything we hold sacred. I cannot believe she has the king in chains.'

'Countess, I do not think Lord Henry keeps his cousin in chains.'

'You think not? I could tell you things about that man. And to think the king is at his mercy. Lord Henry will put him in that tower his brother built at Pontefract.'

'I believe the king is to go to Kenilworth,' I said gently.

'Just as bad.' She began twisting the cloth of her skirts in her agitation.

'Countess, where is your husband?'

'He heard of the killing of his sister's husband and is afraid for his life. He wishes to make peace with the queen but is unsure of how matters stand.'

'I think Lord Fitzalan was regarded by Lord Mortimer with an extreme hatred which I doubt extends to your husband. However it was not prudent for him to remain with the king for so long. Did he not see which way the tide was running?'

The countess looked embarrassed. 'I urged him to stay loyal. He was wavering. He told me it was *my* fault we had returned to England. *My* fault? You know how things were, Lady Margaret. He lured me back with promises of a fresh beginning to our marriage. I believed he wanted me under his roof while all the time he was consorting with other women. He shamed me in front of my household. I said he had no concept of loyalty and I would return to France. I raised my voice to him, Lady Margaret, something I have never done before.'

'Countess, you knew what the queen and Lord Mortimer were planning. Did you not consider what might happen?'

She sniffed loudly and wiped her eyes.

'I saw no further than my own happiness and I have been duly punished. But though he has cheated me a second time, I would not see my husband dead.'

'I do not think the queen will allow your husband to be killed.'

'But what will become of us? Our kingdom is without a king.'

'We have a king.'

'But for how long? Anything can happen when a Lancaster is let loose, anything.'

The countess was becoming panic-stricken and whatever I did I had to calm her before she began screaming.

'You mustn't worry, the queen has issued orders that her husband is not to be harmed.'

'I doubt she'll be able to control those dogs of hers.'

'Which dogs?'

'Lord Mortimer and his like.'

'Countess, my cousin may seem a violent man to you but …'

She leaned forward and grabbled my hands. 'You think you know him, Lady Margaret but you do not. He is like Lancaster, a man who will stop at nothing to get what he wants. You may think me a foolish woman but I tell you, Lord Mortimer would kill the king himself if it suited his purposes.'

'Countess!'

I thought Lady Jeanne sane enough but perhaps her troubles had left her mind unhinged.

'I know you think me fanciful but I have had a long time to reflect on what the queen and Lord Mortimer have done and what they want. They have the boy and they will use him.'

'Which boy?' I said, startled.

'Lord Edward, the king's son.'

'The queen loves her son.'

'That will not stop her from using him.' She put her mouth close to my ear and whispered, 'She will set him up in place of his father.'

'She wouldn't,' I said uncertainly.

'You know she would.'

'But what of her husband?'

For a moment there was nothing but silence in the room but the silence told me everything I wanted to know.

'To kill a king would mean eternal damnation.' I whispered. 'It would be impossible.'

But we both knew that to a woman who had stolen her husband's kingdom and killed his friend, who had plotted and planned an invasion and gathered her husband's nobles to her side, nothing was impossible.

7

VIVAT REX 1327

Our baby was a boy and we named him Edmund for his father. Four weeks after the birth I climbed into a litter and together with my little son and his wet-nurse, set out for London through the dismal white-washed countryside. Snow lingered in the valleys and underneath hedges but on sunny slopes it was thawing fast. River waters were steadily rising and in one place a bridge was threatened by the relentless progress of the icy-grey torrent. I was nervous but my escort assured me I was perfectly safe.

Inside the litter there were furs and heated bricks to keep me warm and I kept the curtains tightly closed. Although it was a summer fever which had taken Aymer, I feared cold also killed little children.

Edmund's note had said the parliament would meet the day after the feast of the Epiphany. He would be at Westminster but our house would be ready for when I arrived and the servants were expecting me. He would come as soon as he was able. He ended with orders to keep his son safe and asked that I should take good care of myself because I was his truly beloved wife.

I had barely settled myself in my room when I had an unexpected visitor. I hadn't seen her for more than two years and had no idea she was in London.

'Lady Abernethy!'

Margery Abernethy sank slowly to the ground in an exaggerated display of humility.

'Countess,' she murmured.

I smiled. 'Get up this instant, Lady Margery. You look extremely foolish down there on the floor. Come and sit beside me and tell me what you've been doing these past two years. I'm hungry for news.'

Before I went to France with Isabella, Lady Margery had been my friend. She was a widow with two children and, like me, had lands beyond the border which were irretrievably lost.

She smiled up at me. 'I think it would be far more interesting to find out what *you* have been doing, Lady Margaret. I leave you in your drab woollen gowns attending to the queen's needs, turn my back for a moment, and what happens? Someone has transformed you into a countess wrapped in velvets and furs and covered in jewels.'

I laughed. 'Come and see my son.'

I called for the nursemaid who arrived promptly with a closely swaddled bundle.

'Oh how sweet!' With a gentle finger Lady Margery turned back the folds threatening to obscure my son. 'I do so want another child,' she said longingly, 'All I have are my two girls, but at my age and with no husband I fear it would be an unspeakable scandal if I produced one.' She looked at me with a wicked glint in her eye. 'I don't suppose you have any more men tucked away in your saddlebags? I'm not greedy. A lord will do. I don't require an earl. I'm not like you.'

'Have you seen my husband?'

'The handsome earl of Kent? She eyed me speculatively. 'You have done well, Lady Margaret. This is far more than you could have hoped for. In truth it is far more than almost any woman could have hoped for. I trust he is generous. Is he an attentive husband?'

I blushed. 'He is most attentive. I think I am very fortunate because I couldn't have found a better man.'

She looked thoroughly disbelieving. To Lady Margery, all men were untrustworthy scoundrels, interested in only two things: a woman's money and a woman's body.

'Tell me,' I said, anxious to divert her conversation from my husband's perceived shortcomings. 'What is happening outside? My maids say people are rioting on the streets.'

Edmund was still at Westminster and had not yet come home so I had no news and was relying on the garbled stories I received from the servants.

'Are you surprised? Their world is being turned upside down. First Lord Mortimer brings his friends to the Guildhall to join in swearing an oath to support the queen and her son; then Archbishop Reynolds distributes tuns of wine to the citizens so there isn't a sober man in the city; and now they hear the parliament has agreed to set aside their anointed king and put Lord Edward in his place. This is not an ordinary day for the people.'

'So it has been done,' I murmured to myself.

'Did you know this was to happen? I think you did.'

I put my hands to my cheeks which felt decidedly warm. 'I knew the queen and my cousin, Lord Mortimer wanted rid of the Despensers, as we all did. But not this.'

Lady Margery leaned forward and said quietly. 'It was not done in silence and behind closed doors as I believe these things often are. Your cousin spoke very eloquently to the parliament. He said the citizens of London and all the lords were agreed on the matter - the king must go. But there was uproar. The bishops were divided. Rochester and York were against it as was old Reynolds, but Bishop Orleton carried the day. Your brother led everyone by the nose like the horse-master he is. He had them eating out of his hand at the end. You should have heard the noise. They were shouting for the king's son, and when Lord Edward appeared they cheered him to the rafters.'

'You were in the chamber?'

'The queen needed someone to attend her. Once she would have chosen you.'

'How was she?'

'In tears by the end.'

Yes, I thought, tears were always a woman's friend at times like this.

'So they will throw down the father and make young Lord Edward king,' I said bleakly.

She smiled as if she was carrying a secret. She leaned back in her chair and watched my face.

'Lord Edward has refused.'

Sainte Vierge! A carefully arranged demonstration of public support and Lord Edward refuses to play the role Isabella has determined for him. She has brought him the crown of England and he has turned it down! My cousin would be furious. To have come so far and be thwarted by a fourteen year-old boy.

'That must have been a shock to the queen,' I said carefully.

'She was shaking from head to toe. Her fingernails were white and you could have crushed a man with the look on her face. She had Lord Edward out of there and into her chamber before you could say "*Ave Rex*". And by the time she dismissed me, she was shrieking that he was an ungrateful pup who had no idea how she had suffered at his father's hands and how all she had ever done was for him. But he was adamant. He would not accept the crown just because she wanted it. He said it was wrong.'

'Oh Lady Margery,' I sighed. 'Where will all this lead?'

'To Berwick, I trust. I need my lands back. The king gave me leave to travel to Scotland two years ago but I have had no success in recovering them. Hopefully Lord Edward will accept the crown and be less of a coward than his father and will mount a campaign against Robert Bruce.'

I had a sudden image of Badenoch, lost in the hills, far beyond my grasp. My dream castle from another time. John's home.

'Now enough of such nonsense,' said Lady Margery. 'Tell me - what is the fashion for sleeves in Paris? Are they wearing them loose and flowing or are they buttoned tightly?'

How like Margery Abernethy. The realm might be falling apart but she always knew what was of importance to a woman.

Edmund returned home two night's later, weary and dispirited.

'My nephew has capitulated. Isabella has worn him down. He has agreed to take the crown if his father offers it to him but not otherwise. So Orleton and his bullies have gone to Kenilworth. Their job is to persuade my brother to resign the throne and God alone knows what threats they'll use to get what they want.'

'Will your brother do that? Will he give away his royalty?'

'They'll have him killed if he doesn't. They've gone too far to turn chicken-hearted now. And Isabella is determined. Dear God, Margaret, if I had known what was going to happen I would never have agreed to any of this. I would have stayed in Paris.'

He looked so miserable I put my arms around him and stroked his hair.

'There was nothing you could do, Edmund. The plan was already hatched and the end was inevitable. At least this way your brother will live in comfort for the rest of his life.'

He made a noise like a stifled sob. 'Do you remember the tower at Pontefract where we first met?' His voice was muffled by the fabric of my shift.

A chasm of memory separated that day from this and yet it was only five years: the freezing cold, a stone stairway to a bare room with a window open to the night sky, the pathetic remnants of a lost life and the shadowed man blocking my escape.

'Of course I do,' I said quietly. 'How could I forget? But Kenilworth is not like that. It is a fine palace and he will have everything he needs.'

'Of course,' said Edmund bleakly. 'Everything he needs. What else?'

He was quiet for a long time and we stayed together, neither of us willing to disturb our closeness.

As the short days of January marched onwards, the fall of a king and the rise of another merged seamlessly one into the other. The bishops returned from Kenilworth with the king's agreement. I heard he had fallen to his knees, weeping like a child and had to be lifted back onto his chair by Lord Henry. When asked to resign his throne in favour of his son he had agreed and asked forgiveness for his many sins. The steward of the royal household had broken his staff of office and the reign of the queen's husband was finally at an end. From henceforth, we were told, he would be known as "Sir Edward, sometime king of England".

One late afternoon I had another visitor - my sister-in-law, the pretty little coroner's daughter from Norfolk. She was now the mother of three children but as painfully shy as she had ever been. She flushed to the roots of her hair when I greeted her.

'I joined my lord for the Nativity celebrations at Wallingford. He said I might attend provided I remembered to behave as he expected,' she murmured.

She spoke with a country accent which betrayed her origins. She was pleasant enough and it was obvious she had learned fast, but it wasn't fast enough. She might have done well as a rich merchant's wife but would never succeed as a countess, poor creature.

She prattled about her husband with a very childish enthusiasm. She clearly adored Lord Norfolk even if his feelings towards her were cool. She bore no resentment for her banishment to his country manors, she was simply grateful for her invitation to the celebrations.

'I love to see my lord in the joust, Lady Margaret, but I am afraid I will disappoint him and disgrace myself. He looks so fine in his armour, so tall and handsome; but it frightens me the way they rush at each other. What if a lance should go astray? What if a horse should fall and crush its rider? Imagine what it must be like to be trapped beneath one of those heaving bodies.'

She admired Mondi, cooing and waggling her fingers over the cradle, making silly noises and speaking nonsense words the way stupid women will. After a while she remembered the purpose of her visit and dutifully came to sit with me though it was obvious she would rather have remained with the nursemaids and the baby.

'I am sure all will be well,' I said, smiling sweetly.

'I am so very nervous of everyone.'

'You cannot be nervous of our new king; he is only a boy. Do you not have younger brothers?'

'Yes, but when Lord Edward … I mean the king, is there, so is the queen and she frightens me. I wish the old king was here. I wish …'

She clapped her hand over her mouth. 'I shouldn't have said that.' Her eyes were wide with alarm. 'My lord said I must never mention the old king again. He said I must keep my mouth shut or he'd sew it up for me.'

'Did you like Sir Edward, the old king?' I said, trying to banish the alarming image of my brother-in-law wielding a needle.

'Oh yes. He was kind. He would invite me to sup with him.' She gave a little smile, her face slowly filling with sunshine. 'Once when my lord was away on his business, the king sent a messenger to bring me up-river, and together we had a small meal and listened to some musicians. When we were alone we talked and he sang for me. It wasn't like being with a king at all. It was as if he was an ordinary man, the kind my father entertained in his house when I was young.'

She overstayed her welcome until I was yawning. Our talk was as limited as I expected from a woman who had done nothing in her life but keep house for her father and lay herself down for her husband. I wondered if Edmund's brother found much delight in her but he hadn't married her for her conversation and in other respects she must still be pleasing. She was amazingly pretty and certainly very willing. She was the kind of woman all men desire but rarely marry, unless she trails a vast dowry in her wake.

As soon as I had undergone the formal rituals of purification I returned not only to my husband's arms but to the queen's presence.

Isabella gave me a cursory glance. 'You look pale, Margaret. Are you sickening?'

'No, your grace. It is only the rigours of childbirth.'

'I gave birth to four children and was never in anything other than perfect health. Nevertheless, I am glad you have returned. I have need of you.'

She made no enquiries about Mondi. I could have been delivered of a bastard in a hedgerow for all the interest she was taking.

'You have heard about Madame of Evreux?'

'Yes, your grace. A girl and unlikely to live. It is most unfortunate.'

'It is many things but it is not unfortunate. I told my brother he would have no luck in his marriage bed and I have been proved right.'

'She is still young.'

Isabella snorted as if Madame of Evreux's youth was nothing.

'Tell me Margaret. What did you think of my cousin, Philip, our new count of Valois? You have a good eye for people. It is one of your talents and why I keep you.'

I thought of the quivering greyhound with his ungainly posture and trembling legs.

'He is nervous of his wife,' I said slowly. 'He may be tall and boast broad shoulders, but he has the look of a man who fears he will fail.'

'Hah!' said Isabella. 'I was right. You saw it too. If Charles should die, God forbid that he should, then long-nosed Philip is not the man to take the throne. And if not him - then who?'

I knew the way Isabella's mind was working. Having removed her husband from the throne of England she was now intent in securing the crown of France for Lord Edward. Of course she would have to get rid of her brother first but I didn't think a small matter like that would stop her. A woman who has invaded her husband's kingdom and stolen his throne could achieve anything.

Sometimes I wondered where the Isabella of yesterday had gone: the sweet young queen who had loved her husband and had welcomed me into her household. When I was first with her she had made much of me, teased me, indulged me and later had treated me as a confidante. But that woman had vanished in the turmoil of these last two years. She had been replaced by this scheming, ruthless, vindictive harpy. But I had long ago decided it was sensible to be friendly with such a woman. Better a friend than an enemy.

'Your noble father had three sons and a single daughter,' I said slowly. 'All three sons have failed to provide a male heir. Thus through your royal person your son would have the strongest claim if anything were to happen to your brother, which naturally we pray will not.'

Naturally,' agreed Isabella.

At that moment the man at the door announced my cousin. The queen looked up and smiled.

'Mortimer, see who is here. Your cousin has come back to us.'

He nodded to us both.

'You are well, cousin?'

'Yes, my lord.'

'And the child?'

'He thrives.'

'Good.' He turned to Isabella. 'Is the boy ready to agree? Have you shut his ungrateful mouth for him?'

For a moment I didn't know who my cousin meant, then I realised he was talking about the young king. I was shocked. This was no way to talk to the queen about her son.

Isabella touched his arm. 'You mustn't let yourself get upset by him, dear Mortimer. He is only trying to do what he thinks is right. Remember, he has had little experience and we need to show him the way things are done. I will keep him in my own household and that way we can be sure he is not influenced by those who do not have our best interests at heart.'

'It is all very well for you, my lady. It was not your sons he was ridiculing.'

'Don't fret. It is all settled now. Your sons shall wear earls' robes at the coronation as you desired: scarlet, green and brown cloth-of-gold with miniver and squirrel fur. They will look utterly splendid as will all the king's newly-created knights. As will you, dearest Mortimer.'

She smiled at him and after a moment his face softened and he returned the smile. But I noticed he didn't thank her.

Earl's robes? I thought. For the sons of a mere baron? How far my cousin had travelled. Almost as far as I had myself.

At the coronation my old friends from the nursery at Wigmore did indeed look splendid in their robes. I could hardly believe how they had grown: tall, well-made men; even young Johnny was up to his brothers' shoulders and already sprouting a beard.

Everything on that first day of February shone: from one end of the abbey to the other, amidst clouds of incense and swirls of brocade, the glitter and sparkle of a thousand precious jewels filled my eyes. This was the day Isabella had been waiting for.

The only person who did not appear to be enjoying himself was the young king. He was solemn and quiet, responding where necessary but with none of the joy and effusiveness expected of a newly-crowned king. At the feast his mother sat beside him and you might have thought it was *her* coronation day - hers and Lord Mortimer's.

My cousin was slapping men on the back and talking his way round the hall while Isabella's son sat mute and wary, watching his progress. The eyes of the young king followed my cousin but the boy didn't move and he said nothing.

There were lavish gifts, as was expected: silver dishes and spoons for Lord Henry and a gilded silver salt cellar for my brother. Bishop Orleton was handed several items from the royal treasury to put in his Episcopal Palace, while a Mortimer cousin, Thomas Vere, received two gilt silver basins engraved with the arms of England and France. Richard de Bethune, now mayor of London, had an engraved gold cup and an enamelled gold ewer. Of course he had not only delivered my cousin from his imprisonment in the Tower four years ago but had recently delivered the citizens of London to him when they were most needed. Did no one else wonder exactly what he had done for the king to warrant these gifts? But all the silver and gold given out that day was nothing compared to Isabella's gift to herself.

'She has taken an income from the crown of twenty thousand marks a year,' said a shocked Edmund. 'Does she mean to beggar my nephew?'

'You forget,' I reminded him. 'When Despenser was in power she believed herself near destitute. Now she behaves in the manner of one who knows what it is to starve.'

'She was always a greedy woman,' said Edmund. 'I trust she remembers her promise to me.'

After the feast a meeting was called by my cousin. Only a select few were invited and the gathering was marked more by those who were absent than by those who came. Lord Henry was missing, as was my brother and so were the other Lancastrian lords.

The chosen few met late in the day and, to my surprise, one other notable person was missing: the king.

'He is weary,' said Isabella fondly. 'It has been a long day for a boy of his age. I sent him to his bed.'

She spoke as if he was six years old, not a young man who had been anointed king of England. But to Isabella he was her son and as such would do as he was told.

'We have problems,' said my cousin, getting down to business at once. 'The parliament is to meet the day after tomorrow and will be packed with Henry of Lancaster's men. Lancaster holds sway in the north and also holds the prisoner.'

Isabella tapped the table. 'My husband is to be called something other than "the prisoner". It is disrespectful to the father of my son, a man who was once your sovereign.'

My cousin flushed a deep red. 'I apologise, my lady. I had not intended the words as an insult.'

Isabella smiled graciously and inclined her head to him. She had reminded him of his inferior position and he didn't like it one bit.

'Lord Edward of Caernarvon would be suitable,' she went on. 'He was referred to in that way before we were married. Or Sir Edward; that would also be acceptable both to me and to the king.'

My cousin frowned impatiently. 'Sir Edward it is then. Are we agreed? Lord Edmund? Lord Norfolk?'

My husband looked up. 'I agree,' he said flatly, as if it didn't matter to him that these men were demoting his brother to the rank of a mere knight. 'It is only words.'

His brother Norfolk nodded and from every side there were murmurs of agreement.

'Perhaps you find you are reconsidering your bishops' invocations, my lady,' said my cousin with a hint of malice in his voice.

'Which would be?'

'That you return to your husband's side in his captivity. We know Sir Edward is anxious for you to bring him consolation. After all, my lady, it would be an honouring of your marriage vows which, we know, you hold in high esteem.'

I knew immediately that Isabella had refused to give my cousin his reward. After Despenser's execution he would have expected her to be more accommodating, perhaps allowing a degree of intimacy, but it seemed she was determined to keep him at a distance and he was angry and impatient. This was a lover's quarrel fought out across the queen's table but the others appeared oblivious to the hidden meanings in the words.

'This has already been discussed, Lord Mortimer,' said Isabella icily. 'The bishops, if you recall, are nervous for my safety. However much I personally may wish to honour and obey my dearest lord, he has, unfortunately, shown himself a dangerous man where I am concerned. My son will not permit me to return to my husband's side. He says my welfare must be his first concern. So I shall remain here with the king to serve him and give him good guidance as a mother and as a queen.'

Her eyes glittered with triumph. I knew she intended to control them both: my cousin and her son.

'Should we not discuss how to handle the parliament?' said the earl of Surrey in all innocence.

Since his return to Isabella's side the earl had been overly anxious to prove himself a loyal and trusted member of the queen's camp. Lady Jeanne said he was cool towards her and seldom visited but fervent in his admiration for the young king and for Lord Mortimer.

'Indeed,' said Isabella. 'Let us get down to business. Lancaster will push for all he can get. He will want pardons for his friends for their actions in the rebellion five years ago and of course for his brother.'

'I thought Earl Thomas had a reincarnation as one of England's newest saints?' said my cousin lazily. 'I've been told they flock in their thousands to his graveside. What more can he possibly need? Surely it is beyond our earthly powers to award him a higher status.'

'What an excellent idea, Lord Mortimer,' said Isabella, smiling. 'I shall write to His Holiness urging him to consider the late dear departed earl of Lancaster as a candidate for canonization. And as the process is a lengthy one, taking many years, Lord Henry will not, in the meantime, wish to incur my displeasure in case I withdraw my support for his brother's cause.'

'Would you do that?' said Edmund's brother.

Isabella ignored the question. 'We shall grant pardons. We don't wish to begin my son's reign with more discontent than is necessary.'

Edmund leaned forward. 'Lancaster will not agree to have Sir Robert Holand pardoned. Holand was a traitor to his brother. He will want him hanged.'

'Very well, but we have had sufficient hangings. I will

deny this Holand his lands but he may keep his life.'

'There is another difficulty,' said Lord Norfolk. 'The lands of the Lincoln inheritance. Henry of Lancaster regards them as his by right.'

'He can think what he likes,' said Isabella. 'Those lands remain with me as do the others the king has awarded me out of the goodness of his heart.'

I nearly choked. I'd been present when Isabella had dictated the list of castles and manors she was taking. There was no question of argument; if she wanted them she was going to have them. Even her son gasped at her avarice but he knew who was in charge and veiled his eyes, dutifully agreeing each gift to his dearest mother.

She took Sir Edward's favourite palace of Langley and the pretty riverside manor of Sheen, as well as the castles of Leeds and Guildford and Porchester. She took Burstwick, which Edmund said was one of his mother's favourite houses. She took Rockingham and Odiham and Bristol and Havering-atte-Bower. By the time she'd finished there was not a single county in the kingdom where Isabella did not own the choicest residences. Except for the far north where she said only a fool would want a house with the Scots breathing down your neck.

'What about the council?' queried Edmund. 'The parliament will get to select the members and as the council will control my nephew, surely it is more important than this matter of pardons.'

'Lord Mortimer, will you put yourself forward?' That was Bishop Orleton.

'No,' said my cousin firmly. 'Neither the queen nor I will sit on the council. We shall have Lord Edmund, Lord

Norfolk and Lord Surrey, and you Orleton. There will be bishops aplenty to argue the finer points of each decision and if we let Lancaster have control he will assume the council will do as he says.'

'Is that not risky?' said Edmund's brother.

'It is a calculated risk, my Lord Norfolk. Lancaster may hold Sir Edward but we have the boy.'

Isabella leaned across the table. 'Lord Mortimer, your tongue will be your undoing. If you are referring to your king, you should choose words suitable to his estate. I have reminded you once, I shall not do so again.'

My cousin glared at her. 'For the particular words, I convey my apologies to his grace. For the sentiments, I do not. We must never forget that he is only a boy of tender years and we, around this table, must be the men who rule the kingdom, not Lancaster and his cronies.'

And not the queen, he was saying silently, because she is just a woman and we all know woman are feeble creatures.

We went home, exhausted.

'She has promised me Fitzalan's lands,' said Edmund as we rode back through the streets. The world was as black as pitch, lit only by the torches of our outriders.

'How wonderful,' I said, thinking of the honour. 'Earl of Arundel.'

'Just the lands, not the title. She's not that generous. But we'll have the castle at Arundel and you'll like that, Margaret. They say it's high up with a sight of the sea, and I believe there's a pretty garden. We'll make it our home if it pleases you.'

'If you are there,' I said, all of a sudden flooded with happiness, 'it will please me, even without the honour.'

The next day saw us back at Westminster hurrying hither and thither through the maze of rooms in the royal palace. Edmund had business with his brother and I was to attend the queen.

I should not have listened, but the door was ajar and old habits die hard.

'I have told you, he is leaving.' It was Isabella's voice.

'Not soon enough.' That was my cousin.

'So you have said.'

'And may I ask, my lady, exactly what you have given him, besides your favours?'

I heard the sound of a woman's hand slapped hard across a man's cheek. This was followed by a quick struggle. A richly-embroidered brocade crackled as if it was being crushed, then a whisper of velvet swept the wooden boards, a muffled groan, and a long sigh.

The Lady Isabella, mother of the king of England, and her closest companion, my cousin, Lord Mortimer of Wigmore, were in the queen's private chamber having one of their not infrequent quarrels. This time the subject was the imminent departure of Sir John and the last of his Hainaulter friends.

Sir John was effusive in his praise for his "beautiful lady", and Isabella, tiring of my cousin's boorish behaviour, had shown Count William's brother a little too much attention. She had smiled at him once too often, held his gaze just that bit too long, and to my cousin's fury, had ordered her son to award Sir John a vast pension in gratitude for his services.

'We all know what services those were,' snarled my cousin.

'He is a more gallant man than you, Lord Mortimer,' she spat.

'And who is to pay for your gallants? By the time you've finished, your son's treasury will be as empty as a drunkard's purse.'

Another slap.

'And it was I who delivered this kingdom into your hands, my lady, not that coxcomb. Don't you forget it.'

Of recent, the quarrels, the slaps and the subsequent embraces had become more frequent and I feared if she did not give way to him soon, their mutual desire would drive them to the brink of something terrible.

'Why in the name of the blessed St Thomas does she not let him into her bed,' grumbled Edmund. 'Then we'd have some peace. Our meetings are racked with their quarrels. She snips and snipes and he retaliates with words I would not use to a fishwife.'

'She cannot. She is terrified of the damnation which would follow. It's not something they could keep secret and imagine what the bishops would say. Not to mention His Holiness. And she remembers what happened to her brother's wife, the faithless Blanche. Adultery is the worst of sins for a woman.'

'Men do not see it that way,' said Edmund. 'Look at your cousin. He's hardly concerned for his immortal soul.'

A picture flashed through my mind of Joan, Lady Mortimer sitting in the hall at Wigmore, her face radiant with joy at the sight of my cousin striding across the floor, still dusty from his travels.

'Men may choose to believe what they like and the church may choose to collude with them,' I said in a low voice, 'but it is still a sin, and a man who loves his wife should remain faithful.'

Edmund muttered something about the earl of Surrey and his many mistresses.

'Don't forget, dear husband, my cousin has no royal blood, no matter what he may pretend. He is like me.'

'And I let you into my bed,' said my husband with a straight face and feigned surprise. 'What was I thinking of?'

I kissed his cheek.

'You married me. That is different.'

'Christ's blood! You don't think he … he can't intend …?'

'What?'

'To marry her.' Edmund's voice had sunk to a whisper and no wonder - what he'd suggested was treasonable.

To marry a queen! What a prize that would be for Roger Mortimer, lord of Wigmore. But of course it couldn't happen. There were far too many obstacles in the way, not least the presence of Lord Mortimer's wife.

My cousin had seen to the release of his family from their various places of incarceration ordered by the king and Sir Hugh Despenser but to my knowledge he'd seen Joan only once since our return. In November he'd gone to Pembridge, the manor where they'd married, but the meeting between the two had been brief. They scarcely had time to greet each other before my cousin was back in the saddle. Since then he'd made no attempt to visit his wife and had not once mentioned her name.

The following day instead of setting out to visit our new castle as planned, I received a summons. With very bad grace I returned to the queen's apartments in Westminster Palace, settled my face into its expected humble demeanour and went to find Isabella. She was in her private rooms examining some objects on a table.

I observed her from my position in the doorway. Her fingers were resting on an exquisite little silver box. To a casual onlooker she was doing nothing in particular, but I knew what was in her mind - she was savouring the riches she had confiscated from her enemies, making a mental inventory of her shiny treasures. In short, she was gloating.

I moved forward. At the sound of my footsteps she turned on her heel and smiled.

'Margaret! At last! I have need of you.'

She waited impatiently as I crossed the floor.

'Your brother is my constable at the Tower.'

'Lord Wake has done nothing wrong, has he?' I asked anxiously.

'On the contrary, he is a good servant: thorough, diligent, a hard man with little imagination. Just what I need in a keeper.'

She moistened her lips with her tongue and regarded me severely. 'I require you to visit your brother, Margaret.'

'Of course, your grace, if that is what you wish. Do you need me to carry a message?'

'No. The purpose of your visit is to be secret, known only to me and to you. You will not mention this to your husband. Do you understand?'

'I shall tell Lord Edmund nothing.'

'Now listen.' Her voice lowered. 'While you are visiting your brother you will also visit the Lady Eleanor Despenser.'

I had almost forgotten Eleanor. Ever since Sir John secured the Tower for Isabella, Eleanor had been deprived of her freedom.

'You must agree it was a stroke of genius to place your brother in charge of Lady Eleanor,' said Isabella, smiling unpleasantly. 'I'm sure he was able to describe the scene of her husband's death much more vividly than an ordinary gaoler. You often said you wished you had known how your first husband died. I remembered your words when I instructed Lord Wake to spare Lady Eleanor none of the more distressing details of Sir Hugh's execution. I thought it would not be kind to leave her in ignorance.'

What Isabella had done was cruel and I felt nothing but disgust for her heartlessness. But it wouldn't do to let my thoughts show. It was never wise to let Isabella know what you were thinking.

'What do you wish me to say to Lady Eleanor, your grace?'

'I am in receipt of a message from Lord Wake. Your brother is a careful and observant man, Margaret, but he is only a man. A woman would have noticed sooner. However, no matter. He tells me the lady has a belly on her. Lady Despenser says nothing but your brother took her maidservant in for questioning and the woman has admitted the truth: another brat to add to the slut's army of little Despensers.'

In my head I did some counting: five months since we'd landed so five months since Eleanor had last seen either her husband or her uncle.'

168

'The child will be born in the summer?' I said enquiringly.

'Ii is not my practice to send a midwife to the dungeons to ascertain such things,' Isabella replied dismissively. 'Naturally it is her husband's brat, but ...'

The unspoken possibility hung in the air and dropped into my waiting hands like a red-hot burning coal. I knew at once what I was supposed to do.

'I understand what is required, your grace. I shall discover what you need to know and I shall report back to you and to no-one else.'

'See that you do.'

Next morning I climbed the stairs to Eleanor's rooms. Tom accompanied me with much grumbling but before I entered, I sent him away. I wanted no witness to my conversation with Eleanor Despenser. It was not that I didn't trust my brother but this was too delicate a matter to take even the smallest of risks. The meeting must be between Eleanor and me and no-one else.

She looked up from the bench where she was seated. She was thinner than when I'd last seen her. The face beneath her cap was hollowed and she no longer dressed as a great lady. In truth, she was very much diminished.

'Oh, it's you,' she said, returning her attention to the child who lay with its head in her lap. Beneath the drab woollen gown I could see the slight swell of her belly pressing gently against the fair curls.

'Your youngest?' I said politely.

'Elizabeth,' she replied, stroking the little girl's forehead with her fingers. Barely more than a babe.'

169

I remembered in Paris someone saying Eleanor had been delivered of another child.

'My uncle named her for his favourite sister, my Aunt Elizabeth. He came to see me two days before she was born and we discussed the matter of my child's name. He was concerned because my husband was absent and my uncle feared for my low spirits.'

I was told how the king had rowed himself upriver to Sheen with a purse of gold to dine with his niece and stayed half the night. It had been a little scandal picked over with great glee in the French king's palaces and we all had our own opinion as to what had occurred between the king and the Lady Eleanor Despenser on that dark December night.

'Your uncle was very good to you.'

Her face brightened. 'He was very attentive and very kind. He paid for all my pleasures and I had so little to give him in return. Yet he said that what I gave him was all he could have ever wanted.'

She had a distant look and I wondered what it was that she had given him. What would a highly favoured niece bestow upon an uncommonly devoted uncle? I had a sudden recollection of the French woman in Paris saying, "Best keep it in the family."

'That winter he made me a gift of a white palfrey, one with green trappings to match my eyes,' said Eleanor, twisting her daughter's curls into little ringlets. 'And goldfinches. Did you know that? Dozens of them. I let them fly round my chamber but then we couldn't catch them and they escaped. It didn't matter because he brought me some more. Have you seen goldfinches?'

'Once or twice. Tiny things. Not really worth the eating.'

She lowered her head and the light faded from her eyes. 'Have you come to gloat over me or have you come to bring me news of my uncle? Your brother is very close-mouthed and will tell me nothing.'

'You have heard about your husband?'

'Yes.'

Her face was impassive and I couldn't tell if she was grieving or not.

'You must miss his company,' I said, trying to provoke a response.

'He was often away.' She sounded as if she had neither interest nor concern in her husband's doings.

'But he was the father of your children?'

She looked at me with her slanting green eyes, saying nothing, showing nothing. If Eleanor Despenser grieved for her husband she was not going to tell me, and if I had questions about the child in her belly I was certain she would remain equally silent.

'My brother tells me you are with child.'

A veiled look crept over her eyes. 'And if I am?'

'You must have proper care. Do you get enough to eat?'

'It is not what I am used to but I'm sure your brother does his best.'

'You wouldn't want your husband's last child to suffer.'

'All my children are suffering.'

At that moment the inner door opened and two little boys appeared together with an older woman who I took to be Eleanor's maid.

'Now you see the whole of my household,' said Eleanor with a sweep of her hand. 'I am well provided for, don't you think?'

I looked through the open doorway to the room beyond.

'Are your daughters not with you?'

I remembered the little Despenser girls running around Eleanor's chambers at various times over the years. Her eldest was married to the Fitzalan boy, once a good match, but not now that his father was an attainted traitor. She would be with her husband's family but I was surprised the younger ones had not been shut away with their mother.

'They were taken.'

'Taken? Who has taken them?'

'Who do you think?'

I had heard nothing of the Despenser girls having been taken by Isabella but it didn't surprise me. What better way to vent your spite on a woman than by removing her children from the households where she had so carefully and lovingly placed them.

'If you are wondering where they are, she has put them behind the walls of a convent,' said Eleanor in a cold precise voice. 'That is my punishment. She has had them forcibly veiled. They can never come out and I will never see them married.'

I was shocked. These girls were only little children.

'They will be brides of Christ,' I said, wanting all of a sudden to be kind. 'It is a worthy life.' Then I remembered the Mortimer daughters. 'And your husband and your uncle did the same to Lord Mortimer's girls.'

'It wasn't the same in any way. Mortimer's daughters only lodged with the nuns, they weren't forced to remain there for the rest of their lives.'

She turned her head away from me but not before I saw a single tear roll down her cheek. I almost felt sorry for her.

I looked round her room. It was comfortable if rather bare. The smouldering sticks in the hearth kept the cold at bay, but in my household, the boy who brought in the logs would have been cuffed for setting such a meagre fire. Gone were the goldfinches and the little beribboned dogs, the gilded cages and the turkey rugs; and gone too were the engraved goblets and silver gilt bowls which had graced Eleanor's sideboard. There were a few children's clothes lying on the table, and on one of the benches, a single book.

'I hear you are married.'

I turned round. Eleanor was looking at me, a sly expression on her face.

'Yes. In Paris.'

'I told my uncle you would ensnare his brother one day.'

'I wasn't trying to ensnare anyone, Eleanor.'

She had a mocking smile on her lips.

'I've known you a long time, Margaret, and I've known many women like you. You have nothing to offer but yourself and you use your body like a purse to be won in the lists. You refused him your bed, didn't you? How it must have enraged poor Uncle Edmund. There you were, all sweetness: demure, obedient, lowered lashes, simpering smiles; a juicy widow just ripe for plucking and then you barred the door to your bedchamber. Cleverly played, Margaret. But I recall you always were a skilful player.'

I should have ignored her but I'd always been too quick to rise to the bait.

'My husband is well pleased with me.'

'Ah, but are you well pleased with him? How does it feel to know your husband ploughed his furrow through every woman in the queen's household? I could name them if you like. I should watch your maidservants if I were you, countess.' She spat out the last word as if it offended her to keep it on her tongue. 'It seems your husband likes women of low birth.'

'At least my husband doesn't …'

'Doesn't what?' Her eyes glinted with pleasure now that she had roused my temper. 'What makes you think my husband was ever lacking in his duty to me. My grandfather chose my husband carefully and he understood the value of strength. I was a good wife who obeyed my husband in every respect and he was a good husband to me.'

'I know what was said about your husband and I saw what he expected of you, Eleanor Despenser.'

'My husband expected nothing from me that I was not happy to give. Did you imagine I was forced to do the things I did? Well, I wasn't. I did them gladly. But what about you, Margaret? Are you obedient to your husband's every wish? As you and I know, those with royal blood in their veins do not like to be denied in any way. Does he ask you to do things which you find distasteful? Men need pleasuring in such interesting ways, don't they? And I'm sure my uncle's brother is of an inventive nature. He always was.'

'You have a foul mouth, Eleanor Despenser.'

She laughed. 'What does he get you to do, countess? Do you tell your confessor? Poor man! How his cheeks must burn to hear such words spill from your lips. And you look so good and so pious. But then, appearances deceive. However, I am not deceived by you for one moment. I know exactly what it is that dearest Isabella wishes to know and I am not going to tell you. I shall leave you to guess just how far I was prepared to go to please my husband. As for your husband ...'

'My husband loves me and I would take him any day over a ...'

'A what, countess? Be careful what you say about the dead.'

She smiled serenely as if we had been discussing the price of cloth and continued to stroke the curly head of the child on her knee.

I couldn't wait to erase the memory of my encounter with Eleanor Despenser from my mind. But first I had to report to Isabella.

'It is as you thought,' I said. 'She says the child is her husband's.'

Isabella peered at me more closely. 'But you have doubts?'

'No. She showed no signs of claiming anything other than what one would expect. But she has been uncommonly favoured by your husband. They appear to have spent many happy evenings together at Sheen.'

'Alone?'

'Privy dining,' I said. 'Just the two of them because the lady's husband was absent. And as we thought, your

175

husband was exceedingly generous in the matter of gifts and money. She lacked for nothing.'

Isabella placed the tips of her fingers together and pursed her lips. After a moment she called for the man at the door.

'Fetch me Mistress Nauntel.'

Juliana Nauntel was one of Isabella's maids and the most valued woman in her household. She knew the queen's secrets and ran the kind of errands Isabella would entrust to no-one else. She was diligent, unassuming and tight-lipped – the perfect servant.

'Ah, Mistress Nauntel. Do you have what I asked for?'

The woman looked disapprovingly at her mistress. Reluctantly she passed over a small leather pouch. Isabella pulled open the drawstring neck and removed a small vial.

'You are quite certain this is what I requested?'

The woman nodded. 'Yes, my lady.'

Isabella removed the stopper and sniffed the contents. She wrinkled up her nose. 'That's it. You may go now.'

She waited until we were alone again before speaking. 'You must go back to your brother, Margaret. Tell him to have his woman use this.'

'I don't know if my brother has a woman?'

'Don't be foolish, Margaret. Lady Wake spends her time with her sisters in their father's castles. I doubt she's seen your brother once since he joined us. He's a hot-blooded man. Of course there is a woman. Tell him she must make up a drink for the Lady Eleanor.'

My eyes widened in disbelief.

'Oh don't look like that. I'm not planning to do away with my husband's niece. This draught is to improve a woman's well-being. It is a kindness.'

I took the small bag and secreted it away. I would go next morning and say nothing to anyone, not even Edmund. Then I would put the matter out of my mind.

Margery, Lady Abernethy was in the queen's apartments at Westminster idly strumming on her lute and singing in a low voice. There was no sign of Isabella but I could hear her.

'You will not go. I command you to stay.'

This was Isabella at her most imperious.

'Don't be ridiculous, my lady. You know I must go. I have business in Abergavenny which must be attended to. If a man does not see to his estates they will fall into ruin in one way or another.'

My cousin's voice was measured but laced with anger and irritation.

'I don't believe you. Tell me where you are really going. I insist.'

There was a long silence.

'It is Lord Mortimer,' whispered Margery, unnecessarily. He has just told the queen he will be absent for several weeks. He is going into Wales.'

My cousin's voice was quieter now, more loving. 'It is not what you think. I am not going to her, I swear.'

The silence lengthened.

'She is beside herself,' said Margery. 'She says he is travelling to Ludlow to visit Lady Mortimer. She says he cares nothing for her and the hurt he is causing her.'

'Surely a man may visit his wife?' I murmured.

'Not if he wishes to retain the favour of his queen and she forbids it.'

Isabella's voice again.

'You are taking her books.'

'I told you before. The books are a gift to make up for my neglect. Christ's blood, Madam! Would you have me throw my wife out and have her wander the countryside in her shift? Is that what you want? For me to insult her?'

'I want you to remember who *I* am and what you owe to *me*, and not go running after a woman who means nothing to you any more.'

There was a moment of silence.

'Or am I mistaken in that as well?'

My cousin's voice sounded weary. 'She is my wife. She is the mother of my children. I cannot deny her a degree of comfort and regard.'

'Very well,' said Isabella in that icy tone I knew only too well. 'Go and lick the hem of her skirts! Do what you like. I shall take myself and my son to Canterbury. I shall spend my days in prayer and my nights in writing letters to my husband. I shall gather up gifts so that he knows I think lovingly of him despite our separation. It would be a sad day, would it not, Mortimer, if a wife could not make love-gifts to her husband when they are apart. What would you recommend? What do you receive from your wife? Does she send you small delicacies for your table? Or fine clothing? Perhaps silk shirts stitched by her own fair hand? Yes that would be suitable for my lord – silk shirts. Or songbirds. It is difficult to express the love and devotion I bear my lord when we are so cruelly parted.'

'Stop it, my lady. We must not hurt each other like this.'

'No, Lord Mortimer,' hissed Isabella's voice. 'You are mistaken. There is only one of us inflicting pain on the other and it is not I.'

Margery raised her eyebrows to me and shrugged her shoulders.

True to her word, two days later the queen's household departed for Canterbury in a great display of royal pageantry. The king and his beloved mother were making a pilgrimage to the shrine of St Thomas to give thanks for their many blessings. And while all attention was on Isabella and her son, my cousin slipped away with barely anyone noticing he had gone.

Delighted by our newfound freedom Edmund and I went to Arundel to view what we had received from Isabella. It was very fine and well worth the burdens we had endured. The approach up the river from the sea reminded me sharply of the finer palaces of Isabella's brother, and nowhere could there have been a stronger, more secure, fortress than this, our new castle. The walls were solid and the gatehouse narrow; and with high ground at our back and a commanding view over the town and river below, an enemy would be immediately apparent.

We spent a wonderful two weeks exploring our home and organising a household for our son. We rode out in the park and in the evening stood on the roof leads, looking down the valley and breathing in the smell of the sea. Our nights were spent in rekindling our closeness and I thought it might not be long before Mondi would have company in the nursery. I would have liked to stay longer but a terse note from Isabella commanded my return.

I arrived at Westminster to find my cousin still absent.

'I wish I knew where he is and what he's doing,' I said to Lady Abernethy.

'You mean you don't know?' She seemed amazed at my ignorance.

'Should I?'

She lowered her voice. 'There has been a plot to free Sir Edward.'

I gasped. 'Free the king? I mean Sir Edward.'

'Yes.'

'But why did nobody tell me?'

Lady Abernethy was blunt. 'If you weren't told, it is because Lord Mortimer doesn't want you to know. Perhaps he worries about your husband's loyalty and thinks he may be involved in the plot.'

'Lord Edmund? Nonsense. He is totally loyal and would never involve himself in something like that without telling me. Besides, what would be the purpose? Why would he want to take his brother away? Sir Edward lives in royal splendour in Kenilworth. He has nothing to complain of.'

'People are saying Lord Mortimer plans to move his prisoner out of Henry of Lancaster's clutches. He believes Kenilworth is not safe which must mean he suspects Lancaster as well.'

'Whom does he not suspect?' I said, bitterly.

'I think the list is short.'

'But I am his cousin,' I wailed.

'Ah yes, but your husband is Sir Edward's brother.'

I could not believe I had been deceived by my cousin and Isabella. I was so angry I decided to ask Isabella for the truth.

I discovered her playing tables with Lady Jeanne in her private chamber. It was not a pastime I enjoyed. I preferred chess, a game of skill and concentration where one could satisfactorily demolish one's opponent.

'Moved?' She raised her eyebrows at my question.

'Yes, your grace.'

'Does this concern you?'

'My husband is Sir Edward's brother, your grace, and it is only proper that he should be told. This was the agreement.'

Isabella narrowed her eyes and a chill filled the room.

'If I remember correctly, the agreement was purely monetary. Your husband was greedy for income, not brotherly love. I think you will find I kept my side of the bargain and rewarded him well.'

I opened my mouth to say something, but Isabella swept me aside. 'However, as you have asked, and, as you are dear to me, I shall tell you. Yes, there were certain unruly elements in the countryside which would have tried to take my husband away and make use of him. They are being apprehended.'

So there *had* been a plot. I wondered if my cousin knew who was behind it.

Isabella was watching my face. 'Lord Mortimer has asked the king to appoint Lord Berkeley and Sir John Maltravers as my husband's new guardians. He is to be moved to a place of greater safety. Everything is being seen to and it is for that reason alone that Lord Mortimer is absent from our side.'

She smiled at me. 'You mustn't worry, Margaret. It is merely a matter of my husband's safety, nothing more. Lancaster has proved a somewhat careless guardian and, as your husband knows, the comfort and well-being of my husband is my foremost concern. Berkeley Castle will, I trust, be a pleasant place for his retirement from the cares of his kingship. I think I shall visit him there later in the year.'

She turned back to her game, all thoughts of my questions banished. I watched as her delicate queenly fingers tossed the dice and then, with great relish, picked up one of her pieces and moved it up the board. Yes indeed, it was a very silly game.

The queen's household moved slowly north through the familiar flat lands of my childhood, travelling along narrow causeways until we reached the island in the marshes where Ramsey Abbey stood. It was here in the chapter room that the king's council was to meet with the king.

There was silence as the king and his mother took their places. Apart from the queen, I was the only woman present and my role was to wait on Isabella, not to speak. The council had come to report on the Scottish problem. Since the disaster of Bannockburn the Scots had been a continual thorn in our sides: raiding, stealing, burning and threatening invasion.

Before Isabella had finished arranging her skirts, the senior member of the council stepped forward. Henry, earl of Lancaster had not aged well. He was grey and bent, and if rumours were to be believed, half-blind. Edmund said he had not taken kindly to having his royal prisoner removed and there was bad feeling between him and my cousin.

Lord Henry pulled himself up to his full height and glared at his king.

'The advice the council gives your grace is to fight the turds.'

The king smiled. He was well used to his outspoken guardian.

'Poor advice,' remarked Isabella.

Lord Henry's eyes shifted to the queen. It was obvious he didn't like her and he didn't like her intervention.

'The so-called peace you brokered in Paris didn't last the year, madam, did it? Norham Castle burned the day your son was crowned. Would you have us pave the way to York for the Scots? Lay down carpets? Bid them welcome? Make them gifts of our cattle and our crops? Let them take our women?'

'War is not the answer to the king's problems,' said Isabella.

'It's the answer to mine.' Lord Henry was not about to be put down by a woman no matter who she was. 'Those of us who've had their Scottish lands stolen, want them back. And we've had enough of those scurvy whoresons storming across the border. It's time to put a stop to it once and for all. Unless you'd care to move your border south, to the Trent, your grace?'

His tone was verging on the rude but he seemed sure of his position. We all knew the king needed Lord Henry and his northern barons to keep the border secure.

'We should make peace with the Scots,' said Isabella firmly.

'We should crush them,' snarled Lord Henry.

The young king turned to his mother. 'The council have put forward their views very clearly, my lady, and their advice is that it is better to fight now and regain what we lost at Bannockburn. Our position on the ground is too weak to negotiate a peace.'

Isabella was having none of this. She leaned over to speak to her son privately. 'Campaigns cost money and your royal coffers are nearly empty. Your father's chamberlain emptied the treasury of gold and you've been left a very poor inheritance.'

I was shocked at her duplicity. This was quite untrue. It was Isabella herself who had emptied the royal coffers. Once she had the keys her greedy fingers had taken practically everything there was to take. She had no intention of allowing her personal wealth to be used in a pointless war with the Scots.

My brother rose.

'Your grace,' he bowed to the king. 'As you know, many of us here have lands near the border. How are we to defend them if we do not make a stand? If we tolerate these raids they will merely increase in ferocity. Soon the north will be ungovernable and what then?'

My brother's northern fortress of Liddell stood in a cold and inhospitable spot in the borderlands. He supported his father-in-law in the matter of the Scots because their interests ran side by side.

The king smiled at Tom. He was always polite, far more so than his father had been. 'Thank you, Lord Wake. I hear your advice and I agree. We shall call a muster at York for midsummer and in the meantime we shall send envoys to Bruce, to see if we can reach an accommodation.'

It was a brave speech for a fourteen-year-old boy but like any boy of his age he wanted to fight. It must seem like a huge adventure, one full of unknown excitement. John had felt the same but John had died on his adventure and I had been left alone.

The royal household left Ramsey for Peterborough where Easter was celebrated and then journeyed slowly on to Stamford for the parliament. As soon as we arrived I received an unexpected royal summons and hastily changed my dusty travelling clothes for something brushed and perfumed.

Isabella was pacing, a sure sign of annoyance.

'I have decided that from now on I shall attend meetings of the regency council in person.'

'But no woman is allowed sit on the council, your grace.'

'Are you trying to tell me what I can and can't do, Margaret?'

'Not at all, your grace.'

'Mortimer and I are agreed we cannot have the council making foolish decisions. They need direction and I shall give it.'

This was highly irregular and the bishops wouldn't like it. Women didn't belong on the council; their place was by the hearth or on their knees. Women were trouble and this woman, they were well aware, was more trouble than most.

Isabella hurried through unfamiliar ante-rooms, sweeping past startled servants and treasury clerks who weren't expecting the queen. She was determined to reach the council chamber before the doors slammed shut and Lord Henry's men barred the way. Luckily there was no unseemly argument on the threshold and Isabella sat down before anyone could raise an objection.

But matters did not run smoothly. Other than the clerks taking notes of the proceedings, there were twelve members of the council in attendance. My husband and his brother had their heads together smiling over some private joke while the earl of Surrey was whispering to Bishop Orleton. Facing the door in the position of maximum importance Isabella sat very upright in a high-backed chair, drumming her fingers on the table. She was dressed magnificently in crimson and gold. Old Archbishop Reynolds was stuttering and stammering, shuffling his feet beneath his robes while she fixed him with one of her iciest looks.

'Would you care to repeat that my lord archbishop. I cannot believe I heard you properly.' She was furious but her voice was deceptively calm.

'Er, in the matter of your lord, Sir Edward, lately king of this realm.'

He stopped.

'Yes.' Isabella stiffened. 'Please continue. What of my husband?'

'Er, my brother bishops and I, feel that as your sentiments are clearly at one with ours, that your lord should receive the most abundant spiritual comfort and the tender devotion of his companion ...'

His voice tailed away. We waited. The queen raised an eyebrow.

'And?'

'The gifts of a loving wife, the letters from one who is still in the utmost harmony with her lord, the genuine remorse felt by the ...'

The old man was rambling but his intentions were blindingly obvious. He thought the queen should return to the conjugal embrace of her husband.

'Er, we understand your reluctance to place your royal person in any temporal danger, my lady, and would never suggest such a thing, but perhaps the greater sin would be not to ...'

'Are you suggesting my lord archbishop that I should defy my son's wishes?'

'No, no.' The archbishop twisted his hands unhappily. 'Not at all. His grace's wishes are ... so, so ... well, obviously. And then there is this other matter, my lady.'

'What other matter?'

'The privy seal of his grace, the king, my lady.'

I smiled to myself. I knew about the king's privy seal.

'It is felt that on occasions it may have been misused. Not intentionally, we would never say that, but perhaps er ...'

'Misused?'

The poor man was becoming more and more entangled in his words. They ran themselves round his tongue and came out of his mouth in an unintelligible jumble. He was clearly acutely embarrassed by what he was trying to say.

'And some of my brother bishops feel your grace is perhaps a trifle too involved in matters concerning er ...'

'Are you accusing me of something?'

'No, no, your grace. It is just a worry that such a thing *might* happen. It was felt that in our letter to His Holiness we should …'

Isabella put her hands on the arms of her chair and stood up. Everyone struggled to their feet.

'I have had enough. I will not sit here and be slandered by my own archbishop. Do what you like. Write to whom you please. Say what you want. But remember to whom you owe your position and don't imagine His Holiness is immune to persuasion.'

She swept out of the room and naturally I had to follow. I could hear a burst of talking in the room behind us as we disappeared down the length of the room back to the queen's apartments.

Of course it was all true. Despite the king having his own rooms and his own people, Isabella kept him on a leading rein. She visited two or three times a day and imposed her will at every turn. Nothing happened in his royal rooms that she did not supervise or approve, and every document which passed across the king's table also found its way into her hands. She used his privy seal as if it were her own and she dictated policy as if her son was just that - her son and not the king.

No wonder the bishops had had enough. Isabella was walking on dangerous ground but with my cousin's support she feared nobody, not even His Holiness. And I asked myself again - where could it lead?

As for me, I knew my destination. The jolting up and down on our journey through the marshes had not improved the unsteadiness in my belly and I could no longer hide the truth from myself. There was going to be another child.

188

8

YORK 1327

It was early May when we rode into York and Isabella was in combative mood.

'I have urged my son to send an affectionate request to Hainault. We shall ask Sir John to return with his men to give us assistance in our hour of need.'

My cousin choked. 'You what?'

'You heard me, Mortimer. Fighting is a waste of our money but if we are to campaign it will be a pleasure to have Sir John at our side. We shall welcome him with a magnificent banquet and my son shall have a new suit of armour.'

'He has half a dozen already,' muttered my cousin.

'They are for tournaments, Mortimer, as you well know. For battle he will need something stronger, more burnished, something altogether grander. And the latest in bascinets. If he is to fight, my son must be well protected.'

At the end of May, Sir John of Hainault rode into York with five hundred of his men. He was in good spirits and eager to do battle once again for the beautiful Lady Isabella. He was a gust of warm wind sweeping up from the south as his army clattered through the streets of the city to the accompaniment of enthusiastic cheers from the crowds.

This time it wasn't only my cousin gritting his teeth. Edmund said the English archers already lodged in the city were even less pleased to see the Hainaulters. They didn't care for outsiders at the best of times and with a campaign in the offing, the idea of sharing the spoils with a bunch of lazy good-for-nothing foreigners was not to their liking.

Name-calling and late-night scuffles became commonplace and several fights got seriously out of hand with men left for dead in the alleyways. It got to the stage where I was nervous of venturing out from our lodgings for fear of tripping over a corpse.

We were lodged, as usual, in the house of the Black Friars, and this time because of my new exalted position, I shared three rooms with my husband instead of being relegated to a back stairs' closet with Lady Abernethy.

But life was no easier because I was a countess. I was in despair over my wardrobe, trying to devise a suitable outfit for Isabella's grand feast. The celebration in honour of Sir John and his Hainaulter friends promised to be a splendid affair. Isabella liked to do things properly and her hospitality would be lavish. All her women were ordered to be extravagantly gowned.

It was a problem to know which of my sets of robes to choose. Isabella outshone everyone so perhaps it didn't really matter what I wore but I didn't want to look like one of those forlorn and forgotten widows, fit only for a bench at the far end of the hall. Edmund was an important man and I must do justice to my position as his wife. I held up my new yellow silk kirtle, wondering if it would go well with the green damask outer gown, when my maid coughed.

'My lady.'

'What is it?' I could have done without her interruption at such an important moment.

'It is the countess of Norfolk, my lady.'

My sister-in-law did not usually visit me at this time of day so I was surprised to see her slip into the room in a state of great distress.

'Please,' she said, clutching me in a childlike fashion. 'I don't know what to do.'

'What is the matter?' I said, detaching myself from her grasp.

'It's the countess of Surrey.'

'Lady Jeanne?'

'She said ...' The girl gulped and gasped and was unable to continue.

I sat her down and called for a cup of wine. I really didn't want to spend my afternoon discussing Lady Jeanne's scandalous stories but I recognised something in this young woman which disturbingly reflected my own situation. We had both been raised up by our husbands and I knew there were many women who thought we were both unworthy of our positions - her, obviously, more than me. I considered it a kindness to sit for a while and listen to her prattle.

'Now,' I said, smiling companionably. 'Tell me what Lady Jeanne has said.'

Her eyes widened. 'She told me the earl is seeking an annulment.'

'The earl, her husband?'

'Yes. She says he is faithless and has a mistress whom he wishes to marry.'

'It has happened before and it will probably happen again,' I said, wondering why Lady Jeanne was unable to hold on to her husband. 'I'm afraid the earl is well-known for his amorous affairs and he and Lady Jeanne don't seem able to live together in harmony. But he won't succeed. He's been trying to be rid of her for at least ten years and I've heard His Holiness won't countenance it. Lady Jeanne has powerful friends and they will speak up for her. She is the king's cousin and His Holiness will not want to offend the English king.'

To my surprise, she started to weep.

'No, you don't understand. It is not Lady Jeanne, it's me! What if my lord wishes to be rid of me?'

I leaned forward and took her hand. It was tiny, just a warm little paw.

'He won't do that.'

'Lady Margaret, I'm not clever like you. People say I'm stupid but I do know why my husband married me. I've always known. I was not a suitable match in any way but he and my father were both determined and I did like him so very much. I would have gone with him without the marriage but my father wouldn't let me. So I became the countess of Norfolk and now my husband is tired of me.'

Tears rolled down her cheeks and I noted with envy how pretty she looked when she cried. There were no blotched cheeks or puffy eyes; she merely looked delightfully tragic.

'I'm sure he's not tired of you,' I said, crossing my fingers against the lie.

'Oh he is. I know he is. The first year we were married he came to my bed constantly but now he is rarely with me. I've always known there were other women but my father says that is the way of noblemen and it is no business of mine. But what if he has found a well-born lady and wishes to be rid of me?'

I considered the likelihood of Edmund's brother discarding this poor girl in favour of a more valuable marriage. Brother Norfolk was not a good judge of his affairs, so Edmund said, constantly making unwise agreements with other men which turned out not to be to his advantage.

'I think Lord Edmund would have told me if his brother had found someone else,' I said, trying to be kind yet not wanting to be untruthful. 'I don't think you need worry.'

I was sure she was the most accommodating of wives. She was not spirited but had a placid charm. She would always do exactly what a husband asked of her, seeing it as her duty. I knew Edmund liked her.

She looked up at me, her eyes brimming with tears.

'I am so afraid. I have no powerful kin and it would be easy for him to put me aside. I've been told that men do it all the time.'

'I think that is an exaggeration. It is an expensive matter to seek an annulment even when there is cause.'

'Lady Margaret, what would you do if you were me?'

I thought her position far from strong. She had given brother Norfolk three children but if he had grown tired of her I wasn't sure what she had to offer. Her family had nothing and she herself had little else to recommend her. And there was only one son.

'You don't refuse him, do you?'

She looked shocked.

'Of course not!'

She was like a piece of old clothing, once desirable, now cast aside in favour of something new. Perhaps Edmund's brother needed a woman with more to offer than this little wide-eyed mouse. Perhaps somewhere there was a secret mistress with a handful of bastard sons.

'My lord is disappointed I am not carrying another child,' she said, tears spilling over again. 'It is three years since the last baby. He says one son is not enough and I must do my duty better. I try, Lady Margaret. I have been to Walsingham to pray for another son and I follow what I have been told by the midwife and by my ladies. I pray every night before I go to my bed but if my husband lies with other women what can I do?'

'As your father says, it is no business of yours. I think you should smile and stop worrying. Your husband won't want to see a tearful face. Be merry.'

She looked doubtful.

'Is that what you do, Lady Margaret?'

I smiled complacently. 'I have no need to dissemble. Lord Edmund is a faithful and devoted husband; I am very fortunate.'

'But I thought …'

She looked embarrassed and didn't finish what she had been going to say.

'What did you think?'.

'It was nothing but at the Christmas festivities my lord said …'

She stopped again and bit her lip. She raised her gaze to mine and I saw reflected in her eyes the compassion

I felt for her. She was sorry for me because she believed my husband was unfaithful to me in the way her husband was to her. She saw us as sisters in our distress; both of us cast aside by our noble husbands tired of their impulsive marriages to lesser women.

The ground shifted uncertainly beneath my feet. What had she heard? Had Edmund's brother mentioned things I didn't know? Lady Jeanne said all men strayed, if not today, then tomorrow.

But Edmund was not like that, he loved me. He was faithful and steadfast, different from other husbands and our marriage was as secure as an iron-bound chest. I didn't want to know what Lord Norfolk had said and I didn't want to know what this young woman thought Edmund had done. He was my husband and I loved him. But a terrible doubt had crept into my mind and refused to go away.

I had brought nothing to our marriage other than myself yet Edmund had promised to hold me and not let me fall. But if Edmund was not faithful, I was diminished and if I was diminished I was no longer the person I thought I was. I would be nothing but a handful of earthshine and dust.

In the echoes a few thoughtless words by a foolish woman, I heard Dame Fortune laugh as she spun her wheel.

The king's final attempts to agree a peace with the Scots failed, and by the middle of June Bruce was once again raiding our lands on this side of the border. Edmund and his brother Norfolk were appointed captains of the royal army under Lord Henry and the king would ride at the head of his men. This was his army and his first taste of war and he was as excited as any fourteen year-old boy would be in the circumstances.

In amongst the chaos of an army about to move it would have been easy to miss the horseman who rode under the gatehouse that evening. His horse was lathered and the rider exhausted. He flung himself out of the saddle and hurried up the steps. Curiosity got the better of me and I dispatched my maid to learn what she could. The days were gone when I could wander at will round the kitchens to discover what I wanted to know. Now I was too grand and no-one would talk to me.

'He been riding five days wi' no rest,' she said, when she eventually returned.

'Where was he from?'

She shook her head. 'Cook said he were Lord Berkeley's man but no-one were sure.'

'Who did he go to?'

'Lord Mortimer.'

I wondered what was so urgent that Lord Berkeley's man needed to ride fast for five days to make delivery. It was a mystery like so much else of what my cousin did.

The following morning the royal army filed out of York on its way north to Durham. Trumpets blared and people cheered, as banners were hoisted aloft and thousands of red and white pennants fluttered in the cool morning breeze. The young king rode at the head of the procession and visible everywhere was his new emblem - the red cross of the warrior St George, the knight from Cappadocia.

I watched until the last man had disappeared and all that remained was a dark cloud of dust drifting into a distant haze. I had made a proper formal farewell to Edmund but, despite the reassuring touch of his glove and the warmth in his eyes, I was overwhelmed with fear. What if he did not come back? What if, like John, he fell under the Scottish pikes and I had to endure the rest of my life without him?

I wandered through the lofty rooms left empty by the king's household where dozens of servants were cleaning. With most of the hangings removed there was very little remaining of a royal presence. I climbed the stairs to the solar rooms and from there up the stone steps to the door which led onto the upper walls. Here I had a view of the city below and the green hills and valleys beyond.

'Looking for someone?'

It was my cousin. He was leaning against a wall, half in the shadows.

'I thought you were gone with the others, my lord,' I said, surprised to see him.

'No, Margaret, I leave tomorrow. I have matters to attend to which cannot wait.'

Into my mind flashed the image of the mud-spattered rider of the previous day.

'Matters more important than the Scots?'

He shrugged. 'The Scots are unimportant. You might hanker after the lands your first husband had, but you know as well as I do that sooner or later we shall have to make peace. And a sensible man will make it sooner.'

I waited to see if he would say more, if he would tell me what he had been doing, but when he spoke it was about something else entirely.

'You have risen high, cousin. I never thought the little girl standing in my hall at Wigmore, who rebuked me over the state of my ditches, would turn into a countess. I had you marked down as some minor baron's wife but I was mistaken. You are far too clever to spend your days stitching napkins for a husband's table.'

'I never planned any of this, my lord.'

'My wife says I spend too much time planning.'

'You have seen Lady Joan?'

'Of course. Do you not see your husband?'

'Yes, but I do not ...'

He smiled at me. It was the old familiar smile which had bound me to him as a cousin through all our fortunes and misfortunes, the smile of a man I could so easily have loved.

'Not what? Your tongue always did run away with you, Margaret. What is it I do that you do not do? Do you think my marriage is so vastly different from yours?'

I pressed my lips together. I did not humiliate my husband as he was humiliating Joan. But how could I tell him his behaviour with Isabella was beyond anything I would do, that it was beyond what anyone would do to someone they professed to love and respect. Then I remembered what my sister-in-law had said.

My cousin took me by the arm and ushered me back through the doorway into the gloom of the stairway.

'You should remember, my little *bwbach*,' he said softly into my ear, 'not everything is always as it seems.'

Half way through August, our men returned. They tried to pretend otherwise but there was no disguising the failure of the campaign. From the riot in the priory which left Hainault and English archers fighting on the stairs and three hundred dead in the streets of York, to the ignominious plodding through Weardale in pursuit of an enemy who refused to come to battle, the whole affair had been a disaster.

'My son blames you,' said Isabella tartly, regarding my cousin as if he had just crawled out from under a stone.

'His grace does not yet understand the realities of war.'

'My son wished to fight and you refused to allow the attack. You overruled Lord Edmund and the earl of Lancaster. You prevented Sir John from advancing his Hainaulters and you stopped Lord Norfolk from leading the vanguard against the enemy. My son had roused his men to fight. He told me your actions were treasonable. And to think I imagined you a brave man, Lord Mortimer.'

'Your son should be grateful to me that he is still alive and not being returned to York in a box in the back of a cart,' snarled my cousin. 'There is no glory in attacking an enemy who has the advantage when there is another day and another hilltop. His grace is inexperienced, my lady. There is a difference between bravery and foolhardiness. Would you have preferred him returned to you in pieces?'

'My son is a young man of great courage.'

'Your son burst into tears like a girl, my lady. He sat on his horse in front of a dozen battle-hardened men and wept. I don't condemn him. It was his first taste of war. The Scots cut the ropes of his pavilion and killed his men around him. He saw how narrow the gap is between life and death and he didn't like it. A bloodied nose in the tilt yard is not the same as a sword thrust in the belly. And a scratch on the hand from a mistimed lunge in the joust does not compare with a friend's life-blood gushing out onto the battlefield in front of your eyes.'

'Isabella,' pleaded Edmund. 'It was an impossible situation. Please try and understand.'

'Understand? I send four of my most able commanders: my husband's brothers, my uncle of Lancaster and my trusted Lord Mortimer, to defeat a rabble of Scotsmen - and look what happens? Now we shall have to agree whatever terms Bruce dictates. Scotland is all but lost to my son.'

'What of those with lands across the border?' I asked in dismay.

'A peace treaty is their best hope of getting some recompense,' said Isabella. 'It is the most sensible way to proceed. We cannot afford to drain our treasury with one costly campaign after another.'

'While your mind is on your purse,' said my cousin drily, 'Have you seen the account your friend Sir John has rendered? I presume you will be pledging your jewels in order to pay for it, my lady?'

'My son's treasury will pay the costs of the campaign. And Sir John is a friend. It is a debt of honour.'

'Whose honour, I wonder,' muttered my cousin. 'Most certainly not mine.'

'Your grace, what of those who do not get their lands back?' I said. 'Where is the honour for them?'

I was thinking of Lady Abernethy and her daughters, of my first husband's sisters and of Badenoch - John's Badenoch, lost forever beyond the mist-covered mountains of the north. With its stone-built towers lapped by the ruffled waters of a distant loch, this was the castle of my dreams; Badenoch, where pear trees blossomed all year round and the sun shone hot on bowers of scented summer flowers.

But mine was a lone voice. Apart from the king who was sunk in gloom at the reminders of his failed campaign, and Lord Henry, who Edmund said had taken himself off to sulk, the others were determined to sue for peace. England would recognise Scotland as a sovereign land. The king would clasp hands with Robert Bruce and to seal matters there would be a royal marriage. I thought of the queen's two little daughters and wondered which one would pay the price for this peace. Which would be the "English wife" sent north to live in that cold inhospitable land and be married off to Bruce's son?

I wept when I thought of the waste of John's life. He had fought for England, for his lands and for his king, but it had been for nothing. The others might recognise Robert Bruce as king of the Scots - to me he would always be John's murderer.

We were a dreary party winding our way slowly southwards from York. At Nottingham my cousin departed, saying he had business in South Wales which needed his attention. No-one questioned his decision, it didn't seem of much importance. He ignored his summons to the parliament at Lincoln and disappeared.

9

BERKELEY CASTLE 1327

She licked her thumb and ran it down the blade. Sharp enough! She eyed the man sitting in the shadows.

'You got a name, Master Sergeant? I like to know who I do business with.'

He ignored her.

She shrugged. No business of hers if a man kept his own counsel.

'I need water.'

The man grunted and went to the door. Before long there was a bumping and groaning as someone made a great performance of bringing up a bucket.

She checked her bag of tools and was surprised when the man pressed something hard and cold into her hand. It was a small bowl.

'What's that for?'

'Heart.'

Ah yes, the seat of courage, of wisdom and all things valiant. She took the battered pewter bowl and placed it beside her jars. Some liked the heart kept separate. French wife probably wanted it.

Now for her customer, the man on the table.

She removed his boots: best quality leather, soft as thistledown, fancy silk tassels, but scuffed and trodden flat at the heels; ill-fitting which was a surprise. It was a job to get them off but with some tugging and heaving she managed it.

Then the clothes. Again, once of the very best but now grubby and unbrushed. The hose needed mending and the sumptuous velvet was threadbare and smelled musty. Removing the silk undergarments, she wondered why it was that lords wore such fine stuff beneath their clothing. What a waste when no-one could admire it.

There was a tear on the shoulder of the tunic as if someone had wrenched the garment off at some time or other. She folded the items carefully and placed them on the chest. They'd be needed later for dressing, though it'd be likely they'd send something more suitable - robes or sacramental garments. It wouldn't be old stuff like this.

She looked at him. A fine man: strong, good shoulders, well-muscled. Hair, golden still, not much grey. Beard a bit straggly, but the chin was firm. Long legs like his father. "Longshanks" they'd called him.

It was hard to ignore the life-giver. Even after all these years she found with men she couldn't help but look and wonder. It was better not to think about the rumours, or what the bishop had said. She didn't like to work with men like that: unclean, unnatural, and everyone knew that sin contaminated.

She looked more closely. How strange! She hadn't seen a man like that before. She'd heard about them. When she was young there'd been a neighbour who others said was less than a man. He was the butt of jokes and wasn't well-liked. But her mother would have dealt with him when he died because it was a long time ago.

Unstoppering one of her jars she added a small amount of bitter-smelling wormwood to the water. Then with the *greatest care, using a scrap of cloth, she began to wash the body, paying particular attention to the face. The eyes were already veiled and under her breath she said a final prayer. His soul had fled and hers would be the last face he looked upon. As always she felt the need to help them on their way. Putting out her hand she smoothed the eyelids shut. The mouth was open but the jaw could be bound later.*

She raised the knife and sliced swiftly downwards. A moment of resistance as the blade penetrated the skin and then the flesh parted. It was better this way, not like the Italian who said he went in through the side. This way you could see what you were doing and nothing would be left behind to fester and corrupt the body.

She probed inside, reaching up and feeling around with her fingers. A few swift cuts and with great care she lifted out the heart and placed it in the pewter bowl. Bigger than expected but he was a big man. It seemed indecent to leave his heart lying open to the gaze of others so she covered the bowl with a piece of linen cloth. Using her hands she scooped out the viscera: the lungs, the liver and the slippery entrails, placing them in another bowl, a larger one brought specially for this purpose. They'd be buried close by the castle walls but nobody had said anything to her about the arrangements.

She worked steadily: cleaning, tidying up the cavity, sprinkling it with salt and wormwood and rubbing sweet-smelling oils into the sides of the wound. It was a strangely pleasing task. When everything was completed to her satisfaction she took her sack of herbs: bell-heather, chamomile, lavender, sage and mint; and the filling: the seeds of barley and flax and special grasses gathered in secret places known only to her. A handful at a time she began to fill the body. Every inch was stuffed tight so that at a glance no-one would know what had been done.

Then came the sewing - quick neat stitches as her mother had taught her. After that, a final wash in case any bloody matter had dripped onto the skin. One more rub with oils to sweeten up the body and now it was time for the cerecloth. This was the last farewell, the moment when he ceased to look like the man he had once been and became something else, something mysterious, a traveller ready for the final journey into the long dark night of eternal rest.

She began with the feet and the legs, then the body, hands and arms. She bandaged expertly. All the injuries that man did to man: the livid scars, the bruises, the old burn marks were hidden beneath these swathes of waxed cloth. Sometimes she thought she was obliterating a man's life and leaving him washed and clean and perfect, like a newborn babe.

When at last she reached the head, the man in the corner said, 'Cover the face.'

She hesitated. 'Surely …?'

'Do as you're told. Cover it.'

It never did to offend one's masters so she wound the cloth tightly over the mouth, the nose and the sleeping eyes; over the broad forehead and the last wisp of hair. She did as she was told but it made her wonder. Somebody would want to come and look. Not the wife if what they said was true. But someone, surely?

Ah well, none of her business. She'd heard enough secrets in her time. One thing she knew was that secrets brought trouble and her life was trouble enough without adding more.

10

AN UNEXPECTED DEATH 1327

'What's that?'

I opened an eye. Edmund's head was off the pillow. I could hear nothing but the usual night sounds of the castle: snoring, snuffling, coughing; the occasional hoot of an owl from the woods beyond the walls and the calling of a fox.

I yawned. 'What is it?'

'Horses.'

'Lord Mortimer?'

'No. He returned this morning, trailing half South Wales behind him.'

'It's nothing then, just Lincoln men celebrating. Go back to sleep.'

A moment later we both heard it: a bang and a scrape as the bolt was drawn. This was followed by urgent whispering. Edmund twitched the bed curtains and by the glow of the night lamp I could see people by the door. Edmund had his hand on his knife but it was only William.

'My lord.' His over-loud whisper would have woken the saints from their slumbers.

'What is it?'

'A messenger, my lord. From Berkeley. I thought you'd want to know.'

I dropped my head back onto the pillow. Berkeley! Another attempted escape! How many more times would these fools persist in their efforts to free Edmund's brother? Why did some men never learn?

'It will be for Lord Mortimer,' said Edmund, putting the knife back under his pillow. 'They'll have missed him on the road.'

'No, my lord. The man had two letters, one for the queen and one for the king. That's why I came.'

At that, Edmund swung his legs out onto the step, pulling the curtain aside as he did so. When William saw me, he blushed and bowed his head, muttering, 'My lady.'

'It's alright William,' I said. 'What is sleep for, but to be disturbed?'

'Where's the messenger now?' said Edmund.

'With the queen.'

This was unheard of. It must be very urgent business to disturb Isabella at this hour.

'Get me my clothes and my boots. I'll go and see what's happened.'

He turned to me.

'Go back to sleep, Margaret. I'm sure it's nothing.'

I lay awake contemplating the possibilities and wondering which would be worse: Sir Edward free and in the hands of those who wanted him king again and us dead in a ditch; or yet another foiled plot which would mean a dungeon like Lord Mortimer of Chirk's for Edmund's brother, somewhere he couldn't be reached - a fate which would cause Edmund oceans of anguish.

I was drifting back to sleep when I heard the door open and Edmund's footsteps. He came and stood by the bed but made no move to join me. I forced myself awake.

'What's happened?' I mumbled, still half-asleep.

There was no reply so I made a valiant effort and opened both eyes.

My husband's face was grey and he was trembling. He looked ten years older than when he'd left the room.

'He's dead.'

'Who?' I sat upright, pushing a tangle of hair out of my eyes, thinking of nothing but Mondi.

'Ned. My brother. He's dead.'

A thousand thoughts tumbled into my mind all at once. The king, dead? No, not the king, the king's father, the old king, the vanquished king; the king we'd pushed off his throne so that Isabella could put her son in his place.

'Oh my dearest.' I hardly knew what to say. Edmund looked beaten.

'It is my fault.'

'No it isn't.'

'If I hadn't agreed to this stupidity he would still be alive.'

'Dearest, there was nothing you could do. When a man is called to God, there is nothing any of us can do.'

'I shouldn't have done it,' he sobbed. 'I should have been steadfast. My mother said I should be loyal to Ned. And look what I did.'

He climbed onto the bed still in his boots, still fully dressed, and fell into my arms.

'Oh Margaret. What have I done?'

I held him against me and stroked the back of his head, making comforting noises as I used to do with Aymer. His cheek against mine was wet with tears as he wept for his brother, for that foolish, selfish, pleasure-loving man who knew nothing of how to be a good king. All the while my heart sang out – he cannot touch us, we are safe. Whatever we did, now we are safe. He cannot reach out from his lonely prison cell and seize us by the throat, throttling the life out of us for what we've done.

At last he raised his head.

'I cannot believe he's dead. It's not as if he was old. He was a man in his prime. He was like a father to me, the best father I could have had. The best father any man could have had.'

'He loved you,' I said gently.

This was not the time to remind Edmund of his brother's follies, of the times he had betrayed Edmund's loyalty and casually disregarded him. There had been very little love or reward for my husband from the king; everything had been poured into the greedy hands of Sir Hugh Despenser.

We sat there for a long time while he talked of the days when he and Thomas were small, when they had followed their elder brother in everything he did: the summer they'd spent crawling through bushes at Woodstock pretending to be wild animals; the water battles in the moats; the mud fights; the dark evenings idling by the fire in the hall listening to stories of magicians and brave knights; and the long hot days spent in the saddle as they'd followed a king who was always on the move.

He told me of the mischievous games they'd played with the king's blood-brother, Piers Gaveston, and of their horror when they learned he had been murdered. And he told me of his brother's grief, how he had clung to the two young boys, trying to claw back the happy times; and then how he'd sunk into a melancholy so deep Edmund feared he would never recover.

Gradually his voice grew drowsy and at last he fell asleep. My arm was trapped beneath the weight of his body but I lay still, not wanting him to wake. With my free hand I pulled the cover over him.

I had no desire to sleep. I was fully awake and thinking. If Edmund's brother had been commanded to God, who, I wondered, had given the command?

My cousin, Roger, Lord Mortimer of Wigmore, was standing with his legs apart and his back to the fire, casually issuing commands as if he were the ruler of all England. The king, meanwhile, was crouched on a stool looking miserable. His face was ashen, his eyes red-rimmed and his bottom lip was trembling. Perhaps, like Edmund, he blamed himself.

Isabella sat stony-faced in the best chair regarding both her son and my cousin with distaste. She had been weeping.

My cousin regarded us sombrely. 'A sad business.'

'Please, tell me what has happened,' I said quietly.

'Letters have come from Lord Berkeley telling us the prisoner is dead.'

'*Requiescat*,' I murmured.

'Indeed.'

'When did he die?'

'Two days ago. The night before Gurney left Berkeley.'

'Gurney?'

'Sir Thomas Gurney. Lord Berkeley's man. The one who brought the letters,'

'Did he say more?'

'What more is there to say?'

Edmund was talking quietly to Isabella and her son and couldn't hear what I was saying.

'Did the letter say how he died? Was he sick?'

My cousin looked at me thoughtfully.

'The letter said nothing. It didn't need to. He's dead. It's finished.'

I shook my head. 'I never thought it would end like this.'

'Didn't you? I credited you with more intelligence, but perhaps I was mistaken.' He started to turn away but then turned back. 'Margaret, a word of warning. Be careful. Do not raise phantoms where none exist. Leave Isabella and the boy to grieve in peace.'

I was about to ask what phantoms he imagined there were to be raised but one look at his face made me close my mouth.

I went over to Isabella.

'Your grace,' I said quietly. 'I grieve for you. A husband is still a husband no matter where he is or what he has done. Sir Edward was the father of your children and as such I know your heart must be full of sorrow at this time.'

She was very pale but quite composed.

'I am truly a widow. No more pretence. It's over.'

She reached out to touch my hand as she had that time on the ship when we thought we might die. I felt the coolness of her fingers and waited for more words but she said nothing.

Edmund was talking to his nephew. They were two young men vainly trying to bring comfort to the other.

'I have written to my de Bohun cousin,' said the young king bleakly.

'And I shall write to my sisters,' said Edmund. 'There are only four of my father's children left. So many have gone.'

'It is God's will,' said the boy, turning his sorrow towards me.

'Your grace?'

'Please,' he half-smiled. 'I don't need formality at a time like this, I need comfort.'

'Dearest Edward,' I said, returning the smile. 'I grieve with you. If there is any service I can do?'

'There is,' he said simply. 'When we return south, bring me your son. I like babies. They are always happy and I need to be reminded that somewhere happiness exists.'

I was surprised. Men have tender feelings towards their own children but it was unusual for a boy to acknowledge a love of all babies.

'It will be an honour for Mondi.'

'Is that what you call him?'

'Yes, Edmund, for his father.'

'I shall call my firstborn son Edward, for *my* father,' he said firmly. 'It will be a way of remembering him.'

'We must make a decision how to play this,' said my cousin abruptly. 'We cannot delay too long in spreading the word. An announcement must be made to the parliament.'

'Is that wise?' said Isabella. 'It's not as if he was king any more. Perhaps we should keep the death hidden until we have settled matters.'

'What matters?' said the young king.

'Nothing which need concern you, dearest,' said Isabella gently.

'The body,' said my cousin with studied callousness. 'We can't just toss it into a pit.'

'Lord Mortimer!' I said angrily. 'Your words are unfeeling.'

'I have no feelings for Sir Edward as he had none for me. He threw me into the Tower and left me to rot. I did not receive justice at his hands. He would have let Despenser hang me. He was a bad king.'

The king jumped off his stool and stood there, his eyes blazing.

'How dare you speak of my father like that, Lord Mortimer. If you were not my mother's friend I would ...'

'Yes, boy? What would you do?'

'Mortimer!'

We all jumped as Isabella's voice sliced like a blade across the room.

'In my presence and in the presence of my son, you will mind your tongue. This is my husband you are slandering and he is not dead a week.'

With no thought for anything but the need for haste, I excused myself and hurried down to the hall where I found one of Edmund's men. I asked the whereabouts of Sir Thomas Gurney and while waiting for him to be brought to me, wondered if he would tell me the truth. He might consider it none of my business, not the preserve of a woman.

'Countess?'

Thomas Gurney was a man with a ferrety face, dark-haired and black-browed, broad in the shoulder with blacksmith's arms. It was impossible to tell if he was more than a simple messenger so I needed to tread carefully. He stood blocking the light, staring at a point somewhere above my head.

'Lord Mortimer said I might find you here.' I put out a hand to grasp a rail, trying to look fragile with my eight-month belly.

'My lady?'

'You are returning to Berkeley?'

His lips twitched in annoyance. 'Yes, my lady. We were ready to leave when I was summoned.'

This was not a good start.

'Please understand, Sir Thomas, my husband, is in great need of consolation. He grieves and, being a dutiful wife, I wish to lessen his pain. If I could tell him his brother did not suffer, it would be a kindness.'

Gurney frowned.

'I lost my first husband, at Bannockburn,' I continued in a low voice as if my words were a long-kept secret revealed for Thomas Gurney alone. 'I didn't know how he died and no-one could tell me of his last moments. Nobody could say if he suffered. I'm sure you understand, Sir Thomas, why I wish to bring my husband any comfort that I can.'

Gurney nodded. 'I'm sorry you lost your lord, my lady. 'Twas a bloody battle. Many good men fell to the Scots that day.'

I hurried on before he could embark on the horrors of Bannockburn. Since marrying Edmund they had disappeared from my dreams and I had no wish to have them resurrected.

'I hear Berkeley is like my childhood home, Sir Thomas - a damp place where fogs creep in from the marshes, and sickness strikes quickly.'

Gurney looked puzzled. 'There has been no sickness in the castle, my lady.'

He seemed very sure but then he would. If there had been sickness everyone would know and would have been afraid.

'Thank you for your assurances, Sir Thomas. My husband's fears will be eased knowing his brother was not lost to a fever. Was it perhaps a fall?'

'I heard of no fall.' A fleeting look of suspicion crossed his face and I knew I'd asked one question too many.

There had been no sickness, no fall. What was it that had caused Edmund's brother to die? Perhaps Sir Thomas Gurney didn't know or perhaps he was under orders to tell no-one.

'The prisoner was well-treated, my lady. He was fed better than my lord. His chamber was heated and he had pen and parchment. They said he wrote verses and would read them to his keeper. I do not think you can fault my lord for his care of the prisoner.'

So Edmund's brother had a particular keeper. I wondered if I could discover his name but Sir Thomas Gurney was anxious to be gone. He took two steps backwards and was beginning his formal farewell. It would do me no good to become an object of his suspicion and perhaps there was nothing of which to be suspicious. I inclined my head and tried to look duly grateful although he had told me nothing of any value.

'I thank you, Sir Thomas.'

He stared at me as if I was worth no more than a laundress. A stupid man. But cunning could easily be mistaken for stupidity. If Thomas Gurney had secrets he was not going to blurt them out to the first woman who asked questions, no matter that she was Lord Mortimer's cousin.

On the final day of the parliament it was announced to a stunned gathering of men in the chapter house of Lincoln Cathedral that on the eve of the feast of St Matthew the Apostle and Evangelist, Sir Edward, sometime king of England, had died a natural death at Berkeley Castle.

Edmund said there were gasps and turned heads and cries of amazement. I wondered how many were genuinely sad at the death of this man they had known, and how many were secretly rejoicing. The timing of the proclamation meant the news would be carried home by every man present and its implications picked over in every hall and every hovel in the land. Each man's wife would want exact details of what was said and by whom; and later, his servants would embroider the tale in the way that servants always do.

'What will happen now?' I asked Edmund as we prepared in a half-hearted way to leave for Nottingham.

'They are arguing about the funeral arrangements. My nephew wishes his father to be laid to rest in the abbey at Westminster where his grandfather and grandmother are buried, but Isabella won't have it. She wants some lesser place, somewhere out of the way where my brother can be conveniently forgotten.'

'And my cousin?'

'Mortimer fears unrest, he doesn't want a funeral close to London. He suggested the abbey at Gloucester where his kinsman is abbot.'

'Gloucester is a great distance from London,' I said thoughtfully. 'Suitable for pilgrimage but not for plotting.'

'I expect it will be as Mortimer wishes,' said Edmund morosely. 'He usually gets his own way.'

'And is your brother's body still at Berkeley?'

'Yes, in the chapel. I am assured a man is watching over him.'

They would have embalmed the body quickly and hopefully Edmund need not dwell on his brother's face. Our viewing of the count of Valois's body two years ago had not been pleasant for either of us.

'Where would *you* like him buried?'

He shrugged. 'I have no opinion. I will grieve for him as much at Gloucester as I would at Westminster.'

'And your brother?' I said tentatively, trying to rouse Edmund from his apathy. 'What would he have chosen for himself?'

Edmund smiled. 'As long as it was suitably glittering and glorious, Ned wouldn't have minded. If he had known he was going to die he might well have chosen to be laid to rest in the chapel at Langley, beside his great friend Piers Gaveston. But no-one would permit that. It would not be fitting for a man who had once been king.'

'So there is your duty, my dearest. Make certain that, whatever happens and wherever it is done, this funeral will be the most splendid glittering affair ever. Talk to Edward, commission a wonderful hearse, call in the king's painter. This need not be a shabby hole-in-the-corner business. This funeral can be as glorious and as wonderful as your brother would have wanted.'

We travelled the familiar road from Lincoln to Southwell, through Sherwood, past Mansfield and on to Nottingham. On every side the fields were bare of crops and signs of autumn were already brushing the trees. In the villages, water dripped from roof thatch, and puddles formed in dips and hollows. Our summer was over and we had begun the long slow march to the turn of the year.

It was six years since I had last ridden these same roads, filled with sorrow at the death of a friend, wondering whether or not I should accept Lord Everingham's proposal of marriage. A lifetime ago John had ridden this way dressed in his finery, overjoyed at the prospect of going to war. I hadn't been there to watch him pass beneath the Sherwood oaks or turn the corner where the stream meandered across the path. I hadn't seen him take one last look back at the rooftops of Mansfield or heard the greeting he shouted to the elderly blacksmith at Southwell. I hadn't even seen his dead body when they brought him home. They said it was not a sight for a lady. All I had was a lead-lined coffin and a tattered blood-stained cloak. Those were the last and only reminders of my first husband. Of Aymer, my firstborn son, I needed no reminders. He was stitched into my heart.

Edmund was riding up ahead talking to his brother, Norfolk. There was no denying my second husband was a handsome man. My eyes followed the line of his calves admiring their taut shapeliness. None of the other men I knew had legs like Edmund's. My cousin's might have been more muscular and Norfolk's longer, but when Edmund rose in the saddle, women's eyes widened in appreciation. He had the straightest back of his family and sat his horse easily. Even his late brother, Sir Edward, could not match his looks: the flowing golden hair, the straight nose flaring slightly at the end, the high cheekbones, the full firm lips and those summer-blue eyes.

'Lady Margaret! You shouldn't gaze at Lord Edmund like that. It is not what wives do. You look as if you wanted to eat him.'

It was Margery, Lady Abernethy. She had ridden up beside me and I'd been so busy thinking of Edmund I hadn't noticed.

She glanced at my belly. 'In your condition it is more than indecent, it is positively dangerous.'

'Lady Margery, he is my husband.'

'Precisely, and as such he has licence. You should be safely confined by now and out of the clutches of lustful men.'

She leant across and tapped me with her riding whip.

'I thought Lord Mortimer would be riding with the queen.' She peered ahead to where Isabella and her son led our royal procession.

'He prefers to keep out of sight.'

'Not for much longer. With the impediment removed there's no further need for evasion.'

'Impediment?' I said wanting to make sure I had understood her correctly.

'The husband. The prisoner. Our late and dearly lamented king. I suppose your cousin will wait a suitable length of time and then claim his reward. God alone knows, he's been waiting long enough.'

So Lady Abernethy, like me, was of the opinion that Isabella had not yet given herself to my cousin. Their apartments were mostly adjoining and they often sat together in private, but in public they were very circumspect.

'I've heard that in Avignon they call her the adulterous royal whore,' she confided. 'The Holy Father is talking of excommunication.'

'I don't know where you heard that, Lady Margery, but if it's true, the queen must tread carefully. Her plans will suffer if there is gossip.'

'Perhaps Lord Mortimer has plans of his own.'

'What do you mean?'

Our procession came to a halt so Lady Margery was able to lean across and whisper, 'If I were Lady Mortimer I would employ a taster for my food and be very careful whom I allowed into my castle.'

The Welsh March was a long way from anywhere, thrown out on the fringes of England, a wild place where lords made their own laws and women depended on the strength of their men. Lady Mortimer would be at Ludlow but my cousin rarely spoke of her and I had learned not to ask. She must still be alive but I didn't know if she was free to ride out or if my cousin had imprisoned her behind those grey forbidding walls.

In my ignorance I had thought my cousin a good Christian, a God-fearing man, but I was beginning to have grave doubts. Two people stood between him and the prize he craved, and now one of them was dead. I thought of my cousin's wife, alone in her castle, waiting for a husband who never came, and wondered if his recent trips to Wales were to arrange matters for his benefit.

As we passed under Cow Lane Bar and entered the familiar streets of Nottingham, I felt the first stab of pain. The royal procession, turned into Low Pavement and wound slowly up the hill to the castle leaving behind cheering crowds and the ever-present stench of the Shambles. By the time we'd crossed the bridge and passed under the gatehouse into the outer courtyard, I was in no doubt. Our child was not going to wait for a more convenient time or place.

She was born that evening on the feast day of St Michael and we named her Joan, for my mother. By the time she was baptised the following day, I had betrothed her several times over: once to a fine English nobleman, perhaps the Pembroke heir, or aiming higher, the elder son of the count of Hainault, still unmarried at the age of twenty. The possibilities for a brilliant marriage were endless when your father was the uncle of the king of England.

She was a beautiful baby with rosy-pink skin and plump cheeks like my mother, and on top of her head was a fuzz of fine golden hair. She had tiny curled hands with translucent pearls for nails and when she opened her eyes they were a dark colour like over-ripe damsons. But I was worried she couldn't see.

'Is she malformed?' I said anxiously.

My brother said Lancaster was almost blind, his vision hidden by a creeping fog. There was nothing the physicians could do, not even with their silver needles. I feared this was God's punishment for what we had done. What if this child of mine was paying for our sins?

'Many of the babes I pull into the world are like this,' said the midwife complacently. 'It passes. In a few weeks her eyes'll be as pretty as a wayside flower, my lady. You wait and see.'

It was a few days later when Lady Abernethy came to see me.

'A girl,' she said, a note of disgust in her voice. 'And after all that shrieking and panic.'

I smiled at her. 'My husband is pleased. He wanted a daughter.'

'Your husband would be pleased with anything you did, Lady Margaret.'

'Have you seen him?' I asked anxiously.

'Yes, he ran three successful courses today. The women in the stand were swooning.'

I smiled with pleasure thinking I too would have swooned at the sight of Edmund jousting. There were great rewards for a woman in having a handsome husband and being envied by other women was one of them.

'And the king?'

'He did well. He has determination and will be a great fighter when he's older.'

'And the others?'

Lady Margery lowered her voice so that my maid couldn't hear. 'Lord Mortimer is keeping his distance.'

'Why? Has something happened?'

'Rumours. Not just one or two, you understand, they are everywhere.'

A shiver ran down my spine as I thought of Lady Mortimer far away in her lonely castle.

'What rumours?'

'People are saying the old king did not die a natural death. They believe he was murdered.'

I wasn't surprised. Any sudden death produced a brew of scurrilous tales and the more important the man the more lurid the telling.

'What is being said?'

Lady Margery Abernethy would talk to anyone. She gossiped with the serving boys and with the men who brought carcasses into the kitchens. When there was a story to discover she could be found whispering to one of the laundresses or asking questions of the men who cleaned out the privy pits. Long ago I had learned to ask Lady Margery if I wanted to know what people were saying.

'The women favour poison. They look at their husbands and imagine how pleasant it would be to feed him a cake to burn out his throat and have him writhing in agony on the floor. And they remember talk of the so-called "loving gifts" sent to Kenilworth by the queen. They believe she poisoned him.'

'And the men?'

'Strangling. What else? Or smothering with a pillow. Men have very little imagination and think it wouldn't leave a mark.'

A mark! I had forgotten to ask if there were marks. But of course, if there were, Sir Thomas Gurney would not have told me.

'Is there no-one who thinks he died a natural death?'

'Only silly girls. They say it was a great sorrow which killed him. They imagine him love-sick for his wife and dying of grief.'

'It could be worse,' I said gloomily. 'At least no-one imagines my cousin wielding a dagger and slicing him into bits.'

Lady Margery lowered her voice and leaned closer. 'Not yet, but wait a while and they'll think of that too. I did hear of one man who told a truly disgusting tale but no-one believed him.'

'Tell me,' I said.

'It will churn your stomach.'

'I'll risk it.'

Lady Margery put her mouth to my ear and whispered.

'They heated a poker until it was red-hot, then held the prisoner down and. pushed it up his … his fundament.'

'Mother of God!'

'I told you it was disgusting.'

I considered the end of Sir Hugh Despenser, fifty feet up in full view of the crowd having his manhood sliced off - a particular punishment selected for a vile and unnatural crime. Was this another punishment chosen for a particular crime? And if it was, who had done the choosing?

For the next few weeks, like all newly birthed women, I was confined to my room. When not admiring my daughter or entertaining the occasional visitor, I lay on my bed and wondered. Who? Why? And how?

Who wanted the old king dead and was prepared to put their wishes into deeds? It wasn't a natural death, of that I was certain. He was a strong man in the prime of life and there'd been no talk of sickness or wasting.

Why then and not earlier, at Kenilworth or in the wilds of Wales where it could easily have been passed off as an accident?

And how was it done so that nobody knew? I cursed myself for the questions I had failed to ask Sir Thomas Gurney.

I wondered how I would have done it. Had I wanted to kill a king, what would I have done? I lay looking at the vaulted ceiling, tracing the curves with my eyes and imagining myself as a woman with murder in my mind. Then I remembered Isabella's vial in the leather pouch. Was that it? Was that how it was done?

Edmund escorted me to Gloucester, as tender a husband as any woman could wish for. He advised me on what would be expected of me as my husband's wife and of the arrangements that had been made but nonetheless I was totally unprepared for the glorious spectacle.

This was a royal funeral like no other. The austere burial of the count of Valois in the church of the Minorites in Paris two years before, paled into obscurity in comparison to this overt display of royal pageantry. Preceded by a procession of black-robed clergy and with six black horses each plumed and trapped with the royal coat of arms, the bier was drawn slowly through the streets of Gloucester. The body of Edmund's brother lay silent in its coffin within a canopied catafalque. There were carved images of the four evangelists with eight gilded angels as incense bearers, and royal leopards in their passant glory.

As Edmund had wished, everything shone brightly with gold.

The magnificently decorated coffin was supported by four sturdy gilded lions, and on top, clothed in royal robes of cloth-of-gold and ermine and wearing a shining copper crown, was a carved and painted effigy of the dead man. With golden hair and flowing beard it was so lifelike I almost believed it was the dead king himself.

Every street in Gloucester was packed with people. Most were openly weeping; some fainted and some even tried to throw themselves against the dead king's bier. It was an extravagant display of grief for a man whom none of them knew. But he had been their king for nearly twenty years and that was a lifetime for many people, they would have known no-one else.

The family walked in slow procession behind the hearse. Isabella, covered from head to toe in a full-length veil of black silk, wept steadily. Tears began to fall the moment we stepped outside her chamber and she continued to demonstrate her widow's grief until she was no longer on display. I was not deceived and doubted any of it was truly genuine.

Her son walked at her side, his head bowed, tear stains clearly visible on his pale cheeks. Behind them came Edmund and his brother, Norfolk, both in black, both dry-eyed, and both with their eyes fixed firmly on the ground.

The younger royal children snuffled and wept. Isabella's eyes occasionally darted in their direction, annoyance flitting across her veiled face. She hadn't wanted the little ones to attend but Edward had insisted. He said his brother and sisters must come to bid farewell to their father.

The Mortimer lord of Wigmore walked amongst the great men looking more splendid than usual and certainly more splendid than anyone else. Whereas the king had chosen a simple black tunic to honour his father, my cousin had ordered a glorious extravagance of black velvet and brocade in which he struck an impressive figure.

The masses and the committal in the abbey church of St Peter were as lengthy and as sombre as expected. The incense was overpowering and I began to feel faint. Abbot Thoky, a simple man, had been overruled by Isabella and my cousin in every aspect of the funeral and the burial. Having decided it should be a display of royalty, Isabella had spared no expense.

As I gazed at the hundreds of fat wax candles ablaze in the north aisle I thought back to John's burial at Mansfield when I had managed only a scant half-dozen to burn around his coffin. It hadn't mattered because no amount of light could disperse the shadows which filled my heart and my first husband had needed no candles where he had gone.

Once the funeral was over we moved to Worcester to spend a dismal Christmas. I would have liked to go home to Arundel to see the children but accepted that soon we must make our way to York for the wedding of the king and the count of Hainault's daughter. I wondered if young Edward's bride was still the same plump little girl we'd seen at Valenciennes or if she'd grown tall and slender and lost her freckles.

By now the party from Hainault would have arrived in London and be starting their slow progress north through the mud and snow of our English winter. The king told me that Lady Philippa was coming with her father and her uncle, Sir John, and would be escorted by his de Bohun cousin, the earl of Hereford. Although he was good at concealing his innermost thoughts, I detected an excitement in this young man, which was unsurprising. He had waited a year and a half for his bride and must be impatient to see her again.

Isabella said he wrote frequently - too frequently in her opinion. As his mother she would have preferred a more measured approach, a more distant, reserved attitude, something less enthusiastic. Isabella had chosen well when she'd selected young Philippa but what she had not anticipated was how much her son would be entranced by his bride. Love in any form had not entered Isabella's calculations.

'The girl is young,' she mused. 'I think she should lodge in my household. Do you not agree, Margaret?'

I selected my words carefully. 'Will they not wish to live together, your grace. The king is of an age and the countess's daughter must be nearly fourteen. I remember her as a ripe girl, very forward in ways which matter. What does her mother say?'

'Mothers!' said Isabella, waving away the countess's opinions as if they counted for nothing. 'She is anxious for a grandchild. She would push them into bed no matter what. No, I think it will suit to have the girl with me for a while. It will save the expense of a separate household for her.'

Isabella was ever attentive to reducing expenditure on others as such economies left more for her and more for my cousin.

'Will she have a coronation when we return to Westminster?'

'Certainly not,' snapped Isabella. 'The girl must prove her worth first.'

That, I thought, would be difficult if Philippa was kept chained in the queen's apartments. If she and the king were not permitted to be together how would she conceive a son. Isabella was a powerful woman and would know how to intimidate a fourteen year-old girl but I wondered if she would manage to control the young king who was showing signs of wanting to do things his own way.

Later we were interrupted by the arrival of a visitor. It was one of the royal clerks and with him was a hunched up figure shrouded in a dark cloak.

'Master de Glanville,' said Isabella graciously. 'What is your business?'

The man was nervous but most people were nervous in Isabella's presence. He looked at me, frowning, doubtless wondering who I was.

'You may speak in front of the countess.'

'Your grace, my apologies but I was told to speak to you alone.'

'The countess is my sister in all things.'

Isabella smiled pleasantly and the man took this as his direction to proceed.

'His grace, the king, has spoken with this woman and he wishes that you too should have information from her.'

The clerk pulled back the woman's hood. She was old with sharp little eyes and a clean white cap, woollen clothing, black boots, but it was impossible to say what sort of woman she was.

'Why should I wish to see a person such as this?'

The man lowered his voice. 'She is Lord Berkeley's woman, your grace. She was at the castle. She attended to the body of your late husband, Sir Edward, may his soul rest in peace.'

It was the embalming woman. At last we would have information about how Edmund's brother had died. There were certain things which could not be hidden from the person who attended a body after death: wounds, bruises, broken bones. Men who were strangled retained the horror in their faces and most poisons left indelible marks. These you could not disguise. An Italian in Paris had told me the secrets of his art and also of the dangers of too much knowledge.

Isabella composed her face.

'You prepared my husband's body for burial?'

The woman lowered her head and made to crouch on the floor.

'Get her up, Master de Glanville,' said Isabella impatiently. 'I cannot talk to her down there.'

The clerk pulled the woman to her feet and gave her a push so that she stood closer to Isabella, I could smell her, an unpleasant sour odour overlaid with the stench of fear.

'You are Lord Berkeley's woman?'

The woman was trembling. She looked as if she wanted to run.

'Aye, m,lady,' she whispered.

'Yes, your grace,' prompted Master de Glanville.

'Yes, y'grace.'

'You were at Berkeley three months ago?'

'Yes, m'lady.'

'And Lord Berkeley called you to attend to a man who had died?'

'They said 'twere him wanted me.'

'Who said?'

'Didn't say his name.'

'One of Lord Berkeley's men?'

'Yes, m'lady.'

'And he brought you to the castle?'

'Yes, m'lady.'

And told you to attend to an important man who had just died?'

She nodded. 'Yes, m'lady.'

'Did you know who this man was?'

The woman's eyes were full of fear and she turned in panic to the clerk.

'There were rumours, your grace,' explained Master de Glanville. 'People talk. You can't stop them.'

'You knew the body was that of the man Lord Berkeley had in his keeping.'

'Yes, I did.'

'You knew his name?'

'No.' She sounded utterly terrified.

'But you knew who he was? You knew he was the father of the king?'

'It were the king,' the woman muttered. 'People said.'

Isabella frowned. 'Not the king. My son is king.'

The woman looked at Master de Glanville.

He spoke very slowly and clearly. 'The young man we saw before - that was his grace, the king. This is the Lady

231

Isabella, mother of the king. I explained this to you.'

He looked embarrassed at the woman's mistake. 'My apologies, your grace. It is hard for these simple people. Their minds are slow. I am sure in time they will know that his grace, your son, is king, but there are still many who are ignorant of the matter.'

Isabella turned her gaze back to the woman and spoke slowly. 'You knew you were attending a royal person, a man who had once been a king.'

'Yes, m'lady.'

'He was a tall man, powerfully built?'

'He had big feet,' muttered the woman.

'Naturally,' said Isabella. 'A well-built man can hardly teeter around on dainty toes.'

'They'm too big,' said the woman.

Isabella ignored her. As far as she was concerned the woman was stupid.

'Were there marks on the body?'

The woman hesitated.

'They'm always be marks. No man's unmarked.'

'But there were no wounds; no sign that he had been hurt.'

'He were dead. You can't hurt the dead.'

Isabella looked at me and raised her eyebrows.

'Ask about his face,' I whispered.

'The face?' said Isabella. 'Was it peaceful? Had he gone quietly to God?'

'He had a good face,' said the woman.

'Nothing unusual?'

'All faces are different.'

'Naturally, but there were no signs of violence?'

The woman's eyes were alive with terror.

'No.'

'Ask her who was there,' I whispered.

'Were you alone when doing your work?'

'That sergeant were there.'

'What sergeant?' Isabella was alert. This was something she hadn't been told.

'Didn't say.'

'Was he one of Lord Berkeley's men?'

'No. He come the day old Will lost his ducks. Wi' a couple of others.'

'And he stayed with you while you worked?'

'Yes, m'lady.'

Having satisfied herself that murder had not been done, Isabella went on to describe the many kingly virtues of this man whom she and my cousin had shut away. Eventually she turned to Master de Glanville and thanked him for his trouble in bringing the woman.

'I have what your grace requested,' the clerk said, bringing out of his bag a beautifully wrought silver vessel with a cover.

'My husband's heart?' Isabella was visibly moved by this reminder of the man who had once been dear to her. I could see a tear in her eye.

While the little ceremony of handing over the silver vessel into the queen's keeping occupied Isabella and Master de Glanville, I spoke in a low voice to the woman.

'Were his clothes clean?'

'Yes m'lady, but his boots were too small.'

'Too small?'

'They didn't fit. I told the other lady. They were too big. Soft leather. Fancy silk tassels. Never seen the like before. The lord don't have boots with tassels.'

Too big? Too small? She clearly didn't know what she was talking about but she was only a simple woman with a useful skill; you didn't need to be clever for that.

'There were only one,' she whispered.

I frowned. One? One what? One boot? One foot?

She looked at me slyly. 'There should've been two. All men have two.'

'Two what?' I asked, moving closer.

Perhaps alarmed at my eagerness for answers, she backed away, pulled up her hood and put her hand firmly over her mouth. I tried more questions but she said nothing, just looked at me out of a pair of terrified eyes.

Master de Glanville, having finished his conversation with Isabella, took the woman by her arm.

'Wait!' Isabella reached into the small silk purse she carried on her girdle and pulled out a coin.

'Give this to the woman for her trouble. My heart is greatly eased to know my husband died at peace.'

I watched the old woman being hurried out of the queen's presence and wondered what else she might have told me if there had been more time and if I hadn't been so impatient. The dead always give up their secrets in the end and I was sure this woman had secrets to tell. Her story was very odd: boots that were too small, feet that were too big or too small and a man who lacked something she thought important enough to mention. I wondered what it could possibly be.

By the time we reached Nottingham where the royal party were to celebrate the feast of the Epiphany, it was snowing hard. There was a mounting sense of excitement at the thought of the forthcoming wedding in York, but in the queen's room, mother and son were having an argument.

'What do you mean, lady mother?'

The king's voice had risen a pitch; it was almost a squeak.

'I mean, dearest, that your bride will stay with me for a little while, until she is rested and ready for the rigours of married life. You mustn't forget, Edward, she is very young.'

The boy blushed a deep crimson. He looked panic-stricken.

'But we promised.'

'Did we? I think you are mistaken.'

'You said Philippa was to have her own household and we would live together as man and wife. I heard you.'

'She will,' laughed Isabella. 'And you will be together, just not yet. Perhaps when Lent has passed.'

'But I am fifteen and I am ready for marriage, mother. And Philippa says …'

'What does Philippa say?'

'Nothing.' He shuffled his feet awkwardly and looked away.

He muttered something under his breath.

Like a lightening flash from the heavens my cousin was across the floor. He didn't lay a hand on the young king but he towered head and shoulders above him.

'Would you care to repeat that? What you said about your lady mother?'

'Mortimer! Leave him be.'

'No, my lady. It is time he realised who is in charge here. Sitting on a throne doesn't make you a king, boy; nor does prancing around in those pretty clothes you wear. You would do well to consider who put you on that throne. Without your mother and me you'd still be in the nursery playing with your toys.'

The young king had turned white and he was shaking.

'Now listen carefully.' My cousin was at his most menacing when he was being polite. 'If your mother says you have to wait then you'll have to wait and so will that little bride of yours. Waiting does wonders for one's appreciation of carnal delights, doesn't it my lady?'

He turned to look at Isabella who by now was simmering with fury. She didn't like my cousin interfering in her relationship with her son. And she particularly didn't like him making allusions to their own private dealings.

I despaired. This wedding was supposed to be a joyous occasion, a celebration, but the remainder of the journey up through Rothwell and Knaresborough to York was conducted in icy silence from the king. He spoke to no-one and never so much as once glanced at my cousin. He was cool towards his mother and it was only with his own friends that I noticed any enthusiasm for the great day ahead.

Despite the herald having given us due warning, the first arrival in York was not the party from Hainault, who were still toiling through the snow and ice, but a lone rider. He brought news from France.

'Good news?' Edmund enquired.

'The best!' Isabella's eyes were bright with excitement. 'Brother Charles is dying. He is coughing up his life's blood, cursed to the end, just as I said.'

Edmund seized the letter.

'He's not dead yet and it says Madame of Evreux is carrying a child,'

'Boy babies die, Edmund,' said Isabella coldly. 'Only girl babies live. You know the curse as well as I do.'

'But if it should be a boy and if he should live?' persisted Edmund.

'Then he won't live long,' said Isabella. 'No mewling, puking child of that little mouse is going to get in the way of my son and his rightful inheritance.'

She was pacing the floor, full of energy at the thought of the vacant throne of France. She had no liking for the probable heir, the quivering greyhound, Philip of Valois, but I thought it unlikely the great men of France would allow Isabella's son to take their throne. I thought of Eleanor Despenser in the Tower, and my cousin's wife at Ludlow, and now Isabella's brother, and wondered for the hundredth time, how far Isabella's ambitions would drive her.

At that moment we heard cheers and the sound of trumpets. The party from Hainault was making its way through the city streets. The king's bride had arrived.

Isabella stood at the top of the steps regarding her son with a degree of displeasure. The boy was waiting expectantly in the courtyard having ignored his mother's wishes and ridden out to greet his future father-in-law. Isabella's eyes slid over the other members of the party, resting momentarily on the handsome figure of Sir John, until she found what she was looking for: the little bundle of velvet and fur that was the count of Hainault's daughter.

'I don't think we'll have any trouble with that one, Mortimer,' she said quietly. 'Barely more than a child. And no looks from what I can see. A fat little dumpling.'

'Nothing to compare with you, my lady,' murmured my ever-attentive cousin, his lips a shade too close to Isabella's neck for propriety.

Both of them had failed to look at the king. Although he was standing very correctly waiting for his bride to be brought from her carriage to meet him, his face was suffused with a naked yearning. He loved her. It was plain to see that this girl, however plump and unprepossessing, however unfashionable her clothing, and however red her little snub nose; this girl was loved.

Unexpectedly, Edmund's hand sought mine and he gently squeezed my fingers.

After the lengthy welcoming formalities for the party from Hainault, Edmund handed me into the care of his brother. Lord Norfolk had offered to escort me back to our lodgings while Edmund renewed his acquaintance with Count William and Sir John. As we walked through the inner courtyard I glanced out of the corner of my eye at this brother of Edmund's. A dark-haired, hard-looking man. I'd not been alone in his company before and felt a certain nervousness as his reputation was terrible and he was rumoured to be violent with women.

'How do you find my brother?' he asked after we'd walked in silence for a little while. 'To your liking?'

'Yes. He is a good husband.'

He looked at me in a way I didn't care for as if appraising me for some purpose or other.

'Treats you well?'

'Very well.'

'And you? D'you treat him well?'

'He has not complained, my lord.'

He barked a laugh. 'By the saints, I'll bet he hasn't.'

I thought in his rough way he was trying to pay me a compliment so I gave him a small smile.

'I never thought he'd do it.'

'Do what, my lord?'

'Have the bollocks to marry you.'

I wrinkled my nose in disgust. Naturally I knew the word. Listening to the gossip of servants and spying on men who thought themselves unobserved, how could I not? But I'd never had it used knowingly in my presence and never by a man such as my brother-in-law.

'My lord, your words are offensive.'

He put a large hand on my arm and squeezed uncomfortably. 'But you're not a coy little maid, sister; you know what I mean, don't you?'

'My lord, I have no idea what you mean.'

He leered at me, smiling with his teeth. 'Oh sister! Come now. My brother's a well-made man. I doubt all your dealings with him are conducted beneath the sheets. Have you not looked, not ventured into unknown terrain?'

'My lord!' I gave him a frosty glance. 'As I am sure my husband has told you, I am a virtuous wife.'

Another bark. 'He has. Warned me off. Told me to watch my manners.'

I stood quite still trying not to show the distaste I felt for his nearness.

'Your manners are commendable, my lord, but your words leave much to be desired.'

At that moment, standing in the courtyard of the abbey at York in the company of my husband's brother, I had a sudden image of Edmund that morning stretching his beautiful naked body, a body which I knew intimately - a very well-made man indeed! And with a leap of understanding I knew what the embalming woman had seen. All men have two, she'd said and yet the man she'd embalmed had only one. Was it possible? Could a man have just one? I shook my head. I didn't know and women didn't talk about such matters amongst themselves.

There was no-one to ask and perhaps I was imagining murder and deceit where none existed. Perhaps there was no mystery, no trickery, just a man dying before his allotted time, a man whose life was of no further use to anyone other than God.

Two weeks later Edward and Philippa were married in the half-finished Minster at York. William Melton, the elderly archbishop, had been a friend of the late king and had protested violently at his removal from the throne. Isabella could ill-afford to make an enemy of a man such as him and this wedding was intended as a friendly gesture. Once the wedding feast was finished, the bride dutifully trailed away at the heels of her mother-in-law while young

Edward disappeared with his friends and, I suspected, got thoroughly drunk.

All through February the council met daily.

'What do you discuss at such great length which keeps you from your wife's side?' I teased Edmund.

'The peace treaty with Scotland,' he said morosely. 'Nobody wants it, least of all my nephew.'

'Of course he doesn't want it. Scotland is part of his realm. He'd as soon cut off his right hand as give it away. Your father fought to keep it and ten thousand Englishmen died for the cause.'

Edmund sighed deeply. 'Unless we wish to send our men barefoot to war with no provisions and nothing but wooden staves to fend off the Scots, we have no choice. The treasury is empty. We can't afford to go on fighting.'

'Has it really all gone? Even Despenser's gold?'

Edmund shrugged his shoulders. 'You know Isabella. As soon as she had the keys, she took the lot. There was barely enough for the campaign last summer and in the end we had to borrow. Nobody will agree to more taxes and without money we have no choice but to accept Bruce's terms.'

'Is everything beyond the border lost?'

'Yes and many men will be disinherited.'

I thought of Lady Abernethy and her daughters, and of John's cousin whose husband would never be earl of Buchan and I thought, with tears, of Badenoch which I would never see.

'They plan to send Isabella's younger daughter to Scotland,' said Edmund.

241

'Poor little mite, she's only seven. Who will have care of her?'

'Sir James Douglas. The one they call Black Douglas.'

I sighed. 'Your nephew won't like seeing his sister marry Bruce's son?'

'He's powerless. He has to agree.'

The next day, as I sat in the queen's room thinking longingly of my children far away at Arundel, Isabella gave me a piece of unwelcome news.

'The king wishes to free the Lady Eleanor,' she said smoothly. 'I do not agree but in this one matter I shall let him have his way. She can do no harm.'

I glanced over to where Philippa was obediently sewing. I wanted to see if she was taking note of the conversation but the girl had a distant look on her face, doubtless lost in thoughts of her young husband.

'Where will Lady Eleanor go?' I asked.

'Some of her lands will be restored, enough to keep her in a degree of comfort. It would not be fitting for my late husband's niece to be begging her way from gate to gate.'

'Will you receive her?'

'No, but she must do homage for her lands and it will be interesting to see how prison has agreed with her. I did my best to ensure her well-being, as you know, but imprisonment can affect a woman in strange ways. I was told my brother's faithless wife liked her gaolers very well. Perhaps Lady Eleanor took a fancy to your brother, Margaret? After all, anything is possible when a woman is caged.'

'My brother did nothing but your bidding,' I said stiffly.

Isabella laughed. 'Would that were true of all men.'

11

One evening, long after the candles had been lit in our lodgings, my husband had an unexpected visitor.

'Sir John Pecche,' announced Edmund's boy.

The man who entered was dressed in dark clothing and looked unwell. His face had a peculiar grey tinge and he was sweating. Unwilling to risk a contagion I made my excuses and left the men together.

I had barely reached my room when I was summoned back. Edmund was standing by the hearth and the visitor was crouched on a stool by the table. His shoulders were hunched and he was shaking. He struggled to his feet, gave a little bow and then sank back onto his seat.

'Tell the countess what you have just told me, Pecche,' ordered Edmund.

The man looked up. His face was full of fear. It was unmistakeable: the flickering glance, the twisting hands, the unwillingness to look me in the eye.

'My name is John Pecche, my lady,' he said in a low voice. 'I am constable of the castle at Corfe. A wild place, near the sea, far from anywhere. My new wife has no liking for it. She says it lacks in everything which give a woman enjoyment.'

He cleared his throat and bit his lip. 'I have been constable there for two years or more but for much of that time I have been absent on business.'

243

I had not heard of Corfe and didn't know where it was.

'Where did your business take you, Sir John?' I asked, trying to put the man at ease.

'The Low Countries, my lady. I was due to remain there until the end of the summer but I became sick. I was in such straits I thought I would die. I believed someone was trying to poison me and once you think that, you don't rest easy. My good wife said we must return to England. She said the food was not of good quality but I believe it was poison.'

'Do you have enemies?'

'Every man has enemies if he looks hard enough. But I never expected to find them in my own castle.'

'At Corfe?'

He looked over his shoulder as if making sure nobody else had sidled into the room, unheard. Whatever it was he wanted to say was making him extremely nervous.

'Tell her the rest, Pecche,' said Edmund.

Sir John dabbed his mouth with the back of his hand and went on with his story.

'When we arrived at Corfe, he was there.'

At this point he stopped and looked at me expectantly.

'The poisoner?'

'No, no, my lady. You see, I wasn't supposed to be there. They thought I was overseas.'

Now he looked positively terrified.

'He was locked away beneath the floor of the hall. I saw him with my own eyes.'

This story was becoming too muddled for me to understand.

'Sir John, tell me slowly. Who did you see?' I hoped this wasn't going to be one of those fantastic tales of hobgoblins and demons, the kind they tell in these wild out-of-the-way places.

'The king, my lady.'

'Sir John, the king is here,' I said gently. 'I saw him this morning. He cannot be in your castle.'

'No, no! The other king. The king that was before - Sir Edward.'

'It is a ridiculous tale, Pecche,' interrupted Edmund. 'Whoever you saw, it cannot have been my brother. We buried him at Gloucester two months ago.'

'I told Sir Ingelram you wouldn't believe me.'

'Who is Sir Ingelram?' I asked.

'Sir Ingelram Berenger, one of Despenser's men,' explained Edmund. 'He advised Pecche to come to me. Said I was the one to tell.'

Sir John Pecche might be a man who had seen ghosts while his wits were astray but it was just possible there was more to this. There was still the matter of the boots. And the one where there should have been two.

'How did you know the man was my husband's brother?'

'Yes, Pecche,' said Edmund, 'How did you know?'

'I'd seen him often enough, my lord, when we were fighting at Shrewsbury. You couldn't mistake him - a head taller than any other man and what shoulders he had, built like a young bull he was. And that head of hair. There was no-one else to match up to him. Not even you, my lord, and you're a fine man yourself.'

'And the prisoner looked like him?'

'No, no, my lady. He didn't *look* like him, he *was* him. I'd swear on the Host it was him.'

245

Edmund shook his head. 'It's impossible. Men do not rise from the dead.'

'Christ did,' I said.

There was complete silence and for a moment neither man spoke. What I'd said was blasphemous and I could feel Aunt Mortimer's switch across my shoulders from a distance of twenty years.

'Look Pecche,' said Edmund. 'To satisfy you I shall make enquiries and in the meantime say nothing.'

'I haven't told anyone other than Sir Ingelram, my lord, not even my wife.'

'Are you returning to Corfe?'

The man looked as if he would faint. 'I have letters of protection, my lord. I shall leave the country and go overseas. It will be safer. I wish I'd never come back.'

We talked some more and eventually Edmund persuaded Sir John to return to Sir Ingelram Berenger and ask him to attend on my husband.

When Sir John had gone, Edmund yawned. 'I have never heard such a ridiculous tale in all my life. It will be interesting to see what Berenger makes of it. What do you think he saw?'

He stretched his arms and folded them behind his head.

I looked carefully at my husband and wondered whether to tell him what was in my mind or whether it would be prudent to keep my thoughts to myself a little longer, until I had more proof.

On our way to York for the wedding I'd pondered the oddity of the feet that were too big or too small, of the boots which didn't fit, and the extreme agitation of the woman who had done the embalming.

Edmund's brother had large feet so why were the boots too small? Or had the woman got it wrong and the feet were too small for the boots. But she'd said the feet were big. I remembered how Isabella had made a joke about large men teetering on tiny feet. So why had he been wearing boots which were too small for him? It didn't make sense. Perhaps they weren't his boots at all. Perhaps the boots belonged to someone else. But if so, why was Edmund's brother wearing them? But that couldn't be right because they were clearly royal boots; the woman had said best leather, silk tassels, not what anyone other than a royal person would wear.

It had taken me all the way to Knaresborough before I'd realised my mistake, and when I did, I'd nearly fainted with shock. It wasn't that the boots didn't belong to Edmund's brother, it was because the feet didn't. Royal boots but not royal feet.

From that thought, the rest followed. A man's feet cannot be separated from his body unless by dismemberment and the woman had said he was not hurt. So if the feet had not belonged to Edmund's brother then neither had the rest of his body.

After we reached York and my conversation with Lord Norfolk, I'd guessed what the embalming woman had seen. That meant the funeral at Gloucester had been an illusion, a trick, something which was not what it seemed. The gorgeous covering which had lain across the body, the gilding on the lions on the hearse, the effigy with its gleaming copper crown, the candles, the solemn ceremony, the weeping - had all been for nothing because whoever was inside that coffin had not been Edmund's brother.

But it wasn't until Sir John Pecche arrived that I knew I was right.

I wanted to go home to Arundel but Isabella needed me and Edmund said he must stay for the Easter parliament. At the beginning of March a messenger in black arrived from France: Monseigneur Charles was dead.

'At last,' said Isabella with apparent satisfaction. 'I thought he would linger all summer.'

She hadn't liked Monseigneur Charles but I found her lack of sorrow shocking. A woman should always mourn the passing of a family member no matter what she feels personally. It was one of the responsibilities of kinship and the dead man had been her brother. I didn't care greatly for Tom but if God should take him I would show proper grief and have a dozen masses said for his soul. It was the least a sister could do.

'How my dear father would have grieved,' said Isabella, shedding a delicate tear for the great Iron King, who everyone knew she had adored. 'Three sons and not a single male heir between them. All his efforts come to nothing because my brothers failed in their duty. They were fools and they were married to fools. And look what they have left us with: my unworthy cousin of Valois who is no more fit to wear my father's crown than a goat.'

When I ventured to remind Isabella that Madame of Evreux might yet give birth to a son, she waved the notion aside as if it was not worth considering.

'No child can rule my father's kingdom nor would my father want his brother's son on the throne; he would want my son.'

On the last day of the parliament, this son of Isabella, with very bad grace, announced that he would recognise an independent sovereign Scotland. He was furious, everyone could see that. I only had to look at the set of his mouth and the expression in his eyes to know what he felt. He blamed his mother and my cousin for the humiliation of losing part of his kingdom but with no control over the treasury or the summoning of an army, there was nothing he could do. He may have been king but he must have been painfully aware how little kingship he could exert. His mother held the purse strings and my cousin had control of everything else.

He was in tears the day he told Edmund how his father had held the kingdom together but his mother and Lord Mortimer were busy giving it away. Soon, he said, there would be nothing left but his lands in England. Scotland was gone, Gascony would be next, then Ponthieu, then Wales. What else did they plan to auction off to the highest bidder?

Poor boy! He refused to speak to Isabella and went out of his way to avoid her company. He ignored my cousin and spent all his time, when he was not with his wife, with the young men who were his friends: his de Bohun cousins, Lady Clinton's son and young William Montagu. They were usually seen together in the tilt yard practising their skills for the jousts. Gradually as the months passed he was growing away from Isabella but she was far from noticing what her son was doing because her eyes were fastened on someone else.

'Lord Mortimer and I shall be absent for a while,' she said to me as soon the parliament's business was completed and the men began leaving for their homes. 'We shall travel.'

'Will you attend the funeral of your brother, your grace?'

'Certainly not! Even if we were welcome, our plans are better served if I remain here. I have trusted men in Paris who can deal with the tedious formalities of royal death and who will advance my son's cause with great vigour.'

'May I enquire where you are going?'

'No, you may not,' said Isabella firmly. 'This is a private sojourn, not a formal progress. I am merely retiring to one of my manors for a rest. You can see how fatigued I am, Margaret. I am worn out. Mortimer and I have had no peace these past two years, what with the constant claims upon our attention. Somebody has always been wanting something. We have been spied on day and night and I have had enough. It has been relentless. We need peace.'

Judging from her heightened colour and the slow secret smiles she gave when she thought my eyes were elsewhere, I deduced that peace was not what she had in mind. After keeping him dangling for more than two years I guessed Lord Mortimer of Wigmore might be about to receive his reward.

My cousin had been very patient and a lesser woman would have been either thrown aside or taken forcibly before now. But Isabella was different. Isabella was royalty. She was his gateway to a life of power and wealth, a dazzling jewel worth serving seven years for if needs be. Waiting to satisfy his lust was surely nothing compared to the rewards that he would reap. I knew myself how easy it was for a woman to succumb to a man's mastery once she had invited him into her bed and Isabella was no different to any other woman.

'My cousin will enjoy a respite from his cares,' I said artlessly. 'He has worked tirelessly in your service these past two years. Will he return to Ludlow?'

I was certain he wouldn't but it was a most unworthy pleasure to see Isabella's face darken.

'No,' she snapped. 'Lady Mortimer will not be visited. Lord Mortimer is to attend me. I am his queen and he will be at my side.'

'Things are different now,' I said carefully. 'You no longer have a husband and are free to place your favours where you will. There can be no objection from interfering bishops. All that is required is a little discretion.'

She looked at me sharply.

'Watch your words, Margaret. You sound more like His Holiness every day. You may be married to my late husband's brother but that does not give you licence to comment on what I do. I shall do what I please and you will say nothing.'

I inclined my head. 'Of course, your grace. Whatever you wish.'

They left two days later.

Returning to Arundel and our children was a joy to both of us. Although Edmund, as the new lord, had duties to discharge and was properly diligent, he liked to spend time with Mondi who was learning to walk. To the confusion of the nursemaids, who were not used to interference, we spent part of each morning in the nursery watching our son master the art of standing and moving. His little fat legs quivered, his arms flailed, he grabbed at his father's hand and then sat down with a thump. A nursemaid swooped to the rescue but Edmund waved her away.

'You have to learn to be a man, my son,' he lectured a laughing Mondi who understood not a word his father said. 'You won't do that sitting on the floor. Come on. Up you get.'

It was a wonderful time but far too short because there were many matters more pressing than our son's progress across the nursery floor.

'Edmund, you remember Sir John Pecche?' I said one day after we had handed Mondi back to a flustered nursemaid.

'How could I forget? A foolish man who'd jump at his own shadow. What do you think he saw at Corfe?'

'I think he saw what he said he saw.'

It took Edmund a minute to realise what I meant.

'You mean a spirit risen up from the dead?'

'No. I think he saw a real live man. I think he saw your brother.'

'But my brother is dead.'

'Is he?'

'Christ's blood, Margaret! Of course he's dead. You were there. You saw him buried.'

'I saw a fine display of pageantry,' I said calmly. 'I saw a hearse with a coffin and I saw an effigy of a king.'

'You saw my brother's coffin.'

'No. I saw a coffin in which I was told your brother's body lay.'

Edmund flushed with irritation.

'Don't be ridiculous, Margaret. Of course it was my brother's coffin. What other coffin could it have been?'

I took his hand in mine. I loved him and I needed to lead him carefully so that he understood exactly what might have occurred.

'Edmund, when your brother died, who was there?'

'I don't know. His keeper. Lord Berkeley. Servants perhaps.'

'And it was Lord Berkeley who wrote and told Isabella and the king that your brother was dead?'

'Yes. You were in Lincoln, Margaret. You saw the letter.'

'What happened then?'

'What do you mean, what happened?'

'What would have happened to your brother's body? Who would have taken care of it?'

He furrowed his brow trying to remember the rituals of death. 'I suppose they would have put him in the chapel at Berkeley.'

'Surely an embalmer attended him first?'

'Yes. Then he would have been placed in the chapel.'

'And men watched over him in the chapel?'

'Yes.'

'But not before. Men didn't watch over him before he was placed in the chapel?'

'What does it matter if it was in the chapel or if it was before? What difference does it make?'

'Edmund,' I said quietly. 'It makes all the difference in the world. Now think. Do you remember in Paris, when your uncle of Valois died and we went to view his body?'

'Yes, of course I do.'

'Do you recall his face?'

'Christ's teeth! Who could forget a last sight of that old bastard.'

'What about your brother? Did you see *his* face?'

He frowned. 'No.'

'Did anyone?'

'Of course they did.'

'Who?'

'Berkeley, some of his men, Gurney perhaps. I can't remember exactly what Gurney said but I think he mentioned having seen my brother's body.'

I roundly cursed myself for not finding out more from Sir Thomas Gurney when he was at Lincoln. But I didn't know then how important it would be.

'There was a royal sergeant-at-arms,' said Edmund.

'Yes, a watcher. The woman who carried out the embalming mentioned him to Isabella.'

'Did she? I didn't know.'

'What was his purpose?'

'He watched over my brother's body. I remember Gurney telling my nephew. The boy was worried in case his father's body was not being given proper care. So there you are, the watcher would have seen him. And the bishops and the town worthies in Gloucester, they would all have come to view the body. So you are mistaken. Whoever it was Pecche saw, it wasn't my brother. My brother is buried in the abbey at Gloucester.'

I had taken Edmund as far as I could today. I would have to let him think about what I'd said. I'd let that little worm of doubt fester, and in good time I would lead him to think about feet: feet that were too big and boots that were too small, and things which were not quite what they seemed.

In the meantime I would turn my mind to why it should have happened. That was what was troubling me.

Why would anyone do such a thing? What would be the purpose of keeping a man alive but pretending he was dead? Who would benefit from the deception and who had ordered it done?

While we were at Arundel I completed the formation of my household by taking two women as my lady companions. Their husbands were knights in Edmund's service and it pleased them to send their wives to me and it pleased me to have company. The women were not skilled at anything in particular but they were pleasant, and good with the children.

Mondi was a delight. He reminded me so much of Aymer that it almost hurt. Little Joan was an engaging baby, beloved by everyone. She lay in her cradle and gurgled happily until such time as she was lifted up.

On our last day, Edmund had a visitor. Unlike those who had crowded in during the day to ask the new lord for favours or pray for justice in some minor dispute, this man came as the candles were lit. He had been with Edmund a long time when I was summoned to the little chamber above the private chapel. It was very secluded, approached by a single staircase and used only by Edmund and myself.

Edmund's visitor was an elderly man, courteous, with a head of sparse lank grey hair and a neatly clipped beard. He bowed and introduced himself.

'Sir Ingelram Berenger, my lady.'

His accent betrayed him as a West Country man.

Edmund was pacing the floor looking agitated.

'You'd better tell the countess what you have told me, Berenger - about Pecche.'

Sir Ingelram put his fingers together. There were old scars and calluses and he had difficulty moving his right arm.

'My lady, as I told the earl, John Pecche is a fine man; you couldn't want for a stouter comrade. Not someone given to fancies, not like some who'd see their grandmothers dance on castle walls at midnight; and not like my daughters who believe in hobgoblins and swear the dead walk in the churchyard. John Pecche is a straight man. If he says he saw the king - the king that was - then that is what he saw.'

'You believe him?'

'I do.'

'Even supposing he was right, which I very much doubt,' said Edmund, 'what would you have me do with this information? We don't know who is holding this man, or why?'

'Pecche says Maltravers has been at the castle.'

'Sir John Maltravers?'

'The same. But that's no surprise, my lord. He's a great man in the district. Has his nose in everybody's business.'

While they talked I tried to remember what I knew about John Maltravers. He'd been with us in Paris. A Dorset man with a connection to Lord Berkeley. Joint keeper of the royal prisoner. If I'd been asked, I would have said he was my cousin's man, through and through.

Had he been at Berkeley on the night Edmund's brother was said to have died? Was it perhaps he who had taken the prisoner to Corfe and if so, who had ordered him to do so? And what of the body placed in the royal coffin?

'Perhaps we should ask Maltravers,' said Edmund.

'No, my lord,' said Sir Ingelram. 'That would be most unwise.'

'If we don't ask somebody we can't discover the truth. Anyhow, the whole thing is ridiculous. If my brother were being held in Corfe, I would know. Someone would have told me.'

'Someone has,' I said quietly.

Edmund looked at me and then at Sir Ingleram, his face full of indecision.

'My lord,' said Sir Ingelram, taking advantage of his age to offer advice. 'If this man is your brother there is only one right thing to do.'

'And what would that be?'

'Free him from his captivity. Whoever is holding him has practised a wicked deceit. By pretending your brother is dead they can keep him there until he rots. No-one would be any the wiser. My lord, it is your right to lead us and I for one am prepared to pledge everything I possess to enable you to carry out this task. My sword arm is of not much use these days but I have some wealth which I can put at your disposal.'

'Berenger,' said Edmund, visibly moved by the old man's sincerity. 'There is no need.'

'There is every need, my lord. And I am not the only one. I know a dozen others who, without my even asking, would pledge themselves to free your brother.'

Edmund shook his head. 'I don't know. I cannot decide. I shall have to consider what I know and I must see what else I can discover. No matter how fine a man Pecche may be it would be foolish to rely on his word alone.'

After Sir Ingelram had gone, Edmund held me in his arms. He kissed the top of my head and I was so close to his chest I could hear him breathing.

'It was easier when we were first together in Paris,' he whispered. 'There were no difficult choices to make. I never had to consider where my loyalties lay or to whom I owed my allegiance. Everything was simple. And then my uncle of Valois died and your cousin came to Paris and everything changed. I wish to God none of this had ever happened.'

My poor husband. I silenced him by putting my lips to his. As the logs shifted and settled in the hearth and the darkness outside deepened, all I could see were the ties of our loyalties unravelling. There could be only one way ahead but which path to choose? Whose cause should we champion and once we had chosen would either of us be safe?

The next day we left the children at Arundel together with their little household and travelled north for the parliament. On the journey we didn't mention the prisoner at Corfe but I was certain Edmund's thoughts were full of him as were mine. Problems wriggled away at the corners of my thinking, disturbing the proper contemplation of my morning prayers and clouding the hours before sleep with confusing scenes of bloodshed and death.

Arriving hot and exhausted at Northampton I was met with two pieces of unwelcome news.

The first was that poor little Madame of Evreux in her white widow's weeds had given birth to yet another daughter. Seeing no direct male heir to take the throne, the great men of France had hurriedly chosen the count of Valois to be their next king. The quivering greyhound and his wife would sit on their matching thrones in Sainte-Chapelle with the serried ranks of French nobility bending their knees and singing their praises. Isabella could do nothing but gnash her teeth in fury. Her son's claim to the French throne had been summarily dismissed but I wasn't surprised. None of the men I'd seen in the palace on the Île de la Cité would have welcomed an English king wearing the French crown and I presumed Isabella's ambassadors had been swept aside as if the matter had nothing to do with them.

The second piece of unwelcome news was waiting for me in my chamber.

'What are you doing here, Lady Eleanor?' I demanded.

Eleanor Despenser turned her slanting green eyes my way and smiled. She was dressed in an appealing dark blue gown and seated comfortably in front of my hearth as if she belonged there.

'I thought I would pay you a visit since you were good enough to visit me when I was a guest of your brother in the Tower.'

'What do you want?'

'Nothing more than you wanted that day. Do you remember? You were looking for answers, weren't you? Not very subtle questions. it was easy to work out what you wanted to know.'

'You lost the child.'

I stated it as bluntly as I could, not wanting any misunderstanding between us.

'Did I? When I last counted, all those I have been permitted to keep were still with me.'

'I mean the child you were carrying that day.'

She looked at me levelly. 'Perhaps you were mistaken.'

'I know the look of a woman carrying a child.'

'But that wasn't what you wanted to know, was it? You wanted to know whose child it was.'

I said nothing just watched her with growing irritation.

'What did you tell Isabella?' she asked. 'Was it you who did her dirty work or did she send someone else?'

'I don't know what you're talking about.'

She turned on me with sudden venom.

'As I bled all over my sheets, I cursed you, Margaret. I cursed you from the bottom of my heart for what you did to me and my unborn child.'

A shaft of terror ran through me as I quickly made the sign against the evil eye. Some people thought Eleanor a witch, her husband's willing accomplice in all his foul doings, a woman contaminated by the acts of an evil man and it was wise to be careful.

'Why have you come here?' I said coldly. 'You are not wanted.'

'Oh but I am. I am the lady of Glamorgan and my kingly cousin has requested my presence. He requires me to do homage for my de Clare lands which he has most generously returned to me.'

'So do it and go.'

She smiled, showing her sharp little teeth.

'I thought I would wait until dear Isabella returns. I hear she is travelling with your cousin. Have they sealed their unholy pact between the bedsheets at last or am I mistaken and they've been mired in sin from the very beginning? You would know as you acted as procuress.

Like a skilled brothel keeper you brought your mistress the very man she desired, a worthy partner for her lust.'

'You disgust me, Eleanor Despenser.'

'Not as much as you disgust me.'

'She won't want to see you.'

'She will. Seeing me humbled and on my knees will please her greatly. And as for your cousin? I'm intrigued to know what makes him so attractive to our queen. I remember him as a plain man, inclined to violence, greedy for power, with no manners and little imagination.'

I thought that description might amuse my cousin but it would certainly anger Isabella.

'You should be careful what you say, Eleanor. The queen will not like to hear criticism of Lord Mortimer.'

'And what of your husband, Lady Margaret? Have you discovered the man behind that handsome face and do you like what you have found? Not a faithful hound I would imagine. Does he lie at your feet in your chamber with his head resting lovingly on your knee, or does he stray? I have heard rumours. It is amazing what people feel they must tell you when you return to court after an absence.'

'I have no wish to hear what other people say of my husband and I do not wish to discuss him with you.'

She gave me another little smile.

'Not quite the man you thought you'd caught for yourself, is he?'

Eleanor always knew where to aim her arrows.

'I am perfectly content with my life,' I said, 'And with my husband.'

'And do you enjoy your view from the top of the dunghill? Is it all you expected it to be? You'd better make the most of it because women like you never last. Take one look at our little coroner's daughter, shut away in a draughty castle watching spiders weave their webs. That could be you, dear Lady Margaret. One tip of the wheel and down you'll fall. And once that happens you'll never rise again. Not like me. Go on - look at me!'

Against my will I forced myself to stare at Eleanor.

She stroked the side of her neck with her long slim fingers and raised her chin. 'Yes, Lady Margaret. I am resurgent, already climbing up from the depths where your cousin and dear Isabella saw fit to throw me.'

'You are nobody.'

She laughed. 'How wrong you are. How long did it take you to find a second husband? Five years? Ten years? I seem to remember it was a very long time. Whereas I already have men squabbling at my feet for the honour of claiming me as their wife. I merely have to decide which one to choose.'

'Nobody will want you.'

But even as I spoke I knew it was untrue. Eleanor was a royal lady, the king's cousin. She would easily find a husband. And despite the months of imprisonment she still had a vestige of beauty.

'My first husband once said you were a dangerous woman but I think he was wrong. I think you are a foolish woman.'

With that display of rudeness, Eleanor Despenser rose in a flurry of skirts and swept out of the room. Imprisonment had not deprived her of her ability to wound and I found my eyes full of tears.

'It's good for a man to have a loving wife,' said Edmund complacently as we stood watching the king and his young wife distribute alms.

'I hope her eyes are not blind to his faults,' I said lightly. 'Otherwise one day she may have an unpleasant surprise.'

Edmund was amused by my words. 'Kings don't have faults, sweetheart. Ask Lady Philippa. She will tell you they are utterly perfect.'

Certainly the young Hainault girl blushed each time she looked at her husband, her fingers constantly seeking his in a way contrary to royal protocol.

'He is only playing at being king,' I whispered. 'Wait until his mother returns.'

'Ah but when she does she will discover that Edward is not the boy he once was. An adoring wife in one's bed changes everything. I should know.'

A week later amidst a flourish of trumpets and banging of drums, Isabella returned. My cousin, flushed with triumph, was more demanding than ever but I observed a new softness to Isabella. Gone was the endless bickering which had marked their relationship for so long and, for the first time since we'd returned to England, she looked happy. If it had not been for nagging thoughts of Lady Mortimer left languishing in Ludlow while her husband shared the queen's bed I would have welcomed Isabella's good fortune.

When the time came for Lady Eleanor to make homage for her lands in Glamorgan, she made a perfect demonstration of the faithful subject. She sank to her knees in front of the king, her head dutifully bent, and placed her hands between those of her sovereign in the traditional manner of submission. I could barely hear the words she murmured because of the appreciative whispering of men nearby. There was no mistaking the fact that the fetching, fertile and extremely wealthy lady of Glamorgan was not short of admirers.

Lord Zouche could not take his eyes off her. His appointment as constable of the Tower in place of my brother would have brought him into contact with Lady Eleanor. Perhaps visiting her in her prison rooms he'd been caught in her toils and now had designs on her fortune. If so, he had a rival. Another of my cousin's supporters, Sir John Grey, was equally smitten. He offered his opinion on the lady's beauty and demeanour to each and every one of his close neighbours. Later I saw the two of them hovering around her like a pair of dogs circling a bitch.

'Who shall we choose for her next husband, my lady?' whispered my cousin to Isabella. 'If we don't hurry, one of those adventurers will have her in a hedgerow and ruin our plans. You have to admit she's quite an eyeful.'

The veil of fine white open-weave silk which Eleanor had pinned over her head barely hid her red hair which she had artfully coiled around her ears exposing her long pale neck. She was certainly every man's idea of a desirable woman. And she had money.

'Are you sizing her up for one of your boys, Lord Mortimer?' said Isabella tartly.

'I have only two still unwed,' replied my cousin coolly. 'Geoffrey is his mother's favourite and she has asked my de Fiennes cousins to arrange a match for him.'

Isabella frowned.

'I trust Lady Mortimer will be an obedient wife and do as she's told.'

This was clearly a well-worn path but my cousin seemed unwilling to tread it.

He turned to me.

'My daughters are to be married at the end of the month. You and Lord Edmund must join in our celebrations. Kathryn is marrying Thomas de Beauchamp, the Warwick heir, and Joanna, the Audley boy.'

I thanked him, noting his self-satisfied smile and wondered how he'd achieved these honours for his daughters. It was a worry because there were many Mortimer daughters still unwed and I didn't want my cousin draining England dry of every titled young man. Not when Edmund and I had a husband to find for our little Joan.

'We travel to Hereford where the young people will marry,' said Isabella, smiling slyly. 'And afterwards, we progress to Ludlow for the celebrations.'

I almost gasped aloud. My cousin must have lost his senses. Was he mad? He was proposing to take his royal mistress to his wife's castle and expecting us to pretend that nothing was amiss.

Once the unsavoury business of the treaty with the Scots was complete, the king and queen departed. Edward was still not speaking to his mother or to my cousin. He had accused them of arranging matters behind his back, giving away his kingdom, disinheriting his people, and selling his sister for a shameful peace. The Londoners were calling it a "fraudulent treaty" and there was talk of what Lord Mortimer had received in payment.

'There's a whisper going around that Bruce has promised to help your cousin make himself king in exchange for his arranging the treaty,' remarked Edmund. 'They're saying he's up to his ears in double-dealing with the Scots.'

'What utter nonsense,' I replied.

But whispers grow louder in the dead of night, and as I shifted myself uncomfortably beside my sleeping husband, I wondered what ambitions my cousin really had. The Mortimers were a proud family and claimed descent not only from a bastard daughter of King John but also from the line of King Arthur. Like all Mortimer men, my cousin believed his destiny was part of the Great Prophecy.

I had a clear memory of sitting in the hall at Wigmore one Christmas, listening to a travelling singer. He was an old man who wore a tattered grey cloak spangled with silver and he sang of the glorious days to come. He plucked at the harp on his knee and wove a tale of such magical beauty that I was entranced. The song spoke of the rise of a great king of the line of Arthur, a king who would come out of Wales to rule over England, a king whose great deeds would shine like the stars in the heavens until the end of time.

To me, as a child, the story was a romance, but Aunt Mortimer said her son believed, as did all the Mortimers, that the family's destiny was written and that it was a magnificent one.

12

LUDLOW 1328

In the early days of summer we set out on our long slow progress across the country to Hereford for the wedding of the Mortimer daughters. It was well known that the royal coffers were empty yet my cousin and Isabella continued to spend lavishly and ignored what was being said.

At Hereford, the four young people were married in a swirl of good wishes, showers of silver coins and noisy trumpet calls. Afterwards we made our merry way to Ludlow. There we would have the feasts, the tournaments and the celebrations which accompany all weddings and enjoy the hospitality of my cousin's wife.

'Very fine indeed,' said my husband as we rode beneath the gatehouse in the warmth of the late afternoon.

Edmund was right to be impressed. Ludlow Castle had changed mightily since I'd been here as a child. My cousin must have spent a great deal of his time and money on improving this part of his wife's inheritance. On top of the old solar wing was a new soaring mass of grey stone and at the end of the hall, where we used to dine in great luxury with Aunt Mortimer, was another building pierced through with tall windows. I was intrigued. I'd seen nothing like it except in the palaces of the French king.

'What do you think?'

It was Joan, Lady Mortimer. She had come up behind me as I stood staring in amazement at a room I would not have recognised. Across the width of the hall stretched an expanse of painted cloth. There were knights on horseback and fire-breathing dragons and men rushing into battle with swords held aloft. Merlin, the wily magician was there as was Llewelyn Fawr, the fabled Prince of Gwynedd, flanked by his sons.

'I don't recognise the scenes,' I said, furrowing my brow in concentration. 'Aunt Mortimer said my grasp of Welsh history was as poor as my stitching.'

Lady Mortimer laughed and kissed me on the cheek. 'I would hardly have recognised you, dear Margaret. You've grown so grand.'

I eyed the impressive tapestries hanging where I remembered something faded and dark. These were a brilliant white and covered with brightly coloured butterflies.

She could see where my eyes had strayed. 'For the wedding couples,' she said with a smile. 'As you see, he has spared no expense.'

From the silver cups and tureens gleaming beneath the new circular wheels of light which lit the hall from one end to the other, to the expensive silk hangings in the bedchambers, my cousin must have spent a king's ransom.

On our arrival I had tried not to notice as Isabella cast her predatory gaze over Lady Mortimer's possessions. The way she looked her up and down as if she were no better than a servant, had been embarrassing to everybody, but the lady of the castle had smiled serenely and behaved as a great lady should when receiving her queen into her home. If she was disturbed at the presence of her husband's royal mistress, none of us would have guessed.

She linked her arm with mine. 'Are you content with your marriage?'

'I could not be happier. Lord Edmund is a good husband.'

She fingered one of the little engraved bowls laid out on the sideboard. When I looked more closely I was surprised. It was new, yet bore both their names – hers and my cousin's.

'He *will* come back to me,' she said softly.

The candlelight caught the ravages of time reflected in her face: the web of fine lines about her eyes and the touches of grey on her hairline. She was no longer the young woman I had known at Wigmore and had suffered greatly when her husband rebelled against his king. After the success of our invasion and the execution of the Despensers, she would have expected him to return to her in triumph and it must have been a bitter blow to discover how his loyalty to her had slipped away. I wondered how she had withstood the shame of being cast aside for a younger, more beautiful woman.

'Is there a great deal of hurt?' I asked shyly.

She smiled. 'He is still my husband, Margaret. When he comes to my bed, he is still my husband.'

I forced myself to show nothing in my face. Wanting Isabella and, since Paris, living with her in the same lodgings, I assumed my cousin had abandoned his intimate relationship with his wife. He had visited her on one or two occasions but, as he had said to Isabella, she could not be thrown out to starve. I thought theirs was a business arrangement not an affair of the flesh, but apparently I was wrong. To survive my cousin's passionate affair with his queen, their relationship must be founded on a deep and abiding love for each other - there could be no other explanation.

'You are the mother of his children,' I said carefully.

She laughed. 'It is more than that, my dear. You do not share what Roger and I have shared all these years without understanding each other. I know exactly what he is doing and why, and although I may not agree with his every step, I am still loyal.' She paused. 'And he, no matter what you may think, is still steadfast.'

I put out my hand and gripped hers.

'You will be careful?'

'My husband will not permit anyone to harm me, Margaret. I am part of his life. He will not put that aside. As for this interlude.' She shrugged. 'That is all it is - an interlude.'

She kissed my cheek.

'She will not hold him forever,' she whispered into my ear. 'He will come back. And when he does, I shall be waiting.'

I wished I was as sure of this as she was.

On the third day at Ludlow we went hawking in the wild lands of the Marches and it wasn't long before I found the opportunity I was hoping for. I edged closer to Lady Berkeley who was gazing disconsolately at her husband's attempts to coax his bird onto his glove. She hadn't seen me approach.

'My lady?' I said softly.

She turned round and a smile filled her face.

'Margaret! How perfect. I was looking for you yesterday but there were so many people and you were busy with that handsome husband of yours.'

It had been sixteen years since I'd last seen my cousin's daughter. I'd been on my way to my wedding and Meg Mortimer had been a tearful nine-year-old, distraught at her friend leaving Wigmore.

'My mother tells me you have children?'

'Yes, two - a boy and a girl.'

'How lucky you are! Here am I, nearly twenty-four years old and I've only been permitted to live with my husband since Easter.' She lowered her voice. 'I told the sisters at Sholdham I was the oldest virgin wife in the country.' She giggled. 'They couldn't decide whether to beat me for saying such a thing or order me to my knees to ask for God's forgiveness.'

I smiled. Clearly her years shut up in the priory for her father's misdeeds had not harmed Meg Mortimer.

'So you were not with your husband when the old king, Sir Edward, died at Berkeley?'

'No I wasn't. But he wasn't there either. He was at Bradley throwing up into a basin.'

That was odd. No-one had said that before. I wondered if it was true.

'Did Sir Edward's death distress your husband?'

'He complained he had to rise from his sick bed. When they told him Sir Edward was dead he was doubled-up with pains in his belly. Of course, being the lord, it was his duty to ensure everything was done properly so he hauled

271

himself up and rode to Berkeley. He was as sick as a dog apparently, poor man, but could hardly leave a servant to deal with a dead man who'd once been the king.'

'Had it been done properly?'

'Oh yes. It seems Gurney and Ogle had everything organised. All my lord did was write and inform the king and the queen, and then return to his sick bed and carried on vomiting.'

So Lord Berkeley said he had seen nothing.

'Ogle?' I asked. 'Is that William Ogle who taught us to fish at Wigmore?'

'Yes. Do you remember the giant pike?' She laughed. 'Oh those were the days! What fun we had.'

'Is he attached to your husband?'

'Ogle? No. I think he is my father's man but I really can't remember.'

I was beginning to think I would glean no useful information from Meg. She had the mind of a grasshopper.

She grabbed my arm. 'Look! There she goes.'

Lord Berkeley's hawk dropped like a stone from the sky onto some small unsuspecting creature below and as his wife ran to offer her congratulations, my hopes of discovering more from Meg Mortimer were extinguished like the life of the prey killed by her husband's hawk.

All I knew that I hadn't known before was that Lord Berkeley said he had not seen the dead man. He was occupied with his sickness. Thomas Gurney and William Ogle, who were both my cousin's men, had been in charge of whatever was done. I wondered who had told the embalming woman to cover the face.

Later, after a pleasant afternoon's sport, Isabella ordered me to attend her in her chamber. I was there to admire the green rugs with their red and white roses, the delicate silk bed sheets stitched with flowers and the heavy green silk hangings.

Most beautiful of all, and what I had clearly been summoned to take particular note of, was a magnificent white bedcover embroidered with pictures of the *Siege of the Castle of Love*. Richly dressed ladies in gowns of every colour hung over the castle walls throwing flowers to armour-clad knights who massed in the field below. Men fought to gain entry through an undefended gatehouse while to one side a young couple embraced passionately. From a tower, high above, a fat little Cupid fired his tiny arrow, aiming at the heart of a beautiful lady who, when I looked closely, bore a striking resemblance to Isabella. She held a shining crown over the head of her beloved who knelt on the ground in front of her.

I had to admit I had never seen anything quite so splendid or quite so disturbing.

'He had it made especially for me,' said Isabella, smiling provocatively. 'He knew I would be amused.'

She stretched like a cat in the sunshine. Juliana Nauntel pattered around the room retrieving Isabella's clothes from where her mistress had cast them, while three of the other maids stitched industriously in a corner by the window. A fifth girl was selecting combs from a small silver box. Light flooded into the room casting great golden bars across the floor. It was everything I had imagined it to be. It was glorious. And my cousin had created it for Isabella.

'Mortimer says we shall hold a Round Table tournament here next year,' said Isabella languidly. 'He wishes to have me arrayed in gold as the Lady Guinivere. The tournament will be the most magnificent ever and Mortimer and I shall be at its heart. He will be King Arthur and I shall be his queen.'

I wondered what roles she would assign to her son and his bride - probably two lowly obedient servants. And what of his wife? What role would she have?

Isabella's lips curved in a secretive smile as the maid began to comb her hair. She turned her head this way and that, running her fingers down her bare neck. The gown she was wearing was a waterfall of embroidered silk designed to accentuate rather than conceal the female form. I thought it wholly indecent but of course a woman may wear what she pleases in her private chamber and there was no law which said she must cover herself up in thick cloth. I thought of Joan, Lady Mortimer in her sturdy brocade and old-fashioned veils and understood only too well the extent of my cousin's dilemma.

Before we left Ludlow I went to pay my respects to my aunt. She was old and rarely strayed from her own hearth but had wanted to see her granddaughters marry. She did not accompany us on the hawking expeditions and I was told she found tournaments too noisy and too tiring; she preferred to rest in her own rooms. Remembering the years when she had cared for me and the obligations of a dutiful niece, I climbed the stairs to her small solar.

'My lady,' I said, kneeling for her blessing.

'Margaret.' She stroked my face with her wrinkled old

fingers. 'My son gives me a good account of you. He says you have done well.'

'I try to remember the things you taught me, my lady.'

'Hmm. Is that so? Your marriage was most useful to my son.'

'So he told me.'

'And you will continue to be of use to him, Margaret. My son was born for great things and your marriage was only one small step for him. There will be others and you must be there to help. Do you understand?'

'Yes, my lady.'

'You are my sister's child. Remember that.'

I nodded obediently. 'I shall always remember our ties, my lady. How could it be otherwise?'

'There is no more important lesson in life, child, than to hold fast to your kin. Friends may be faithless, husbands may prove a disappointment, but one's kin are always there.'

'I don't know what my cousin has told you, my lady, but my husband is not a disappointment to me.'

She smiled. 'Oh Margaret! How much you still have to learn. Husbands are always a disappointment in the end. Yours will be no different.'

'I think your son's wife would disagree,' I said.

'Ah but Roger is a special man and Joan is a clever woman. She respects my son. She will do anything to help him as must you. You will put your other desires aside and do what my son requires of you. Do you understand?'

Her voice was that of a querulous old woman but she spoke with fire in her belly. The Aunt Mortimer who had

275

so often terrified me in my youth was there still, hidden somewhere inside this bent and faded old lady.

I didn't stay long. Aunt Mortimer summoned her private chaplain so that we could say a prayer together and then I left. She was an old woman and it was sad to see her fading when I remembered her as strong. But that is what happens to the old.

We left Ludlow, travelling slowly and in great splendour and by the time we arrived at Worcester, the king and Lady Philippa were waiting for us. Everywhere I went there were whispers of how over-mighty my cousin was becoming. He had taken to wearing the kind of robes more suited to a king than a baron and that evening at supper wore a silk tunic covered with yellow velvet and emblazoned with the Mortimer arms. Beside him the young king looked insubstantial, a mere boy playing at being a king.

'You are looking pleased, my lord,' I said to him when he greeted me later. 'Are matters going well?'

He looked surprised at my question as if he had almost forgotten my existence. 'Yes. Since you ask, they are going very well. I've just acquired the roof lead from Despenser's castle at Hanley for my new chapel at Ludlow.'

'I told my son it would be a charitable gift,' explained Isabella. 'The chapel is to be dedicated to St Peter ad Vincula in recognition of dear Mortimer's escape from my husband's clutches. It is, after everything that has happened, the least a grateful king can do for one who has done so much for him. But what a pity Lady Mortimer will have the use of it.'

I wondered how many visits to Ludlow "dear Mortimer" would make to check on the progress of his chapel and whether he would tell Isabella where he was going. Knowing about his continuing relationship with his wife and the sharing of intimacies, I thought he would be wiser to keep Isabella in ignorance.

We spent an increasingly uncomfortable week at Worcester amidst endless rows between Henry of Lancaster and Isabella, and between Isabella and her son. The king surprised us by raising his voice to his mother, something he had never done before.

'This your doing,' he yelled across the chamber. 'Yours and that ...'

He was momentarily lost for a word that was acceptable in public to describe my cousin. I was certain that in private, with his close friends, he used suitably vulgar terms, but he had been raised to respect his mother and could not bring himself to use words like that to her.

'As always, I have your best interests at heart,' said Isabella placidly.

'It was not in my best interests to give away parts of my realm,' he shouted. 'I shall not recognise this treaty.'

'It is too late,' said Isabella. 'It is done and cannot be undone.'

'And I don't agree to the selling of my sister. I say she stays here.'

'Joanna is a royal daughter. She will do as she is told. We are to travel to Scotland where she will be married. It has been agreed.'

'I shan't go.'

Isabella raised her eyebrows.

'Indeed?'

'I refuse to watch my sister handed over to those warmongers.'

'Very well,' said Isabella equably. 'Stay here. Lord Mortimer and I will take the child.'

That stopped the king. Clearly he couldn't prevent his mother from going, and having once said he wouldn't go, changing his mind would be seen as a display of weakness. Poor Edward! Isabella would always win their arguments because she was skilled at twisting words. How humiliating it must be to be treated as a child when he was the king.

I thought Isabella would relent but two days later, with no further discussion, as far as I was aware, she and my cousin departed for Berwick. Their party was bound for the Lady Joanna's wedding to the little son of John's murderer, the so-called Scottish king.

I watched the vast procession pass under the gatehouse of Worcester Castle and out into the morning sunshine, flags waving, trumpets gleaming and everyone dressed in their best clothes. Isabella, I noticed, had dropped any public pretence of grieving for her late husband and was wearing an amazingly splendid outfit of dazzling blue and gold with a travelling cloak of fur-lined green velvet. Included in the party were Isabella's younger children as well as Bishop Orleton and the earl of Surrey together with their retinues. Accompanying them were the chancellor and hundreds of lesser knights and clerics, all eager for the opportunity to prove themselves friendly towards my cousin and the king's mother. It seemed everyone knew who really held the reins of power and it wasn't the king.

Edward stayed behind in the care of Lord Henry who was his guardian. But Isabella and my cousin were careful; they took the Great Seal with them and without it the young king was powerless and so was Lord Henry. How Edmund and I laughed when we heard what they'd done.

'Home!' said my husband, kissing me fondly on the cheek. 'I've had enough. We'll return to Arundel where the air is fresher.'

I enjoyed my summer at Arundel with the children. The sun shone over the walls and gardens of our new castle and I'd not felt so happy for a long time. Edmund went away twice on matters of business but I remained behind. Most days I rode out accompanied by William de la Mote. I preferred having a strong man beside me because despite Isabella's new laws there were unsavoury elements still at large in the countryside.

The people we came across on our rides were convinced I was a Fitzalan lady. They muttered a greeting, pulled off their bonnets and sank to the ground as if I were the queen herself which was very gratifying. I enjoyed their deference.

'They've known nothing else, my lady,' explained William. 'Some of them don't even know who the king is. The man who rules their lives is their overlord, the man in the castle, and he's always been a Fitzalan.'

'Why are they so ignorant?'

'The priest fills their heads with warnings of hellfire and the lord's man tells them what they can and cannot do.

They don't think, not like you or I do. They're like oxen: dumb and plodding.'

'But useful,' I said, thinking that these people were like my tenants at Mansfield all those years ago. They too might have been ignorant but they weren't at all like oxen.

'Yes,' he agreed. 'That is God's purpose for them. They are here to work.'

I thought that in William's eyes my sole purpose was probably to bear children for my husband. He wouldn't see me valued in the way that my cousin valued his wife or rather how he had valued her in the days before he'd became enmeshed with Isabella.

Towards the end of July, Edmund returned. I heard the sound of horses in the courtyard and men's voices on the stairs and before I knew what was happening, there he was, pink-cheeked, wind-blown and smiling.

'I thought you were going to York,' I said after I'd kissed him.

'I was but I changed my mind. I went to see my brother.'

I waited for the explanation as to why, when there seemed no urgent reason, he had decided to visit Lord Norfolk. He sat himself down, called for a boy to take off his boots and ordered some wine.

'We decided not to go to York. There's no point. The council is ignored whatever it says. The only voices are those of your cousin and Isabella. Cousin Henry can do nothing.'

He cuffed the lad who was pulling at his left riding boot. 'Mind what you're doing, you fool.'

He picked up his cup and tipped his head back, taking

the wine in huge gulps as if he hadn't drunk for a week.

'You saw what happened over the Scottish treaty,' he continued. 'And as for Edward? He's powerless. He couldn't stop Isabella marrying his sister to Bruce's son so there's no hope of anything being different.'

'But he is your nephew,' I protested. 'If you and Lord Norfolk were to …'

'It's too late, Margaret. Cousin Henry is determined to have the boy under his control. He's already gathering an army. This time he means to get what he wants but I think he underestimates Isabella and your cousin. They won't give up the king.'

'What will you and your brother do?'

'Try and make Cousin Henry see sense. We don't want another season of killing. It's barely two years since we got rid of Despenser and already everything's falling apart.'

Edmund called for his cup to be refilled.

'And we've decided to send a man to Corfe,' he said, almost as an afterthought.

'You told your brother?'

I was astounded. This was to be kept secret. No-one was to know of our suspicions.

'I thought he should know.' Edmund was defensive. 'Ned was his brother too. It was right to tell him.'

'And what if your brother is loose-tongued and tells others?'

'He won't. Stop worrying. It's all organised. We found a man who will worm his way in with the men at Corfe and find out what's happening. We've got to stop this rumour before it spreads any further, and the quickest way to do that is to prove it false.'

'And what if it's not?'

He laughed. 'Oh come Margaret; there's not a single speck of truth in what John Pecche said and you know it. He was a frightened old man who thought his enemies were out to poison him. No wonder he saw monsters lurking beneath the flagstones in his hall.'

'Sir Ingelram Berenger thought he was telling the truth.'

'Sir Ingelram is a man yearning for the old days. He would jump at any chance of a return to what he remembers as the good times of the Despensers. He is suffering from nostalgia, Margaret, nothing more.'

And so I told him. I told him what I had failed to ask Sir Thomas Gurney at Lincoln and what the embalming woman had said to Isabella at Worcester. I told him about my cousin's visitor on the day the army left to fight the Scots last summer and what my cousin had said to me on the walls at York. And I told him what I had learned from Meg Mortimer at Ludlow and what I thought had happened that night at Berkeley Castle.

'There was one thing they didn't reckon on - the size of your brother's feet. The boots didn't fit.'

'The boots didn't fit?' he repeated in disbelief.

'They were too small and the embalming woman noticed. She probably said nothing at the time. I doubt if they'd have let her live if she'd said anything. But she didn't. She kept silent until she saw Isabella.'

I could see Edmund was having difficulty believing any of what I was saying. I put out my hand to hold his.

'And there was something else, something they couldn't possibly have known because it was hidden.' I paused. I didn't know the words to use even to my husband. When Edmund and I lay together we whispered endearments to each other; we didn't list his private parts in intimate detail. 'His … equipment,' I faltered. 'His manhood. He had a member like other men but as for the rest - there was only one. There should have been two.'

'Only one?'

I hurried on to hide my confusion. 'They weren't to know. A man would keep that secret. But the embalming woman noticed.'

'My brother was not like that. He was …'

'He had two?'

'Of course he did. All men have two.'

'Not all,' I said quietly. 'The dead man didn't.'

'My brother did. He was perfect.'

'You're certain?'

'Christ's blood, Margaret! Of course I'm certain. He was my brother. We bathed together, we swam together. I'd seen him naked a thousand times. Of course I'm certain.'

'Then the man in the coffin at Berkeley was not your brother. He couldn't have been.'

Poor Edmund was utterly bewildered.

'But if he wasn't my brother, who was he?'

'It doesn't matter who he was. They just needed someone who was tall and well-built, someone who in the shadows could pass as your brother. There must be plenty of men like that, men who wouldn't be missed. And they'd have hidden his face afterwards to make certain no-one would ever know.'

'But why? Why would anyone do such a thing?'

'I don't know. But there could be a dozen reasons.'

'It was your cousin's doing.'

Edmund had jumped to the same conclusion as I had but that was not surprising.

'I don't want to believe it,' I said miserably.

'If what you say is true then it must be him. There's no-one else who would do something so evil.'

'Unless it was Isabella. But I've watched her carefully and I'm certain she believes she's a widow. She wouldn't allow my cousin into her bed if she knew her husband was alive. It would be too great a sin.'

Edmund kept shaking his head. I could see he was struggling to believe anything of what I had told him.

'But the funeral at Gloucester?'

'A trick. Something designed to deceive.'

'But we were all there? *You* were there.'

'Whoever planned this needed us there. We had to be convinced your brother was dead and there had to be no room for doubt or suspicions.'

Edmund put his head in his hands. 'I don't understand,' he said. 'Why would anyone do such a thing? What would they gain from it? I thought it was murder, we all did. I don't think there was a single person who thought my brother had truly died a natural death. But this?'

'Perhaps the proof you seek is at Corfe.'

Edmund sat thinking for a moment, then straightened his shoulders as if gathering himself up for an imaginary battle.

'If the proof is at Corfe, we'll find it. And in the meantime you must stay here. Trouble is brewing between Cousin Henry and Isabella and Mortimer and I need you and the children kept safe.' He leaned forward and kissed my lips. 'You are very precious to me.'

I wondered how precious we really were or if the age-old ties of love and loyalty which bound him to his beloved brother were stronger than those which he had joyfully woven round me and his two children. If it came to a choice, who would he choose?

13

ENDGAME 1329

That winter saw Isabella finally triumph over her enemies. Shortly after Christmas and despite Edmund's efforts to broker a peace before the fighting began, Lord Henry surrendered his sword to my cousin. Having seen the size of the advancing royal host and hearing that the town of Leicester was lost, the remnants of the demoralised Lancastrian army laid aside their weapons and went home to their manors. They'd had enough. My brother and Lord Beaumont were loyal to the end but when they saw Lord Henry weeping on his knees in front of a laughing Isabella, they turned and fled for their lives.

It was several weeks before I heard from Tom. The letter was water-stained and had passed through several hands before arriving at my door but at least I knew he was safe. He and Lord Beaumont had ridden across a countryside covered in snow and ice, making for the nearest port. There they'd taken ship across the Narrow Sea and found refuge with Lady de Vesci close to Paris.

The rebellion was over. Lord Henry was stripped of his offices and his wealth and the exiles stayed where they were, afraid to return and face Isabella's wrath. But for my cousin there was nothing but good news.

'Lord Mortimer has been given the earldom of March,'

said Lady Abernethy, making herself comfortable in my best chair.

She swore she had come to see my children but I suspected it was more to do with wanting to share the latest gossip.

'You have never seen anything like it, Lady Margaret. If the occasion had not been so solemn I swear I would have laughed. There was Lord Mortimer puffed up with importance in his ceremonial robes.' She thrust out her chest and blew out her cheeks in a fine travesty of my cousin at his most commanding. 'And there was the king, expected to exchange the kiss of peace with this man who had seduced his mother and usurped his royalty. He had a face on him as if he'd sucked a lemon.'

She pulled in her cheeks and pursed her lips in a grimace of utter disgust. Then closing her eyes she offered me her lips.

I laughed and pushed her away. 'It can't have been as bad as all that.'

'Oh it was, believe me; it was every bit as bad. We could see the king wasn't happy. But just think - earl of March! So much for the earldom of Gloucester. No-one can compare with Lord Mortimer now.'

'He will be very grand,' I said slowly, wondering how much higher my cousin planned to climb.

'He was very grand before,' said Lady Margery, signalling to my girl to bring the bowl of dates. 'But now he has the title to prove it.'

I smiled to myself. Lady Mortimer would be a countess. I wondered if Isabella had thought of that when she had ordered her son to ennoble my cousin.

In early February I left the children at Arundel and travelled to join Edmund at our house in Kensington. I liked the position. We were close to Westminster but there was no danger of meeting Isabella tripping along the paths; and no chance of bumping into my cousin and his increasingly vast entourage sweeping through the cloistered walkways. Here we could be as peaceful or as busy as we wished and entertain only those whom we chose to see.

Edmund said that apart from venting their anger on the Londoners for supporting the earl of Lancaster in his rebellion, my cousin and Isabella had been surprisingly merciful. There were no executions. But he reckoned Lord Beaumont and my brother were wise to fly the country as Isabella's anger was known to be fickle and you could never be certain.

Huge fines were levied on any of the rebels who could pay and this money would go some way to replenishing the royal coffers. As well as fines and forfeitures, oaths were to be sworn by those who had dared to oppose the king: oaths to protect the king, his mother, the earl of March and members of the king's council.

I felt nervous. How would I be received as the sister of a known traitor? Edmund's position would shelter me but I was beginning to fear both Isabella and my cousin. There was a time when I would have done anything the great Lord Mortimer asked of me, when I would willingly have died for him. But that was a long time ago. Now I knew him for what he was. Once I had been close to Isabella, her confidante in all things. Now I felt cast out and unwelcome.

I had barely unpacked my chests when I received a summons. Someone had told Isabella of my arrival and she ordered my presence at once, this minute, without delay. I would much rather have stayed and organised my household but I wearily changed my gown and rode once more through the familiar precincts of the royal palace to visit this woman I had once thought was almost my friend.

I was given a chair at the king's high table, seated between my cousin and Countess Jeanne. On my cousin's other side was Isabella, a sparkling iridescent Isabella.

'You are trembling,' said my cousin, taking my hand in his. 'Do I frighten you that much or are you merely cold?'

'Of course you don't frighten me, cousin,' I said untruthfully. 'I am nervous at returning here after so long an absence.'

'Ah yes, you have been with your children. You are fortunate, Margaret. You doubtless heard about my boys?'

The news had come late to Arundel. Two of my friends from the nursery had died at the end of the summer: young Roger from a brief fever and Johnny, handsome, carefree Johnny, killed in a jousting accident.

'I had masses said for their souls, as you must know I would; and I wrote to their mother.'

My words seemed inadequate but I didn't know how to give comfort to a man like my cousin who seemed impervious to grief.

But across his face came a fleeting shaft of pain. 'I wish I had more sons,' he said quietly. 'All I have are two and Geoffrey is often away. He sees his mother more than he sees me.'

'Once you have lost a child you fear daily for the others no matter how old they are,' I said, thinking of my little dead son, Aymer.

He was about to turn away when he hesitated.

'A word in your ear, Margaret. Warn your husband to tread carefully.'

My stomach lurched. 'Has Edmund done something to upset you, my lord?'

'Not yet. I have forgotten his unwise peacemaking of last year. But I should hate the king's uncle to be seen as anything other than totally loyal. And you already know what happens to meddlesome women.'

With that odd remark he turned to Isabella.

'Lady Margaret?' It was Lady Jeanne.

After we had made our greetings she insisted on telling me the latest gossip.

'The Lady Eleanor has disgraced herself again,' she said, her eyes gleaming at the thought of more scandal. 'She has run off with an inferior lordling.'

'Lady Despenser?'

'Alas, Lady Despenser no longer. She claims she is now Lady Zouche. Abducted or more likely eloped.' She lowered her voice. 'They are saying she had the two of them. Wanted to sample the goods before she purchased.'

'Two what, Lady Jeanne?'

'Two men, of course. Lord Zouche was one and the other was that handsome Grey fellow. And it wasn't a matter of conversation. She took both of them to her bed.'

'At the same time?'

Lady Jeanne looked suitably shocked. 'Oh surely not? A lady would never. Would she?'

I smiled sweetly. It was such fun teasing Lady Jeanne. 'And Lady Eleanor picked Lord Zouche?'

'Yes. Although Grey refutes the marriage. Claims he had her before Lord Zouche and that he and Lady Eleanor are man and wife. Says he will pursue the matter through the courts.'

'Did she have the king's permission to remarry?'

'No and Isabella is not pleased. Lady Eleanor was raised back to her previous position, had her lands restored and now she does this. It's a disgrace.'

'Perhaps it was love?' I suggested.

'What? With two of them?'

After the meal was finished I accompanied Isabella back to her private apartments.

'You have heard about the Lady Eleanor?' she hissed.

'Yes, your grace.'

'I have her in the Tower.'

'For marrying without the king's consent?' This was harsh even for Isabella.

'No, you fool, for stealing my jewels and my plate. When she was last my guest in the Tower she had the temerity to help herself to some of my treasure, valuables that evil man Despenser inveigled from my late husband. She claims they are hers by right. She is wrong. They are mine.'

I murmured something about base ingratitude.

'I haven't decided what to do with her yet but I think a further period of incarceration will cool her inclinations in all directions. And Margaret?'

'Your grace?'

'You would do well to note what happens to women who incur my displeasure. I haven't forgotten about your brother. See you redeem the reputation of your family. It wouldn't do for you to be branded as disloyal.'

With that she let go of my arm and swept ahead, leaving me wondering what, if anything, she knew. Isabella wasn't stupid and if I had worked out what had happened that night at Berkeley Castle, probably so had she. And if she had, she would know I was a danger to her. She would have noticed me talking to the embalming woman and having private conversations with Lord Berkeley's wife. Perhaps I had unwittingly betrayed myself.

A yawning pit of horrors opened up in front of my eyes and I wished I had left well alone.

In the weeks after we left Westminster, we followed the king as he moved from one palace to another. We were bound for Isabella's castle at Guildford where the king was to host a splendid tournament. Now that she had humbled Lord Henry and satisfactorily punished his followers, Isabella was in the mood for merrymaking. There were to be two days of feasting, jousting and celebration in honour of her victory: hers and Lord Mortimer's.

'The crown cannot afford such generosity,' said the king, setting his lips together in a firm line as if he didn't wish the conversation to continue.

This was the second cool exchange between mother and son over the matter of a special presentation to Lord Mortimer. The gift was intended as a reward to my cousin for his part in the defeat of the Lancastrians and had been decided on by Isabella.

'Don't be ridiculous.'

'My coffers are empty.'

'Lord Mortimer has just won a great victory for you. He has squeezed those who rebelled so that your treasury is full. Of course you can afford to be generous and Lord Mortimer is the most deserving of your nobles.'

'I cannot reward him so handsomely, lady mother. He is only one man among many and has already been given an earldom. What more does he want?'

Clearly the king had no desire to give further expensive gifts to his mother's lover when he had probably given him a king's ransom already. But of course he couldn't say that. He may have whispered such things to his wife on her pillow but he would not dare say them to his mother.

I wondered how long it would be before the king rebelled. Weak sons remain cowed by their strong mothers all their lives but I didn't think Isabella's son was weak - merely young.

I shifted somewhat uncomfortably on my cushion. Though I was surrounded by other women in the royal stand, I didn't care for my close proximity to Isabella. I was certain she could read my thoughts. On my right Lady Philippa was watching her husband succeed in the lists and I had to admit the young king was becoming one of our most skilful tournament riders. Of course Edmund was taller and stronger and would usually defeat his nephew but today the king triumphed.

I slipped out of the stand and holding up my skirts, walked across the grass to Edmund's tent.

'Are you hurt?'

He grinned at me. 'Covered in mud and grass, nothing more.'

'It's not like you to fall.'

'I didn't fall. I slid off.'

Despite being still half-harnessed, he put his arms around me and nuzzled my cheek.

'It was purposely done. I need to go into the town,' he murmured against my ear. I tried to pull my head back but he held me fast against his shoulder. 'I'll take William with me. If anyone asks, say I was shaken after my fall.'

'Where are you going?' I said lightly, pretending nothing was amiss.

'Our man is back. He's at the Angel.'

He kissed me hard on the lips and walked away, cursing and holding onto his arm.

Our man? Of course - the man from Corfe.

It was some hours later when Edmund returned. His face betrayed nothing as we mixed with the king's guests at the evening entertainment. The music swirled, the acrobats danced and my husband was as charming and as talkative as ever. But as soon as we could, we retired, Edmund pleading exhaustion and a sore arm.

'What did he say?'

I was impatient but Edmund insisted on making sure no-one was listening. He checked the window shutters and instructed William to stand guard. The maids and the grooms were ordered out. Eventually we were alone.

'John Pecche has a nephew,' said Edmund. 'One Harry Pecche.'

'And?'

'He is to be found at Corfe.'

'Not unexpected if his uncle is custodian.'

'He has a special position, this Harry Pecche.'

'Which is?'

Edmund hesitated. 'He guards the prisoner, the man hidden beneath the flagstones in the hall. I say guard, but he is more of a companion as the man sees no one but him.'

'Why did Sir John not mention this nephew?'

Edmund shrugged. 'Who knows? Perhaps he forgot or perhaps he didn't want to get him involved.'

'What else did your man say?'

'Harry Pecche and the prisoner arrived at the castle more than a year ago. They came with the lord of the district, John Maltravers.'

'You are certain of this?'

'Our man is quite certain. He says it is common knowledge but nobody talks much about it.'

'And the prisoner's name?' This was the most vital piece of information. Edmund had given his man no clue as to the identity of the prisoner, not wanting to influence him one way or the other.

'They call him "King Folly". When there is a feast they bring him out of his dungeon and sit him in the hall. They put a crown on his head and drink his health. My informant tells me it is a very merry affair.'

'He has seen the prisoner?'

'Yes. At the nativity celebrations.'

'And what did he say?'

Edmund's face was bleak. 'He said, "He is the dead spit of your brother, my lord, him that were king." Those were his very words - him that were king.'

'But how did he know?'

'I chose a man who *would* know, a man who had once served in my brother's household. They are ten a penny nowadays, men who served my brother. Margaret, what am I going to do?'

Now there was no doubt. Edmund's brother was not dead as everyone believed, but alive and imprisoned in the bowels of Corfe Castle. A great deceit had been practised and knowing what we knew placed us in terrible danger. I knew what I would do but the prisoner was not my brother.

We had been a week at the royal palace of Woodstock but this was the first time we had walked to the pavilion at Everswell. The paved floor was littered with debris from last autumn: dried leaves, small twigs, dust. The grass had that dried-up winter appearance and the water running through the stone-lined channels looked icy.

Edmund took my hands and sat me down on a stone bench.

'My mother used to bring me here. She told me that my grandmother planted the trees to remind her of home. My grandfather adored her and when she said she was homesick for the plants and sunshine of Provence, he sent for two dozen pear trees. He wanted her to be happy.'

The leafless branches moved in the wind, and the dust on the floor drifted into a corner. I shivered.

'In spring the trees are covered in blossom but it doesn't last. My mother said it is a reminder of the importance of love. One moment the person you love is alive, the next they are gone to God, fallen to the ground like the petals. For a short time they are remembered and then gradually they disappear as if they had never been. Remembering the blossom gave her comfort. She told me you cannot choose how long you keep those you love but you can remember them for as long as you live.'

I felt my eyes fill with tears. These were John's trees, the ones I would have planted at Badenoch and they always reminded me of him. But now there would never be a Badenoch and John had been dead for fifteen years.

There was no-one to hear us where we sat. The men and women who had ventured out to keep us company were huddled together against the shelter of the cloisters and were too far away to be aware of our conversation.

Edmund took my hand.

'I cannot leave him there, Margaret.'

I had been waiting for this. There had never been doubt in my mind as to which path Edmund would choose. He couldn't endure the thought of this man he loved shut away from the light, left to rot in a dark hole. He couldn't leave his brother where he was and continue his life as before, treading on the lies and deceits my cousin had devised. It was horribly dangerous, not just for Edmund but also for me and the children.

'What would you have us do?' I said.

'He must be released.'

'And what then?'

There was silence. I doubted Edmund had thought further than the joyful reunion when he pulled his brother out of his dungeon. But I had.

'Edmund, if you free your brother, what will he do? Will he travel overseas and lodge with someone kindly disposed to him.'

'Our French cousins?'

'Would you not think that might be dangerous?' I said. 'Your cousin, Philip, would dearly like to have the king of England's father in his clutches. Nothing would give him greater pleasure.'

'Then who?'

'His Castilian kinsmen perhaps?'

Edmund looked doubtful.

'Or,' I said slowly, 'Are you entertaining the idea of restoring him to his former glory?'

He was shocked as if the thought had never occurred to him.

'Because,' I said, 'you can be quite certain that is what your friends such as Sir Ingelram Berenger have in mind. They want your brother back on his throne.'

Edmund said nothing for a moment. Then, 'I hadn't thought.'

'No,' I said sharply. 'I didn't think you had. And what if you fail? What if your plot is discovered? What then?'

When he didn't reply I gave him the answer. 'My cousin will pursue you to the ends of the earth. He will hunt you down the way he hunted Sir Hugh Despenser and his father, and when he catches you he will dispose of your body to the dogs.'

And just to make sure he had no illusions, I added, 'And Isabella will stand by and watch.'

Edmund turned as pale as the bleached grasses.

'And what of your nephew?' I said relentlessly. 'What will you do with him? Pat him on the head and tell him to go back to being his father's son? Wait his turn?'

Edmund put his head in his hands.

'What shall I do?'

'Leave matters be. There's nothing you can do unless you wish to sacrifice us all.'

I didn't have a bond of feeling with my brother as Edmund did with his and couldn't imagine risking my own life and the happiness of my husband and children on some wild rescue plan. Perhaps my years alone had made me a hard woman or perhaps Edmund was too kind, too loving, too easily persuaded by others. All I could do was hope he would make the wise decision.

Isabella was in a bad mood. Her annoyance with her son had spilled over and affected us all.

'In the summer the king will travel overseas to make his homage to that foundling who sits on my father's throne,' she said.

"Foundling" was the term of abuse for Philip, the new king of France, and Isabella delighted in its use. It was sufficiently rude without being vulgar.

'I told him the son of a king has no business bending his knee to the son of a mere count, but my son wants us to live in harmony with those vultures across the Narrow Sea. They confiscated our tax revenues from Gascony but my son intends to send our envoys with gifts for them. And now he has just announced he will go to Amiens to do homage to the Valois pretender.'

'Will you go with him?'

'Never,' she said. 'When my son sits on the throne of France, then I shall return but not before. I will never recognise their Valois king.'

It was when she turned away that I saw. I wasn't certain, of course I wasn't. It was far too soon for anyone to know. Probably Isabella herself didn't know. But to a woman who has lived with other women for all of her life there is an indefinable something: a way of walking, of holding oneself; a particular sheen on the skin, a fullness around the face and the breasts. Before the sickness starts and the second course is missed, there is an unmistakable air about a woman carrying a child. And Isabella had it.

I stood frozen to the spot, not daring to speak in case my voice betrayed me. A child! My cousin had said he wanted another son. But this? This would spell disaster for us all.

Early next morning we left Woodstock. I kept my horse close by Edmund's, hoping to be able to speak to him privately, but it was impossible. William was in conversation with him for most of the journey. They were discussing the fortifications at Arundel and whether the gatehouse should be strengthened. Then they moved on to the planned extensions to our house in Kensington and the purchase of some more horses.

That night as I lay in our sparsely-furnished chamber in the priory's guest house, I reminded myself how lucky I was to be sharing a bed with my husband who held me close rather than with Lady Abernethy who kept me awake with her snoring. But through the walls I could hear every rustle and groan from the adjoining chamber so judged it safer not to discuss my suspicions about Isabella.

When we arrived at our town house and before I had changed my mud-spattered travelling clothes, I heard William come running and bang on my husband's door. Curious, I peeped out of my chamber.

'Bring him up.' Edmund was standing in the doorway in his clean silk shirt.

William turned and retraced his steps, disappearing rapidly from view. A boy came into sight carrying a jug of hot water. Edmund shouted at him to hurry.

'Who is it?'

'Berenger.'

So Sir Ingelram Berenger had returned. Was this good news or bad?

'Shall I come?' I hoped the answer would be yes.

Edmund nodded. I withdrew into my chamber and quickly stepped out of my filthy clothes and put on something clean, brushed and lavender-scented. I decided to leave my hair and veil as they were. Sir Ingelram was an old soldier and unlikely to pay heed to female vanity.

As I stepped across the threshold I saw Sir Ingelram was not alone. He had brought another man, someone familiar, and I rather regretted the decision about my hair. The man's eyes lit up in appreciation as he stood to greet me.

'Lord Zouche, my lady,' said Sir Ingelram.

Lady Despenser's new husband! What was he doing here? I inclined my head graciously and sat down. He turned his attention to Edmund, giving me an opportunity to examine this man who had married Eleanor. A pleasant open face, long legs, sturdily built and not in the least perturbed by my presence. I wondered why he'd married her. Money of course. Hardly love as I had suggested to Countess Jeanne. I couldn't imagine anyone loving Lady Eleanor. It had to be money.

'I thought there would be a need for funds,' explained Sir Ingelram. 'Lord Zouche and I have spent a pleasant couple of days with money men in the city.'

'Relieving them of their bags of gold,' laughed his friend.

He was a cheerful man. I wonder if he'd used his wife's lands as surety. I wasn't sure how these things worked but Edmund would know.

'I think I should explain Lord Zouche's presence,' apologised Sir Ingelram. 'He came to me.'

'There are a lot of men who think like I do,' said Lord Zouche. 'Nobody says or does anything because what would be the point? Nothing will change, not after Lord Henry's humiliation. But we yearn for the days as they were, when your brother was on the throne. My wife's first husband was a rogue, no matter what Sir Ingelram may say, but your brother was a good man, my lord.'

'You told him,' I said, accusingly.

The old man looked shocked. 'No, my lady. I promised the earl I would tell no-one.'

Lord Zouche was curious. 'Told me what?'

As Isabella had once said, I possessed a talent for reading people, and I could see a valuable ally in Lord Zouche. I didn't like his wife but that didn't mean I had to dislike the man. I reckoned he was trustworthy.

Edmund and I exchanged glances. I gave a small nod and Edmund proceeded to tell him the story of the prisoner at Corfe.

Lord Zouche raised his eyebrows and sucked in his cheeks. 'God's wounds! The scoundrel! To think I …'

'We were all deceived, Lord Zouche,' I said, smiling.

'Does he intend to keep him there until he rots?'

'Possibly, but I rather think he wants him alive. That way he is more useful.'

Edmund had not spent the hours I had mulling over this problem. He was a more straightforward person than me and the devious twists and turns of my cousin's mind would never occur to Edmund.

'In what way, my lady?' Sir Ingelram was intrigued.

'Lord Mortimer controls the king because the king is just a boy and my cousin is powerful and very threatening. But as the king becomes a man he will wish to make his own decisions. So Lord Mortimer must find another way of keeping him under his thumb.' I let them think about that for a moment.

'I don't understand.' Edmund was floundering.

'What better threat can there be than having possession of what many see as the "rightful king". The son can say nothing and do nothing because he knows my cousin holds his father. There are many threats Lord Mortimer could make to ensure the king does what he wants. The son would not want His Holiness to be made aware. Or the king of France. Think what they might do if they knew.'

They fell into a discussion of what to do if they freed Sir Edward from his underground dungeon. Sir Ingelram, as I had predicted, was all for restoring him to the throne, while Edmund wanted him out of England, somewhere safe. Lord Zouche had as yet, no opinion on the matter but was quite ready to consider either possibility.

'You will need help,' I said calmly. 'You cannot do this alone. Whom can you trust?'

'Melton.' Sir Ingelram didn't hesitate before naming the archbishop of York.

'Fitzwarin,' said Lord Zouche.

'My brother-in-law Lord Wake, Lord Beaumont, his sister Lady de Vesci, Pecche and Roscelyn.' Edmund was tallying up names on his fingers. 'And Lancaster, naturally.'

I thought of the half-blind man kneeling in the mud. 'Lord Henry won't be much use to you.'

'His name commands support. Remember his lineage.' Edmund was dismissive as if I could not be expected to realise the importance of the earl of Lancaster. I was a mere baron's daughter, and a lowly baron at that.

'Donald of Mar.'

There was silence. Donald of Mar was Robert Bruce's nephew, brought up in the household of Edmund's brother. He was branded an enemy rebel and if he came to help he would bring thousands of men pouring across the border from Scotland. My stomach turned over and for the first time I was truly afraid. This was no small affair they were planning but a full-scale attempt to change the face of the kingdom. They were not going to stop at freeing Edmund's brother, they were going to put him back on the throne.

As they were leaving I touched Lord Zouche's arm.

'How is Lady Eleanor, Lord Zouche?'

'I have no idea, my lady. I am not allowed to see her.'

His tone was light. For a man recently married, he didn't seem too concerned at the loss of his wife. He had her lands under his control and doubtless that was what he had wanted from the marriage, not the lady herself.

That evening I told Edmund we needed to talk. I called for the candles to be lit and the fire made up and threw the servants out. William was to guard the door because I wanted no one else to hear what I had to say.

I told Edmund my suspicions. The muscles around his mouth tightened.

'A child?'

'I cannot be sure, but I think it probable.'

His eyes flickered to my belly assessing the state of my womb. It was eighteen months since Joan's birth and I knew he wanted another child.

'Does Mortimer know?'

'Isabella herself may not be certain and most women keep their suspicions to themselves until they feel the child move.'

'Now she truly is a whore.' He was coldly furious.

'She desires him.' I shrugged. 'She always has but as long as she considered herself a married woman she held back. Now she believes your brother dead she is no longer constrained. It may be distasteful but there is nothing other than good manners to prevent a widow from taking a lover.'

'What about your cousin? You think he is also caught in an overwhelming passion?'

'No. I think, for him, it has been a calculated gamble from the moment they first met in Paris. I think he is using her.'

Edmund drove his fist down hard onto the table. The cups rattled against each other and the hound asleep by the hearth lifted his head in annoyance, then seeing it was only his master, settled down again, nose between paws.

'He takes what he wants and then flaunts himself in front of us.' Edmund was really angry.

'She has used him too,' I said, keeping my voice gentle not wanting him to become even angrier.

Could Edmund not see how this adventure had been to both their advantages? My cousin disposed of his enemies and regained his position and wealth, while Isabella was able to return: her husband emasculated, her worst enemy horribly put to death and her biddable son on the throne of England. She was powerful, rich and unassailable. Their passion may be pleasurable but it also served as a silken rope to bind one to the other. They used their lust as a weapon: a snare, a line, one snap, one snatch and the fish is caught, floundering, helpless unable to escape.

'I will not allow this insult to my brother and my nephew.'

'There is nothing you can do, Edmund,' I said. 'If there is a child, it will be born.'

I banished memories of a drawstring pouch and the little vial, and the gently swollen belly of Lady Eleanor Despenser.

Edmund walked to the door. He called William and told him to find his clerk.

'This has made up my mind. We shall leave.'

I smiled. Life was definitely more pleasant away from the dangerous presence of Isabella and my cousin. 'I shall give the orders. The children will be delighted to see us.'

'We are not going to Arundel, we are going overseas: Paris, Avignon, Aquitaine, Santiago di Compestala.'

He had given me no warning and hadn't asked my opinion. I wasn't sure I wished to go to Avignon or the

Aquitaine. And why Santiago di Compestala? I didn't want to tread the pilgrim path and I certainly had no desire to add my coins to swell the coffers of avaricious monks at the tomb of St James. If I wished to make a pilgrimage, the bones of the blessed St Thomas at Canterbury would do me just as well.

I protested vehemently, but Edmund was adamant.

'I need to see Beaumont and your brother who I've been told are in Paris. And I need to visit the Holy Father on private business. When we've done that we shall fulfil my mother's dying wish.'

'But why Avignon? What business do we have with His Holiness?'

'I will tell you when we get there. Until then it is nothing to do with you. You will have to be an obedient wife and do as you're told.'

I closed my mouth. When Edmund was in this mood there was no point in saying anything. If he wanted us to go to Avignon and Compestala then I would have to make the best of it and perhaps it would be enjoyable. I had never been further than Paris.

We needed letters of protection from the king to enable us to cross the Narrow Sea in safety. I listened as Edmund lied smoothly about the deathbed promise made to his mother and how he desired to visit the shrine of St James at Compestala to fulfill her last wishes. He said nothing about visiting my brother in Paris.

He would also, he explained, take the opportunity to further the cause of his late cousin of Lancaster with His Holiness. Doubtless his urgings would hasten the path towards sainthood for Earl Thomas.

'Do we want it hastened, Mortimer?' Isabella was proving difficult.

I watched her closely trying to decide whether or not I was right about the child. She sat with her hand protectively on her belly. I thought her face a trifle smoother, her breasts a little fuller. At meals she picked at her food, but she had never been a greedy eater. I still wasn't sure.

My cousin smiled lazily. He was grander than ever with luxuriant fur-lined robes cast carelessly over his powerful shoulders and jewelled rings sparkling on every finger. If either of them betrayed knowledge of a forthcoming child, it was my cousin. Here was a man who had achieved more than the young Lord Mortimer of my childhood memories could have imagined. And the next step?

'I see no reason why not.' My cousin's words interrupted my thoughts. 'Lord Edmund will make a good advocate. And with your son bending his knee to the foundling in Amiens, you and I will remain here to ensure matters run smoothly.'

We stayed at Windsor for the Easter celebrations where I sat beside Countess Jeanne at the tournament. The cushions were plumper and more comfortable than usual and despite my worries I was enjoying myself.

'I hear you plan a pilgrimage?' Lady Jeanne sounded wistful.

I dragged my thoughts back to my neighbour.

'It is to fulfill a vow which my husband's mother made. She was dying and Lord Edmund promised he would go in her stead.'

'It has taken him a long time,' observed Lady Jeanne. 'Dear Marguerite! It must be ten, eleven years since she went to God. Such a good woman. She saw life in a simple way. Be charitable, she used to say to me; be merciful; and most of all, have faith in God and the love of the Blessed Virgin.'

We watched Isabella toss a favour to my cousin. Her gown strained across her breasts as she leant forward, the folds of rose-coloured silk catching the rays of the sun. The brooch of rubies and sapphires at her neck glinted and sparkled.

My cousin's horse side-stepped at the unfamiliar exchange but he kept the animal in position. The great Lord Mortimer inclined his head, saluted his queen and rode off to the end of the field where his squire waited patiently holding his helm.

Now his entire head was encased in burnished steel but somewhere behind the narrow slits which allowed him sight of his opponent, the darkness of unfulfilled ambition burned fiercely in his eyes.

I considered the new fashions: voluminous skirts, tightly-buttoned sleeves which drew the eye away from the body, sideless outer gowns which swung as a lady walked. I did some counting in my head. It would be winter when the child was born. Enveloping cloaks, furred mantles. Yes, it could be done with most people none the wiser. They would wait until they knew if it was a boy before allowing people to know. A girl wouldn't matter, but a boy – a boy would change everything.

And what about Lady Mortimer? I shivered as I thought of her alone at Ludlow, watching her meals and lying at night in her great marriage bed, wondering if her husband would come back; or if he would send a man to end it all, a man with a knife concealed in his belt. There were so many ways to kill a woman: a push down the stairs, a slip over the battlements, an accident out hunting, or a dose of wolfsbane in the wine. So many ways to rid oneself of an inconvenient wife.

We spent two months making our preparations. Edmund was constantly in the saddle, travelling to see his men of business, first at Arundel, then at Kensington. If he had more meetings with Sir Ingelram Berenger or Sir John Pecche he didn't tell me and I heard nothing more of Lord Zouche.

I made arrangements for the start of Mondi's education with the children's guardians who managed their little household with commendable efficiency. My son was nearly three and the time had come to stop playing with toys and start learning to be a man. He must receive instruction in his catechism and attend mass on Sundays. I left instructions about the children's food and the number of sweetmeats I would permit and I discussed buttoned winter coats for Mondi with the tailor. The nursemaids, I knew, would be kept in good order. I would have liked to have put my son up on his first pony but thought that could wait until we returned.

All this and there were still three weeks to go until June and our departure for Avignon.

It was magnificently ornate. The sun shone relentlessly out of a clear blue sky and all around the courtyard, white walls and tiled floors reflected the heat. It might be October but my stockings were clinging to my legs and sweat was trickling down my back. Light silks would have been more comfortable but the Holy Father's palace on the hill at Avignon was somewhere a woman must dress decorously and modestly. Images of the Blessed Virgin were everywhere, reminding me of my sole purpose in the eyes of these men. My brocade gown was cut high at the neck and instead of my usual crispinettes I was covered in an all-encompassing conventual veil. I felt trussed. And bored.

We had spent six weeks in Paris making polite visits to Edmund's cousins during the day and having clandestine meetings with my brother, Lord Beaumont and Sir John Roscelyn in the evenings. They had put forward no plans, just expressions of support for some unnamed action at some unspecified time in the future. There might be money, but naturally their positions were not what they once were. They simply wanted anything other than what they had at the moment, which was exile, impoverishment and humiliation.

I visited Lady de Vesci's manor outside Paris and found her much frailer than I remembered. She received me kindly and offered help to whatever extent she could at whatever it was my husband wanted to do. I don't think she fully understood what was happening because several times she called me Lady Abernethy.

After the dullness of the Valois and Evreux ladies and their pointless contemplation of fashion and the doings of people I had never heard of, I was certain I would enjoy Avignon and the fabled splendour of the papal court. I found I did not.

'My lady?'

I was jolted out of my reverie. A familiar accent. A slight burr of the West Country? I looked up. At first I couldn't place him. He was someone I'd seen before but I couldn't put a name to the face. Youngish, about the same age as Edmund; straight nose, brown hair and eyes, nothing remarkable. Then he smiled and I remembered.

'Sir William Montagu!'

He gave a small bow.

'Countess.'

Sir William Montagu, the king's closest friend. What was he doing in Avignon?

'How pleasant to see someone from home,' I said. 'You are here on affairs of state?' It was not my business to know, but I was curious and as always, alert to danger.

'I am here to see His Holiness on a small matter for the king and also one for the Lady Isabella. And I am searching for the Lord of Cuyk.'

'Alone?'

He laughed. 'Hardly, my lady. I have brought the chancellor's brother, Sir Bartholomew Burghersh, with me. Or if you like to put it another way, he has brought me. It all depends on who you think holds the leash.'

I didn't think he was going to tell me any more but he must have decided I was trustworthy or else the matter was not confidential.

'The king is keen to employ Lord Otto of Cuyk, and the dowager queen is anxious to make repayment of a debt to His Holiness. So you see I shall be busy.'

'And Sir Bartholomew Burghersh?'

'He is here to keep an eye on me. He has no other role that I know of.'

I presumed Sir Bartholomew was my cousin's man. Chancellor Burghersh was most definitely a devotee of Isabella so it made sense that his brother would be in the same camp. But why didn't they didn't trust Sir William Montagu and what was he doing here? I thought the story about Lord Otto of Cuyk was a thinly veiled attempt to hide his real intentions. If the king had sent his most valued friend to visit the papal court, what did he want from His Holiness?

I considered the young king's dilemma. He was dominated by his mother and by my cousin but there would come a time when he would break free and when that happened - if it happened - my cousin's days of glory would be over. Perhaps, in secret, the king was already planning for that moment. Perhaps Sir William's mission to the papal court was designed to see where His Holiness stood in relation to the growing antagonism between the king and my cousin.

Which way? Cousin or king or neither? Perhaps I should encourage Edmund to risk our money on the prisoner at Corfe. I wondered how trustworthy Sir William was. Not everybody was what they seemed in this life. I had learned that the hard way.

'How fares the king, Sir William?'

'Pleased to be back in England after our trip to Amiens, my lady. His grace annoyed King Philip and his council and left a host of problems in the wake of his homage. You must know what it's like: the words weren't quite what they wanted, his hands were in the wrong place, the bow wasn't deep enough. It's a vipers' nest at the French court.'

I smiled. 'And the dowager queen, the Lady Isabella?'

'Well.'

He didn't elaborate. Either he didn't know or he wasn't going to tell me.

'And my cousin, Lord Mortimer?'

This time there was a slight hesitation. 'As always, my lady, busy with matters of importance.'

He didn't like my cousin, that was clear, but he was perfectly polite.

'And you, my lady?'

'To be truthful, Sir William, I am bored. The delights of Avignon are greatly overrated. I have found little to do but we are leaving soon to make our pilgrimage to Santiago di Compestala and as far as I am concerned it will be a welcome relief.'

Sir William hadn't moved and nothing had happened, but with no warning a chill ran through my veins, and fingers of dust brushed the back of my neck. I felt afraid.

'Don't go.'

His face was serious. He didn't smile. He wasn't even looking at me. He was watching a man stride across the courtyard towards us: large, sweating and angry, the heels of his blood-red boots ringing out loudly on the paving tiles.

'Why not?'

His voice low and the man was still too far away to hear. 'If you go, you will not come back.' He raised an arm. 'Burghersh! I wondered where you'd got to.'

Edmund wanted to know every detail of my encounter with Sir William Montagu. 'Did he say nothing else?'

'Not then. But as we were taking our leave, I made sure I left my book on the bench. Sir Bartholomew kindly went back to retrieve it at my request. That was when Sir William said something very odd.'

'What?'

'He said it is better to eat the dog, no matter how unpalatable that may be, before the dog eats you. Just that. He didn't explain what he meant and before I could ask, Sir Bartholomew returned and Sir William began talking of something else.'

We didn't go to Santiago di Compestala. My nausea had settled into a familiar pattern and when I told Edmund he said no child of his was going to be born on the pilgrim path. Instead we came home and set out almost immediately for Kenilworth. The royal party had been there a month, we were told, and Edmund was anxious to discover what was happening.

'You mustn't go alone,' I said fearfully. 'I shall come with you. Remember my love, I have spied many a time for Isabella and if there are secrets to uncover I shall find them.'

It was yet more days of gruelling travel, this time through the cold of an early English winter. When we arrived we were informed that Lord Mortimer was absent, departed that morning for Ludlow but he would return shortly. The queen was resting. The news suited me. It was easier to ask questions without either Isabella or my cousin watching.

I knew what I was looking for but after a day of subtle and not-so-subtle questioning, I had discovered nothing.

Isabella's women were the same as ever: industrious, quiet and smiling. They asked had I enjoyed the wonders of the papal court and had I seen the Holy Father? Was the sea crossing calm and were the ladies in Paris still wearing gowns close-cut to the body? And what of their necklines? As to their own lives - oh, nothing much. A tear in the queen's favourite blue silk robes which was difficult to repair and the kitchens reported a lack of cinnamon for the queen's favourite sweetmeats - nothing unusual.

'Have you heard?' whispered Lady Jeanne as I took my place at the table for supper. 'One of her women told me this morning.'

'I have heard nothing,' I said cautiously.

'There is to be a child.'

It was like a blow with a hammer. My belly lurched and I began to shake. How did Lady Jeanne know? I'd found out nothing.

'Are you certain?'

'Oh yes and anybody looking at the two of them will be bound to guess. See how solicitous he is of her comfort.'

I followed her gaze expecting to see my cousin but all I saw was the young king helping the Lady Philippa into her chair.

'Lady Philippa?'

'Isn't it wonderful. I've said nothing to Isabella but I'm sure she knows. One of the maids will have told her. She pays them you know.'

'Pays them?' I said stupidly, trying to recover from my mistake.

'To bring her information. She will have someone in *your* household too. With Lord Wake's reputation I doubt she places her trust in you any longer. Of course she trusts me, but that's different.'

'How is it different?' I asked, increasingly bewildered at how foolish I had been.

'Lineage, my dear Lady Margaret. I am a king's grand-daughter.'

That evening I confessed my mistake to Edmund.

'There is no child. Perhaps there was one and she lost it. It happens.'

But Edmund was not impressed with my news. 'If there was one child there can be another. Mortimer won't give up.'

'No, he won't,' I agreed. 'And people are saying he preens himself like a peacock. Sits higher than everyone else and acts as if he was already king.'

Edmund grasped my hand arm and led me to a settle by the hearth, away from the door.

'What are we going to do?'

'We could be dead if it hadn't been for William Montagu,' I said morosely.

'And where do you think the warning came from? Someone must have told him.'

'Edward.' I kept my voice low. 'It must have been Edward.'

'And if the warning came from Edward who do you think is plotting our deaths?'

Many times I had imagined an assassin picking his way through the shadows and in my waking dreams, the face beneath the assassin's hood was always that of my cousin.

I wanted it to be someone else. I couldn't believe it of him. I was his cousin. I had loved him when I was a child. He couldn't mean to have me killed. I could believe it of Isabella. If it suited her purpose she wouldn't hesitate. I could imagine her twisting the knife in my cousin's own heart if that would get her what she wanted, because Isabella loved nobody but herself. Once she had been a loving woman who had held my hand in the dark. But not now. Now she was hard and cold and merciless.

'You know, don't you?'

I nodded. 'Yes. But why?'

Edmund thought for a moment.

'Because we are a danger to him and when planning a campaign you pick off your enemies one by one.'

'Like in a game of chess. Remove the foot soldiers then the knights and the castles until all you have left are a couple of bishops and the king and queen, isolated and alone.'

Edmund nodded. 'First Cousin Henry who is old and blind, then me, then my brother Thomas.'

'You forgot the softest target of all.'

'Who is?'

'The prisoner at Corfe. He baulked at killing a king but eliminated him just the same. Dead men can't come back.'

I thought of us all stationed on the board. Who were we protecting? Who must be saved at all costs? The king of course. Young Edward asking me on the borders of Hainault whether my cousin was a good man. And what had I replied? How wrong I had been.

'Isabella won't allow him to hurt her son.' Edmund spoke the truth.

'He doesn't need to. He can control the king as easily as if he were a piece on the board. And one day he may have a son of his own - a royal son.'

The thought of Isabella giving my cousin a son was too much for Edmund.

'He mustn't be allowed to get away with this.'

'How will you stop him?'

'I shall take my brother out of Corfe.'

The little chamber echoed with his words - out of Corfe. Sir John had told us about the castle which was vast and impregnable. A mighty fortress, perched high on the rocks, guarding a gap in the hills and a path which led down to the sea. Edmund's brother would never be brought out of there alive.

'Dearest, think carefully. You could be putting all our lives at risk. Think of the children.'

'My son will not want a coward for a father.'

'If you go ahead with this he may not have a father at all.'

We stared at each other in horror. Whatever Edmund did was dangerous. To do nothing might still result in a plot to dispose of us as Edmund's relationship with the one-time king and his antagonism towards my cousin made him an obvious target.

Ice filled a pit in my belly. I had been horribly naïve to think my shared past with my cousin would save us. If Edmund was discovered trying to free his brother, his life would be worth nothing. My cousin wouldn't let him live. And trying to restore the prisoner at Corfe to the throne could only lead to more bloodshed.

Edmund spoke gently. 'I am not alone, Margaret. I have the blessing of His Holiness. He was glad to give it.'

'You told him?'

'That was the purpose of our visit.'

He had hidden this from me. I presumed his lengthy discussion with the Holy Father had concerned Earl Thomas.

'Did he believe you?'

'He gave me his blessing.'

'Will he help?'

'No. But he won't interfere. I think he is uncomfortable at what Isabella and your cousin did and is pleased someone is to put matters right. It offended him greatly to have an anointed king put aside in the way that my brother was.'

Once we returned to Arundel Edmund went ahead with preparations for the rescue of his brother. And because I knew he would do it better with my help, I became a party to his plans. Late night meetings occurred in shadowy alleyways and secret conversations were held while men rode side by side along the highways. Messages were passed furtively from hand to hand when no-one was looking and here at Arundel strangers entered quietly with no fanfares and slunk up the stairs in silence to join Edmund in the private chamber above the chapel.

Late January. It was bitterly cold and I was wrapped in my warmest fur-lined mantle, crouching by the fire.

'Who have we got?'

Edmund turned over his list.

'Melton. He's arranging the money and the clothes. He assures me there's a merchant in London who will supply what is needed. My de Monthermer cousin; Stephen

Gravesend, the bishop of London; a host of men you've never heard of, men who were in my brother's household. Zouche whom you know; Fulk Fitzwarrin who was with me in Gascony; the abbot of Langdon; dozens of lesser clergy: friars, monks and the like; Hamo Chigwell, the Londoner. And not least, Sir John Gymmynges - he's providing the boats.'

'Boats? More than one?'

'We need three: a shallow-draught boat, a coastal cog and a sea-going vessel; one for each stage of the journey. We'll take my brother from Corfe out into deep water, and round the coast to here. Once he's rested and changed his clothes I'll travel with him across the sea.'

Because I was a woman who never trusted anyone to arrange matters properly, I couldn't let it rest there. 'Pecche said the coast at Corfe is wild. Are you sure it's safe for your boats?'

'Gymmynges says we go through the marshes to a large inland pool and from there the tidal race will take us out across the sandbar. He says it's safer than making directly for the sea because if the escape is discovered that's the way the guard will assume we've gone. He says his is the least dangerous route. Once over the bar we hug the coast keeping far enough out not to arouse suspicion. We make for Portsmouth and from there they say it's just a short journey round to the mouth of the Arun.'

I couldn't imagine entertaining Edmund's brother here at Arundel. Would he expect a king's welcome? Probably not. If I had spent two years in an underground tomb I would want rest and food and nothing more. But I had to decide which rooms to set aside and have them made ready.

Edmund took my hands in his and raised me up. 'I know you would rather I didn't do this, Margaret.'

I looked him straight in the eye. There was no use in pretending. 'No. I wish it didn't have to be done. I wish it had never happened. But it has, and although I think you are being careless with our lives I can understand why you feel it necessary.'

He pulled me close. 'It is a matter of loyalty. I love you, Margaret.'

'Do you? Are you sure it isn't your conscience pricking you?'

I blinked furiously. I would not let him see me cry.

'My dearest. How long have we been married? Four years? Four years, two children and this.' He patted my belly. 'How could I regret it?'

'But I sometimes fear you do.'

He sighed. 'No, Margaret, I don't. But what about you? Do you feel more for me than simple gratitude?'

I stood still within the circle of his arms fighting the memories.

He tightened his hold. 'Do you love me, Margaret?'

'What do you think?'

He stroked my cheek with great deliberation, running his fingers slowly down my skin. For a soldier, his hands were amazingly gentle.

'My mother used to say that love is a most uncomplicated feeling. Don't fight it, she said. Accept it. You don't choose who to love. I didn't choose to love you, my dearest Margaret; it just happened. But your heart is so full of the memories of that boy you married more than fifteen years ago that I sometimes fear you have no room for me.'

'That's not true. Of course I love you.'

I pulled myself away from him. I knew I was going to cry and I didn't want him to see me weep. I crouched down by the fire where he couldn't see my face. Did I love him? He was my husband, the father of my children and I had wanted so very much to marry him.

I had loved John with an uncomplicated love in those far away days at Mansfield. But with Edmund there had been evasion and pretence, right from the start. He had not wanted marriage, he had merely wanted to possess me, and despite his protestations, he had not been prepared to go against his king. It had taken pressure from my brother to persuade him otherwise and that still hurt, even after six years.

He knelt down beside me. 'Margaret.'

Tears trickled down my cheeks and onto my hands. Why was it so easy to cry and so difficult to tell him how much he had hurt me? Why could I not tell him what I truly felt?

'You'll put out the fire if you carry on like this,' he said gently.

The plan was almost ready. We spent the evening going through it in detail making sure that nothing was forgotten. There would be horses where horses were needed and boatmen to man the boats; provisions in case the prisoner was weakened by hunger; warm clothing and boots because nights were cold by the sea; and small coins for bribes because you never knew who you might stumble across. And our men would be well armed.

We waited for the Lady Philippa's coronation at Westminster because Edmund was to ride in the procession. He and his brother were to escort the new queen as she rode through the city streets from the Tower to the royal palace at Westminster. Then there would be the parliament at Winchester and after that Edmund said he and his men would make a move.

The moment had almost come. Every morning I expected discovery and soldiers at the gate, but everything remained peaceful. The days passed in quiet domesticity and I tried not to worry.

'They don't suspect me,' Edmund said after a meeting where my cousin and Isabella had been present. 'Now, come and sit down. I need you to write a letter for me.'

I fetched the ink and parchment from the corner table where I kept my chest of private things, and sat down. Edmund stood behind me, his hand resting lightly on my shoulder. I could hear the creak of his leather boots as he shifted his position, and to one side there was a movement as the logs in the hearth slid and settled, disturbing the bed of ash below.

I felt the brush of his fingers as he pulled aside my veil; then the warmth of his breath on the back of my neck. His lips touched my skin with infinite gentleness. Once, twice, three times. Small kisses. I sat very still not wanting to disturb the moment.

'*Worshipful and dear brother.*' Edmund began with a formal greeting. '*Soon you shall come out of your prison and be delivered … I have the assent of almost all the great lords of England …*'

'Is that true? Almost all?'

'Just write, Margaret. I wouldn't say it if it wasn't true.'

He continued dictating and I kept silent. He didn't need my questions.

'... *so you shall be king again as you were before, and all of them – prelates, earls and barons – have sworn this to me upon a book.*'

'You told me he would go overseas. You said he wouldn't remain here. Are you mad? Do you plan to host a rival court at Arundel?'

I was angry, but Edmund was calm.

'Margaret, you don't know my brother. Do you imagine he will want to slink off across the Narrow Sea? If I want him out of there, I have to make him believe he is going to be king again. Otherwise he might as well throw himself off the castle walls. Squatting at Philip's feet in Paris for the rest of his life would not be an attractive thought.'

Pushing my worries to the back of my mind, I finished the letter and passed it to Edmund to sign. He handled the quill inexpertly; he didn't care for writing. I had been his scribe in private matters since the early days of our marriage when he discovered what I could do. In my bleaker moments I had comforted myself with the knowledge that I was necessary to him for some things.

He sealed the packet with his personal seal and tucked it into his jacket.

'I'll get this to John Deverill.'

'Is he one of us?'

'He's being paid well and is anxious to help. We were lucky to find such a man in the garrison at Corfe. Only a few more weeks now, sweetheart. Stop worrying.'

'And Donald of Mar?'

'We've had a message. He is sitting on the northern border promising forty thousand men if force is needed.'

'And your brother Norfolk?'

'Ah, Thomas. Now there's a problem. Caught in a bind, is Thomas. Did you know he married his boy to one of your cousin's daughters? Last summer while we were overseas. A Mortimer daughter-in-law! He considers it a good match.'

I nodded. I had been told. Two more great marriages for two of my cousin's girls: Beatrice to Lord Norfolk's son and Agnes to the Pembroke heir, young Laurence Hastings. These alliances were yet another rung up the ladder to the very top.

Edmund frowned. His brother Norfolk was continually giving him cause for concern.

'He tells me he must consider his ties to the Mortimers as well as his loyalty to our brother. So you see, my brother Thomas is committed, but not doing much to help. And he says his wife is sick.'

A poor excuse. I couldn't see Norfolk at the bedside, tenderly wiping sweat from the brow of the little coroner's daughter. He'd more likely be off with his wild companions, drinking and gambling. I had always thought him a fair-weather friend but it worried me if he was distancing himself from Edmund. Did he know things that we didn't? Had he heard something?

Edmund was gone a week and came back weary from too much rich food and too much celebrating. Philippa, he said, had looked very lovely and every inch the queen of England. He was an obliging husband and described, as best he could, the fur cape and cap she wore, the sumptuous gowns of crimson and green and silver and gold, the jewelled clasps, the crowns - everything.

It had been a hardship to miss such an occasion but I truly was too far gone with this child. I would have looked like a dumpling waddling about and I didn't want women sniggering behind their hands - so inelegant, such a poor marriage!

'I never thought her a pretty girl but she did Edward proud,' said Edmund, leaning back while the boy pulled off his boots. 'Even Isabella was put in the shade, and that takes some doing.'

I smiled to think of Isabella's annoyance. She had never wanted Philippa to have any of this: no separate household, no dowered estates, no money, no coronation. If she could have produced an heir for her son without allowing Philippa into his bed, she would have done that joyfully.

We passed the next two weeks checking and rechecking the plan. Edmund said he had received private visits from would-be supporters while he was in London and many offers of money. The last day we spent together with the children and then it was time for Edmund to leave for the parliament in Winchester.

I went out into the courtyard to see him go. As he rode out under the gatehouse he turned and raised his arm in salute. Edmund was twenty-eight years old but still heart-stoppingly handsome.

Just before he disappeared into the shadows under the narrow archway, a shaft of sunlight caught the polished hilt of his sword and slid off the scarlet and blue of his clothing. It reminded me of a morning a lifetime ago - the same colours, the same cheerful wave, the same refusal to consider the danger. It was John riding off to war up the sandy track at Mansfield, John who said I mustn't worry, John who promised he would return but who never came back.

I remembered that day as clearly as if it was yesterday. I was young, he was young and we were very much in love. I thought our marriage was blessed and would last forever and that the strength of my love would keep him safe. But I was wrong.

Edmund said he would come back and I believed him. Ten days he said. Ten at the most. There wasn't much business to deal with at the parliament but he would let me know if he was going to be delayed. Winchester wasn't far. That morning in bed he had kissed me in my drowsiness and promised he would be back for the birth of our child.

And so I waited.

14

ARUNDEL 1330

On the sixth day, I was resting in my solar when I heard footsteps running up the stairs. One of my women burst into the room.

'There are soldiers in the hall, my lady. They are asking for you.'

She was wide-eyed and breathless. Of course none of them knew anything about Edmund's plan but she was afraid. I could smell her fear.

I swung my legs off the rumpled day bed and struggled to my feet.

'Help me with my clothing.'

I had no wish to entertain visitors in my solar and would have to make the effort to go downstairs. Holding tightly to the rail I walked slowly down to greet these men, whoever they were. It was as well I did because, as I appeared at the turn of the stairs, one of them already had his foot on the bottom step.

'Please return to the hall,' I said in my firmest voice.

He was half in the gloom, his back to the light, a typical man-at-arms: burly, rough and mannerless.

'Ah! The lady of the castle. And not a moment too soon. I was coming to get you.' His voice was deep with an accent I couldn't place.

He retreated a few steps until finally we were both

standing in the hall. The servants were gathered around the edges of the room looking nervous. My steward was helpless with a man at his back.

'What is this?' I demanded.

'You are Margaret, wife of Sir Edmund, earl of Kent.'

'I am.'

My legs were trembling but I felt fire warming my belly. How dare this man interrogate me! Then I noticed the keys to our castle in his hand.

'My name is Nicholas Langeford. I have here a warrant for your arrest, my lady. You are to come with me, you and your children.'

He held out a letter. It bore the royal seal. There was no doubt it was official. It was short and very much to the point. I was to be taken by these men to Salisbury Castle and delivered into the custody of the sheriff. I was to bring my children and two damsels, no more. My jewels and all my goods were to be seized.

'Where is my husband?' I said, my thoughts rushing about wildly. 'Where is the earl?'

Master Langeford exchanged a glance with his nearest companion.

'The earl is imprisoned at Winchester, my lady. I understand he is to stand trial for his crimes.'

It had happened just as I had feared. Edmund in prison. A trial. Sweet Holy Virgin! Who had betrayed us?

'My husband has done nothing wrong.'

The man's face was impassive. 'It has nothing to do with me, my lady. I merely carry out my orders. Now if you please - your jewels.'

330

He was looking at the rings on my fingers. I quickly withdrew my hands into the loose sleeves of my gown.

'No use, my lady. We'll be taking them all. That's what our orders are. I am to deliver them to Master Holyns here. He indicated a man in black, clearly the king's clerk. Now, are you going to make this easy for us or not? I have no wish to use violence on anybody, least of all a woman, and especially not with children in the house.'

I turned to my maid who was hovering behind me. 'Go and fetch my silver coffer from the solar and give it to this man.'

As she turned to leave, Master Langeford nodded to one of his men. 'Follow her. We don't want any of this stuff disappearing.'

He looked me straight in the face. I knew exactly what he was doing. I'd seen animals look at other animals this way. He was assessing my strength as an adversary. Eventually he smiled.

'Now my lady, the items on your person if you please. Those rings and the jewelled clasp.'

I kept my hands where they were. He took a step towards me. One of my men made a move and was struck a blow to the head. He collapsed on the floor.

'Order your household to behave, please, my lady. It really would be best for everybody. Don't forget, this is an order given under the king's seal. Resisting such orders can be seen as treason.'

There must have been at least a dozen of them crowded into the room; all armed and clearly ready to use violence if necessary. The king's clerk, the man in dusty black, looked mild enough, but I was sure Master

Langeford would delight in ripping the rings off my fingers if I didn't surrender them quietly. Slowly I twisted the little emerald from the middle finger of my left hand. The flesh had become swollen these past weeks but whatever it took I would not allow Master Langeford the satisfaction of laying hands on my person.

'That's better, my lady. Now the other one.'

The twisted gold band studded with sapphires came off more easily. Then I unfastened the pearl and ruby clasp on my shoulder. As I dropped it into the hand of the clerk's assistant, my maid returned silently, holding the silver coffer.

I waited. I would offer them nothing. They would have to ask for every single thing. Master Langeford tried to open the lid. It was locked.

'The key, if you please, my lady.'

I smiled at him. 'The key?'

'A pretty little box. I doubt my lord would be pleased if it got broken. So, please, the key.'

Slowly I raised my gaze to the hanging at the far end of the hall. I stared at it as if contemplating a problem.

With frightening speed his face was thrust into mine. His filthy boots brushed the folds of my skirts and his rough soldier's jacket pressed hard against my body. I could smell the sweat on him.

'Don't play games, my lady. Give me the key or I'll rip your fancy clothing apart.'

I had no doubt he would do just that. Slowly I lifted up the purse I kept fastened to my girdle and removed the small key which opened the coffer. I handed it to the clerk's assistant.

'That's better.'

The rage I felt at seeing them count out my treasures was enormous. How dare they put their dirty hands on my beloved jewels? As the heavy gold and ruby ring was removed I felt a stab of pain. Edmund's mother's ring, the one he had given to me as a token of his love. Every one of these jewels had been a gift from Edmund; all except for the little garnet ring given to me by John on the day we were wed.

While the clerk and his assistant busied themselves with my valuables, Master Langeford was looking round the room, his eyes pausing at each sign of wealth.

'Right my lady, we'll deal with this later. In the meantime, tell your women to get the children ready. I've ordered a cart. You can have two women to travel with the children. You will ride alongside me.'

Oh how sweet it was to defeat a man like Master Langeford. I put on my most docile face and unwrapped my mantle so that he could see the vast extent of my swollen belly.

'I think you might be making a mistake. Unless, of course, you are skilled at midwifery. I don't recall how many days journey it is to Salisbury but giving birth in a roadside ditch is, I think, a strong possibility. I cannot imagine the king meant you to subject me to that.'

He looked in disgust at my belly.

'How soon?'

I smiled. 'One day, two days, a week. These matters are in the hands of God but I would wager a jolting ride will hasten matters along. Have you ever seen a birth, Master Langeford? Bloody affairs. Not for the faint-hearted.'

He had a hurried conversation with one of the other men, then turned back to me. My thoughts were darting around in my head. If Edmund had been taken did that mean the whole plot had been discovered? What of the others? Could the rescue from Corfe go ahead without Edmund? What if men arrived at Arundel bringing Edmund's brother?

Whatever else, I must strive to remain here and to remain calm. The children would be better cared for at Arundel. I knew nothing of Salisbury, but whatever the castle was like I doubted my accommodation there would be comfortable. Perhaps two rooms, like Eleanor. Two rooms, and for how long? And where would they put Edmund? The Tower in all probability, or a cold northern castle, like Pontefract. My poor Edmund.

'You are to remain here under guard until your child is born, my lady. Then we shall travel to Salisbury. I have sent a man to pick suitable accommodation for you and your children. I regret it may not be what you are used to but that is the way for those imprisoned by royal command.'

'I am certain you will have a care for my comforts. It's never wise to incur the enmity of those who appear to have fallen as men and women can rise high again. Fortune's wheel turns for us all, Master Langeford.'

We were locked in two of the smallest and meanest rooms in the castle, at the top of one of the towers. Master Langeford's man must have taken great delight in selecting them. There was one small window in the larger room, too high to give me a view of anything other than the sky. And it was cold.

Our comforts were meagre and the guard on the stairs ensured that nobody could smuggle in any luxuries. The maids shared a small pallet while the children and I took the bed. Food and ale were brought to us once a day by one of Master Langeford's men. There was precious little meat or fish; it was mostly bread, and a bucket of indifferent pottage.

For our personal use we had a covered pail in one corner. I had never lived in such conditions and found it utterly disgusting. Even when fleeing from Paris, our rooms in the inns and hostelries on the road had been better than this. I was not allowed to leave my prison rooms so had no way of discovering what had happened to Edmund. There were always travellers and someone must have had news from Winchester but shut away like this, I was helpless. My maids made occasional visits to the laundry but were always accompanied and not permitted any conversation.

Each evening as it was getting dark, Master Nicholas Langeford came to see me. He would sit himself down on a stool, fold his arms and wait for me to speak.

'You have news of my husband?' Every evening I asked and every evening the answer was the same.

'No.'

I might have wanted something from my gaoler, however he wanted something from me.

'No child yet?' He eyed me suspiciously.

'No.'

'Tonight perhaps?'

'Perhaps.'

The conversation never varied.

After two weeks Master Langeford had had enough. Infuriated that he could not just order this birth, I could see him wondering if it was just a pillow beneath my gown.

He usually found me lying on my bed which is where I spent most of the day trying to rid myself of the pains in my ankles. At first I would spring up, unwilling to be found at such a disadvantage but as the days passed I became too weary to move.

'Still nothing?'

I smiled sweetly, although I was feeling anything but sweet.

'No.'

'I have my doubts you have a child in there. I think I shall send a woman to examine you, then we'll get to the bottom of this. And if I find you've played a trick on me, my lady, I'll make sure you regret it.'

'Would you not rather place your hand on my belly, Master Langeford?' I fixed his eyes with mine, challenging him. 'I'm sure you know the difference between a woman's flesh and a feather bolster.'

He was tempted. Oh how he was tempted. I read it in the flicker of his eyes and the moistening of his lips.

'We can settle this matter here and now. You've degraded me in practically every other way. Why not go one step further and violate my person? Would you like me to draw back my robe? I'm sorry I cannot actually show you the child but I would imagine that once you see my belly in the flesh you will be satisfied I am telling you the truth.'

His eyes slid away.

'I shall send a woman.'

But he never did.

Eight days later my son was born. Mercifully it was quick. In that stinking little room, with no herbs to numb the pain and no midwife to help me, I could not have endured a lengthy birth. My maid did her best while the younger girl kept the children in the other room.

I screamed. What woman does not scream at a time like this? I hoped the whole castle could hear me scream. I particularly hoped Master Nicholas Langeford could hear me scream.

'It's a boy,' said my maid busying herself with the child.

John, I thought. I shall call him John. Edmund would be happy because it was my father's name and therefore entirely suitable. But I also named him for my first husband, for the young man who had left me long ago. Tears rolled down my cheeks and I wondered why I was crying when, despite everything, I should be joyful. I had a live child - Edmund's child.

That evening Master Langeford returned. He brought with him a small wooden object.

'For the child,' he said awkwardly holding out a little carved animal.

I lay there, cradling the baby in my arms and felt generous. If he was making amends then so could I.

'Thank you,' I said, as graciously as one can, lying propped up on a single pillow, covered by a grubby coverlet.

'I have arranged for a priest, my lady'

A hasty baptism and some furtive questions! At last there was hope of news. A priest, however miserable a man he might be, would know something of what was happening outside the walls of his church.

'My lady. The matter of the child's godparents. As there is no-one suitable, if it is agreeable to you, I myself would …'

What! A low-born man like my gaoler! I shuddered.

'Master Langeford, a man like you is not worthy to kiss the hem of my child's swaddling cloth. My son and my daughter will carry out this duty.'

He flushed and it occurred to me, too late, that he was simply trying to be kind.

But his kindness did not extend to allowing me a conversation with a priest. On his orders, the baby was carried by one of my women while the other took the hands of my older children and led them away. I was left utterly alone.

'It was the priory church, my lady,' whispered my maid on her return. 'The prior himself named and blessed the babe and laid him in the arms of young Lady Joan. I were that worried she'd drop him.'

The days passed slowly. I had nothing to do but attend to my child. He was a puny little thing, not strong like Mondi, and it was a strange experience to put him to my breast. I had no wet-nurse so needs must feed the child myself. At first I was shocked by the visceral tugging at my nipples and the way he pummelled my flesh, but gradually I began to enjoy it. It was a strangely satisfying feeling. I watched the tiny fuzz of hair on top of his head as he sucked greedily and admired the way he always knew where to find my breast. Yes, I thought. In many ways he is quite lovely.

Mondi and Joan were fascinated by the baby, always hovering over the bed, wanting to touch him. Eventually, tired of the fuss, I snapped at them and then wept because I had been unkind when there was no need. The maids stared at me fearfully, unused to this strange tearful woman.

I expected to be ordered to Salisbury Castle at any moment but Master Langeford said nothing. The days dragged by with unbelievable slowness and with each one, my hopes of release diminished. I had been forgotten by everyone except by my gaoler who still visited daily.

It was getting warmer. Summer must be here. I tried to keep a tally of the days but without the rhythms of the church to remind me, each day was like the one before and the one after. I could hear bells but it was hard to know one from the other and gradually, without my even realising, the days lengthened into weeks and the weeks into months.

One day, when I despaired of things ever changing and thought we would be shut away like this for ever, I had a visitor. I heard a commotion from down below, a man's voice shouting, a clatter and some more noise. I'd not heard horses but my heart leapt. Edmund had returned! He would throw out these interlopers and rescue me.

'Make haste!' I said to the maids. 'Take the children into the other room in case there's violence.'

I stood with my back to the wall furthest from the door to the stairs and tried to calm myself. Edmund wouldn't want me to be cowering in fear, he would expect me to be brave.

But it wasn't Edmund. It was my cousin.

The door swung wide open and he walked in: tall, commanding, magnificently dressed, and looking distinctly annoyed.

'Lady Margaret, I didn't expect to find you here.' His voice was rough with irritation.

'I didn't expect to be here.'

I wasn't going to let him frighten me. I pushed to the forefront of my mind the fact that he was my cousin and had once cared for me.

'They tell me you've birthed that inconvenient child you were carrying.'

'I have.'

'And are you enjoying your new living quarters? I'm sorry if they disappoint you but I told the men you were a resourceful young woman and needed locking up well if you weren't to escape.'

Anger rose in my throat. 'Have you come to tell me what you have done with my husband or have you come merely to gloat?'

He began to walk round the room looking at my few meagre belongings. He picked up a pair of hose which needed mending, turning them over in his hands as if he had never seen such things before. What a change from the magnificence of his own existence this must be? All that finery, all those silver goblets, all those embroidered silken sheets!

'You don't have to stay here, you know,' he said casually. 'I could arrange for you to be released.'

I was immediately suspicious.

He tossed the hose back onto the table. 'The Lady Eleanor used to live like this with no warmth, no light,

340

just the most basic of comforts. I expect her gaoler fed her; they don't like their prisoners to die, it spoils their fun. But I decided to make it possible for her to leave. She has returned to conjugal bliss with Lord Zouche, much good may it do him.'

So Lord Zouche had not been taken. My heart leapt. There was hope for us yet.

'Where have you put my husband? What have you done with him?'

He ignored my question.

'The Lady Eleanor proved very sensible. She took some persuading but in the end had the wit to see that my solution was for the best. She had no greater desire to spend the rest of her days locked up in the dark than I had to keep her there. So we came to an accommodation.'

'What did she give you?'

'Give me? My dear Margaret, you must think I have no sense. And before you ask, I didn't lay a finger on her. She didn't look too pretty when I saw her but I understood she had been unwell.'

He pulled the stool over with his foot and sat down, hitching up the fur trimming on his cloak so that it didn't brush the floor. He thrust out his legs and leaned back against the wall, half closing his eyes.

'The Lady Eleanor agreed to return her lands to the crown - all those lovely fertile acres in Glamorgan.'

He smiled, relishing the thought.

'I don't believe you,' I said. 'Lady Eleanor would never give up Glamorgan, least of all to you.'

'But I was very generous; she can have it all back one day.'

'How? What terms did she agree to?'

He smiled. 'Oh you are quick, Margaret. How I like your mind. I was never much attracted by your body, you've not enough flesh on you for my taste, but I've always admired your intelligence. Fifty thousand crowns and she can have her lands back.'

'She'll raise that. You won't keep them.'

'I haven't finished. Fifty thousand crowns to be paid all on one day.'

He smiled. 'You should have seen her face when she realised what that meant, but by then I had the release order in my hand. So, admittedly with a certain degree of reluctance, she signed.'

It was obvious he had come to bargain with me but what did I have that he could possibly covet?

'I suppose you want my manor.'

He laughed.

'Mansfield? That dog-hole? What on God's earth makes you think I'd want that? No, no, Margaret. I don't want your lands.'

I started to shiver. Despite what he had said, surely he wasn't going to violate me? Not here?'

'You've taken my jewels.'

'Indeed I have. Isabella was pleased to receive them; you know how much she appreciates trinkets. She was greatly taken with your gold and ruby ring. Perhaps she's wearing it this very moment.'

He gave me an assessing look, weighing something in his mind.

'What I want from you, my dear cousin, is information.'

'I'll tell you nothing.'

'Oh I think you will. I know how much you care for your husband.'

'What have you done with him?'

'All in good time. First, the name of the man who told you about my prisoner.'

So he didn't know about Pecche. I wondered if he knew anything at all or if he was just guessing. He must have discovered something or he wouldn't have risked arresting Edmund and imprisoning me. But Edmund would not have talked. Edmund was far too loyal to have betrayed his friends.

'You are so transparent, dear Margaret. You are thinking your husband told me nothing but I can assure you he sang like a little bird.'

'You're a liar.'

'No. It's God's truth, my dear. Men do. There are ways and means to extract information and no man is immune. Your husband told me a lot but I think there is more. He was most unwilling to reveal the name of his informant, spun me a story about friars who conjured up devils. I didn't believe him so I thought you might like to tell me. To avoid further unpleasantness.'

'You can do what you like but if my husband won't tell you then neither will I.'

He got up and walked across the floor towards me, smiling. I remained as still as I could, trying in vain to stop my legs from trembling. He had me trapped against the wall and there was no possibility of escape. He put up his right hand and pulled the cap from my head leaving my hair and neck exposed. Then with the infinite slowness of a lover he placed his fingers delicately round my throat.

He didn't squeeze, but the threat was everywhere. It permeated the air between us, thick and menacing. With his thumb he began to stroke the tender pulse at the base of my neck. I lowered my lashes, not wanting to see the look in his eyes.

'It would be so easy to break you, little cousin,' he murmured. 'I could rip off those fragile feathers you wear and crush your bones with my fist. I might even find a degree of pleasure in doing so. But that's not why I'm here. I'm offering you a deal. You want something from me and, provided you do as I say, I'll give it to you. How's that for a kindness?'

I didn't trust him an inch.

'What do you want? You've taken my jewels and my plate. I doubt there's anything of value left to steal.'

'Not valuables, cousin. Information. Names, dates, places. That's what I want. We have most of your husband's friends already: faithful Archbishop Melton, and poor Fitzwarin; old Sir Ingelram Berenger and the Despenser crew. They'll soon be under lock and key singing their hearts out. But I remembered about your prodigious memory and I'm sure you have a list of your fellow conspirators, right here.'

He placed his hands across my brow and squeezed very slightly. It was agonisingly painful and I almost screamed.

'If you think I'll give one single piece of information for you to use against my husband, you are very much mistaken.'

He took his hands away and gripped my shoulders.

'This is your own fault, Margaret. I warned you often enough. You should have left well alone. You shouldn't have interfered. People who get in my way get hurt. Now …' He pushed one of his legs hard up against my skirts so that I couldn't move. 'The name. Before I lose patience.'

'No.'

I kept telling myself he wouldn't really hurt me because I was his cousin and a woman. I kept telling myself to be brave, to be strong.

His eyes glittered with anger. Then with a sigh he stepped away.

'Very well, if that's the way you want to play the game, that's how we'll play it. But don't say you weren't given a chance.'

He'd reached the door before I realised he was leaving. I ran swiftly across the floor and grabbed hold of his sleeve.

'For pity's sake, cousin, tell me what you've done with my husband. Where have you put him?'

He shook me off like an intrusive insect. He stood there, one hand holding the iron ring of the door, the other adjusting the collar on his robe, and smiled.

'Your husband? Didn't I say? We had him executed two months ago.'

I opened my mouth but no words came out.

'He was a traitor and he confessed. He had to, the evidence was overwhelming. Mind you, it was a beautifully written letter, Margaret, you must have taken a great deal of care in writing it. Naturally it wasn't intended for me and I'm certain you never expected it to end up in my hands.'

'Deverill,' I whispered.

'Yes. John Deverill. A sensible man. Gave his loyalty to his king, which as you know means giving it to me. Unlike your husband, who seemed unsure as to where his loyalties lay. I thought he was still with us but I was mistaken.'

'How could you do it?'

'Me? I did nothing. The king signed the order, not me. I merely brought matters to the attention of the court. And yes, Margaret, it was a proper trial. The king's coroner was there. When your husband realised they were going to have him killed, he wanted to make amends; he offered to walk to London with a rope around his neck in just his shirt. It was a pathetic sight, him pleading for mercy. The lords were unanimous in their verdict: loss of life and limb and nothing for his heirs, save for the king's mercy and clearly the king was not feeling merciful on that particular day.

'It was you. You and Isabella. You don't fool me. Edward would never have done this. She made him sign. What did she do, hold a knife to his throat?'

'Oh come, Margaret. Can you really imagine the queen harming her beloved son? She didn't need to threaten him.'

'What did she do?' I whispered.

'She talked to him. And you know how persuasive she can be when she sets her mind to something. She could see the danger for us all in what your foolish husband was trying to do and she ensured her son knew what would happen if his uncle was successful. She told him a good king had to make difficult choices and that in the eyes of his people he would be judged, not on misguided merciful acts, but on his strength. Then she gave him the order to sign.'

I raised my hands to claw at his eyes, at his face, at any part of him I could reach. I hated him more than I had hated anyone in my life and if I'd possessed a knife, I would have killed him. But he caught my wrists and twisted my hands to one side until I cried out in pain. Then he pushed me away and rubbed his hands down his tunic as if to rid himself of the stain touching me.

He stood looking at me for a moment and in his face there was no trace of my cousin any more. This man was the ruler of all England, the man who controlled the king, and there was nothing I could do.

'When I get out of here I'll hunt you down and tear you apart,' I said in a low voice. 'And if I don't, my curses will follow you to your grave.'

He laughed. 'You won't get out. I shall have your children removed but you will stay here. And remember, little cousin, in the years to come as you grow old and withered and pale, that it was your choice to die here, shut away from the world. Your choice, not mine. You could have told me what I wanted to know but you chose to keep silent. Sweet dreams, Margaret, I doubt we shall meet again.'

The door clanged shut. The sound of his boots descending the stone stairway could just be heard. Then another bang as the lower door slammed.

I was perfectly calm. I felt as cold as ice. The words my cousin had spoken remained somewhere else, somewhere where they had no meaning.

Edmund was dead. Two months ago and I hadn't known.

I endured six months of penance. There was time to examine each one of my sins and time to pray to the Holy Mother of God who in her goodness would surely show me what to do. But she didn't answer.

It had been my fault. I could see that now. Without my interference Edmund would never have known his brother was alive in Corfe Castle. He would never have heard of the boots which didn't fit and what the embalming woman had said. He would never have heard of the man who was not his brother who had been put in the coffin at Berkeley to deceive us all.

He would have dismissed John Pecche as a stupid man with too much imagination. He would never have encountered Sir Ingemar Berenger and they would never have hatched their ill-conceived plan. Everything that had happened had been my fault.

Time slipped by in an endless void. I completed my daily tasks. I talked to my children and spoke occasionally to my maids. But every night I crouched low on my knees, trying in the eyes of God to right the wrongs I had done.

Edmund would not have joined with my cousin and Isabella if I had not persuaded him to do so, and without Edmund the invasion might not have taken place. It was Edmund who brought his brother Norfolk with him and opened up the landing grounds of the east to our ships. Without his name on Isabella's letters and petitions her words would not have carried the weight they did. The queen and the queen's son might have been a welcome sight to the king's enemies but it was the support of the king's two brothers which added legitimacy to their rebellion.

If, in Paris I had urged Edmund to come home to England and retire to our country manors, we would have raised our children together in peace. We would have loved and lived and grown old and none of this would have happened.

As I prayed my face was awash with tears of grief and shame until I realised that tears were self-indulgent and what I really deserved was punishment. I should have been the one who suffered the executioner's sword, not my beloved Edmund.

The days became colder, the daylight hours shorter, and Mondi became sick. Our nights were full of his whimpering. He developed a fever and began coughing. I pleaded with Master Langeford to fetch a physician but he said his orders were clear - no visitors under any circumstances. It was more than his life was worth to disobey Lord Mortimer.

'I could bring the boy a cordial,' he said. 'One of the men says he knows a woman in the town who brews them.'

I was touched by the thought. It was unexpected and these days little kindnesses moved me to tears.

The contents of the jug smelt familiar. At Wigmore I was an expert on the various herbs and berries used for medicinal purposes but over the years I had lost my skill. I placed a drop on my tongue. Sweet with a rich smoothness and a burning aftertaste. I gave Mondi a little to drink and he seemed easier. His face was flushed and, although his skin was hot, he complained of the cold.

There was nothing else I could do but pray for him. I didn't sleep but kept watch over him in the night which was when he suffered most. His eyelashes fluttered as he tossed and turned. I prayed for forgiveness. I had sinned but my children were innocent. They had done nothing. This was my doing. Everything was my fault.

We passed the day when the souls of the dead are said to walk the earth and the first frosts were already threatening. One night as I lay, trying to keep warm, wrapped tightly in my coverlet, I heard noises: faraway shouting, banging, a man's footsteps on the stairs. It was still dark but it must be nearly morning as there was a faint greyness lapping at the window high on the wall.

Hurriedly I slipped out of bed and threw on my robe and thrust my feet into my shoes. A moment later the door opened and there was Nicholas Langeford holding a lantern. With half my attention I noticed he hadn't closed the door. Usually he was scrupulously careful to make sure I was well locked into my prison, even if he was with me. I also noticed that his boots were polished and his jacket, which had become rather grubby in recent days, had been replaced by a finer one, dark-red with a blue hood. He set the lantern down on the table and then stood very upright holding out a roll of parchment. The seal was broken.

I raised my eyes to his.

'This came, my lady' he said. 'A royal command.'

'What is it?' I was frightened in case this was something worse than what we were enduring at the moment. Was this the order to take my children? Or for my execution?

'It is from the king, my lady.' I barely noticed the softness and the respectful tone of voice. 'It is an order for your release. You are to be …'

I heard nothing else. My knees trembled and my legs gave way and I collapsed on the floor, weeping. I could see nothing. My eyes were blinded by scalding hot tears. This was a trick. This was like the funeral at Gloucester, something designed to deceive. It couldn't be true. He said I would die here. He said I would never come out.

'My lady! Please.' Master Langeford bent over me and placed his hand gently on my shoulder. 'My lady. Don't weep. Please don't weep. This is good news for you. Good news. It is the best of news. I have ordered your chambers downstairs to be prepared and a meal cooked. The boy is bringing in the logs for your hearth this moment. Soon everything will be ready. You are free, my lady.'

He helped me to my feet.

'Free?'

'Yes, my lady. Free. You do not have to stay here. This order is for your release. You are to be brought to the king at Westminster.'

'To the king?'

'Yes, my lady. Lord Mortimer has fallen. A week ago. The royal messenger said the king's friends seized him at the point of a sword. He's in the Tower this very moment awaiting trial.'

He settled me on the stool and hovered over me like a mother hen with her chicks.

'The king wanted him killed on the spot but it's said the Lady Isabella begged for his life. Bets are on he won't last the week. They say it'll be the rope at Tyburn and there's not many who'll be sorry. He was a bad man.'

'Where is the Lady Isabella?'

He shook his head. 'The messenger thinks maybe Berkhamsted but doesn't know for certain.'

It was over. Oh sweet Holy Mother, it was over. A new day had dawned and they couldn't hurt me any more. I was free and I would be reborn.

351

15

WESTMINSTER 1330

We travelled to Westminster but I was weak and, after so many months shut away, found the light and the noise difficult. I was told the king was busy, much involved in matters of state and making preparations for the parliament. I would have to wait.

When, after two days, our meeting took place I was surprisingly nervous.

He had grown, not just in height, but in royalty. When I had last seen him a year ago, he was a boy, afraid to open his mouth, afraid to look you in the eye, afraid of his own shadow. Now he was truly a king.

'Lady Margaret.' He held out his hand to assist me to a chair. He was full of thoughtfulness and concern.

'Your grace.' I inclined my head, thinking how formal this was. And everything was so glitteringly bright. So many candles.

'Is your son recovered? the queen tells me he has been unwell.'

'Yes, your grace. The Lady Philippa in her kindness called her physician to advise on what should be done and Mondi is much better.'

'We will remember him in our prayers. Now about your estates.'

I thought he would tell me about Edmund but it

seemed he wanted to talk about my dower lands.

'Your grace, may I ask you a question?'

A look of surprise crossed his face.

'Certainly. Subjects may always ask. A king of course cannot guarantee an answer.'

'My husband.'

There was a long silence. I didn't know how to ask what I wanted to know without insulting him but surely he must understand.

'I know things cannot have been as I was told,' I said carefully. 'Lord Mortimer had his own reasons for what he said to me. But there are many things I still do not understand.'

He considered his fingers for a moment and then looked up at me and smiled.

'Do you recall a long time ago when we were in foreign parts, Lady Margaret? I asked you a question and you gave me an answer.'

It was in another time, on our journey to Valenciennes. I remembered the boy asking whether my cousin was a good man.

'Yes,' I whispered. 'I remember.'

'It wasn't true, the answer you gave me; it wasn't true.'

'I wasn't to know, your grace. People change. I truly thought my cousin had your best interests at heart, and later, when I found out that he didn't, it was too late.'

He didn't lose his smile. 'No, you misunderstand me. What I am saying, Lady Margaret, is that an answer is meaningless. You may think it is true but it may not be. So, there is no point in asking me the question, is there?'

'But …'

353

He spoke before I could say anything else.

'My clerks are drawing up a petition for you and your elder son to present to the parliament for the restoration of your lands and your title. You will be wealthy, my lady, and you will be safe.'

'May we go back to Arundel?'

'That will not be possible. Arundel will be returned to the Fitzalan's. It was their castle before it was taken from them and fairness dictates it should be theirs again.'

So Edmund's favourite castle was to be lost. But castles were nothing other than blocks of stone, it was only people who truly mattered.

'Is Lord Mortimer to die?' I asked, already knowing the answer.

'There will be a trial, but yes, he will die. There can be no forgiveness for the sins he committed. He was not the anointed king, yet he behaved as if he was.'

'And your lady mother?'

He smiled. 'My mother has been unwell. She is resting at Berkhamsted, regaining her health and her strength. She is very devout so she will recover, of that I am certain. It may take a while but the queen and I hope she will be well enough to join us for our tournament at Guildford before the Epiphany. The preparations are well under way. It will be a great spectacle. We shall have a mock hunt this time with boar and deer. You must come and bring your son. It is the kind of entertainment a boy would enjoy. Or is he too young? Mine I'm afraid is only a baby.' His gaze softened. 'Have you seen him?'

'Yes, your grace, I have. He looks like you.'

'He does, doesn't he? I named him Edward just as I

said I would. I didn't forget. You see, Lady Margaret, I never forget anything.'

'Your grace, what of your father?'

I had never noticed before how veiled his eyes were - blue as the summer sky, just like Edmund's, but curiously opaque as if there were thoughts he wanted kept hidden.

'My father is dead, Lady Margaret. We buried him at Gloucester. You were there. Surely you remember?'

'But the prisoner …?'

'My mother has my father's heart in a silver vessel. It is a great comfort to her and she says she will take it with her to her grave. She grieves for him, as we all do.'

So this was to be my answer. I was not to know.

I would never know what was found when the king's men went to Corfe. Was the prisoner dead or had the chickens already flown the coop? Whoever had been at Corfe, if anyone had been there at all, I was not to be told. Whatever my cousin had ordered done or not done that September night three years ago was to remain a secret and if I was sensible I would keep my thoughts to myself.

'Yes, your grace,' I said looking down where my hands lay in my lap. 'I understand.'

It didn't matter now. Nothing mattered at all, not now that Edmund was dead.

'What of Lord Berkeley and Sir John Maltravers?' I said bitterly. 'Will they be called to account? Will anyone pay a price other than my husband?'

'Lord Berkeley is to answer to the parliament as is Maltravers. What I believe they and their henchmen did at Lord Mortimer's command was treasonous.'

I should have felt glad. Gurney and Ogle and the

unknown watcher who forged the deceit which led to Edmund's death would be brought to justice. Maltravers would die, as would Meg Mortimer's husband, as would my cousin.

'A word of advice, Lady Margaret.' He hadn't finished with me. He wanted to be sure I understood what was required of me. 'Don't look back. Look forward to the years ahead. You have three children. You are young enough to remarry if you wish. Thank God that you came out of this alive. Not everyone has been so fortunate.'

'I do, your grace. I thank God on my knees each night that I and my husband's children have lived through another day.'

I wondered if any of us would ever know exactly what had happened at Berkeley and at Corfe. Soon my cousin would be hanged; Gurney, Ogle and the watcher would be dead; Maltravers, if he could be caught, would be silenced and nobody would be left alive to tell the tale.

Edward was right. Nothing could undo the past and I must look to the future. I could plant a garden. It would be a suitable penance to dig in the earth again as I had at Mansfield after John died. Perhaps in the long empty years ahead I would have my pear trees. What else was there left for me?

Epilogue

NINETEEN YEARS LATER

The seasons are unravelling. This morning I watched through my tiny solar window as the night sky slid from deepest black to grey to the gauzy violet light which comes before dawn. When the sun rose blood-red above the forest and stained the earth's rim from Clipstone round to Three Thorn Hollow I knew I was afraid. We thought the laws of God were mutable but we were wrong and now death crouches beside every hearth and my friends are dying one by one. In Avignon the papal court lies empty and people say the streets of Paris are full of corpses with no-one left to dig the pits.

It is late and the day has gone from my garden. Soon they will come to carry me in. They disapprove of my staying outside as the shadows gather but I like the peace and in the silence I can escape from the horrors. The evening is warm yet from somewhere amongst the trees a small chill whisper of wind drifts slowly across my hands, disturbing the silk of my sleeves.

Fruit hangs heavy on the boughs of my pear trees, jewels of dull green flushed with gold; a fine crop this year, more than I expected in these dreadful times. The smell of autumn grasses fills the air mixed with the delicate scent of a late summer rose.

It is nearly twenty years since I returned to Mansfield and I have lost so much. Mondi did not live through that

357

first winter. The cough never left him entirely and when the snow came, he closed his eyes and didn't wake.

Our men have gone: Edmund, his brother Norfolk, my cousin Roger, Lord Beaumont, Lord Zouche, and four years ago Earl Henry. He never recovered from what Isabella did to him, we none of us did. He lived on in darkness for more than fifteen years which was probably a greater punishment than any she could have devised.

Now the pestilence has taken the last of them, my brother, Tom. He died quickly, no time for farewells. His wife wrote a letter but I didn't care to read it. What could she say that I didn't already know? Despite my aching bones, I made the effort to travel to Westminster to pay my homage for his lands and see Edward and Philippa for one last time. Four boys and three girls they have, lovely children. As I hoped, they have been truly blessed.

We women have fared little better than the men. This year my friend Lady Abernethy was called to God, leaving me alone. Eleanor didn't live to enjoy her freedom or her wealth but they say those last years with Lord Zouche brought her a degree of happiness. I can't imagine it; she was too much a vixen to be content with a simple man like Zouche.

There are just we three left: Isabella, my cousin's widow and myself. Each one of us is waiting for the others to die; each one of us clinging to life, determined to dance on the grave of her enemy.

I have seen Isabella once since my cousin was hanged. She looked much the same but her sort of beauty wears well. She lives the life of a great lady and it is said she never mentions my cousin. Joan, Lady Mortimer I've not seen.

She asked the king for her husband's bones and took them home to Wigmore, so you could say she was right all along - he did come back to her.

A single flake of snow has settled on the sleeve of my gown. It doesn't melt. From the trees and from the sky more are falling but I see they are not snowflakes, they are blossom - delicate petals of the pear, drifting and circling and softly descending. Around my feet, brushed by the hem of my skirt, the ground has become a carpet of white.

And now, from out of the darkness between the trees, they come. I'm not surprised. I've been expecting them for some time.

First John: my dearest one, the young man who left me far too soon. 'When I return we'll go to Badenoch and make a garden,' he had said, and true to his word he has come back for me.

My cousin Roger: young, fresh-faced, happy, the lord of Wigmore as he once was, stretching out his hand. 'Come little *bwbach*, it's time to go.'

And Edmund, my golden-haired, blue-eyed, handsome husband. Edmund, who brought my frozen heart back to life and gave me my precious children. I did not realise until it was too late how much I truly loved him.

And the children: Mondi, smiling and laughing. Beside him, holding his hand, is Aymer, my firstborn. Their little feet tread softly on the petals as they run. Aymer's face breaks into a wide smile. 'Mama!' he calls. 'Mama! Come here Mama!'

AUTHOR'S NOTE

Only two men paid the ultimate price for the murder of Edward II and the entrapment and execution of Edmund, Earl of Kent - Roger Mortimer and a little-known man called Simon Bereford. If you want to know more about the mystery surrounding Edward II's death and possible afterlife, I would urge you to read *Medieval Intrigue* by Ian Mortimer published by Continuum or *Long Live the King: The Mysterious Fate of Edward II* by Kathryn Warner published by Amberley.

Isabella died at the age of 62, some nine years after Margaret. She was buried, not in Gloucester with her husband, but in the fashionable Greyfriars church in London. According to her wishes she was buried with the clothes she had worn at her wedding some fifty years earlier and with her husband's heart in a silver casket placed on her chest.

Joan, Lady Mortimer died two years before Isabella at the age of seventy. She was probably buried at Wigmore, possibly with her husband.

Several of the people who appear in this book you will meet again in *The Fair Maid of Kent*.

ACKNOWLEDGMENTS

A book, particularly one about a real-life person from the past, does not appear fully formed in an author's mind. Among the many hundreds of books and websites I consulted when writing Margaret's story I would particularly like to mention the following:

Ian Mortimer	*The Greatest Traitor*
Ian Mortimer	*Medieval Intrigue*
Kathryn Warner	*Edward II: The Unconventional King*
Kathryn Warner	*Isabella of France: The Rebel Queen*
Alison Weir	*Isabella: She-Wolf of France, Queen of England*
Kathryn Warner	*edwardthesecond.blogspot.com*

I cannot thank Jackie, Jane, Kat and Ken of the writing group enough for their advice and for their assistance with the editing (not to mention coffee and cake on Wednesday mornings). My thanks go, as always, to Richard for acting as unpaid chauffeur, celebrity photographer, chief publicity agent and part-time chef, and for his unstinting support in what I do.

Also by Caroline Newark

THE PEARL OF FRANCE

It is 1299 and as part of a treaty of peace between England and France, Marguerite, the nineteen-year-old sister of the French king, is married to her brother's enemy, the elderly Edward I. Marguerite expects nothing from this marriage other than a lifetime of dutiful obedience. But Edward is a man experienced in the art of pleasing a woman and awakens unexpected passions in his young bride.

Used by her stepchildren as a peacemaker and by her husband as a vessel for the sons he craves, Marguerite believes she is content until she comes to desire a man who is not her husband and whose interests run counter to those of the king. But when the quicksands of a Scottish war move beneath her feet and her beloved stepson rebels against his father, she is engulfed in a nightmare of brutal conquest and barbarous retribution.

The Pearl of France tells the story of a royal marriage where passion runs high and jealousy bites deep but nothing can protect you from your husband's world of treachery, murder and hideous bloody revenge.

THE FAIR MAID OF KENT

It is 1341 and Joan, the beautiful young cousin of the king of England, is poised on the brink of marriage with the earl of Salisbury's son. While plans are made for the king's continuing war against France the families gather to celebrate the wedding. But the bride is in tears. For unknown to everyone, Joan has a secret and it is one so scandalous, so unspeakably shocking, that discovery could destroy this glorious marriage and place the lives of those Joan loves in danger.

Faced with a jealous and increasingly suspicious husband Joan must tread a careful path precariously balanced between truth and deception, where love is an illusion and one false step could spell disaster.

From the glittering court of Edward III to the lonely border fortress of Wark and the bleak marshlands before the walls of Calais, *The Fair Maid of Kent* tells the story of an enduring love in a dangerous world where a man may not be all he seems and your most powerful enemy is the one you cannot see.

Coming Soon

AN ILLEGITIMATE AFFAIR

It is 1374. The prince is dying, the king is in his dotage and the vultures are circling the throne. The heir is not the powerful duke of Lancaster but seven-year-old Richard, half-brother of Alys's husband, Thomas Holand.

Alys is the daughter of the earl of Arundel and does not care for her husband. She considers him dull, unambitious and a disappointment in every sense and yearns for the young man to whom she was once betrothed. But her view of a golden past is shattered when her father dies and she learns of a monstrous deceit.

Later when her husband's brother, John, is accused of murder, Alys offers to help despite her instinctive disgust at his wild and unprincipled behaviour. She has been warned of the dangers and thinks she knows how to protect herself but ultimately knows only half the story.

From elegant riverside palaces to the wilds of the Yorkshire moors and a shabby upstairs room in a London tavern, *An Illegitimate Affair* is a tale of infidelity, deception and the true nature of love.

About the Author

Caroline Newark was born in Northern Ireland. She has a degree in Law from Southampton University and her career spans such diverse activities as teaching science, starting a children's nursery business and milking Jersey cows.

In the 1950's Caroline's father began researching his wife's ancestry and Caroline has used his findings as the basis for her series of books about the women in her mother's family tree. There will be one book for each generation starting with *The Pearl of France*, the story of Marguerite, the young sister of the French king who marries her brother's enemy, the elderly Edward I. Marguerite is Caroline's 19 times great-grandmother.

The Queen's Spy tells the story of Marguerite's daughter in-law, Margaret, and *The Fair Maid of Kent* that of Marguerite's granddaughter, Joan, the first English Princess of Wales. *The Illegitimate Affair* (to be published in 2019) is the story of Alys who marries Joan's son.

Caroline Newark lives in Somerset with her husband and their border collie, Pip. She has two daughters and five grandchildren.

Website:	www.carolinenewarkbooks.co.uk
Contact:	caroline@carolinenewarkbooks.co.uk
Follow:	caroline newark on Facebook
	@CaroNewarkBooks on Twitter